CLUB DED

NIKHIL SINGH

Luna
Press
PUBLISHING

First published by Luna Press Publishing, Edinburgh, 2020

www.lunapresspublishing.com
ISBN-13: 978-1-913387-06-8

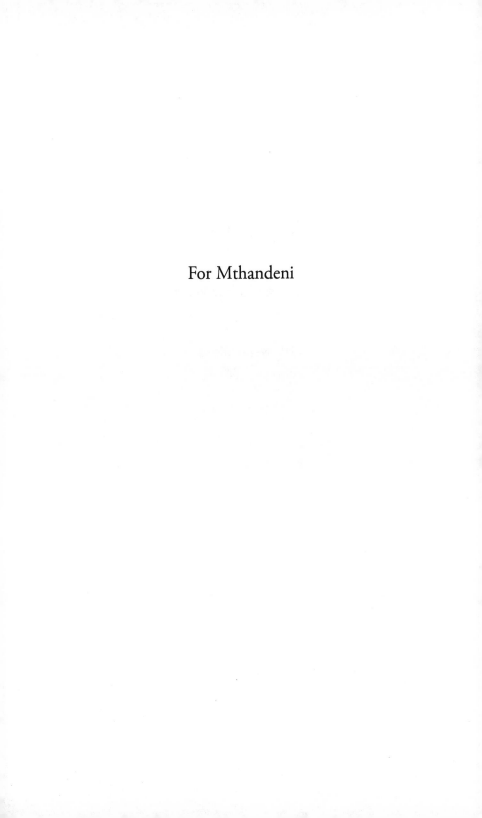

For Mthandeni

Contents

'*Like most of the painters in Ciraquito and Vermilion Sands, I was passing through one of my longer creative pauses. I had stayed on in the town after the season ended, idling away the long, empty afternoons under the awning at Café Fresco, and was already showing symptoms of beach fatigue—irreversible boredom and inertia. The prospect of actual work seemed almost a novelty.*'

JG Ballard—from 'The Screen Game'

I

The Hopeless, The Helpless and the Holy

The Fish

Trill follows the fish. Ghosts the inner city. A clear bag swinging from its fingers. The plastic swells with water. Within are the fish.

The Two Des's

Desmond met Despierre in a crater, somewhere in Afghanistan. The foreign correspondent for a British broadcast service was also present. He immediately began referring to them as the 'two Des's'. It stuck. In hindsight, the pair had a lot more in common than a nickname. Both were competent, hard-boiled and unforgivably maverick. Superficially, they seemed an unlikely pair. Kenny Desmond was a dwarfish, sunburned Mile-Ender. Lupi Despierre, a towering Basque country bad boy, with the semi-ironic beard of a suicide bomber. The charm of glamorous failure was written all over them. It didn't take much to turn their legendary drinking bouts toward serious partnership.

The shared nickname took on a notorious flavor. After the duo's exposure of rape, at the hands of independent military contractors. Desmond's field work yielded a paper trail to key policy makers. The affair opened up a hornet's nest. There was a certain amount of recognition and critical acclaim. In the end, however, the material was considered too 'sensitive' for the mainstream press. Of course, Desmond had foreseen the snub. All the same, it hit him hard.

His contacts in the private arms sector dried up. Doors to military organizations closed forever. Despierre had already made a name for himself with an Associated Press award. He'd earned it in the rebel advancements on Freetown, Sierra Leone. But that was at the turn of the Millennium. When he was still a young lion. By now the bottle, if nothing else, had bled him out by degrees. The double act was well on their way to becoming a losing hand. The next time they were caught in a crater, it wasn't so charming.

A piece of shrapnel put Desmond out of commission for three months. He ended up with lifelong limp. For a time, he wallowed in a relief clinic. Drinking on the sly, reading Len Deighton on his phone and watching his career die a slow death. Late one night, in the television lounge he caught the tail-end of a Delany Croeser picture. It was the famous one: *Game Over*. Where Brick Tynan Bryson transitioned from action-star to celebrated writer. Bryson played an existential, drug-addicted superhero, on the road to an apocalyptic suicide. He had penned the screenplay himself. The big budget existential sci-fi film was a phenomenal summer hit. An industry game-changer. Perfectly of its time. It elevated the winning Croeser/Bryson team beyond blockbuster status—well into the mythical sphere of critical acclaim. *Game Over* went from strength to strength, eventually garnering two Oscars in 1997. One for art direction. The other, out of nowhere, awarded Croeser with best director. Yet, despite the stupendous follow-up potential, side-offers and bankability, the winning combination of Del Croeser and Brick Bryson fell apart almost immediately. All Desmond could think of though, while he sat watching the film, was the time he unexpectedly encountered Croeser in a Viennese brothel.

Desmond was on assignment. The establishment had been flagged as a child-trafficking station. The journalist was working with a sympathetic, middle-aged sex worker. She allowed the reporter to pose as a customer. This way, he could safely observe the comings and goings. The sex worker specialized in dominating middle-aged accountant types. Desmond's visits didn't draw too much attention. On one of these occasions, the woman surprised the reporter with a webcam recording of Croeser. He was seducing a fourteen-year old. The girl was a good six months above the age of legal consent in Austria. The sex tape would have also compromised the dominatrix had it aired. So, in the end, nothing came of the situation. In any case, she had only showed it to him as a kind of novelty. She didn't expect that it would merit investigation. Desmond noted that Croeser was not cruel or abusive with the girl. In fact, she seemed to enjoy his bearish company. There was something distinctly paternal in his attitude toward her. The interaction sickened the reporter to an unanticipated degree.

The trafficking investigation escalated soon after this episode. Desmond's attention was diverted from Delaney Croeser. It was only years later, in his shrapnel-induced convalescence, that the indignation took root. The reporter could never admit it. But his righteous wrath stemmed from a species of envy—towards Croeser's commercial success. It was a jealousy compounded, no doubt, by unpaid convalescence in a third-rate clinic. Desmond had inherited this hatred for the privileged. He viewed 'them' as morally corrupt. Part of this had to do with a low-income upbringing in the grey suburbs of east London. It was a trait he would dispute in conversation. Yet, an acute awareness of class division remained a natural facet of his personality. It was all too obvious to anyone who knew him. When Desmond was in the war zones, his inbred furies transmuted into a resentment of authority. But, stripped of the hierarchies of armed conflict and reduced to the status of an invalid, Desmond seemed to finally find his level. Memories of the sex-tape fermented. They catalyzed the 'two Des's' most infamous and enduring career change; from war correspondents to paparazzi.

Magic Castle

The location of fake castle is memorable. Chiefly because it is littered with haunting formations of standing rock. They lend the landscape an enchanted atmosphere. Since day one, studio executives have been lathering themselves over the bargain-basement cost projections. Croeser's latest project was pushed forward on location price alone. Set construction happened faster than anticipated—primarily due to a lack of film labour unions in the Western Cape. You could work a crew till they dropped. Still, they would still thank you for the dollar compensation. For the US co-producers, South Africa acquired the lustre of ripe fruit. Something to be pulped, packaged and flogged off at discount prices. 'Thank God for cheap African labour' became the guiding mantra during the film's inception.

Of course, the magic castle is just a facade. Once viewed from the side or back, its majestic battlements reduce—to a cable-ridden sideshow. In relation to the rest of the picture (and its overinflated budget), the castle is a minor location. Demanding only a few key days out of the schedule. Shooting had commenced on time and wrapped early. Dismantling is underway. The property is owned and maintained by Oracle Inc. When Anita originally caught wind of the leasing enquiry, she positioned herself carefully. She made sure to negotiate the tenancy agreements personally. Oracle real-estate had been her division once. So, it was nothing for her to assume control of the deal. Anita went to great lengths for the production house. She cushioned the contracts, bent over backward. All with the precise intention of seducing the famous director. She was mortified when Jennifer informed her that the '3rd girl' had ended up on his arm.

'If you visit Africa, I suppose you expect to eat dark meat,' was Anita's automatic racist response.

She made a show of being livid and kept tabs on the fling. It wasn't long before Anita had another fox in the coop—one who would do her bidding. Finding new and creative uses for date-rape drugs was a hobby she didn't get to indulge that often. Though dosing Croeser turned out to be less challenging than she anticipated.

Chloe calls around four in the morning. Anita is in the Response Room. She is dressed in black and crunching cookies. Using an inarguable exit strategy, she quickly abandons Jennifer and the 3rd girl to the black box. Despite her watertight excuses, Anita thinks she catches a suspicious glance from the 3rd Girl on her way out. She decides it's just the PPP (powder-panic-paranoia) talking. She did dust her nose rather excessively prior to departure. All the same, the look gives her jagged edges. All the way out to the city limits. It's a week night. The roads are dead. Ghosts of old hijackings haunt the four-way crossings. Anita runs every red light, making international calls. She has to drive up Sir Lowry's pass and through orchard country to reach the magic castle. By the time she enters the property, the sky is bruising lilac. Security minimized the day the set wrapped. Anita had been quick to come to a cash arrangement with the remaining detail.

She meets a pair of silhouettes at the gate. The bulbs in the watchman's shed have been extinguished. They make the old farm entrance appear derelict. One of the guards accidentally brushes her hand with his. While she is making payment. She is shocked at how cold the flesh feels. In the dimness, the men have the substance of shadows. Touching one, delivers an unpleasant reminder of reality. She does a line off her finger—just to get over the incident.

A dirt road leads up. Through the murk of an abandoned vineyard, into a wilderness region. Ancient rock pinnacles loom against a paling sky. Their formations are breathtaking against the half-light. Anita barely registers their impact. She is the first to admit that her only real gauge for beauty is resale. The rocks pass in and out of the headlights. She drives a company issue BMW VISION NEXT 100. It has changing skin. A concept car, that Anita somehow wangled for top Oracle operatives. By now, the castle silhouette has begun to loom. It is perched atop a rise. Anita has to negotiate a steep lane, just to make an approach. The car adjusts. Chloe waits at the threshold of the make-believe palace, with a sword and winged headdress. She texts on a slim device, toying with long, chestnut braids. Skimpy armour catches the headlights. It reveals fine filigree in the car's approach. Anita can't help but notice (with cocaine-heightened distaste), that Chloe's sandaled feet are lashed with mud. For some reason, this offends her immensely.

'He made you wear a costume?' she calls, rolling down a window.

'It's from the movie! The alien princess wears into in battle.'

'With what? Her dildo?'

'Dressing like an alien slut doesn't contradict any of *my* feminist values, Anita...'

'Where's Svengali?'

'Come.'

Anita parks. Chloe leads her up a crew path. Purple light rises. The birds are waking up. Croeser is out cold in bike leather. His face pressed against a sheen of mud. He lies somewhere in the grass behind the castle.

'How does he look?' Chloe whispers nervously.

Clearly, she is concerned about the dosage. But Anita has a feel for Rohypnol. She inspects the figure while Chloe swings the sword at a passing fly.

'He looks like Rutger Hauer,' Anita eventually replies.

Distant headlights announce the arrival of the 'Two Des's'.

Eye-Detail

'We process neurosis. From all those hellholes to here.'
The Oracle Helpline runs 24 hours. The online response is monumental. Everyone knows that the world is ending. Broken hearts, broken heads and broken lifelines. They settle behind the tinted windows of Oracle Inc.—like blood at the bottom of a glass. Yet, despite a churchy flavour of sanctuary, management continues to outsource from face-agencies. They scoop up the short-timers. Lost cam-girls with oblique skill sets and save-the-world complexes. Those too industrious for industry. 'After all, it's still sales' is the justification. *Prettiness* remains an awkward joke round Switchboard Control. Though the job does afford more dignity than the whole 'squirming naked on a soundstage' routine. In Control, lip-synching to shampoo copy is just a bad memory. Well, that's the pitch at least. Space shuttle pay-slips and perks you'd kill a dog for — that's what gets a girl through the long, dark night.

Jennifer likes the awkward joke. It's what got her out of casting hell. She thinks about it when she's underwater. She's been swimming in hotel pools lately, anonymous blue afternoons. People wonder why her hair is always wet. Chloe used to ask her why—down at Control. But Jennifer hasn't been in the Control Room for three months. She likes to wait in the car these days. Buffing her nails and vaping vanilla pods.

'Chalk it over to chronosystolisis, cell hibernation, time moves funny in Faery... And it's more than just the coke, its time-travel, honest-to-dog...'
She'll whisper these little mantras when she's levitating in the bathroom.

'I was swimming in a pool on the forty second floor' has become the alibi for almost everything. Designer goggles and basic black—all the bubbles that leave her head like empty speech bubbles. Still, no matter how deeply Jennifer drowns, she can't quite escape Control. All her flight patterns are mapped there. Control is in the mountain. Window walls overlook the city from a great height.

Daily orders circulate through a network of laser-carved chambers. They lead deep into the flesh of the mountain. *Eye-detail* populates this wasp's nest. They, like their Response Room counterparts, are exclusively female. Their dress-code, however, is not black. Ceremonial white instead. They log the testimonials of the desperate and lost. Masked by therapy and augmented-reality helmets. They communicate with all the antiquated restraint of nuns or air hostesses. Control swells with clipped, switchboard whispers. A perpetual stream of data. Tens of thousands of traumas are edited, sorted and filed daily. Time-catalogues. Everything edited down to essentials. Mostly questions. These are filed in *primary-phase* envelopes—*black* envelopes. The envelopes are loaded into a *12 hour-black box*. There is a kind of assembly line in play. Black boxes are processed during the day. Then delivered to drop points by dusk. By the time *Eye-detail Alpha* clocks off, the sun is melting postcards, in the acid bath of the Atlantic. *Eye-Detail Omega* takes over. The nameless blackbirds. The suicide-watch. Diametrically opposed to their sisters in white—both in dress and character. Omega teams slink around. Black cocktail ensembles. They carry passkeys and quality narcotics. Working in six teams of three, each is issued with a black box.

Standard protocol runs six Omega triads per city. Though special attention is awarded to regions where the Oracle maintains a regular presence. So, even though the company head migrates from time to time—to offices in Greece, Japan and Canada, she maintains the mountain as her official home-base. The blackbirds process their final products. Then wing it all to the Oracle by morning—so that she can give these essential messages her personal attention. Jennifer is amongst their number. Wet hair slicked back. Blood alive with psychoactive substances. Ready to relay.

Champion of Earth

The rain drags flags beyond the glass walls of Charles De Gaulle. Brick can feel the Northern winter coming on. He'll get one last taste of it before stepping through the airlock. A nostalgic 'escape-to-paradise' feeling resurfaces. For a moment, it's just like the old days. Then time catches up to him. *Escape to Paradox*, the old inner voice chortles. He wonders when he picked up such an annoying voice. Did it come out of rehab? Was it perhaps a fossil of some half-defined character sketch, the career-relic of a younger self? Brick prefers to ignore it in any case. Inner voices are way too Hollywood for Paris in the rain.

The coziness of the airport café, in relation to its freezing views, only accentuates the unreality of his situation. Flying out to a shoot used to be a daily grind. But after years of inactivity, Betty Ford and a splendid array of mid-life crises, the whole situation had started to morph into memoir-potential. Something a young writer could breed a rom-com out of—*a real touchie-feelie*. Brick realizes that he is finally playing the starring role, in the nostalgic sequel to his very own life. Looking back at the golden years with a bitter aftertaste; 'Just south of cliché' was what he would have grumbled twenty years ago. Or was it fifteen? Exactly how many golden years did it take before the ripest of grapes turned to dust in his mouth? He could recall all the dates. The numbers stayed solid. It was just actual memories he was having trouble with. The colours and tones escaped him. Lost time, he ruminates, the ultimate special-effect. He tries to avoid being cynical. He even listens to his wife and attempts yoga here and there. Yet, despite his obvious sincerity he is still haunted by the age-old sensation of feeling like an imposter. It's a sensation that took him back to when he was a young lion and the world was still his tuna fish. This was back when the fame had really hit hard, leaving technicolour bruises over everything. But even in the glow of those golden days, Brick was always waiting for the penny to drop, waiting by the phone, or in the wings. When fans looked up and saw their 'dapper Hercules', fresh from outer space or slick with the blood of an enemy, the man behind the action idol remained in silent doubt. Brick waited patiently to be exposed for the cheap Hellenic mirror-portrait that he struggled to maintain. He was continuously on the watch for the critic, reporter or love interest that would finally unmask him for the stand-in he felt he had become. It never happened. Instead, his career took off.

Brick's life descended into corporate wangling and backroom deals. Fame crystallized around him; that most exclusive of amber's, slowly asphyxiating his personal freedom and pickling him in 'type'. But that was all in the Jurassic—light years ago. Now, Brick has been exiled to the land of Nod. He regards his wife Lisa-Marie, who wafts beyond the wasteland of a wilting cappuccino. She looks so cinematic, he thinks. He begins to mentally construct an opening scene: *camera tracks slowly through a large crowded airport. It finds a man and his wife. They sit at a corner table of a cafe. Isolation in a crowd* (or is that too obvious for an opener?). *The man is Brick Tynan Bryson (early 50's) and the bottle-blonde ex-swimwear model, is his wife, Lisa-Marie Liszt (mid 40's). She faces in towards him while he sits facing out, feet apart, uncomfortable and shifty in the hubbub. In dress, both are sleek and well turned out. He, every bit the 'aging action movie star', large, statuesque, standing out almost comically against a tide of urbane human traffic....* A 'dapper Hercules, lost amongst suburbanites' was how the Times described him in '95 (the description still sticks—'like bubblegum on a shoe'). *She, on the other hand is* (what any callous casting brief would describe as) *the 'mature trophy-wife'.*

Perhaps Lisa-Marie had been content to wear the trophy tag once. But 1995 was a lifetime ago. By now the routine has worn thin and died. Her strategically disguised intelligence turned to melancholia, in the same way wines age. The ingredients remain the same, but an irrevocable alteration had occurred after fermentation. She was like that—a real California red. Still, Brick couldn't help but cartoonify her anxiety. He is incapable of interacting with the morbidity of her yoga-toned body, which to him, is a pointless strategy against the onset of age. Her withering silences had only brought him closer to the shore of death. It's all too Ingmar Bergman for an old-school action legend. This sensation of mortality became the excuse he offered his reflection. When she was crying in the lounge next door, quaffing dong-qui or nostalgically watching reruns of the sitcoms she had despised so much in her youth. Brick often dwells on her old reflections. He remembers a lush Amazon, bounding un-catchably through the Malibu surf. Or winking down from billboards across Scandinavia. Of course, he loathes the fact that he objectifies his wife. But these judgements are played close to the heart. After all, Lisa-Marie could always be counted on to remind him of his affair with alcoholism. All his neuroses are, by now, just so many dirty glasses to her. 'Take off the mask, we need the hood' was still her oldest insult.

'...This is why I don't like people coming to see me off at airports anymore,' Brick sighs.
'In the old days, you'd just fuck me in the parking lot,'
He can't help but laugh. She mirrors his smile wanly.
'I remember,' he acknowledges.
'Do you remember if you still love me?'
'Well, of course I love you, you're my wife!' he replies, caught off-guard.
'It sounds like you're delivering a line,'
'Believably?'
'Depends who's directing I suppose,'
'Who *is* directing?'
A voice interjects and they both turn.
'Brick Bryson!'
It is virtually every wife's nightmare made manifest; late teens, attractively predatorial, marking everything with her scent. Lisa-Marie notes her husband freezing in the cross-hairs and smiles wryly. She decides to lean back and enjoy the show.
'I would like very much your autograph,' the girl foxes (positioning herself strategically between them).
She's tropical, colonial French (Reunion island?), seasoning a Creole husk throughout her broken English like a pro. The all-black ensemble is cheap, but well arranged. Probably an art-student, Lisa-Marie guesses. She's a little rough around the edges, but clearly minor-league mistress material (Nothing like buffing up a diamond in the rough). Brick is taking it well. He has inserted the 'serious and clearly concerned about the state of things' look into his kaleidoscope of faces. A dead give-away, in his wife's opinion. A slice of the girl's bare stomach shines through at eye-level. He seems incapable of withstanding its tactical assault.
'He's still hot, isn't he?' Lisa-Marie confides to her. '...Like he just saved the world from a bug-eyed monster.'
The girl glances back over her shoulder, smiling dangerously, sensing a potential alliance. Lisa-Marie begins to enjoy herself. But clearly wishes she had a vodka on standby.
'I noticed some discreet toilet cubicles near the parking lot,' she winks at her husband.
The girl manages to flick her blue dip-dye photogenically. It's all a bit tragic—just the sort of bit-part an aging, misogynist might cast. This is what he is thinking.
'Where do I sign?' he mutters, unimpressed, glaring stonily across

at his smiling wife.

The girl surprises them both. She fingers open the stomach slice. Exposing a snowy belly adorned by a tiny, emerald navel ring. It's a youthful party trick and they back off a step, recalling how they had once also tossed manes on the old hunting grounds of vanity. It's an elemental moment. An acknowledgment of life's great continuities. Despite this, Brick is still perplexed. The girl hands him bright blue lipstick and hip-lines her torso closer to his face.

'Go on,' she smirks. 'I take snapshots in bathroom.'

He signs dutifully. Lisa-Marie half expects her to kiss him right there and then. Instead she slips something behind his tie. Brick investigates. He discovers a sticker mounted QR code. Her calling card, he assumes.

'Call anytime,' she air-kisses, stalking off, stomach smudging with every step.

Lisa-Marie studies her ass, making stylistic notes. When she looks back, her husband is contemplating the sticker.

'Cute,' he mutters, feigning amusement.

She glares at him, flicks at her coagulating coffee.

'I spoke with our former-son last night.' she decides to announce dryly.

Brick seems to age several years within the space of a second. But quickly manages to recover his stride.

'Isn't there some point where we are supposed to start referring to him as our daughter?' he enquires diplomatically.

'Yes, of course. Soon he will be a she. But, this is Billie. It's complicated, I think he still wants to feel as though he is our son, even after they...you know.'

'So he's really going to let them slice it off?' Brick practically whispers.

No matter how many times it's discussed, the image still manages to alarm him at some primal level.

'Oh, his dangling days are most definitely numbered,' Lisa-Marie sighs, swatting at an invisible fly.

'Well, he's a braver man than I am.'

'Probably the worst thing you could say to him.'

'Or the best—I haven't seen my kid for over six months. Is he ever going to come home?'

Clearly, the thought troubles her too. She leans in sympathetically.

'You might not even recognize Billie after the hormones. They get them from horse piss, you know. It's all a bit futuristic.'

'My God, has he changed so quickly?'

'Took him sports-bra shopping last week.'

'The horror, the horror,'

'Welcome to the Stepford.'

'Strange. In the eighties guys would take steroids to get more masculine. Now it's the other way round.'

'Progress.'

'Nothing to say to his old Dad, I suppose?'

'He said some things. Not to you, but certainly at you. I did my best to be a secret agent and taped the video chat. It's all in your email.'

She fixes her husband in an icy glare. As though suddenly reminded how irritated she is supposed to be with him.

'Well, I suppose I'd better say bye,' she snips. 'My basil need watering.'

And that, as they say, was that.

Response Room

The day starts around midnight. Jennifer has been living the lunar life. Suffering nosebleeds. Swimming the crystalline blue universe of urban alienation. 'These days' she sighs. She can only think when she's underwater.

'Everything is high-resolution down there.'

Happiest in slow motion. Moving within a bright, soundless sphere. Maybe it's the suicide pills. Jennifer can't tell. Time runs backward when she's submerged. At least that's how it feels. She watches nosebleed clouds suck back into her face.

'I only work when I'm underwater…'

She whispers this—into a glass phone-plug. Somewhere in the future.

Dress-code: one hundred percent vampire-city. Oracle Inc. forks out fat stipends. Hair and cosmetics. Its photo-finish till dawn (In a wilderness of mirrors, what will the spider do?).

'We process neurosis.'

This is Jennifer's go-to slogan when asked to describe her work. Not that anyone asks. They might as well be working in the coldest reaches of the asteroid belt. Collecting comets. Taking plasma readings off collapsing stars. Maybe it's the night grind. Nothing alienates faster than broken sleep. Except, perhaps, knowing the future before it's happened. Jennifer thinks about *that* when she's underwater. She thinks about all those loose strands. Future events, waving anemones against a sea of possibility. Which strand will survive this time? Fossilized by the past. Forever ravaged by future analysis. The Oracle reads the secret harmony of these filaments. She knows their outcome. The Oracle *always* knows.

Anita and the 3rd Girl pick her up in the VISION NEXT. Anita drives, Cleopatra bob reflecting the night. A real storm-trooper helmet. The daily grind starts with a line off her compact—'get the nerve-juice flowing'. Then its fat bass and cigarettes. All the way down to the electric mess of town. Neon oils the shapeshift of the coppery car. They sit in tight focus. That watchful, paranoid silence of Mach-one thought. Jennifer takes the backseat these days. The world shuffles past. A deck of terrible playing cards.

'From all those hellholes to here...'
She chants her various slogans, eyeing a parade of ghostly tenements.
She sees all the lonely people. The midnight rooms. A blue glow of a
television comes at her—through curtains. A hundred alleyways. All
these stolen glimpses. Little slices of night.
'I hear your voice.'
She pops a suicide pill, fast-forwarding deeper into the cryptic
labyrinth of humanity. All of a sudden, the Lexus takes a dive. Landing
somewhere, downwind of Quan's Superior Emporium...

Quan's: A lavish, dragon-infested Schezuan restaurant on the seedy side
of nowhere. The structure is old, draughty. People die on the pavement
outside. Red lanterns sway swollen glands against a night breeze. The
girls move in tight, cocaine formation. Under tarnished gold arches—a
real military unit. The 3rd girl lights a cigarette by the door. Jennifer
leans longingly against the glow of an aquarium. Anita approaches
reception. Jennifer watches, distracted. She wants to be amongst the
fish. Someone once told her that goldfish have four second memories.
She envies them that (if it's true). Much of Jennifer's time is spent in a
kind of mourning for the sub-aquatic realm.
The other day she saw something at the bottom of the pool. She'd
been swimming at the Lexington. Drifting through the deep end,
sometime around midnight. The pool was deserted. A small, dark blur
became apparent—against the white slope of a wall. It was really rather
tiny. Situated at a point where the pool walls began to shift to floor.
She swam closer. The patch remained illegible. She fetched her goggles.
The blackness coagulated, becoming words. Someone had written 'IT
IS WRITTEN'—on an otherwise unblemished curvature. Jennifer
studied the sentence in a slow and fascinated way. She mouthed it in
bubbles. A little mystery had opened up. It spoke to the detective part
of her, penetrating like a meteor. Wholly unknown. She knew of no
cure to this kind of mystery.
Anita jabbers in Mandarin. She trades catty barbs with the house
matriarch. Anita picked up the lingo at a Chinese freight company.
Somewhere in the Namib waste. One of her clients ran a traditional
crematorium service for wealthy expats. She had to make regular trips
to the People's Republic on their behalf. Delivering ashes. 'Dining on
ashes', she would joke. Once, she told Jennifer how she used to smuggle
uncut diamonds out of the country. It would have been out of character
to be caught. Anita was one of those intense human calculators—a
factor-cruncher. She consumed technical manuals. Did arithmetic
to clear her head. When she and Jennifer met, they clicked instantly.
Two long lost vertebrae, snapping satisfactorily into place after years of

inexplicable stiffness.

Jennifer takes too long to order. Even though she always goes for the salmon roses. The 3rd girl is ready with her usual dig—something about sinking low enough to order sushi from a Chinese restaurant. You could set a watch by her wisecracks. Anita was quick to start up the whole '3rd girl' thing. It was a facet of her alpha dog routine. The fact that the 3rd girl was Congolese only raised the stakes. It wasn't that Anita saw herself as racist. Far from it. 'Hey, I'm the first to get off on interracial porn' was the usual excuse. But the '3rd girl' had a mouth on her. Attitude was something Anita could respect. Not enough to drop the patronizing nickname. But, certainly enough to share her last line of coke. The trio ended up becoming a unit, despite a shaky take-off. All part of the plan—Jennifer figured (Their employer *did* see the future, after all). Quan's was an important launch pad. Something to kick off the night grind. Something management wouldn't approve of, and therefore, in Anita's book—a worthwhile team-building experience. After shooting the obligatory breeze, the dragon lady retracts. Back to murky depths. Five minutes later, Jennifer is in the backseat. Her arm on three boxes of imported fortune cookies.

They set up a different *Response-Room* every night. It keeps things 'spontaneous'. Step one: finding a no-name brand motel. Like a smoker's lung, no-one cared what blew through those places. Cheap beds and carpet burns. A boxy tube. Screams in the night. The perfect place for secrets. Anita has a new place in mind. Somewhere in Seapoint. They haven't tried it yet. It's dirt cheap. Catering to low income holidaymakers and hookers. They quickly convert a room into an office. Anita rigs the hardware. The 3rd girl unseals the black box, dumps envelopes. Jennifer loses her heels, configures networks, chooses music.

'*No-one can save the world to witch house...*' is her regular.

As soon as the system is up, Anita begins to pace like a warlord. Fielding calls and responses. They process systematically. Take-out boxes of Chinese sushi pile up in the bathroom sink. The television vomits. Muted celebrity news. One of the laptops runs a nature documentary loop. Something about an ant's nest. Work ethic stuff.

Suicide-watch rotates 48 hour shifts. Anita, Jennifer and the 3rd girl comprise Team Omega 5. They keep contact with the other Omega's in play. Though the groups rarely socialize. Each cultivates their own unique approach. Omega 5's style organizes responses into three groups; 'the HOPELESS, the HELPLESS and the HOLY'. At that point, they deviate from proscribed protocol. They begin to cheat. Methodically cracking fortune cookies, they start to transfer paper futures—to the HOPELESS envelopes. Broken cookies crunch underfoot. This is the volume. The girls trawl in and out of dingy bathrooms. They do lines off upturned screens. Clocks speed up. Time blurs. Sometimes, they document cocaine usage on-cam. Those not-so-secret diaries everyone keeps. Anything to stay on track...

Always thirteen 'Holies" (standard protocol). These are the special messages. Stored in *secondary-phase* envelopes—*white* envelopes. They are to be read aloud—to the Oracle. The Oracle spends many hours a day, reviewing global readings. The HELPLESS are accorded different treatment. They are not subject to any special treatment. They are answered in short, cursory notes. Pledges of support. This is the most time-consuming and taxing of the blackbird tasks. The teams work efficiently, 'helping the Oracle to alleviate the suffering of those lost in the wasteland'. All, except the HOPELESS, of course—who Anita feels are beyond help. The Fortune Cookies were her idea. After a few weeks, just the sight of one was enough to make Jennifer sick.

'You have no idea how many we go through a week.'

Jennifer repeats this phrase into a glass phone-plug. Somewhere in the future.

'I only work when I'm underwater...'

In the future, her face lit by deep blue light. One cough away from vomiting. Still, she manages to swallow another suicide pill. Water patterns flicker—across the ceilings and walls. Jennifer pulls herself to a sitting position. A bedroom by the sea. The large room is drenched with shadow. Blue light through a bubble-curve window-wall. A moonlit ocean-expanse glitters. A girl laughs somewhere outside. There comes a muted splash, followed by the distant tinkle of water. Incoherent conversation. A circular bed occupies the center of the chamber. Figures snake, in and out of darkness. A broken helmet reveals Anita. She makes no sound. Jennifer crawls to an area, somewhere between the bed and the bubble-wall. Her hair is ruined. Her swimsuit torn. Propping herself against the wall, her earplug catches glare.

'All these broken cookies...'

A door opens abruptly—the future has already been written.

Game Over

Naturally, everyone had expected a sequel. Following *Game Over*'s massive critical and commercial successes, a follow-up seemed unavoidable. The split between Bryson and Croeser scuttled that pipe-dream. There was a reshuffle at the studio. Numerous pleas and deals were negotiated between agents and the producers. In the end, in light of Bryson's alcohol abuse and the insoluble animosity between star and director, a spin-off was quickly green-lighted. Characters, previously sidelined in *Game Over*, were now developed and brought to the fore. Croeser took to the helm once more. The resulting reboot raked in double the profits of its predecessor on opening week-end. *Game Over*'s anarchic twist on blockbuster standards, had created a fan-base. They were expecting more of the same. In the end, most were disappointed. But the numbers were already in. The sugary, watered-down version was selling. What did it matter that the narrative was pre-chewed? It was peppered liberally with the intricately constructed action sequences that had become Croeser's trademark. '*A mind-blowing set-piece of calculated excess*' was the response of one notable critic. The rest were not so accommodating. Though, critical acclaim hardly mattered at that threshold point. The follow-up film was already a massive summer opener. A franchise had been launched.

Brick lounges in his first-class cabin, reading the trades. Gossip about the much anticipated fifth installment of the *Game Over* series, is rife. Production has been cloaked in secrecy. Yet, despite all the precautions, speculation had already arisen about the overinflated budget. Damage control is out in full force. It's been this way since the film went over-schedule. Controversial images of the infamous director have also emerged. They show Croeser naked and comatose on the set of a castle. The leak is a double-whammy, if you take into account the spoiler. Fan blogs are already afire with theories about the castle's role in the mythos. It appeared in a previous episode, but was thought destroyed... A cartoonist has wryly caricatured *Club Ded* as a white whale (with cyborg implants), harpooned by investors, stars and studio alike. It is saddled, cowboy-style, by Croeser. He is dragging everyone down to the bottom of the ocean floor. Much to his surprise, Brick takes no pleasure in the director's shaming.

Discarding the magazine, he turns on the monitor. *Game Over* is headlining the bouquet. He reflexively deactivates the screen. Marketing must have all the old pictures circulating in anticipation of the next release, Brick reasons. He hasn't been able to watch the film since the premiere. Even then, he was seething and remembered little of the final cut. The entire situation begins to breed a familiar sensation—a panicky hunger he has not experienced for some time. Now that the fear is refreshed and out of its box, the sensation turns to appetite. Brick is already fingering the drinks menu. He swallows the remains of his lemon cola, decisively ploughing ahead with his online research.

The first thing to pop up is a publicity still of pouty, leading man, Sasha Styles. Sasha's reprisal of *Jack Andro* is two movies deep into the franchise. He plays an android version of Brick's original character 'Z-hero'. It was the role that had Marty Uber made famous in the first spin-off. The idea was that after Brick's superhero committed suicide. A robotic replica of him was constructed. It went on to adventure throughout time and space. Uber was already a big name in many sci-fi fan bases, having come out of a very successful space-opera. The '*Andro*' role was designed specifically for Uber, in the hopes that production could build upon his pre-existing foundation. The strategy ticked all the exec's boxes. Unfortunately, the star was notoriously difficult to work with. In the end, his spectacular clashes with Croeser and cast assisted the franchise by generating tabloid attention. But when Uber entered into litigation with a pop chanteuse over charges of assault, the financiers started pushing for an injection of fresh blood.

Enter Sasha Styles—the studio's go-to celebrity handyman. Sasha Styles was Mr. Fixit. He had a rep for being professional. He also had the requisite bankability to headline a blockbuster franchise. A teetotaling, fully audited scientologist and former college tailback, Sasha was more interested in his collection of sports cars (and girlfriends) than Stanislavski. Despite this, he had a background in show business. He had been forced into ballet at a very young age by his mother. She had had been a Broadway hoofer in her youth. Sasha loathed the practice, but was quick to realize that it was the dance regime which had honed his football skills to a unique degree. He was a star player in high-school. In private, he gravitated toward hip-hop culture. It improved his dancing skills. Sasha began showing up in music videos. Through his mother's theatre contacts, he found bit-parts in a contemporary street-style shows. His cavalier straddling of fences lent him a unique edge—football ladies' man by day / studious dancer by night. It wasn't long before someone suggested acting. He did a year at the NYFA, acquired a good agent and in due time went from Sasha Petrov to Sasha Styles. After diligently working his way up, he eventually made a name for himself—playing second fiddle to established stars in the noughties. When Uber dropped out of the franchise, the young, up and coming star was ripe for a lead outside of romantic comedy. Sasha proved shrewder than his predecessor. Through his agent, he was able to secure a contractual agreement which sidestepped many of the caveats that Croeser usually used to entrap his stars. The fan-base also took to Styles while Croeser, unsurprisingly, didn't. They disagreed famously, but somehow managed to remain civil and get the job done. It wasn't until *Club Ded* that Sasha started to walk off the set. The situation became critical. Production hovered in stalemate while the great white whale bled out.

The second member of the cast to dominate search engines was Delilah Lex. She had the requisite fresh face, was bright-eyed and oozed a Disney-esque vitality. Delilah was famous before she turned fourteen. She was a famous mermaid, in a syndicated YA adventure series. Figurines of her cluttered the corners of schoolgirl's (and middle-aged men's) rooms all over the world. By the time she hit seventeen, teen comedies and popular sitcoms had propelled her into the A-list. It was par for the course that she would wash up on the shores of an action blockbuster like *Club Ded*. Even though the chances of her bankability taking a critical hit were growing exponentially with the production's uncontrolled spiral.

Brick was studying write-ups on Delilah when a call came in from LA. It was his agent Sal Stark.

'So how does it feel to be back in the saddle, space cowboy?' he asks.

'After five years in the phantom zone, it's a little sobering…'

'It's amazing that I still represent you.'

'That IS amazing.'

Sensing weakness, Sal switches to a more maternal mode.

'Listen, baby,' he cajoles. 'I know you haven't been in front of a camera for a thousand years and the press is still hot for your whole…*funny farm phase*. But any possibility of you and Del Croeser collaborating again is worth chasing down.'

'I suppose it will get some fan-base reaction.'

'Are you kidding? This is massive.'

'Mo must be desperate to pull me out of the hat.'

'I always forget that you call him that, where's it come from?'

'Gimme mo.'

'Simultaneously hilarious *and* poignant—how Hollywood of you, Brick. Anyway, you guys made each other's careers. It makes sense that he would reach out. Now that you are out of Farmville.'

'Amazing how you manage to miss all the arteries, every time you cut so close to the bone...'

'Don't be a bitch. It's why I get the big bucks.'

'Mo hasn't made a decent picture since we worked together.'

'He's made *money*. This is movie-making we're talking buddy, not cinema.'

'Unfair enough.'

'Save the moments of clarity for group therapy.'

'It just smacks of some emergency measure to me. I mean, they must have reworked the whole script to get me in at the 11th hour.'

'The writer is suing.'

'Well you know Mo and writers.'

'Has he been in personal contact?'

'No.'

'So, we are in the dark about the role.'

'The cameo.'

'...The groundwork for the mythical sequel.'

'My character killed himself!'

'This is Hollywood, Brick.'

'Sorry, I keep forgetting.'

'Well the fee is secure. Worst comes to worst, you score a paid vacation to the ass-end of nowhere and get to take selfies on safari. Anyway, I have to rotate—meeting at some new Icelandic grill.'

'Enjoy your seal kebabs.'

'And you don't get mugged, murdered or taken hostage—It's a fucking jungle down there!'

'I heard aggressively middle-class...'

'Well, you should feel right at home then mister Box Office. Toodles.'

Brick finds himself procrastinating when it comes to 'the email'. He lets half the night bleed away before plucking up enough fortitude to face his shifting child. Opening the video, he is treated to a sideways glimpse of his ghostly reflection. The porthole becomes a still from *Game Over*'s long-awaited sequel. Instead of the recognizable fringe-flicking Z-hero, the audience is treated to a hangdog, middle-age actor. The ex-addict. The sensation is duplicated, somewhat ironically. He realizes that Lisa-Marie was right about him not recognizing 'the artist formerly known as Bill' (an insensitive paternal nickname that had come back to sting Brick on more than one occasion). The webcam view of a doll-like, blue-haired girl takes him by surprise. She is on her stomach, bare legs upturned against a wall of posters. Brick's eye is instantly magnetized to the bulge of her cleavage. It takes the parent in him several moments to attune to the fact that the nubile changeling is, in fact, his son. It only gets worse.

'It's the raging pussy-hound routine,' Billie is remarking, toying with one of his newly acquired breasts. 'But anyway, I mean, let's face it—he only looks right with, like, a laser rifle or... groping supermodels on Mars, or jumping out the fucking window!'

'How is that bad?' Lisa-Marie laughs off-camera.

'He's not real. The man's not real. Don't you get it?'

'So, you don't want to speak to your father again because he's unreal?'

'Let me contextualize this...'

'This isn't campus Billie. I'm just a dumb blonde, remember—let's please *normal-talk*.'

'Do you think I look hot?'

'Of course, I think you look hot! I'm your mother!'

'But as a former swimwear model, toast of Malibu, ex-queen of the runway, bla-bla—do I make the grade?'

'Billie, those things don't make anyone an expert. Don't be one of the sheeple—Awaken your inner Pleadian.'

'Mom, I'm *not* an alien.'

'I'm not going to lie to you simply because you're my child.'

'Can we stay on-topic, for once? I don't feel like discussing my *extraterrestrial heritage* every single time we have a conversation!'

'Fine, though you're a Hollywood brat—you should get used to the alien thing. And regarding your new hotness, I'd like to remind that I have had a very deliberate hand in it. I've been very supportive. By the way, I was speaking to Julie today about that little shoot you did with whatsisname at Coachella. Want me to arrange some castings?'

'Putting me to work already? Anyway, I *hate* Coachella. I don't want anyone to know I was there.'

'I didn't mean it like that.'

'We're rich, mom! Why do I need to work?'

'You might not need to, but I need to relive my teens—always wanted a hot daughter,'

'I'm not some psychological squeeze-toy.'

'Of course, you are! And there are lots of perks sweetie. I mean, just remember who bought you that Simon Preen you are wearing—Work that peachy ass now, my little Barbie.'

'What a political, Hollywood wifey you've become.'

'Anyway, I still don't see what all this has to do with your father.'

'As the raging pussy-hound we all know him to be; how do you think old Brick is going to relate to my new tits, for example?'

'I don't know what you mean,' Lisa-Marie fences, taken completely by surprise.

'*You know what I mean!*'

'Billie, I honestly don't know what you mean and don't think I want to.'

'His first reaction will be to sexually objectify me.'

'Jesus! Stop! I wish you could see how liberal your father is at heart.'

'I saw him bring home a hundred hot girls while you were away. *I know how he liberal he is with hot girls.*'

'Well, he treated me fine, and as you know, we have an agreement. We chose not to live like everyone else and...'

'He didn't have to flaunt them to me. All his little show-ponies that he, you know, might let me play with one day.'

Lisa-Marie goes quiet and sullen as the conversation mines a nerve. Brick can picture her unseen face. It stings him deeply.

'My dad, the suicidal superhero,' Billie continues. 'Last man standing.'

'That's enough, young man.'

'Young lady.'

'WHATEVER!'

Brick enters the toilet cubicle. As soon as the door is secured, he sags against the droning panels. He withdraws four miniature bottles of Scotch from his jacket. With all the sneakiness of a schoolboy. The first quenches him deeply. His insides loosen. Of course, Billie was right about what he noticed first. The pain of the situation is vague and volatile. His newly unlimbered guts twitch like snakes. He swallows another, lets the empties tinkle in the basin and unlatches his belt. The liquor has cut a knot in his bowels. He voids himself, flushing away what anxiety he can along with it. Washing his hands, he catches himself in the mirror. The lens of alcohol adds a glisten. He realizes that the QR code is still attached to his tie. Re-buckling his pants, he collapses onto the closed lid and cracks his third Scotch. What time was it in Paris? He scans the code. After a few rings, a dingy room crackles into focus. He's old and drunk enough to appreciate the unreality of the crystal ball. He didn't have crystal balls like this when he was... how old was she? He is pondering it all when she steps into frame. For a moment, her face is low res with dimness—cold cooking fat in water. When she recognizes him however, her smile lights up the glare of the screen. It still comforts him to know that celebrity carries such power; the power of instant love and acceptance (*particularly with the young fillies*, his inner voice cackles).

'You called me!' she beams, catching him mid-swig.

'Aren't you just from rehab?' she adds, eyeing the bottle.

'I left my heart in San Francisco.'

'Oh, me too, wow, I'm too amaze you call me back. Brick Bryson! Honestly, I wish my flat-mate was here...'

'I'm glad we're alone. Are we alone?'

'Just you, me and the NSA.'

Brick polishes off the bottle and sighs heavily. She looks just fine to him. Her breasts aren't quite as upstanding as his son's, but at least he doesn't experience any guilt when he looks at them. She is weighing him up.

'How many whisky you have?'

'Clearly not enough, but I'll slow down.'

'This the spirit. You can do it!'

'I don't need a cheerleader.'

'My name is Alix.'

'You're beautiful Alix.'

'Maybe you do need a cheerleader,' she smiles, flicking up her skirt.

It gives him a cheap twinge. She leans closer, eager to push more buttons. He lets her. Though, when she is finally naked in the bulb-glare, she resembles a ghost or an impressionist painting. The impoverished, bohemian squalor of her dingy room irritates him. He wonders how long it will be till Alix starts cadging holidays and clothes out of him.

'You're old enough to be my son.' He mutters, tearing off the last whiskey cap.

'You mean daughter?' she giggles. 'Or, you like the boys maybe?'

'No, I like girls.'

'Ladies', man on the moon.'

'Catchy. You should write screenplays.'

'I do.'

'Of course, you do. Turn around.'

She obliges, cupping some flesh.

'So, are you *recapturing youth*? You know, chasing hot, young girls?'

'You can't recapture what was never lost.'

'How you mean, old man?' she laughs.

Perhaps she is expecting to offend him. But he smiles. Brick knows how to take a dig. He's made a living off charm.

'My youth is pickled in celluloid.'

'Is all digital now, baby.'

'See? Even technology is conspiring to preserve my youth…'

'That shit isn't real, you know—all that shit. But you, you know. You are real. You are the shit!'

'My son seems to think I'm not real.'

'Well, you're a super hero, dummy.'

'That's me,' he nods, toasting himself.

'You don't do this so often, do you?'

'What, cybersexing?'

'Nobody calls it that, except old froggies.'

'The expression is 'old fogies'.'

'Should be name of skiffle band; *fowg…ees.*'

'Not only am I old, but I'm also old fashioned. So is this whole Flash Gordon video television talk, let's be honest.'

'You realize I could be recording this chat?'

He straightens up.

'Are you recording this chat?'

'No, I would never. My Venus is in Scorpio. I'm, how you say, secretive.'

'You sound perfect.'

'Though, *if I was* recording this chat… I could make a fortune. You should be more careful who you call.'

He clears his throat then grumbles sincerely:

'Thanks for setting me straight with that,'

'Doesn't mean I'm not taping you…' she teases.

'No games. I've had a rough day.'

'I can tell.'

'My son has breasts.'

'Are they better than mine?'

He checks.

'They are.'

'Misogynist.'

'I didn't mean it that way.'

'Just teaching you about equality, mister Champion of Earth.'

Bricks drains the bottle, flings it in the sink. She is watching him, smiling at her little upper hand, fondling parts of herself.

'If only I could live up to the whole Champion of Earth thing.' He ruminates.

'It's your dark side makes super-heroism believable in you.'

'How do you mean?'

'Keeping the planet safe is tough work, *n'est-ce pas*? Whoever does, has to *really* understand the darkness.'

'Never saw it like that.'

'You can't lie to me. I've seen all your films.'

'And I appreciate that. Turn around again.'

Asteroid

Sunlight dapples a washing line. Starlings coo and detach. The line bisects an inconsequential corner of an overgrown plot of land. Starved chickens roam. A military garrison had been constructed here in the seventeen-hundreds. Now the magazines lie abandoned—except for vagrant communities. Most of the area is derelict. The buildings clutter with the accumulation of a hundred human magpies. One of them created the old road-sign: 'PHARM'. Of course, nobody remembers who named it now. Part of The Pharm acts as an animal shelter. All manner of dismal creatures can be found, haunting the groves. Permaculture festers amongst trashcan fires, sustaining rats. The old base is situated at the gut end of an old German neighbourhood. The locale had once been obscure. Now it's prime residential. Colonial-era architecture, situated between town and the fair foothills of the city's smaller peak. This mountain was once described as the head of a lion. No-one ever saw the resemblance. Instead, it picked up a more fitting name: Shark Fin. Or simply—the Fin. Its shadow is an uncomfortable place for a farm. Urban decay lurks beyond the tree line. Street children hunt in packs.

The washing line is heavily laden. Wallets, purses, watches and similar items dangle. They drip with bubblegum-pink paint. A coated figure stands at a remove—Pat Ziqubu, otherwise known as Ziq. He has held the position for some time now, engrossed in his handiwork. Ziq is the type to freeze within silences. A bright wind lurches out of the Pharm. It tousles his coat, but fails to move him. He has learned to ignore time. He likens it to a starving child in the street: 'serious—but I can't afford it'. When his reverie breaks, Ziq moves with surprising swiftness. He goes down to the city. Springtime. A rare and beautiful day. Fragrant winds nose down from the mountain. They sway lavender shadows across all the sidewalks. Within this somehow artificial light, contours clarify. The entire city, along with its two, unreal mountains, take on a similarly artificial quality—as though generated 'in post'. The larger mountain is long and flat. It dwarfs the Fin. Ziq swims pleasurably through the rich beauty of the day. He relaxes his stride, moving in an inertial drift. Ziq's expression is characteristically mask-like. It shows little of the colours within. He is wary, yet distracted by details. There is something feline about his close observation of events. His actions continue this predatorial motif. He walks as though followed, moving loosely through the streets, watching their flow. His eyes tag loose watches and open pockets. He auto-calculates the angle of hands, replacing wallets or purses. He notes checks being paid in restaurants. Glimpses handbags through glass, in passing. He watches surreptitiously, losing himself in the crowd.

A tourist exits a café. He enters a sunny, tree lined boulevard. There's a newspaper under his arm. Street drummers provide a weary backdrop. The tourist stops, hovers on a street corner. Lights a cigarette against the unpredictable wind. Ziq forms behind him. He approaches in a careless manner—a leaf blown across a pond. Pretending to lose his balance, Ziq brushes against the man. The foreigner puffs, glances. Taking a call, he recedes—a sign on a highway. The pickpocket continues upon his way.

Ziq strolls through sunshine. He balances the freshly acquired wallet on an upturned palm. Tossing it absently, up and down, he walks. Engrossed by the day. Flocks of pigeons seem to mirror his thought processes. They sweep and fragment. Closer inspection would reveal mutilations. People are unkind to scavengers in this town. Ziq navigates the tangled nether-quadrant of the Company Gardens. He walks, till the cake-like structure of the museum comes into view. Homeless people speak to themselves in its easy shadow. The city is really unpacking beauty today. Ziq can see it in the glow-gilted leaves. In the flight of birds. The concept of alienation in a place so beautiful seems absurd. Yet, a kind of misery pours down daily—into the coloured boxes of the town.

Ziq had once spent some time in New York. Back when he used to 'exist as a human being'. A specific moment often haunts him. He remembers stopping in a subway, hands jammed into rainy pockets. He was staring at one of those escape-to-paradise bills. The kind you find on the walls of the great subway systems. In this particular one, Ziq rediscovered the great, flat mountain of his city. It had been digitally spit-polished—ripe for tourist exploitation. Ziq felt truly lost at that moment. Because he had escaped that mountain to get to New York. Now, staring at the rock faces, the memory repulses him. The mountain had been bleached—transformed into revenue. This particular mind-set reflected itself throughout the city. Relentless tourism, nationalist pride campaigns and advertising. All designed to sell. They had reduced the ancient peak to an affordable postcard. One which, Ziq liked to say, 'rendered its viewers two-dimensional'. Somewhere in every picturesque day, there existed for him, a tiny seed of mourning. A timeless monument—to the systematic cheapening of beauty.

Foliage sways in the magic light. Ziq breathes it in. He loiters at the edge of a rose garden, unsure which way to walk. He often finds himself pondering the many crossroads that fate will present during the course of a single day. The concept of a seemingly inconsequential decision, laying the track for a vastly different future fascinates him. It also fills him with doubt. Ziq never dwells on the concept. He imagines himself as a stubborn train—locked to a route that cannot be switched. Life, to him, is a long metal line. It winds nonchalantly through a wasteland. Full of gaudy, inessential stations. He plucks a rose, wandering in the direction of the museum. The magic of the day clings to his every random action. Along with the pollen of a thousand flowers.

There is a circular chamber in the center of the museum. Sunlight enters the high windows of its domed ceiling. Three whale skeletons suspend in this antiquated glare. A macabre illusion of floatation. Electronically reproduced whale-song dissipates, down somber halls, completing the image. A child laps an ice-cream cone. Just beyond the window of the marine specimen gallery. The boy distracts Jennifer. She is watching the skeletons. But he is staring. Her hair drips—a recent underwater interlude. She is still doesn't know how she ended up in the museum. A panel beater had her car. She needed it back in forty minutes—to meet Anita. That morning the blackbirds had convened, as usual. Delivering missives to the Oracle. V was scheduled to do a little airport welcome wagon for a movie star. Anita had been snarky about it all day. But Jennifer was happy to give 'the 3rd Girl' a lift. She hit a dog on the way back in, damaging her bumper. The incident depressed her. Anita's barrage of snide SMS's didn't help. Jennifer wanted the vehicle seen to as soon as possible. She'd invested a lot in her sports car over the years. Even now, its condition is vital to her sense of wellbeing. Her head follows the line of a blue whale's spine. Her nose is bleeding. She doesn't even notice the warm fluid. It quickly covers her face and neck. The look of terror on the boy's face betrays her predicament. Jennifer pinches her nose, stalking off in search of a bathroom.

Clattering up dingy, marble staircases, she enters a Victorian-era hallway. Movement distracts her. Jennifer peers down a line of glass cabinets. They vary in size, encapsulating stuffed animals. The silence seems especially dense in there. Dust-beams poke from skylights. They illuminate a thin, coated figure. He is at the far end of the chamber, his back to her. He is unaware of being observed. Something in his posture alerts Jennifer to clandestine activity. She looks closer. He is defacing the lion cabinet glass with a laundry marker. Losing interest, she gives the scene a cursory once-over before leaving.

Jennifer learned to love bathrooms at an early age. Chronic nosebleeds made cleansing sanctuaries of them all. She could play hide and seek with the whole world in just one toilet cubicle. Later, narcotics opened up new vistas. Things, previously hidden behind dirty white porcelain and mirrors, emerged. Magic made rabbit holes out of drains. Turned bacteria into a religion. '*You can't judge a girl by her secret worlds*'—Anita used to say.

Jennifer rinses blood from her face. When the bleeding is staunched, she runs cold water over her wrists. Staring her reflection straight in the eye. Then she gazes at her hands for a long time, dipping them in and out the flow. She does this often. It's a private ritual—indecipherable to an outside observer. She imagines there must be millions of girls like her. Each, engaged in their own private mirror duels. Those silent, commonplace moments of existential tension. The secret faces of humanity. Jennifer pulls herself out of the moment. She dries off, strolling back.

She hesitates outside the taxidermy hall. Something compels her to investigate the defaced glass. A black patch suspends on the glass of the lion cabinet. It separates into words: IT IS WRITTEN. Jennifer freezes. She experiences a giddy, unreal sensation. It feels as though she has been sleepwalking—perhaps since the Lexington pool. The wonder of a mystery, suddenly solved, overrides all thought. She glances around in bewilderment. Somehow, she is expecting the coated figure to be present. But the room is deserted. Her responsibilities dissolve. She begins to stalk agitatedly through hallways and atriums, searching of him.

She finds him near the asteroids. Then she hesitates again, suddenly unsure of her intentions. Ducking behind a pillar, she observes from a safe distance. A schoolteacher guides a flock of schoolchildren through a gallery of deep-space specimens. Jennifer becomes distracted by the commentary. The coated figure is oblivious. He studies star-charts. Profiled against white window glow. Jennifer peers, trying to make out his face. The teacher's voice intrudes:

'*...Sometimes an asteroid will appear out of nowhere, penetrating the atmosphere and falling to earth. No one is sure where most asteroids come from, except to say that they have been travelling through the coldest reaches of outer space. They could have travelled for centuries before striking the earth. Most burn up on entry. But the strongest manage to survive the ravages of extreme heat. Their impact often leaves behind devastating craters. Some completely destroy the environment they land in. Scientists believe that the dinosaurs...*'

Jennifer realizes that the mystery is far from being solved. It has only yielded its tip. Like an iceberg, she finds herself in strange waters. Ziq turns and leaves. Jennifer delays a moment. Then follows him out into the bright, gusting day.

Jennifer trails Ziq through sun-washed gardens. She slips on sunglasses, passing like a cat through the rose maze. He is clearly accustomed to walking. He gives the impression of a person who strides leagues each day. Jennifer considers noting this detail on her phone. The thought amuses her. She hadn't realized what an aesthetically pleasing day it was—'*crisp as an apple and twice as bright*'. A line from childhood. She used to visit the gardens when she was at the dance academy. Sometimes she'd eat pasta on the wrought-iron benches. It feels like another life. She has the sense of being a ghost, accounting for wasted time. Sometimes her cynicism overwhelms her. She ignores the squabble of her mind, concentrating instead on the novelty of private investigation. He passes an ornamental koi pond. Enters the park café, taking a table beneath a twisty blue gum. Jennifer lingers in the lane. She peeks discreetly through leaves. His table is partially obscured. Like everyone else, she can only see his back. A deliberate act of obfuscation. A waitress approaches. Jennifer ducks. She lights a cigarette in the lee of a cycad.

Ziq orders an espresso, waits for the waitress to leave. He likes this table in the afternoons. The cove of shrubbery affords privacy. He darts a sip, producing pilfered items. A gold watch, an ivory rosary, three wallets. Then Jennifer's vinyl clutch. He arranges them. The initial perusal always gives him a stir. He savours his coffee, fingering the lives of others. Ziq couldn't be certain when stolen merchandise became his only real contact with society. He blatantly uses the money to survive. Though survival is far from his focus. Perhaps secret knowledge—of the people around him It has turned him into an outsider. He identifies with this concept—'the stranger in paradise'. Particularly on beautiful days. Sometimes a person can drift. This is his reasoning. They wash up on shores unknown. Forced to survive on meager fare. Ziq no longer yearns. He feels as though he has passed some unseen barrier. The borderline stands, a wall of one-way glass. Between him and the rest of humanity. Ziq watches from the darkness of his side, observing the passage of millions.

He unsnaps the vinyl purse first. Then methodically dissects its contents. He finds a premium-service medical card. For a private clinic in Constantia. The card is printed with an ID snapshot. A young woman with pale eyes. Her bottle-blonde hair is scalloped. The face is all logic and response. A marked lack of emotion—a calculated quality. Here is a person that measures the impact of their appearance with precision. 'JENNIFER BECKETT' is printed alongside. Ziq looks her over with little interest. It's a media town. Many faces, selling many ice-creams. Across many billboards. Everyone has a price-tag—when the right phone call comes in. He replaces the card, noticing a substantial billfold. Flicking a thumb across, he stops counting at two thousand. Various items follow; an Oracle 24-hour helpline card, some designer cosmetics and an envelope of cocaine. He also finds a Polaroid—also of Jennifer. The image had been snapped in the city, at night. The amateurish flash captures a vastly different aspect to the medical card. Jennifer's hair and clothes are torn. Her face smeared with blood. She weeps. On the edge of a dark street. Ziq is thrilled—hidden treasure. He takes the Polaroid gingerly, rummaging for the medical ID. Holding the photos alongside one another, the mask-face dissolves—a cake layer. Ziq frowns, analyzing the discrepancy. He loses interest in the other items on the table. He studies the Polaroid for almost an hour.

Jennifer smokes on a park bench. For a few mad moments, she contemplates approaching him. She nurses the moment, watching it grow cold. After a while, she checks the time. Eventually she just leaves.

The 3rd Girl

Brick disembarks before everyone else. Production is rolling out the carpet. His head is still ringing with Scotch when the hostesses put him on a runway cart. He is whisked toward a small party. They are waiting for him outside one of the main structures. The air is bright, the sky a penetrating blue. Brick feels instantly revitalized. '*Africa!*' is what he is thinking. A girl takes form at the head of the approaching team. She wears a smart little suit and holds up an ostentatious welcome sign. It reads 'GAME OVER' in large, semi-ironic letters. Brick's focus is so captivated that he barely notices the flunkies and press until he is amongst them. He throws out the old photo-face, taking refuge behind sunglasses. The sign is irritating him. He catches the girl's eye. There are some forms to signature and photos to take. The girl has by now sidled up to him. She is being a professional about it all, smiling like a geisha.

'Croeser's idea?' Brick mentions, indicating the sign.

'You can tell?'

'Pissing on his territory, I suppose.'

'Children can be *very* territorial,' she winks. 'Especially the grown-up ones…'

He is caught unawares by the complicit barb. Her eyes hold him steadily. He senses strength there. A local official extends his hand, breaking the moment. Someone takes a snap. The girl snatches the opportunity to signal some luggage porters (and ditch the sign).

The limo is new and white as a tooth.

'All that's missing is the pool,' Brick jokes.

The girl calls it the 'Croesermobile'. The name fits. Brick sees an Asiatic twist to her features. He comments on her high cheekbones and the wide spacing of her up-slanted eyes. She tells him that she has, what some would describe as, classic Congolese features. He can't tell if she is making fun of him.

'I'm V,' she adds, extending a supple hand.

The mountain swivels behind smoked glass.

'It's really something,' Brick mentions.

She nods, still smiling. A sense that Croeser has rigged the cabin with secret cameras has occurred to him. Brick realizes why he feels so comfortable. It's the old 'Croeser-control'. He's back on set. All the old routines have already begun to take on water and send out roots.

'Espresso?' she asks.

'Sure.'

She slides a wooden partition, operating the compact machine enclosed within.

'There's a video message for you, from Delaney.' She mentions. 'Would you like to watch it while you take your coffee?'

'By all means,' he nods, accepting a tiny china cup and saucer.

The espresso comes complete with vegan biscotti and a blinding white linen napkin.

V reseats herself—a little too close, he thinks. She leans over to flick some switches. A cabinet opens, revealing a widescreen monitor. He is, by now, uncomfortably aware of her physical proximity. The sensation intensifies when she appears naked on the large screen. Brick freezes at her chuckle. Onscreen, V stands in a large, white hotel suite with an ocean view. A gleaming collar binds her throat. The hand-held camera tracks along its slim-link leash, until Croeser abruptly turns the lens on himself. A ruddy, lined smile fills the entire screen.

'Brick, if only you could see your face,' the director growls.

Croeser switches hands on the leash, wobbling the lens. Brick catches a glimpse of his old friend in a nearby mirror. The award-winning director is somewhat obscenely attired in a pith helmet, loud stars & stripes boxers and biker boots.

'Jesus,' Brick has time to mutter before Croeser starts up again.

'Consider this jungle goddess my welcome gift to you Brick,' he smiles. 'A trophy I personally captured in the teeming back-alleys of Darkest Africa!'

'Turn it off,' Brick mutters.

V laughs, killing the screen with a flick of a button. She moves back to the couch across from him.

'What are you so amused at?' he mutters irritably.

'You have just won me a wager."

He frowns.

"I told Delaney the video would embarrass you. We could not agree. We made a little bet.'

'He would have won—ten years ago.'

'Oh, I've been a fan since I was a teenager. I knew you would not let me down.'

Once again, Brick finds his irritation neutralized by the girl's cool resonance.

'Forget Delaney,' she says. 'I'm happy to show you around. Perhaps after you have freshened up?'

The offer makes him wary.

'I'm exhausted—another time?'

'I understand. I also apologize for Delaney's joke. He is so colonial sometimes...'

'Racist, you mean.'

'Was he ever racist towards you?'

'I don't think he sees me in racial terms.'

She laughs.

'But you are a black man! How could he not?'

'I'm too all-American for him to racially profile. It would short-circuit him.'

'That's ridiculous.'

'That's Del Croeser.'

'I don't allow him to offend me. I know that he looks down on everyone with perfect equality.'

'That, at least, is true.'

'Even this proposition has a selfish motive.'

'How so?'

'He's been seeing a lot of his leading lady. Perhaps you've seen the tabloids?'

'Delilah Lex? She's barely out of high school.'

'Perhaps she has daddy issues. Who knows? I suspect that this idiotic attempt to palm me off onto one of his famous friends is his idea of reconciliation.'

'That sounds like him.'

'I didn't mean to embarrass you. I just wanted to win.'

'How much did he bet?'

'A thousand dollars.'

'Not a bad day's work.'

'You were a sure bet.'

'Is he always this discriminatory towards you?'

'He's just finding his South African groove. As a foreigner, I find that almost everyone is racist here—in their own special way. You will never guess what my squad leader calls me.'

'What does he call you?'

'She calls me the 3rd Girl.'

'Third wheel, eh?'

'That's the general idea. My other colleague has no judgements or preconceptions. Anita is simply...Anita.'

'I thought it was all rainbows and Mandela-magic down south.'

'Don't believe everything you read.'

Brick regards her for a moment.

'What would you have done if I'd decided to lose your bet?'

She meets it unflinchingly.

'I meant what I said—I would be happy to host you. Just let me know.'

'I think at this point, the most exciting thing I can think of is falling asleep,' Brick parries diplomatically.

'No problem.'

'Sorry to be so prudish—I've been off-planet for some time,' he adds, quoting himself.

'In that case, welcome back, *Champion of Earth*,' she quotes in return.

The limo heads in the direction of Cape Point, where two oceans merge. Brick is suitably impressed by the kelp-rich surf, epic mountain vistas and white sanded beaches. He compliments V—as though she had manifested it all herself. She finds this amusing. She reminds him that she is 'a stranger there herself'. The hotel is positioned on a wild and elevated stretch. The surrounds suggest an unspoiled nature reserve. Brick remarks on this.

'How did such a luxurious hotel come to be situated on such pristine, undeveloped land?' she repeats with a smirk.

'It seems a little out of place.'

'I'll let you in on a dirty secret—the mountain, and much of its surrounding area, are privately owned.'

'You're joking? Who owns it?'

'If I knew, I'd probably be in a limo with one of them.'

Brick isn't sure whether to laugh. The limo lands outside the lobby. A small army of porters rushes out. A drunken man is leering at the entrance. He is flanked by a pair of women. They appear dressed for the track. Brick notices one of them remove some cigarettes from a gold case. The drunk begins to take an interest.

'You're Brick Bryson!' he calls, unsteadily approaching.

'What is that horrible accent?' Brick mutters sideways.

'Western Cape Afrikaans.'

The drunken man breaks Brick's nose, taking them all by surprise. The action star finds himself sideways in the gutter. Shell-shocked porters and a mortified concierge stare down at him. Blood is leaking prodigiously from his now throbbing face. The women drag their cackling comrade into a nearby sedan before the lawsuits start flying.

'Sorry! He's very drunk!' One of them calls.

'Who's the action hero now?' the assailant jeers, vanishing into the back seat.

Brick rises unsteadily, assisted by V. She is firing orders at the help. One of the women steals over. She stuffs a wad of cash into Brick's top pocket. He realizes that she is also quite drunk. He fumbles at the money, not quite understanding its function. By now, she has scampered back. Security arrives as the gang drives off.

'I don't want your Mickey Mouse money!' Brick yells after them.

'But you need new tights!' the drunk shouts back, receding.

'Welcome to Africa!' his girlfriend adds, somewhat guiltily.

A security guard chases uselessly after them. He slows to a trot near the gate. Shrugging to his colleagues, they all watch the car exit the drive.

'Let's get Mr. Bryson to a doctor,' V announces.

Everyone is catalyzed into action.

Brick allows himself to be led. Many gleaming glass doors are held open for him.

Messages from the Deep

Jennifer lolls. Steam scarves. Sleeplessness. Five am, and V is at the far end of the sauna. She doles eucalyptus infusion onto sizzling rocks. She asks Jennifer to drop her at the airport before eight. Jennifer agrees—a decision that will cost a dog's life. But now it's all minty steam and a sanctuary of windows. Anita is in there somewhere as well. Anointed with precious oils. Jennifer and V don't want her to overhear their plans. Dawn cracks the mountain. At quarter to six, all three are scrubbed down. Rock salt and rose petals. They are made to lie in volcanic mud. Once cleansed, they prepare for their audience with the Oracle. Hydrotherapy suits Jennifer's aquatic disposition. Her thoughts float free, in misted spaces.

The blackbirds arrange. A terrace in the hotel's largest suite. The quarters are removed from the central structures. They perch on a crag. Elevation affords the rooms a 180-degree ocean view. Freed from their nocturnal plumage, Team Omega dons soft, white towelling robes. Hooded, they line like Maries. A vestal atmosphere. Morning sets out across the sea. It illuminates urns of fruit, freshly drawn spring water and nectar. The Oracle takes her place at the head of the long, sea-facing table. There is an ageless and elfin quality to her. Her silver hair is turbaned. Her robe is snowy silk. Her nails are curved and white as teeth. Her eyes are colourless quartz. A teenage girl attends her. Anita and V take up lotus positions. The HOLY box lies open. A tray of torn envelopes sits to the right of it. Jennifer stands and faces them. Using a long, silver dagger, she slits one of the envelopes. The Oracle watches. Her attendant pours out a slim tube of nectar. After a moment, Jennifer begins to read:

There are large inanimate objects that have intimidating effect on what you would consider normal. All I can remember, when I think of these things, is shouting out loudly, so violently, that I terrify myself and everyone else around me. I have no control of my surroundings. I can see them everywhere. Even large boulders sometimes. Once there were these rockets. Large rockets in a dark place. A very empty place. And in the bottom of this dark and empty place, you see the rockets from the front—dark, navy-blue rockets. They are dotted in and around the crystalline gravel. And you're panicking and shouting and screaming. You can't let the rockets go off. You can't, but they do. They are vast. But they move so quickly. I can't understand how objects so vast could be gone so fast. With only one deep flash. You can't even think of stopping them. In the end, it's though they had never moved. Like they never been there in the first place. As though they had retained their essential in-animation by denying you the sight of their moving. Even so, they leave their reverberations. In that dark and empty place. They leave echoes.

Jennifer stops. Looking up at the Oracle, something passes between them. The moment is broken. V takes the opportunity to select a carambola from a tureen. Jennifer re-folds the letter. She places it on a silver tray, reaching once more for the dagger.

'The Oracle asked us to watch out for this kind of message.'

In the future, Jennifer will mumble these words. Into her glass phone-plug. She will collapse against a wall. In a house, full of blue light. Figures entwine. A shadowy bed. The door will open. But before this happens, she will say:

'She calls them *messages from the deep*. Not the voices of individuals. These are the voices of cities. Cities sometimes speak through people. Did you know that cities speak through people? Well, of course you do. You're always trying to feed yours lines... I suppose, even I can hear the cities talking, sometimes...'

A distant crackling distracts her. For a moment, it is as though Jennifer is able to hear the past listening in. The sensation describes a confluence of time-streams. Where the future informs moments, which have ceased to exist.

'These are the only messages she answers.' Jennifer finishes, tiring of the sensation of déjà vu.

The future has become the present. A surge of water, somewhere outside. Aquatic light-play. It flexes around the room.

'The Oracle told me that she lives in the spirit world. She says she isn't really here at all.'

Jennifer hesitates again. Her brow knits with perspiration. The crackling radio of the past seems louder.

'Nobody knows *how* she answers these messages...'

Jennifer and Anita go to the mall on an off-day. They lounge around in jeans and sunglasses. Even 'out of uniform', they are unable to shake the look of playing on the same team. Jennifer is tense. She handles a take-out smoothie like a hand-grenade. They drift sharkishly, through clothing stores.

'She's mad you know,' Anita says.

Jennifer pulls a top from a show-rack. She looks it over. Anita waits for a response. Her chlorophyll coloured eyes sharp and mobile as sniper mounts.

'I love her, I do,' she adds cautiously. 'But she's mad.'

Jennifer glances absently at Anita. Then sidelong at a sales clerk.

'Can I try these on?'

The shop assistant points out a door. They pass into a long, white passage. Jennifer selects the last mirror-cube. The lock activates a drift of pulpy music. Anita folds neatly into the only seat. She snaps open her purse. There is a general watch-work precision to Anita's movements. She performs each task with mechanistic efficiency. As though programmed for it before birth. Jennifer peels off her t-shirt. She regards herself critically in the three-way mirrors. Using her compact, Anita prepares a small amount of cocaine. Different faces travel across Jennifer when she steps into a mirror. They traverse like fish. She tests each against the garment. Anita angles a Minora blade.

'I'm not saying I don't believe,' she continues diplomatically.

'You don't *want* to believe,'

'I can't believe that she speaks to spirits…'

Jennifer turns, inspecting herself from various angles. Eventually she flicks off the top, swimming into another.

'Spirits are always speaking to us,' she murmurs. 'We need someone to answer them, to translate what it is they are trying to tell us.'

Anita glances at her exasperation.

'Jen, we're the ones answering those letters. *We're* the ones alleviating the burden of the common man. Not her. I'm sure she feels what she is doing is somehow important. But the fact is—it just isn't.'

She pauses for a moment, struggling to express herself.

'She doesn't help anyone,' she eventually mutters.

Anita resumes her intricate chopping, blustering on:

'No-one gives a fuck what the spirits are saying! I mean maybe they did once. But they just don't anymore. People want someone to understand their suffering. To say something supportive. They don't want absurdist nonsense.'

She abruptly dives her head. Does a line. Jennifer is reminded of nature documentaries. Cormorants skewering fish. Anita offers the compact. Jennifer is indecisive. Then some face swims across her. She bends to inhale the offering in a single, sharp breath. Anita packs up surgically. Jennifer sways. She pulls off the latest top, inspecting her nudity with microscopic intensity.

'How can we understand what god is saying if we've forgotten god's language?' she asks her reflection.

Anita fidgets, self-absorbed, adjusting unseen wrinkles.

'Look around you, babe,' she mutters. 'God doesn't live here anymore.'

Jennifer cannot take her eyes from her reflection.

Anita sleeps like she's in a coma. When she's on her stomach, it's a murder scene. Jennifer's head tucks under Anita's jaw. Late afternoon filters through terrace doors. Jennifer can't sleep. A muted television spurts old cartoons. Like toothpaste from a tube, she is thinking. Sitcoms loom. It's one of those fat, faceless, cruise-ship afternoons. Cargoed heavily with inertia. Once-solid slabs of sunlight retract. Jennifer watches them inch across the ceiling. She's been tracking them for an hour. Palm trees rustle beyond wood-slatted screens. Anita's place is spartan. It could have come in a box (and probably did). They lie, bundled in Egyptian cotton. A tennis racket balances against the sun sliced cupboard. Really, it's really the maid's flat, Anita jokes. 'She spends more time here than anyone else. Sweet lady. Excellent weed connection. Even makes tea!' Although clearly from a conservative household, the maid happily accommodates Jennifer and Anita's 'playing-house' act. And it's more than just the role of the 'matronly domestic' Anita has enforced. Jennifer feels that the woman *understands*—in a sisterly sort of way. Who knows how *it* started anyway. Or what *it* meant. Maybe it was just the expense accounts. Free clothing, coke and complimentary spa treatments did go a long way. Or maybe it was just one of those mirror-games. The kind that slowly that turn into someone to watch television with on Sunday evening. Life is lonely in the outer reaches of space. Neither of them would admit to loneliness. Years of cynical detachment had hardened Anita to bullet-proof porcelain. She was her own one-man chess club. Jennifer didn't like sleeping alone. But behind the Venetian masks lay genuine affection—the universal intimacy of sisterhood. Taken to pathological extremes perhaps. But still heart-felt and sincere. A clever girl can get tired of being called a feminist. Some canaries just want a cellmate. Jennifer can't sleep. She lies, entwined by troubling thoughts. The light drains. Edges fuzz with dusk. Anita awakens in the dim half-light.

'How long we sleep?' she murmurs.

'I didn't sleep.'

Anita squirms onto her stomach. They lie face to face. Mirrors in the gloom.

'I could eat,' Anita mumbles.

Jennifer rummages for a cigarette. Lighting it, she slumps. Breathing coils into the gloom.

'I'm on Eye-detail,' she replies.

She stares blankly into the television glare. Anita rolls, coughing into the pillow. In the dimness, her ruffled hair lends her an unusual frailty. Jennifer is disturbed by this image of vulnerability. The air is so still in here, she thinks. It feels pressurized. She can actually hear her cigarette crackle.

'Do you believe in predestination?' she asks Anita.

In the future Jennifer will ask the same question of Ziq. She will be slouched in much the same position. Smoking in her own bed. Black sheets will twine about her legs in dead of night. Ziq will be lying to her left. A similar position to one Anita holds. It's one of those replications that cause a person to doubt the supposedly chaotic nature of the universe. After staring into darkness, and much consideration, Ziq answers:

'Yes. I believe our destinies are already written. I don't think that we are afforded the luxury of choice. Free will is an elaborate illusion—to keep us in line. We live in a cage of time. All we have is the curse of inevitability.'

He pauses for a moment. Then continues.

'I knew from the moment that I saw your true face. I knew that one day we would be lying in a bed like this, speaking like this. That's the curse of inevitability. There is no choice.'

He turns. His face falls into shadow.

'Didn't you also know?' he asks.

Jennifer looks down at Anita and sees the future. She feels an ice-cold strand of possibility. It fossilizes—into an unquestionable certainty. The world becomes a life-raft. Unsure of rescue, yet hopelessly bewitched by the ocean. Jennifer suddenly understands. This is how the Oracle must feel—every moment of her life. Cold, starry draughts blow in from the future. They bathe her in ice. Jennifer senses this quantum pull, as one would the cries of distant children. Children she is incapable of comforting. The future has petrified the Oracle. It has transformed her into something *other*. Now she is a kind of sphinx. A sphinx with false nails and autocratic tendencies. Jennifer has to admit—the Oracle chills her to the bone. Anita murmurs in her half-sleep.

'I have to go,' Jennifer announces abruptly.

Life Underground

Ziq receives a cryptic SMS around one am. He follows its directions. Down into dingy, industrial districts. He carries his tantō balisong loosely. Following barbed wire racks. There comes a distant screech of trains. The words *black angels roost* pattern the supports of an underpass. Ziq senses these inner-city angels. They sharpen wings against rooftops. A faint, orange firelight manifests in the distance. It is out of kilter with the drabness. He approaches its glow. Watching it furl along the sides of an old brick tower. A tortured column of smoke pushes into the shadow-sick sky. A warehouse is ablaze. Men cluster, agitated. Ziq enters the glare. The blister and crack of wood come into focus. An antiquated siren begins to clang—in the depths of the burning building.

'What happened?' he asks a nearby guard.

The watchman's response is incoherent. Old wood floors, vagrants. Conspiracies trade hands around the fire. Ziq gets the gist. He drifts from the blaze. The men fluff about, bleating and chattering. Smoke vomits from a fractured window. Fragments fall several stories. They shatter against the roar of the blaze. Moving shadows increase the confusion. Ziq distinguishes a spindly silhouette. It squats in litter, beside the burning factory. He approaches the figure. It wears a hideous papier-mâché bird mask. The visage gleams eerily out of the trash. As Ziq draws closer, the figure removes the mask. A malnourished, boyish face. Damaged spectacles. He squats in the garbage, his clothing soiled. The word: JAYBIRD is scrawled across the back of his shirt in permanent marker.

'Well, hello,' Jaybird calls out cheerfully.

He has a New Yorker twang. It lends his voice a discordant sitcom cheeriness. Ziq stands, hands in his pockets. He is not quite prepared to enter the stinking passage of trash.

'You have to stop doing things like that,' he complains, indicating the burning building.

Jaybird glances down thoughtfully. He examines his dirtiness in the dark.

'I've been getting these pains,' he mumbles. 'In my stomach...'

Ziq listens, a blend of concern and revulsion.

'I think I have a worm,' Jaybird confides.

Ziq eyes the fire. Sirens approach.

'Let's get out of here,' he mutters.

Jaybird was an art student when Ziq met him. He'd make enormous sculptures out of meat. Then leave them to rot in the faculty basements. Once he tried to steal a vulture from the zoo and was arrested. At the time, Ziq had been working as the projectionist in a small art-house cinema. He had fallen into a comfortable rut. Sometimes, he doubled as an usher. When the owner's nephew was too drunk to work. He liked the solitude of the projectionist's booth. Very few people visited the place. When they did, it was mainly at night. Once, during a screening of 'The Birds', Ziq noticed a scrawny figure stealing into the cinema. He had a large sack. Halfway through the film, the sack was untied. A multitude of kidnapped sparrows was unleashed. Some girls screamed. Management kicked up a fuss. Ziq decided to stay quiet about the identity of the culprit. Some friendships are like plane crashes. Although the danger is apparent, it is ignored. Perhaps, like a large majority of crash victims, they assume 'it could ever happen to them'. Eventually, the friend becomes like a bad tooth. They hurt and discolour. But one is always hesitant to extract.

Ziq and Jaybird cross the city at night. The bird mask bobs in the gloom. Jaybird shuffles and rattles. Loping, he apes the gait of a wounded animal. Ziq is silent, withdrawn. He emits no sound whatsoever. Even when he walks. Jaybird stares up at the mountain.

'That fucking rock,' he grits. 'Everywhere you go, it's there. Dominating the top edge. Watching."

'Ignore it,' Ziq snaps.

'How can you ignore a six-hundred-million-year-old wall of rock! It's six times older than the Himalayas! Bad Feng Shui. I tell you. That thing is influencing us now—even as we speak."

'Ignore it,' Ziq mutters in exhaustion.

'These things must be dealt with…'

Around them, streets yawn with desolation.

Back on the Pharm. They cross a ruined sports field. Sheep loom. Ziq empties the day's haul into a bucket near the washing line. The mad cockerel will crow soon, thinking that it's day. It is blind and cannot remember the dawn. The pair move off, encountering a knot of vagrants. They huddle around a garbage bin fire. All greet wordlessly. In the manner of medieval pilgrims. Drawing closer to the larger structures on the rise, the pair enter a broken building. For a while, they tread lightly. Complete blackness. Eventually, Ziq seals them behind a heavy door. Sightless, they padlock it. Once secure, Jaybird ignites a hand-held spotlight. A ramshackle graveyard of junk. Decaying corridors nuzzle away from the light. Together, they pick their way through the flotsam and jetsam. Mobility is slow. The passages are fraught with obstacles. Ragged holes gape in the floors. Some months ago, an enterprising hobo had arrived. He carried with him lengths of copper telephone wire taken from poles in the desert. He and a few others had attempted to jury-rig illegal electricity for the Pharm. Despite the odds, they had succeeded. Now, usage is kept low to avoid attracting attention. Those in the know, limit access. Jaybird's idea had been to create a secret lair—deep within the junk. His sanctum is surrounded by booby traps. They hobble through this minefield. After some time, a watery glow appears. Pipe-gorged aquariums, housed in an ante-chamber. Ziq feeds vivid fish specially prepared food. When he is done, the pair penetrate deeper into the nether regions. Darkness rocks and jerks in the spot. It threatens constant engulfment. More clutter. Broken toys and car bumpers. Vast bulbs of corrupted polystyrene. Moth-eaten sofas hunch like fallen cattle. A hundred stacked bottles threaten perpetual collapse. Rotting magazines invent dwarf walls and passages. Fatigue swamps this phantasmagoria of used things. Ziq slogs through. Moving against a heavy current.

Eventually, they emerge. The catacomb is stacked with sculptures and life-size papier-mâché figures. Axe-carved wooden idols stand to. Totem masks haunt mildewed corners. Each sculpture has been pilfered systematically. From the pungent markets, downtown. The lost American sets his bird mask on a special hook. He collapses into a wicker chair. There, he cradles his stomach. Ziq drifts into the idols. He settles against a wall. The stillness of dead things jellies the cellar. Jaybird reaches down. He finds a cigarette in a bundle of scraps. Every sound is amplified. Cave acoustics. He lays the hand-spot on the floor, rocks it with his foot. The movement flutters the room with eerie syncopations. Ziq sinks to his haunches. He listens to the sound of the cigarette. In the light-lurch, he watches smoke invade the sculpture garden.

'I've seen the faces of tapeworms,' Jaybird announces. 'I've seen them through electron microscopes.'

Ziq ignores him. He is sullen. He feels like he is sinking into the earth.

'Arsenals, those faces. Hooks, beaks and claws. Glowing little horns. Geometric mandibles...'

For Ziq, the words press home the insanity of their existence. Down, amongst these broken images of humanity.

'I don't understand how burning down buildings can be considered creative,' he points out bitterly.

Jaybird fidgets. He considers with great seriousness, the consequences of his actions.

'The sun is burning as we speak,' he eventually reasons.

Ziq remains inert.

'I've been eradicating the rhythms of language,' Jaybird continues. 'I'll soon be able to put into practice a method that verbalizes subtext, whilst simultaneously doing away with the cerebral virus, commonly referred to as *small-talk.*'

Ziq searches for his sleeping bag. It lies, concealed in the space between two mannequins. He eases off his shoes, inching into the battered hollow-fiber pocket. Tomorrow he will bathe with home-made glycerin. In a stream, partway up the hill. He will wash his clothes in a tin pail.

'By removing key-letters, I can alter the supposed meaning of words. I can re-forge them, into something organic. Something entirely new. Something coherent and spontaneous.'

Jaybird begins to gesticulate. He invents hand signals. Smearing perfect smoke patterns.

'Instead of *fuck* for example, I would say *uck*. Instead of *spectacles* I would say, perhaps *pectacs*, etcetera, et a Sarah, its Petra...'

'How are people supposed to understand you?' Ziq asks, disinterestedly.

'Nobody understands anybody!' Jaybird shrieks.

The noise is deafening.

'Empathy was crucified long before Christ! That's the whole fucking point!'

His words chain into a tirade. They slur against one another like drunks in a crowd.

'The only real meaning we communicate is in the cadence of our voices! The retarded singing we call speech! The unspoken eech which ee tuck en hazz, tantic un...cun...'

He disintegrates into incoherent mumbling. Then furious silence. He clutches his stomach. There is a moment of quiet. The moment multiplies. Time passes without seeming to move. As it sometimes does, underground.

'Hi cun eep,' Jaybird announces solemnly.

His foot catches the spotlight. All the shadows jerk. Ziq lies in the shaking darkness. In the warmth of his sleeping bag, his hand touches the Polaroid of Jennifer. Sleep spreads. A dream of moth's wings.

Oscar Night

The suite is one of their best. Brick notices something familiar. It's the same room in which V had been collared—in the video. The thought makes his nose throb, though not unpleasantly. He reaches a hand to his face, tentatively exploring the bandage.

'Welcome to Africa,' he mutters to his reflection.

He eyes the bottle of complimentary champagne. His alcoholism had made headlines. Management could have been more tactful, he thinks. Then he realizes what old news he must be. He rips up the card of apology. It had arrived with an ostentatious rose bouquet and the obligatory fruit basket. By the time he drifts to the sea-view, the telephone is ringing. He observes it semi-ironically. He has little or no interest in speaking to anyone—perhaps ever. After a while it stops. He is contemplating a bath when someone knocks at the door. Despite the obvious logic of the manifestation, Brick is stunned to find his old friend Mo skulking in the corridor. A gratuitous bandanna wraps around the large man's ruddy neck. He is clad head to toe in biker leathers. These are simply too new and shiny to be authentic. Upon the director's head is a gleaming winged helmet—clearly rooked from the costume department. For a moment, Brick cannot help but be happy to see his old buddy. Then he notices the Oscar statuette in Croeser's hand. The embryonic smile dies on his damaged face. Croeser is clearly affected by this. He layers over his reaction. That famous smile—the one no-one could ever refuse.

'Already getting into fights with the locals. This is why I love you, Brick.'

'Come in, Mo.'

Croeser strides in, instantly dominating the room.

'Where are you hiding, my little black panther?' he yells out, much to Brick's irritation. 'Come on out baby, I've seen it all before!'

'V's not here. Fix you a drink?'

Croeser whirls around, incredulous.

'You didn't like her? I'm sorry! I thought a fat slice of jungle pussy would be just the thing after…'

Brick cuts him short, holding up the champagne.

'Hotel sent this up to apologize for nose. Seems appropriate, considering that garden gnome you have there.'

Croeser goes quiet and pensive. He regards the Oscar as Brick peels gilt from the cork.

'I suppose this has been a long time coming,' Croeser announces.

Brick glares at him, disliking the theatrical undertone. Croeser is unable to meet his gaze. He turns his head away. The helmet, Brick notes, creates a calculated illusion. It describes a fallen Olympian. He tenderly touches at his bandaged nose. What a pair they must make, he thinks.

'You know it as well as I do, Brick; this guy is as much yours as he is mine. Christ, he's our bastard lovechild!'

'I suppose you have plenty of experience with bastard love-children.'

'Damn it brother, I'm trying to apologize to you!'

The cork pops abruptly. A gush of champagne drenches the roses.

'Got to be some flutes in the kitchenette,' Brick mutters, exiting the room.

Croeser hovers. He rubs the statue affectionately. It seems to be a regular ritual of his. He abruptly removes the helmet, setting the statuette upon a mantle. Free of the winged helm and with his scuffled hair, he radiates a sudden, dejected impression of age. Brick notices. He wordlessly hands Croeser his champagne. Croeser sees that Brick's glass is filled with orange juice. He does not comment. Their eyes meet for a moment. The pleading quality in Croeser's face accosts Brick. He realizes that the director is trying to release the statuette, in spite of his all-consuming self-interest. Perhaps it is simply a token sacrifice. Nevertheless, the act chimes a chord somewhere in Brick. Maybe it's all Croeser can do to make amends. His anger gears down a notch. The director raises his glass quickly, almost telepathically, recognizing that Brick is ready to listen.

'Brick, if you only knew how sorry I am. I know that if you just give me one more chance, I can make it up to you.'

'You took all the credit for the work I did on *Game Over*. When it came to the crunch you didn't hesitate to take it and run. Everyone told me that it's what you would do. I just didn't listen.'

'Don't torture me Brick. I already have one leading man putting me on the ropes…'

'And to balance the books you are putting a leading lady on the ropes?'

Croeser simply stares.

'Delilah Lex?' Brick continues. 'Is she even out of her teens?'

Croeser cracks a mischievous smile. It takes him a second or two to realize that Brick is not paying him a compliment. He strides to the windows, his face clouded. Brick turns away too. In doing so, he notices the Oscar on the mantle. It is as though he is seeing it for the first time. It gleams. Freshly polished, it begins to exert some unwelcome enchantment upon him. Brick drains his glass and realizes unexpectedly that it isn't liquor. He regards the vessel in an unsatisfied manner. Then tops it up with sparkling water. Croeser starts to speak. Again, there is a somewhat rehearsed quality to his wording. Only this time, Brick is listening.

'The picture was falling to pieces Brick. Hell, I was falling to pieces. We'd worked together so many times it felt natural for you to take the reins when I couldn't get it up. That hole I'd dug for myself in Laurel Canyon. All that fucking sugar. I was in the ass of dreamland, baby. Sure, I promised you a co-directing credit. I would have promised you anything! Don't you see how scared I was, Brick?—How much I needed you? How was I to know that you'd show actual talent? I promised the world without thinking…but then, I saw how well we were working. I liked it. *Game Over* was game on! Big time. We were spinning gold, Brick. We were making the kind of picture I'd always wanted to make…'

'You mean I was making the picture you'd always wanted to make.'

'Come on, Brick. Give me my due.'

'Fine, I admit it. When you're in the zone, nobody can move a camera like old Croeser-control. Even flamed out on speedballs and after twelve days of binge-drinking, you can still land the plane on the edge of a studio dime.'

He raises his glass in a mock-toast.

'…But lost your edge in the 90's. Hey, you were gold in '87, but the bottom dropped out when your nose started running the show. All that pre-production you used to insist on, the pencil sketch bibles, all of it. You died on the vine and you didn't even know it, brother. By the time you asked me to step in, you were just another bloodsucking robot looking for a lifeline.'

'1996. We were a wonderful team, Brick. We struck gold.'

'It was *you* who got greedy when the buzz kicked in. Nobody expected we'd get in the running. Maybe the string-pullers, sure—but certainly none of the roaches at ground zero. All those famous Croeser appetites kicked in and just kept on kicking.'

A moment of silence.

'Sure, Brick,' Croeser finally admits. 'That's exactly what happened.'

Brick drains his glass reflexively, again. He stalks over towards the bottle of champagne, circling it. Croeser observes him closely.

'So now you want us to work the old magic again, is that it?' the star mutters. 'Some rooster is fucking up the magic castle and its radio for back-up time…Well, I got news for you, sunshine; my radio's deep fried. It's been bashed and battered—for decades. You're reaching for smoke bringing me down here.'

Croeser seems to derive a kind of sure-footedness from his Brick's weakness. He shifts effortlessly into the role of a director, comforting his troubled star.

'Brick, you underrate yourself. Always have. Sure, pride kept me from getting in contact, but I've wanted to make it up to you for ages. There just hasn't been an opportunity.'

'Well, that's just it with you, isn't it, Mo? —Opportunity. Del Croeser doesn't lift a finger unless there's something in it for him.'

'You've forgotten how the industry works, Brick. There really wasn't a solid window until now. I really think it could work between us.'

'How could I ever trust you again?'

Croeser approaches Brick slowly, circling the stem of his glass in his fingers. He stops just short and looks closely into Brick's eyes.

'Grow up, Brick. Sooner or later we'll both be dead. Everyone we've ever fought or fucked will be dead. We're sinking ships. It's taken me this long to figure it.'

He sets his hand weightily upon the actor's shoulder.

'How long do you plan to hold a grudge, brother?'

Brick looks over at the statuette. It seems to stare back at him.

'We can win this thing, Brick.'

Brick turns to Croeser.

'Fuck it,' he mutters. 'Let's get drunk.'

Spice Trades

V picks her way up through the darkness of the Pharm. The ruin makes her wince. A mouldy tire emerges from the gloom. It overflows with baby chickens and rotten lettuce. V scowls, redirecting the blue flare of her cigarette torch. It catches Fortunato, as he emerges from a broken wall. The wiry man sports sunglasses, despite the pitch blackness. It amuses her. She knows the glasses are purely for her benefit. He can't stand for her to see his eyes—even if it reduces him to blindness.

'How can you spend so much time in this garbage pit?' she laughs.

'How…Insensatez,' he sings wryly.

He tosses her a packet. She is turning to leave when he calls her back.

'The great white hunter is in the car?'

'He is. Come say hello.'

Fortunato makes a show out of kicking a nearby bucket. It flies into the darkness, disturbing some goats. The action strikes V as a little overdone. She senses that he is curious—perhaps even bored. What *could* he have been doing before she came, she wonders? In a *garbage dump*, no less!

'Come on,' she says, taking him by the hand.

Despite his outburst, he allows himself to be led peaceably down the muddy path. After a while he retrieves his hand. On the pretext of adjusting his collar. She smiles in the dark.

The limo is parked just outside the Pharm gate. On Military road. Despite the squatting, the area is still government land. Law enforcement agencies utilize the lower region as a paddock. Police horses sleep in rows. Pretty, German-colonial houses come into view, near the gate. Their pristine colours clash starkly with the rural wreckage of the Pharm. None of the locals seem to register the contrast. Perhaps constant exposure creates a kind of vintage uniformity. Most of the buildings are old, after all. One of the limo's back windows un-scrolls. Fortunato is stunned to find an inebriated Brick Bryson.

'What's the matter, dear?' V smirks.

'You didn't warn me that *he* would be here…'

'I thought it would be a surprise. Come on, let me introduce you.'

'But he's drinking,' Fortunato complains, somewhat cryptically.

'Everybody suffers in their own way, Fortunato.'

'What's going on out there?' Croeser bellows.

His high-volume American accent invades the quiet neighborhood. It lends the car and its company an uncomfortable, proprietary air.

V entices Fortunato to the window. Croeser blatantly ignores him. By now Brick is a bottle down and red around the gills. He is laughing uproariously at the screen. Wire-frame trolls beat the stuffing out Sasha Styles. A girl at the back meets Fortunato's eye, before returning to her phone. He recognizes Jennifer from a previous buy. Another man, in his mid to late fifties, occupies the far corner of the car. He, like Jennifer, is also absorbed in the operation of a hand-held device. A name-tag on his lapel reads: Greenbaum. Though most refer to him as 'Greenie'. Perhaps because he resembles something of a leprechaun (by way of a lawyer).

'Brick,' V announces. 'I would like to introduce you to Fortunato,'

Brick notes her prim, air hostess hand gestures. He finds them exotic.

'Hay! How're you doing there, buddy?' Brick smiles, holding up the bottle. 'Champers?'

'No,' Fortunato scowls, turning instantly from the group.

He shoots a final loaded glance at V, before vanishing into the darkness. Brick appears confused. Croeser, who has observed the entire interaction, slaps his old friend's back.

'Fuck these teetotalers, old pal of mine, fuck them in the face!'

'Fuck them in the eye!'

V re-enters the vehicle, surreptitiously passing the bag of suicide pills to Croeser. Then they are upon their merry way again.

'So, where is your *third friend* tonight?' Croeser sneers.

'Work,' Jennifer responds curtly.

'*Work*? Too bad,' the director drawls. 'It's a shame she couldn't tag along. Though I have to say, she irritates me.'

The hilarious scene with Sasha repeats. This time Brick's face is serious. He has become drawn in by a technicality. He mentions it to Greenie, who feeds him background information.

'Be careful Delaney,' V warns 'Anita has ears everywhere—she might even spike your drink!'

Her comment elicits a panicky look from Jennifer. V winks slyly at her. The complicit exchange misses Croeser by a wide margin—just as V calculated.

'Come on, girls,' the director growls. 'Don't tease me about that paparazzi incident. I won't deny that skirt her dollar for dosing me— she clearly had a mouth to feed. I'll weather it. She gave me enough in return.'

Jennifer scowls at V, who smiles. Both precisely aware of how little Chloe had to 'give' to get him drugged.

'Delaney's a Leo with an Aquarius rising— he can't take personal criticism.' V says.

'My star sign is a lobster,' Greenie mumbles enigmatically.

'So, how are you finding our country?' Jennifer asks Brick.

'Don't you mean *your* country?' Croeser adds maliciously. 'After all, you're the only native in the car.'

'Actually, I come from the ocean,' Jennifer explains matter-of-factly.

'She does!' V laughs. 'She's always in the pool!'

'Well, I was born on a yacht, somewhere near New Zealand,' Jennifer explains.

'Interesting,' the director nods. 'Maybe that's why you remind me so much of Delilah.'

'Be careful Jen. Next thing he'll be fixing you up on dates with his best friend!'

Brick looks away to avoid laughing.

'Hay, I'm being serious!' Croeser protests. 'Don't you agree Brick? From the back, we could have Delilah's body double here.'

'I'm afraid I don't know Delilah's body well enough to comment,' Brick comments.

He turns to Greenie, who is trying to show him an image on his phone.

'Ah, this glorified backwater!' Croeser rants at the world beyond the window. 'It's clear that apartheid never ended.'

'Didn't it?' Brick asks, bemused.

'How could something like apartheid disappear so fast?' V mentions, siding unexpectedly with her former lover. 'Things like that don't just vanish overnight..."

Brick catches a glimpse of their private relationship. So, a bone of seriousness did lie concealed. What agonizing pillow talk they must have shared, he thinks.

'Heard of the xenophobic riots?' Croeser asks Brick.

'Sounds like something out of the film. Is it?'

'Hell, no!' Croeser barks. 'This is reality, Brick. A new generation of racist swine has shuffled toward Bethlehem to be born—perfectly tutored by their former white oppressors. These entitled fuckers have decided that they are better than the Africans from other parts of Africa.'

'Even the Congolese?' Brick teases.

'It's no laughing matter,' V say's seriously.

'She's right,' Croeser says. 'People were decapitated in the streets, out on the East Coast.'

'Decapitated!' Brick exclaims. 'Why?'

'The usual bullshit. Immigrants taking our jobs—that sort of thing,' Croeser replies.

'Unbelievable,' Brick sighs, taking another swig.

'There's more racism in the US, to be honest,' Jennifer pipes up. 'I mean, of course there's going to be generational scar tissue here.'

'People will tell you Nigerians are drug dealers and pimps,' V tells Brick. 'Now, I used to live in Lagos. I know a lot of good Nigerians. But not so many on Long Street. Though the thing is, with crime syndicates—they sometimes favour their countrymen. Especially in strange countries. And if they are strong—they tend to give a false impression of their National character—to anyone who doesn't know better…'

'But the keynote of this place is still prostitution,' Croeser points out. 'Just like Italy.'

'Fuck is that supposed to mean?' Jennifer asks.

'It means that here, people will prostitute anything for a buck— old churches, cultural institutions, bodies, languages, you name it! Just like Italy!'

'A real bargain basement fire-sale, for anyone with foreign currency,' V adds, elbowing Croeser in the ribs.

'Hay, I'm not denying that I'm taking a fat slice here and there,' he laughs, slapping her thigh.

Tiring of the conversation, Jennifer pops a vape-pod and starts typing on her phone.

'So, it's not just these Afrikaner types, then?' Brick asks, unsure of his footing.

'If you stand on your average person's head their whole life, they are going to aspire toward standing on someone else's head—just to get even,' Croeser tells him, snatching the bottle out of his hands. 'It's the basic psychological mechanics of a system like apartheid. It's built to last. In any case, the old controlling powers didn't just dissolve. They just went into the private sector.'

'Africa is ruled by foreign economics,' V adds. 'Just look at Congo.'

'How so?' Brick asks, completely out of his depth.

'Ever heard of Coltan?' she asks him.

'Can't say that I have.'

'It's an ore—and it's found in my home country. It also just happens to provide a vital component for smart-phones. Without Coltan—none of these new devices will work. Coltan mining has financed many wars in my country.'

'Corporations are the new colonists,' Croeser belches. 'Or, rather the old ones—wearing different party costumes. They'll ruin entire populations for a fat slice.'

'Pass me that bottle,' Brick says. 'I think I need a drink after all these conspiracy theories.'

'Oh, don't be so *American*, Brick,' Croeser scolds, handing him back the champagne.

'He's right,' V nods. 'Exploitation is the reality of Africa. You are now here and you cannot simply bury your head in the sand. Someone will steal your pants!'

Croeser bursts into laughter. For a moment, Brick can see them as the perfect power couple. The effect doesn't last long.

'I suppose, it all started with apartheid,' Brick rationalizes. 'At least we know who to blame.'

'It's tempting to put everything on the shoulders of the Boers and the British for constructing such an unforgivable system of oppression,' V tells him. 'The truth is that almost every single tribe who entered Southern Africa—with the exception of the San, of course, were colonists; many of them quite ruthless.'

'The San?' Brick asks.

'Also known as Bushmen,' Croeser explains. 'Though I've heard 'San' is viewed as a derogatory title these days. Some tribe called them that to mock them for not owning cattle, can you believe it? They are kind of a first nation here, an aboriginal and ancient people. In Victorian times, they were classified as a species of monkey. You could buy a license to hunt them. In fact, it was quite fashionable in the salons of Paris and London to carry a money purse fashioned out of a Bushman's scrotum.'

'Insanity,' Brick says, shaking his head.

'Oh, we haven't changed all that much as a species,' his old friend grins. 'We just hide our savagery beneath red tape now. The old monkey skull is still there—grinning back from beneath the skin.'

'Don't be so hard on monkeys,' Jennifer scolds. 'I mean, that's such a *First-world* way of looking at things…'

'Oh, touché, Blondie,' Croeser toasts. 'I'll remember that next time I see some heads roll the street!'

'I think, you are all generalizing,' Greenie chips in. 'It's just a place, like any other—full of people, good and bad. You can't judge an entire culture by a handful of zealots. It's like saying that everyone in Israel is in favour of the Palestinian occupation.'

'Aren't they?' Croeser jokes.

'Of course not,' Greenie says. 'People are individuals. Those that are strong enough will curry individual opinions—for, against or perhaps, even, without any interest whatsoever!'

'That's true,' Croeser nods. 'Not everyone chooses to be a sheep…'

'Or a lemming,' Jennifer mutters.

'…We each create our private universes,' Croeser muses.

'Or get others to create them for us!' V teases, causing Brick to chuckle involuntarily.

'…Though, there is a kind of national identity to various places that, I suppose, the landscape itself imposes,' Greenie rambles thoughtfully. 'I've noticed a kind of fraternity here that I've only ever seen in war-zones.'

'Because of the crime?' Brick asks.

'Yes, exactly,' Greenie nods.

'Well, crime springs from need,' V points out. 'Isn't the creation of that need, a crime in itself?'

'How so?' Brick asks.

'Like these Nigerian drug dealers,' she shrugs. 'You think most expats had criminal intentions when they came here looking for a better life? Of course not. But when you are on refugee status, can't open a bank account, can't get proper work, can't rent, are harassed continually…I mean, one has to survive.'

'I suppose the fraternity I mentioned comes out of an acute sense of life and death,' Greenie observes. 'When you are living in fear for your life, you build strong bonds with people you feel you can trust.'

'Or those you can milk!' Croeser cackles, pinching V's closest nipple.

'…Or you become paranoid and start building walls,' Greenie thinks out loud.

'This part of the world has always been run by predators,' Croeser explains. 'Even before people came. The same primal games of hide and seek were going on with the animals— it's part of the land's identity.'

'I'm not sure I understand—or agree that a landscape can inspire crime,' Brick frowns. 'But I think get your point. At heart, it's still a wild place.'

'In any case, foreign markets have a lot invested in South Africa,' V points out. 'They need to paint it a certain way in the press. To attract revenue.'

'I wouldn't put too much stock in the rainbow nation, Mandela-fication of it all,' Croeser tells him. 'That's just retail. Economically, the place is a sinking mess.'

Brick glances out of the window. A series of royal palms and blue-glass fronted beach houses drifts past.

'Looks alright to me,' he says.

'It's the ultimate, corrupt, vacuous, nouveau-riche society,' Croeser booms preachily. 'These assholes want what the first world has. But they've never experienced it first-hand. They can't experience it!—to do that you need to travel. And you can't do that very easily on a South African passport.'

'It's difficult to travel on an SA passport,' V agrees. 'Only the privileged get to do it.'

'Even if you eventually manage, the economy is so choked that your currency will be worth peanuts wherever you go,' Croeser adds. 'It's the end of the line here. Bottom of the known world—trapped between bare ocean and the rest of Africa. Keep moving South and your next stop will be Antarctica.'

'How do the locals handle the physical isolation?' Brick asks him.

'They don't see themselves as isolated. They have a kind of islander's insularity. They imagine that they are at the center of the world. In this case, I would say it's more how are *they* handled.'

'It's a media monoculture,' V sighs.

'Could they compare to Fox-choked Middle-America?' Brick laughs. 'I doubt it.'

'Your average middle-class South African's reference for reality, being so navel-oriented and bourgeois, is the mainstream media,' Croeser points out. 'But, there is no bar of excellence—no standards. These can only come from a global frame of reference. I mean, there's practically no cultural cross-pollination from the rest of the world! Christ, even the internet connectivity is shit for most people!'

'How come?'

'Geographical isolation—Start-ups are always competing to control the internet. They've tried everything—piggybacking off television signals, drones, you name it. Whoever gets control of Pan-African connectivity will rule the roost.'

'So, the media diet, for most of the population, is heavily regulated—due to these restrictions,' V explains.

'And the corporates are right in there,' Croeser grins. 'Selling the middle-class their own diluted version of a first-world lifestyle. With all the beads and trinkets that go with it—at extortionate prices. This whole country's sense of national culture is a nothing more than a cheap ad campaign. Designed to line the pockets of fat cats. There's no room for niche-markets. I'll bet some even feel privileged at being able to side-step generations of cultural development—just to get at a dollar bill lifestyle.'

'A prefab class structure,' V nods.

'What do you think of all this?' Brick asks Jennifer.

She looks up from her phone and shrugs.

'Hey, it's easy to point fingers at other countries,' Jennifer says 'It's what tourists do.'

'But, how do you feel about apartheid?'

'Probably the same way you feel about drone strikes in the Middle East.'

'Unfair enough,' Brick nods, too drunk and bored to pursue the topic much further.

'I'll tell you an Afrikaans story,' Croeser says.

'Fine, let's hear it,' Brick sighs, finishing off the bottle.

'Back in the 1800's, a feller by the name of Josh Slocum was navigating the globe in a homemade sloop,' he begins.

Croeser extracts another bottle of Cristal from the fridge. V obligingly unwraps it.

'Wasn't Slocum the first person to circumnavigate the globe on his own?' Brick checks.

'That's the feller,' Croeser nods. 'He stopped here, after a hiatus on the east coast, took a few weeks to see the sights.'

'Coconut milk and fair maidens,' Brick toasted.

'Well, it's hardly the South Pacific,' Croeser chuckled. 'More like aloe ferox, guano and gold! Aloe was a big export around the turn of the century. Whole towns along the coast used to stink from the cauldrons that they boiled the stuff in.'

'This place as well?'

'No. Cape Town was a refueling point on the Spice route—somewhere to let loose steam and replenish supplies. It became sort of hedonistic halfway house. Ships from every port stopped here. There was a kind of lawlessness.'

'Leopards would steal meat right out of the butcher's shops,' Greenie mentions, his eyes flickering across his phone.

'It would have been a sort of high-end Casablanca in those days, I imagine,' Croeser ruminates. 'Saloons decked out with priceless, Oriental spoils, antiques nipped from all corners of the globe. A place for rare pleasures.'

'Exotic,' Brick nods.

'Not really Slocum's cup of tea though. The man was a loner. Couldn't survive in decent society, obsessed with natural patterns—you know the type. But anyway, since he was a respected captain, his voyage had, by then, attracted attention in the press. He was taken to meet the president—Paul Kruger.'

'Krugerrands?' Brick asks.

'That's the feller, one of the Boer folk heroes—a real cultural icon.'

'Ok.'

'Well, Kruger believed the Earth was flat.'

'How contemporary of him,' Brick jokes.

'Numbskull interpreted the bible literally. Can you imagine it? So, anyway, Slocum is introduced to him as the guy who has just sailed around the world. Kruger replies: 'don't you mean across the world', then snubs him entirely.'

'What's your point?' Jennifer asks, irritated.

'My point, sugarplum, is that this attitude still represents the general mind-set of Afrikaans culture; if it doesn't fit into an accepted provincial, small-town mentality, the majority just pretend it doesn't exist!—or works to suffocate it.'

Jennifer mulls this over.

'Can't argue with you there,' she concedes, returning to her phone.

'It's a shame though,' Croeser sighs. 'They were surrounded by highly developed indigenous cultures. Who knows how it could have all turned out if the Brits hadn't bought them off and turned them into the landed gentry.'

'Civilizations generally survive through assimilation and adaptation,' V notes. 'Those that practice isolationism since their inception, usually end up totalitarian.'

'It's is not even a real language!' Croeser laughs. 'It's more a kind of Creole...'

'But then why is it accepted as one?' Brick asks disinterestedly, his attention drawn back to the dailies.

'It was recognized by the British in exchange for a monopoly on resources,' V explains. 'It's barely a hundred years old, cobbled together from Dutch, German and whatever else was lying around.'

Brick nods. A soundless, onscreen argument erupts between Croeser and Sasha Styles, prompting a walk-off by the star.

'Hey, can we un-mute this?' Brick asks.

Croeser glances over at the screen. His face clouds instantly.

'Fuck that guy,' he snarls. 'I need you to work some enchantment on him, Brick. You know how to handle actors. Let's get a repeat performance of our Oscar days. What do you say?'

'I thought I was here for a cameo?'

'Well, that too, of course. I'd love to write you a little walk-on, get all the fan-boys creaming. But really, I was hoping to make use of your other talents.'

'What talents are those, exactly?' Brick replies coyly, refusing to make this any easier on him.

'You direct the actors, in the scenes we have left, streamline the script—I'll handle everything else.'

'You're over-schedule *and* over-budget!' Brick laughs. 'How can you still have scenes to write and shoot?'

Brick looks over to Greenie for support, but the man remains tight-lipped and avoids his gaze.

'You just let me worry about that, Brick,' Croeser smiles. 'I'm playing the suits just how I want them played.'

'Oh, I don't doubt it,' Brick nods, retrieving the bottle. 'But if you want me, you're going to have to get hold of Sal and make it official.'

'It's a sensitive studio issue, Brick. We can't just dole out a co-directing credit, you know.'

'I want it in a contract by this time tomorrow or I'm on the first plane out of here.'

V smiles hungrily at their exchange. Everyone else is also tuned in.

'Buddy, you're being unreasonable,' Croeser cajoles.

Brick gestures at the fight scene taking place on the screen. 'Looks action-heavy,' he points out. 'Are you talking about an overhaul of pivotal scenes?'

'Actually, I want you to rewrite about forty percent of the dialogue,' Croeser replies soberly. 'Maybe even seventy.'

Brick looks incredulously back and forth between Croeser and Greenie, who still refuses to jump in.

'You are *over-budget and over-schedule*, guys!' he laughs 'How is this going to work?'

'Not much dialogue,' Croeser shrugs. 'What's there needs sharpening—a couple weeks to bring in the boat, but twice the manpower. I'm telling you, we can do this in our sleep.'

'And how is the crew going to take my direction?'

'It's the same crew I always use, they know you. You could literally walk on. We all won those Oscars together! Let's do it again.'

Onscreen, Sasha throttles a green, latex goblin. Spittle flies from his bared teeth as he delivers an unheard, macho ultimatum.

'Clearly Oscar material,' V smirks.

'Everyone's a critic,' Croeser snaps. 'Why don't you start a blog?'

'Are you also involved in production?' Brick asks her.

'No,' V admits. 'But I've been around the biz for a few years. My ex, Fortunato, was also a director, back in Nigeria.'

'I didn't know your boyfriend directed,' Croeser teases. 'What? Music videos?'

'Why don't you ask him sometime,' she replies neatly. 'I'm sure he'd love to chew the fat with you.'

'I don't fraternize with film students.'

'You sure do chew fat, though…' Greenie mutters from his phone.

V leans forward and places a hand firmly on Brick's knee.

'This production needs some class,' she tells him. 'You should help Delaney.'

'What kind of films did…'

'Fortunato.'

'That's right,' Brick nods. 'What kind of pictures did he make?'

'I'll show you some. You can judge for yourself.'

'When did you break up?'

She shrugs, leaning back against Croeser.

'It was Delaney who persuaded me to break it off,' she winks. 'After all, only one jockey gets to ride the prize ponies in the lost kingdom of

Croeser...'

'Don't pay any attention to her,' the director chortles. 'She knows she's too wild to bridle.'

'Unlike some ponies,' V smiles, indicating the screen.

Delilah timeously appears, flicking about a freshly acquired mop of platinum locks.

'I thought she was a brunette,' Brick frowns.

'Delany liked her better as a blonde.'

'Hay, it was a studio decision, ok?' Croeser retorts.

'Did the studio tell you to put your dick in her as well?'

'You know I can't resist anything handed to me on a silver platter,' he grins.

V fixes him in with a cool look. Brick notices that the space between the couple has widened subtly since their previously complicit, political antics.

'How would you know if you've never tried?' she asks him quietly.

Sulette is in a state. Someone has stolen her cocktail dress and heels. She left them on a deckchair by the pool, but now they have vanished, along with her purse. She scans around the party in a panic. She's dressed only in wet, designer underwear. It's an important event for her—the first time Delilah Lex has ever invited her out. But now it's all going to hell and the drugs are kicking in...

Six months earlier, Sulette celebrated her twenty seventh birthday. She started by quitting her job as copy writer. She'd been in the employ of a luxury supermarket chain. All in all, it was a cushy job. Nevertheless, she decided that she would prefer to settle down to some serious housewifery. It was pretty in the old German suburb, beneath the Shark Fin. Her mother owned an antique block of jacaranda shrouded apartments there. Sulette inherited the top floor on her twenty first. She and her husband, Tinus Malherbe (Sulette had retained her maiden-name, Labuschagne), lived in one of the two ground floor garden flats. A pomegranate lined alley connected it to Brownlow at the bottom, and Belle Ombre at the top. As soon as the upper level came into Sulette's possession, her mother, Charlize, set about knocking down adjoining walls. This industrious woman swiftly transformed the entire space into a spacious penthouse. She was also quick to find tenants; a couple of baby boomers, both in marketing. The area used to have a bohemian quaintness. But an influx of tourism following the 2010 World Cup soccer, quickly transformed the old neighbourhood into a cash run. Rentals inflated exponentially, sometimes quadrupling within a couple of years. Foreigners were learning—South Africa was more than mud shacks and brown, lion-haunted veldt. There was real opportunity here—and it was cheap (by first world standards). Charlize was quick to capitalize. She arranged her only child's income dispassionately. When the rental was transferred, she settled down to watch her offspring blossom into adulthood.

Privately, of course, Charlize considered Sulette a lost cause. She had watched the girl waste years, accumulating student debt. First, she wanted to become an actress, then a painter. Finally, Charlize was able to persuade her to enroll in advertising school. She had some contacts at the supermarket chain and was able to get her daughter in on the ground floor. She cleared the student debt without a word. It was a new slate. Unfortunately, Sulette had, by then, become engaged—to her varsity sweetheart. Charlize was of the opinion that they were too young to marry. She opposed the union. However, when she saw how hardworking the fiancé was, Charlize pushed for a summer wedding with all the frills.

Malherbe started out as a runner on film shoots—mostly advertising. While he did this, he also moonlighted as a rope-monkey, dangling tourists off the mountain every summer on rock-climbing tours. Eventually, he was able to fuse his interests and find work as a rigger. Malherbe was a dedicated, salt of the earth type—a real farm boy made good. People trusted him. It wasn't long before he started getting regular gigs in the film industry. After five years (and a loan from Charlize), he had his own company, supervising rigging on-site and offering top-notch consultancy. *Club Ded* was a feather in his cap, his first real blockbuster. He meant to go the extra mile for Croeser, no matter what it took. So, when he heard that Croeser was looking for a picaresque, out of the way crash-pad to avoid the press, Malherbe suggested his wife's 'penthouse'. The baby boomers had moved to Australia and Sulette was dragging her heels about finding new people. Charlize refused to get involved. As a result, Malherbe found himself supporting the household. He wanted to invest in a fishing boat when he turned thirty-five, so something would have to be done about the vacant spot. Being a good sort, he also had it in mind to involve his wife, albeit tangentially, in his work. He could tell that she was envious. It was tragic sometimes, to come home and finding her watching tabloid television while he was out rubbing shoulders with real-life stars. After Sulette quit work, she stayed at home. She claimed to be working on a novel—some dystopian science-fiction thing. It didn't get very far. He bought her a pug and that worked for a while. Malherbe didn't think much would come of his penthouse offer. But when Greenie came back with a positive response, he sprang immediately into action.

Sulette was an impeccable hostess. It was the single legacy her upper middle-class upbringing had afforded her. She excelled at it. Polishing her domestic skills like heirloom spoons, she transformed herself, over the years, into a real kitchen courtesan. She envisioned herself as the perfect wife. Many men agreed. Malherbe was envied his pretty, charming wife (who also came with property). When Malherbe explained Croeser's interest in renting her apartment, Sulette threw her arms around her husband's neck and declared her undying love. She then put on her most expensive high heels, shortest vintage Versace and proceeded to charm the director around her maisonette in the trees. She pointed out the turn of the century architecture and newly installed blond-wood flooring. She showed him the view across Brownlow, which, she explained, had once housed a Victorian tram rail, running to the white sands of Camps Bay. Sulette walked him past the former stable of this old transport line. It was situated halfway down the citrus lined street. The building had been converted into a Parisian café called the Daly Deli. It came complete with striped awnings, wrought iron furniture and Edith Piaf on repeat. Perfect for breakfast, Sulette pointed out with a wink. Croeser was sold. They had a coffee together at the little café, chatted with the owner and strolled back, talking all the while. When Croeser asked Sulette for a blowjob in the back of his limo to seal the deal, she snapped instantly to attention.

Of course, the whole event was watershed bragging-fodder. Sulette kept her friends and family entertained for weeks. Privately, she had juicy ambitions of divorcing Malherbe and becoming the notorious director's new love interest. She would move in with him at his place in Hollywood and settle into the sort of lifestyle she had always foreseen for herself. Eventually, she would divorce him too and find herself a pop-star or something to raise brats with. Unfortunately, Croeser did not proposition her again. In fact, his attitude cooled, quite dramatically, after their episode in the back of the limo. Perhaps she hadn't done it properly, Sulette thought, panicking. She took to consulting guides in the glossies and practicing on bananas. The maid caught her fooling around with fruit in the bathroom. Sulette almost fired her. It was a bad week. However, when she discovered that the one and only Delilah Lex was a regular houseguest in her upstairs apartment she quickly cheered up. She didn't mind playing second fiddle to a celebrity princess. In her mind, Croeser had wanted to continue seeing her but had been forced in line by the hierarchies of social status—hierarchies that Sulette herself, religiously adhered to.

Despite her best efforts and position as landlady, it was difficult for Sulette to get herself an audience with Delilah. She became a kind of Nancy Drew, paying close attention to the comings and goings of the celebrities upstairs. It perplexed her because all the tabloids and celebrity news channels informed her that Delilah was practically engaged to the famous rapper, Real2Reel. Now it looked to Sulette as though the young star was running around with someone three times her age. Knowing something about Delilah, that even the entertainment-news people didn't, excited Sulette supremely. She had even started to get on Malherbe's nerves with her Delilah-this and Delilah-that at dinnertime. She began keeping a notebook and using her phone to photograph her tenants through windows. She had fantasies of selling some of the clearest ones to the press. She prayed to catch them having sex on the balcony. She made detailed notes of their various entourages. Delilah was usually in the company of a taller girl, slender, coffee-coloured, with long black hair. This girl would also spend many nights upstairs with the pair. Sometimes she would even go out with Croeser, alone. Sulette was fascinated by the whole situation. She started writing it all down in the hopes of producing some sort of unauthorized expose.

Things changed when she ran into Trill at a mall. Trill was the name of the other girl. Only, she wasn't a girl. Trill's gender was obvious when you were up close and personal, but it was quite difficult to tell from afar. Sulette was impressed by the new narrative hook that her unwritten novel had acquired. She accosted the strange character after some stalking, introducing herself as the landlady of Croeser's apartment. She was surprised to find Trill demure and self-effacing. Despite he/she/it's close celebrity consorts, Trill still seemed to treat Sulette as some sort of social superior. Sulette found that there was an inbred trashiness to the boy-girl's speech and mannerisms. 'Ghetto', was the only word she could attach to it. Sulette began to wonder whether they had found Trill out on the street. She wondered how celebrities could be in the company of this thing. She couldn't even think of it in terms of 'he' or 'she'. Rather it was an 'it'—like that Gollum creature from *Lord of the Rings*. Only Trill was pretty, like a doll. Of course, its prettiness made it all the more perverse.

She invited Trill out to coffee. They sat at a seafood restaurant overlooking the harbour. The creature was coughing a lot. It sounded congested (possibly contagious). Sulette tried to broach the subject of Delilah, but quickly realized that Trill had no idea who the actress was. Of course, the creature understood that Delilah Lex was 'famous'. It just didn't, to Sulette's mind, fully realize *what that meant* exactly. For her, this was an almost incomprehensible concept. She took the position that Trill was simply too ignorant (or conceivably, too inhuman) to understand the perks of an association with celebrity. She also enquired about the name 'Trill', which she found a bit weird.

'The tunes are cool,' was all the creature could offer.

Not wanting to appear 'un-cool' herself, Sulette nodded knowingly. 'So, what are you doing at the mall?' she asked. 'Doing some shopping?'

'I work at the hotel sometimes,' Trill replied.

There was deadness to the entity's almond eyes that both intimidated and interested her.

'Oh! What do you do in the hotel?' she asked. 'My mother is on the board of trustees.'

Trill frowned.

'In the rooms,' it said quietly. 'I work in the rooms.'

Sulette opened her mouth and then closed it again.

They bought a couple of ice-creams and wandered about. The passages were thick with tourists. In its tiny skirt and split-toe, triple white Nike Rifts, Trill received many strange looks and sometimes even outright mockery. Construction workers, in particular were very vocal. Trill took little notice. Sulette was titillated. She linked arms with her new friend and greedily absorbed some of this raucous attention, smiling at staring passers-by.

'Sometimes we party in that parking lot,' it told her.

It indicated an isolated wing of bays, just behind the concrete shoreline.

'Can I come?' Sulette asked breezily.

Trill looked her up and down. It was a clinical scan, like someone appraising a vehicle for roadworthiness.

'No,' it replied.

'Why not?' she laughed.

'How many men have you had at once?' Trill asked.

Sulette was taken aback.

'...One?' she fumbled.

'Well you'll have to be able to handle at least three if you want to party in the parking lot.'

Trill flitted away for a moment. Leaning on a rail, it watched the sea. It had a small coughing fit and spat something blue and sticky over the rail.

Sulette studied the being closely. She made mental notes. She was completely hooked.

'I don't like the sea here,' Trill scowled, over its shoulder.

'You don't like the sea!' she smiled, joining it at the rail.

'It's cold. I like a warm sea.'

'I went to the Maldives with my husband last June. That sea was warm.'

'I'd like to go to the Maldives.'

'Let's go!' she laughed.

Trill's face grew serious. Sulette realized that it was trying to decide whether or not she had made a proposition. Somehow this amused her.

66

She took the Trill's arm, laughing.

Sulette had originally intended to use Trill to get to Delilah. She hadn't expected to become attached to the creature.

'I made a new friend in the shoe shop!' she announced to her husband, the night following the mall episode.

Malherbe was locked in the bathroom again, sneaking a cigarette. Sulette enjoyed tormenting him while he was trying to find a quiet moment. He fanned smoke away, irritated.

'A friend?' he called back.

'He was trying on shoes,' she sang provocatively.

The effect was more or less instantaneous.

'HE?' Malherbe protested, cocking instantly to attention.

'He was trying on girl's shoes.'

'Oh.'

'What are you doing in there?' she yelled with a smile.

'Oh, there's ants in here…'

The ant thing was becoming a fetish. Just the other week Sulette had caught him on his computer. From his shifty attitude, she'd assumed that he was watching porn. But, after quickly snatching the laptop from him, she was surprised to find a time-lapse video of a mouse corpse being devoured by ants. Malherbe was incredibly embarrassed. He turned a peculiar shade of greenish-pink before yelling at her.

The entire situation was comically reversed, only the next day. Deciding to research her newfound friend on the internet, she chased up a link Trill had sent her. It had tenuously described the site as one of its 'profiles'. Thinking it would lead to social media, she was shocked to find pop-up ads for transsexual strippers and live webcam tabs clotting up her browser. The 'profile' was headlined by a nude and tactfully gender-less picture of Trill. A kaleidoscope of fetishistic peccadilloes followed, many of which she had to research to understand. The name of the profile was *Trillzone*. The word seemed to describe an entire realm. She found herself mouthing it in fascination, while she trawled through a succession of increasingly compromising photos. Malherbe walked in at one point. On reflex, she slammed her laptop shut.

'You watching porn?' he asked, bewildered.

'Nature documentaries,' she sneered.

It was a boring Tuesday, the night her life changed. She was texting Trill. The creature was out hooking in town. Even now, she couldn't get her head around the fact that she was becoming pals with a real-life prostitute. Trill was in one of the Nigerian clubs on lower Long Street. Sulette started nagging to be invited along. Delilah hadn't been around for a couple of days. Sulette was hideously bored. Usually, Trill refused her outright. This time, however, it relented. Malherbe was surprised to find his wife donning denim hot pants and stilettos on a weeknight.

'Going for some shots with your trannie buddy, eh?'

'He's a girl,' she snapped, confusing him completely.

They met on upper Long, which, Trill explained was safer than the lower side. That end tapered grimly down to the deserted foreshore. The foreshore was a region of concrete spaces, highway underpasses and barbed wire. Some Nigerian clubs and sailor's karaoke holes were dotted around there. Sulette had always considered it a no-man's land.

It was the beginning of summer. The street was flush with neon and music. The pair linked arms, pushing past fried food vendors and pedestrians. Many languages networked the pavements. Trill pointed out a trio of Nigerian coke pushers. The men mingled with a gaggle of, what the creature referred to as, 'sex tourists'. These were uniformly blonde, dreadlocked European girls. They had the look of university students. Trill explained that sex tourists were a 'regular type'. They drifted in haphazardly from the North, looking for tall, dark strangers to base a thesis on—or bear children with. It was practice, Trill explained, for refugee Romeo's to 'accidentally' impregnate European or American girls in order to pursue a passport. Sulette nodded excitedly, making notes on her phone.

The street had its own peacock fan of beggary. There were the heroin addicts, worn to ghosts. Almost all were neatly packaged. Some in freshly laundered clothes, all peddling stories of broken-down cars and stolen wallets. They polished these stories every day, until they gleamed. Street children roved like wild birds throughout. And on the aprons of turn-of-the-century pavement corners, you could find, those obligatory old salts, common to every port.

'These clubs used to be cool,' Trill muttered, pointing out a couple of dancehall/hip hop establishments at the top of Long.

'What happened?' Sulette asked.

'Soldiers come in. Congo, Uganda, Rwanda, everywhere,' it complained. 'They get jobs as bouncers.'

'Why?'

'They were killers.'

'Hectic.'

'Don't ask who runs the company that provides bouncers…'

Sulette nods.

'Foreign powers come, arm militants, destabilize governments, take resources,' it continues.

The statement sounded vaguely second-hand. Sulette wondered whose opinions Trill was airing.

'Used to be a party here,' Trill continued 'But in homelands these soldier guys shoot trans. Some Congo bouncers they don't like my

Tanzania friends. Fuck knows. I got nice Congo friends. But these guys misrepresent. Make trouble with this macho shit. Then one gets stabbed. Suddenly its xenophobia…'

'They won't let you in?'

'Five years I've danced here. Now this shit.'

'But you can't pick up men in those places!' she scolded.

'I go to dance.'

They sidestepped a fight. Sulette found herself being pulled energetically up a flight of black-lit stairs. She emerged onto a colonial-era balcony, overlooking the street. The foot traffic seemed even more chaotic from above. Couples smoked shisha in cool corners. A marimba eight-piece band was deafeningly everybody. People were constantly spilling off the dance-floor and lurching against the rickety iron railings. Trill had to shout to be heard.

'I seen people dance on cars, smash them. Political holidays. Someone got thrown against a window—died.'

'No! Didn't the glass break?'

'Thought it would. It didn't. They threw him over and over. He broke.'

'Where?'

'Restaurant down that side.'

'Police sorted it?'

'Too dangerous.'

It was becoming unbearably loud. The floorboards were rattling. They went downstairs and danced on a small, empty stage beside the bar. Sulette was feeling positively teenaged. She couldn't remember the last time she'd gone out like this. She lived less than five minutes' drive from this place. When had her life reduced itself a chain of gym, restaurants, television and the dog, she wondered? She pulled Trill into a corner and kissed the entity spontaneously. The mouth she tasted was cold, molded from plastic or rubber. Its tongue moved languidly, but there seemed to be no undercurrent of emotion. Sulette wiped her lips off and wrapped her arms tightly around a waspy midriff.

'Tell me about Delilah,' she smiled naughtily.

She explored the wiry body with her hands while she talked. Trill's muscles were lax, but there was a nervous tension in the creature—as though it might bolt at any moment. Trill remained passive, somehow unconscious of being handled.

'Delilah's on a voyage,' it explained.

In the roving multi-coloured spots, Trill's face took on a mask-like quality. Sulette realized that she was more than a little tipsy.

'What do you mean?' she giggled. 'Is she going somewhere?'

'You could say that.'

They had drifted into a dark corridor, just off the dance floor. They settled near the restroom landing. People pushed past.

'You know Fortunato?' Trill asked.

'No?'

'He and a few others, they have a plan.'

'A plan for what?'

'For everything. For reality.'

'Sounds like a cult.'

'I suppose.'

'Is Delilah a cult member too?'

'They are all voyaging.'

'What are you talking about?' she laughed, lighting a cigarette. 'Where are they supposed to be *voyaging*?'

'Beneath the waters,' Trill whispered. 'Beneath warm tropical waters.'

She nagged a little more. Trill eventually related the story of how Fortunato had found something in a small coastal village. Trill didn't remember the name of the place, but it was somewhere in Western Africa. The item was a kind of small, dazzling, reef fish. It was pregnant. Fortunato had managed to keep it alive somehow and nurse the fry when they hatched. Witchdoctors used these fish, Trill explained. They cut out a pair of their glands. If you swallowed one, the fish took you places. It was all starting to make sense to Sulette now. These people were members of some exotic drug cult. Her book was going to be a best-seller.

'Are you on these fish glands now?'

'I micro-dose in the mornings.'

'What's it like?'

'Try it.'

'I can't just get high!' Sulette giggled. 'It's Tuesday, for god's sake! Anyway, I have a lot of things to do in the morning. I have to buy dog food and...'

'It's the only way you'll get in with Delilah,' Trill explained.

Sulette smoked. She stared into those dead almond eyes. Dangerous thoughts were entering her mind. She reached over and stroked the creature's eyelids closed for a moment, just to break its gaze.

'Can I micro-dose too?' she asked.

'You have to eat a whole gland first time.'

'Why?'

'Those are the rules.'

She laughed, fidgeted and moved away. Ending up back on the dance floor, she didn't feel Trill come up behind her. Black-nailed fingers settled around her hips. They moved together, low to the floor. She was exhilarated to be the only white person in the club. Everything seemed to be new, fresh and vaguely taboo. She caught flashes of Trill in the strobes, moving in perfect synchronization with her, checking a small phone constantly. Text messages flooded its cheap, throwaway phone. Sulette supposed that they were clients. Somehow it had all been completely normalized; this whole 'letting strangers fuck you for money' thing. But she had chemistry with the night creature. They were becoming girlfriends. Sulette always believed that girlfriends should share everything, like sweets. Almost telepathically, Trill's fingers came from out of the darkness. They entered her mouth. The creature left something on her tongue; a smooth, sugary little globe. She took it out and studied it. It was pink and glossy, like a little dieting pill or an antihistamine. It made her suspicious. Trill noticed what she was doing. It plucked up the pill, placing it once more at the back of her mouth. Its cool palm closed over her lips. She play-fought against it, giggling. Was she resisting, or pretending to resist, she wondered?

'Tastes sweet!' she shouted above the music.

'Candy coated,' Trill answered.

'Are you trying to drug me?' she asked, half-serious.

Trill regarded her un-readably before dancing away. She watched the ambiguous, elfin figure swim through pools of moving light, drawing and repulsing drunken men in equal measure. After a while, Sulette swallowed decisively, chasing her new girlfriend into the center of the floor.

The street had started to remind her of a tropical reef she had seen on a scuba diving vacation. Here could be found the same holes, the same toothy heads poking out. Sulette started to remember what the dive instructor had told them all about moray eels; how they hid in crevices, darting out occasionally to eat things. Sometimes they would fix their jaws on a diver's hand and never let go. Sulette thought of it when she saw her hand in Trill's. She began to feel exactly like the vivid little reef fish whose gland she had eaten—The kind you might see half-in, half-out of a moray's mouth. Only now, she was the one with the poison gland.

She hadn't realized that she'd been stretched out on the dance-floor, lying on her side as though in bed. Trill pulled her up. She was dragged into a filthy toilet cubicle and pushed to her knees. Trill held her hair back while she vomited. Apparently, detoxification was a natural side-effect. Sulette felt terrible afterward. She must have been very toxic, she thought. Her mouth was washed out for her. As soon as they were outside however, the sea breezes caught up with her. They buoyed her up like warm, tropical water. She felt great.

She was being dredged along by her wrist. It made her stumble. Where was her bag? She saw it in Trill's hand and panicked. All her things were in there. Her designer blouse had come undone. She struggled out of it so that it could be replaced properly. A gust of wind came up fast through a side-street, caught it, and ripped it away. Trill looked over at its tumbling form.

'Gone,' the creature announced childishly.

Sulette couldn't stop laughing at this fairy book monster of hers. Looking up from the pavement she suddenly noticed that they had drifted from the street. They were deep in the dark forest of the foreshore. A broken building came and went. Plastic pennants trailed hypnotically from high racks of wire. The streets were completely deserted. They finally emerged from the warren of dark streets. An unfinished highway overpass dominated the harsh environment. It jutted dizzyingly above deserted, fenced off areas. Sulette felt as though they were caught in the gravitational field of this structure. Trill hefted her over concrete crash barriers and through ripped fences, moving them consistently toward it. A car rocketed past at one point, blinding her. Then they were wading through canals of trash, just to be able to grasp the edge of it. Floodlights split the night above a concrete verge. As they cusped the monolith's edge and crawled into this naked light, Sulette felt as though she had finally left the tropical reef. They were now in open water. Whales might be navigating beneath this raised motorway. Looking down to check, she saw that she had lost her expensive stilettos. Her bare feet, once so manicured and pretty, were now lathered in muck and garbage. Her hot pants were skew. Her lush brassiere kinked up to one side. She flung loose her breasts. Trill was quick to cover her up. But her ringing laughter had already begun to draw the attention of the shadows beneath the highway. These shades watched from boxes and blankets. It was just the kind of wasteland Sulette had glimpsed from the windows of cars all her life. The sort of place she had prayed she would never break down in. Now she was out on the highway like a whore. She let out another whoop, pulling down her bra once again. Trill was more forceful with her this time. They wrestled across the macadam. She was manhandled back into what was left of her clothes. Eventually Sulette flopped back, allowing herself to be manipulated. It seemed so natural to be out here in the dark, half-naked with this thing. Shark infested water must be Trill's natural habitat. She tried to ask it where she was being taken, but the words didn't formulate well. They slurred out of her on glassy webs of drool. She found herself playing with them. Trill seemed to understand what she was saying perfectly, however. She was heaved to her feet again and pushed back into the tidal current.

'Going to see a band,' Trill told her.

Sulette started to imagine a club. But they didn't go to a club. The landscape around them degraded further. Scrap yards and corrugated iron. They followed the edge of a railway line into a dismal galaxy of industrial warehouses and rotten, old houses. There, a tenement resolved out of the gloom. She was trawled toward it. Sulette realized, as they made their approach, that she was being taken into this ghetto block to 'fuck strangers for money'. Yet, despite this nugget of certainty, she made little effort to resist. She had succumbed to the inevitability of it. Perhaps she even looked forward to it. It's exactly what a little reef fish like her would do, she reasoned: go into a hole in the ocean floor and let the eels devour her.

The lobby guard eyed her semi-nudity with suspicion, but acknowledged Trill. On the second landing, they found a junkie. He was adrift in a puddle of his own fluid. A shopping trolley hung off the banister rail. It nosed down toward a dismal garden. Junkyards and vacant lots extended. Sulette could hear a sound. It was coming from far above her. A grinding, white-noise sound. Heavy and deafening. It seemed to emanate from the concrete itself. It grew steadily as they climbed. On the third floor, the Shark Fin showed in the distance. Sulette had never seen it from that angle. It looked like the set-piece of some fantastic, alternate universe. She began to scan the area between her and the mountain. Have I really walked all this way, she thought— dressed like *this*? The sound above became the voice of this new, strange city. And it was as if, she was hearing the city for the first time. Despite having lived in it her entire life. Trill started to tell her something. There was an Industrial noise festival. One of the bands was from Poland. They were doing a side-gig in a flat upstairs. The information washed over her—a vague and insubstantial footnote to her own fantastic visions. She was taken into that apartment. Figures in black loitered and jerked. Stacks of high-end sound equipment. The racket was deafening. Her skeleton was alive with its physical force. Vintage war footage was being projected. The ceiling swam with aeroplanes. A ragged thermal sheet doubled as curtain, People spasmed against the moving light. Sulette struggled to light a cigarette. When she finally accomplished this task, she realized that the shrieking was not the voice of the city at all. It was more as though some terrible angel had descended. It had exited the void and landed in this tenement. There, it started to speak about terrible, angelic things. Sulette felt as though she would never understand what the voice was telling her. This lack of understanding made her desperate. Why would an angel come down to this dingy tenement, she asked herself? Why would it speak to people like *this*? The black clad people jerked against a rough wall of almost physical sound. Outside, one of the hooded figures told her that she was hearing the natural sound of the universe. It was being amplified. Breaking like a continuous wave against them. Sulette turned away roughly. She didn't want to contaminate her understanding of the phenomenon. Again, she was stunned to find herself overlooking a tundra. One that was irradiated by the signals of another world. Solar rays, echoes of the Big Bang, all joined in the onslaught. She nodded vacantly. At some level, in her state, she understood. She was wrong, after all. She could understand everything the angel was describing. She pulled away, not wanting to hear any more. She staggered back into the machine-cramped flat. The windows were rattling. One of them had cracked. A heavily tattooed man in sunglasses. He operated banks of instrumentation. He attenuated the noise. A strobe flickered. Images immediately began to take hold. She listened to the glare of the speaker system. The voice was describing a living wilderness—a breathing, screaming emptiness, upon which the neatly defined structures of reality were built. Behind these false shells, a monstrous, yet somehow comforting ocean of nothingness seethed. It was the first time Sulette had glimpsed the void. It howled beyond the fences of her mind. It communicated a simple truth: she was the one intruding upon the sterile cleanliness of Paradise. She and everyone else she had ever known.

She woke up alone in her car, off Long street. It was not yet dawn. She still felt high. Trill would later explain. One of the band members had transported her in the back of a van. They had bribed a car guard to watch over her. This figure knocked on the window, startling her. She waved him away, covering herself, throwing money. Then she went home and fell asleep in the bath. Malherbe found her there in the morning, jabbering excitedly, transcribing notes from her phone.

Later that evening there was a knock on the door. It was Trill. It had brought along Delilah Lex. Both wore matching black bikinis and heavy sunglasses. Delilah was smiling. A welcoming smile. She had made a garland of frangipani flowers. She hung them around Sulette's neck. They all went swimming at Llandudno's secret beach. They ate fish glands and coconut cakes in the caves. Till the day she died, Sulette would describe it as the happiest period of her life.

She didn't see Delilah or Trill for a week. In any case, she needed the time to recover. Repeated use of the psychedelic had left her reeling between worlds. That weekend they invited her to a house party in Clifton. She spent several hours getting ready. As soon as she arrived however, Delilah commanded her to strip and join them in the pool. Somewhat shy around one or two familiar, local faces, Sulette left her underwear on. She hated to ruin her carefully put together ensemble and freshly blow-waved hair. But she couldn't disappoint the celebrity. In the water, Trill fed her a pink pill, with its cupid lips. This time, she swallowed it unquestioningly, happy to be included in their clique.

It's only when Sulette looks to the deckchairs and sees that her clothes have been taken, that she panics. Trill joins her in the search. She watches the creature waft naked. Through marble pillared Grecian grottoes. Its waist-length hair coils like seaweed around its hips. Sulette is becoming distracted by the changeling again. What rabbit hole is she being taken down this time? She turns to check on Delilah. The star is floating behind the infinity pool's waterfall feature. From Sulette's perspective, and under the growing influence of the glands, it seems as though Delilah has transformed into some enormous sea goddess. She reclines near the horizon. A gaggle of faces lily pads around her. A tall, dark stranger approaches. He squats beside the waterfall's edge. He taps Delilah on the crown of her white-blonde head with an abandoned plastic sword. Delilah becomes excited. She swims over, wrapping a wet arm around his collar. Despite his fastidious appearance, he allows it. Sulette observes him pass Delilah a package. The pair chat together a moment.

'Who's that?' Sulette asks Trill.

'That's Fortunato,' the creature tells her.

'What's he giving her?'

'Delaney bankrolls her fish gland supply, but never gives her the herbs that are supposed to go with the pills.'

'What do they do?' Sulette asks greedily, feeling her joints and vision begin to loosen under the first waves of the psychedelic.

'If you eat glands every day, you have to take herbs to protect your endocrine receptors and lymphatic system.'

'Do I need those?'

'Only after a few months of continuous use.'

Sulette gazes at the young movie star in awe.

'She's been on fish glands, every day, for that long?'

'She is a committed voyager, Trill explains seriously. 'A real mermaid. We must look after her when she is beneath the waves.'

'We must,' Sulette nods eagerly.

Suddenly she clutches Trill's arm.

'Oh, my fucking god!' she hisses. 'Isn't that Brick Bryson? What happened to his face?'

The place reminds Brick of LA—in a bad way. They were made to ride a private elevator up a small cliff. All terracotta tiling and royal palms. The moon-glitter sea beyond elevator's glass enriches the night with the stink of kelp. Balinese sculptures line cool white corridors. Each seems to lead to its own sea view. The incense-stricken dimness at first carries a fragrance of New-Age temples, but quickly degrades to a publicity-still for a questionable lite-beer. Too many blonde dreadlocks. Too many amethyst bouquets. The place is also infested with half-naked models.

Brick touches his bandaged nose, suddenly feeling conspicuous. Deep house throbs soporifically. It makes his wound throb too.

'It's like someone photocopied a Santorini villa onto a marinara pizza box,' he mutters to Croeser.

But the director has already moved off. The sight of Fortunato has set him striding angrily in the direction of the pool. He'd pulled the winged helmet back on in the limo. Now it lends his seriousness a comic edge. By the time Brick has registered Fortunato's toothy smile, the dealer has already vanished in a puff of joss.

'Wasn't that the guy...' he begins.

'This city is a very small aquarium,' V smiles. 'You're always bumping into the same fish.'

'I'm already starting to feel a little like Pat McGoohan...'

'I used to call Kloof Street, airtime street.'

'Why?'

'Because if you walk down it, you'll eventually bump into everyone you needed to call.'

'Small towns are all the same,' Brick quips drunkenly.

They begin to ascend a series of terraces. Jennifer joins them, but only for a moment. She vanishes into a bathroom to change into her swimwear. Greenie spots the bar and mumbles a quick apology. He strands Brick and V on an Italianate landing, overlooking the pool. In chambers alongside, oiled bodies move by candlelight, sometimes in water. The blue glow of the pool lights up the undersides of more royal palms. Outside the pull of Croeser's immediate orbit, the hedonistic atmosphere of the party starts to sober Brick up.

'So, what went wrong between Mo and Sasha?' he asks V.

She shoots him an amused, 'oh, you don't know' expression. The haphazard traffic on the staircase causes them to draw against a wall, into an intimate, frescoed niche. Brick sights Mo over the banister. The sylph-like, naked figure of Delilah detaches from a clot of slowly revolving bodies. She fins over to the edge, where Croeser waits. Trill joins them.

'Delilah and Sasha were an item once, around the beginning of her career,' V tells Brick.

'It all begins to fall into place,' he nods.

'It's worse than you think...'

As though on cue, Croeser produces the bag of pink pills V purchased earlier at the Pharm. He dangles the bundle like a carrot. Trill and Delilah reach for it like a pair of Waterhouse nymphs. Croeser pulls them from the water. He lifts one under each arm—the friendly ogre from a fairytale, carrying them off beneath the waterfall to devour. Brick observes them vanish- into the low cave of a lounge.

'He's got her on drugs?' Brick asks.

'The medicine is shamanic, it produces visions.'

'So, he's got her on drugs.'

'The glands of the Ipi fish can heal a person.'

Brick shrugs, clearly irritated.

'Is that all she's on?' he asks.

'She's on opiates too—I think.'

'Heroin?'

'I think so.'

'Was it Mo who got her on smack?'

'There's no reason why he wouldn't encourage it. A star like Delilah Lex, eating out of his hand—how would he be able to resist?'

'Did he try it with you?'

'He suggested I use it for sex. But I refused. Not my style.'

Brick rubs at his eyes, massaging his temples. All of a sudden, he is angry at himself. For allowing Croeser to seduce him into drinking again.

'This place is like quicksand,' he mutters.

'Many clandestine trade routes run through this city,' she says.

She extracts her e-cigarette.

'They have done so for centuries,' she continues. 'It's the only reason this place exists! Everything is so cheap and plentiful—by first-world standards, of course...'

'By the time the picture wraps, that kid's going to have a drug problem.'

'She already has.'

'Are they even sleeping together?'

'It's what he wants people to think. Who knows? Maybe he feels paternal toward her.'

'Whilst supplying her with heroin? I don't buy it.'

'She has a reputation of being hard to work with. She's young, but she's a control freak. His ability to control *her* is a trump card he can use against producers. He needs all his aces, now that the film is in trouble.'

'So, what's your honest opinion? Should I trust him?'

She drags deeply off her electronic cigarette. The end glows an unnatural blue. It mirrors the pool.

'All his talk of the good, old Oscar days,' she muses. 'It's pathetic. He is clearly attempting to manipulate you.'

'To what end?'

'That's the real question.'

'This whole situation is fishy. I'm mystified as to why production hasn't just cut its losses and pulled the plug.'

'There's that.'

Brick gazes down at the pool and sighs heavily. He feels like another drink, but resists the urge to cut and run to the bar.

'We lucked into that award,' he confesses. 'A drug-addicted superhero who may, or may not, be the actor who plays him. Is he real?—Or is it just a movie…There was so much of that Moebius-Strip style, meta-narrative going on in the late nineties. Science fiction psychosis, rendered in big-budget blah blah—the picture suited the climate of the time, suited Mo's style and my image. A few years earlier or later—it would have probably tanked.'

'Listen Brick,' she says, taking him by the arm. '*Club Ded*, if handled correctly, could still do well at the box office. I've heard the back-room talk. They want to open next year, as a summer blockbuster. If the script and performances have integrity, it *will* get the right attention. Delaney's whole spiel about winning awards and serious acclaim—it's absurd. But this film could certainly get both your careers back on track. Everybody knows what you both can achieve together. Everybody wants more.'

'Is he paying you for this?' Brick smiles guardedly. 'Or do you only do it out of love?'

'Why not give it a chance?' she pushes, ignoring his cynicism. 'I mean, what do you have to lose?'

The thought leaves Brick in a serious disposition.

''I've barely been here a couple of hours and I've already lost two years of sobriety.'

'Well,' she sighs. 'The night is young.'

The Leading Man

Fade in on the Chrysler building at sunset. The statuesque figure of Z-hero. He stands in silhouette, on the sleek head of one of the gargoyles. His ragged cape flags against the red line of dusk. Cutting in closer. A red-gloved hand. Z-hero releases the rubber hose that has been wound around his arm. It falls away. A titanium syringe juts for a moment. Then it follows the hose. A bouquet of slow-motion CGI blood droplets. The face beneath the mask catches the wan, end-of-the-world light. The jaw is unshaven. The neck is bowed. Z-hero's eyes remain hidden. We get the impression that he is transfixed by the view below. Cut to street level. Fast-edits highlight the dramatized chaos. The kind that usually precedes an apocalypse in New York. There are the running policemen. Army personnel. High-res close-ups of teenager's faces. All stare upward, in a perplexing mix of hope and horror. Safety barriers domino. Helicopters circle. The White House is on the line. Racial equality is the most noticeable characteristic in the screaming crowds. A fashion model cum television anchor yells above the din. She's as serious as a person can be, in a low-cut, cherry red (but somehow 'secretarial') two-piece can be. Back to the top of the skyscraper. It's a tightly framed shot. The back of Z-hero's head. The coy manner in which his eyes remain hidden, accentuates a build-up of orchestrated menace. The score simmers. Discordant strings, laid thick, over low-end rumbling. A lone, militaristic trumpet refrain comes into focus, in the distance. At certain intervals, it subtly apes both the American national anthem and the funeral dirge of fallen marines. Now the camera dollies cautiously, over the crown of the superhero's head. Soundtrack swells. Eventually, Z-hero's POV is revealed. Instead of an aerial shot of New York, we are presented with a mindscape. The Chrysler building recedes endlessly. Down into infinite blackness. There is no city for Z-hero to look down on. No world at all. Only a yawning, chthonic gulf reaching out to the far horizon. Finally, we cut to a sharp close-up of his mad, bloodshot eyes. Dilated pupils rage their black suns. He stares, mesmerized. Into the fathomless, swirling abyss beneath. Cut to title (sound mix drops to rumbling): GAME OVER.

Brick sits beside Croeser. They are in a screening room at the Cape

Town film studios. A joint ghosting between them. A half bottle of bourbon. The pair are joined by a dapper, Saudi businessman. He wears a grey silk suit and the obligatory keffiyeh. He occupies the seat next to Croeser. Brick had been introduced to Saud Al Qantani at the restaurant they had ended up at after the party. Brick understood that he was involved in the production in some way. Still, he didn't make any attempt to clarify the man's position. Saud remained with them for most of the evening. He made clever jokes and toasts. He was very touchy-feely with Brick. Though not at all in homo-erotic fashion. Rather he was the sort to hold a handshake too long. Brick sensed Saud had pull. A financial backer. Or something along those lines. A surly man in a tuxedo accompanies Saud at all times. He joins them in the cinema, but sits apart. Near the exit. V has also elected to sit on her own. The blue light of her cigarette marks breath in the center of the middle row. Vape catches the projection rays. Greenie is in the back, working on a laptop. As the familiar musical themes build, Brick finds himself sighing. He floats in a haze of weed and liquor. Pleasantly induced nostalgia. Seeing his younger self makes him touch the lines around his eyes. After ignoring the film for so many years, he is surprised to find himself engrossed. He is reminded of the admiration he'd had for his old friend's skill. This respect is still there. The realization touches Brick. He reaches over and squeezes Croeser's shoulder, handing him the joint.

'You're a goddamn genius, Mo.'

The statement elicits a smile and a nod from Saud. Croeser is surprisingly sullen. He sucks ruthlessly at the marijuana. His regard for the film seems to approach disdain. As though he were capable of being jealous of himself.

'Maybe I was…then,' he growls. 'Maybe I only had a taste of it.'

Z-hero's voice-over emerges from the low rumble:

'I was lost above. In a world of phantoms.'

The glittering curvature of the earth appears. As seen from space.

'You wouldn't know the place,' comes Z-hero's basso murmur. 'It's where only the superheroes get high.'

When Brick comes to, the screening room is dark and deserted. He sits up abruptly and rubs his face. Sharp pain. He had forgotten about his nose. He looks around, disgusted with himself. Luckily, his sunglasses are still in his jacket pocket. He manages to quit the building with minimal human contact. A thin, grey dawn colours the sky. It filters through the masts of a pirate ship, left over from a cancelled television series. Despite it being summer, the wind is cold and troublesome. It gusts at Brick from all directions, making a nuisance of itself. He strikes out for the limo, which is still parked at the far end of a lot. A gang of crew members crosses the concrete. They carry between them the immense effigy of a dagger.

'The sword of Damocles…' Brick mouths dryly.

He eyes the set piece warily, arriving eventually at the limo. Expecting to find it deserted, he is surprised to discover V and Jennifer. Both are alert and hard at work. Jennifer is on a laptop, typing furiously. A line of cocaine waits on the cover of a fashion magazine. There's a film playing on the car's big screen. V watches it out of the corner of her eye, typing on her phone, drinking black coffee. She smiles when she sees him. Jennifer merely nods, barely breaking stride on her keyboard. Brick recognizes an old Vicente Minelli picture; 'Two weeks in another town'.

'Espresso?' V offers.

'Kombucha?' Brick asks, collapsing onto the seat beside her.

'How about a green juice? It was squeezed yesterday, but…'

'That'd be great.'

Brick recognizes the scene on the monitor. It's the part where Kirk Douglas's character realizes that he is not alone in the screening room. An Italian girl, Veronica, is seated behind him. She has something in her eye. He moves to assist her.

'Haven't watched this in ages,' he comments.

V passes him a chilled bottle and a painkiller.

'It's one of Delaney's favourites,' she mentions. 'It's also the reason he decided to get hold of you.'

'What do you mean?' Brick frowns, swallowing the pill with a mouthful of juice.

'An old director reaching out to his former star. It gave him the idea to try work with you again. I was with him when he suggested the idea. Life imitates art—that's what he said.'

'I thought his Oscar spiel in the hotel sounded a little stagey.'

'I think he would like to remake it with you.'

V picks up the telephone handset. Brick drinks deeply from the chilled bottle.

'Take us to the hotel,' she tells the driver.

The fact that she didn't feel the need to say 'please', somehow sticks with Brick. They leave the studio gate. V opens a window. They watch the mountain turn to gold. Irregular blasts of wind revitalize the stale interior. They fluff at V's hair. Brick realizes that he is eyeing her.

'You know, you didn't have to wait,' he says.

'It's no problem. I miss this limo. Delaney used to let me use it all the time.'

'It suits you.'

'Breakfast by the beach?'

'I think at this point, the most exciting thing I can think of is falling asleep…Wait a minute, I've used that line on you already, haven't I?'

'Yes. And I've had more than enough award-winning dialogue for one night, thanks.'

'Touché. Where's Mo?'

V looks away.

'Trouble in paradise,' she replies, enigmatically.

They kiss hungrily. But even this hunger is moderated. They employ a certain delicacy. Neither wants to aggravate Brick's wound. Collapsing across the hotel bed, he scoops at V's flesh. She rolls over abruptly, breaking contact. The interruption distracts him. He opens his eyes. They had drawn the curtains too hastily. A sliver of harsh, morning sunlight knifes across the bed. V arches her muscular back. The action causes her to rise apart from him.

'What is it?' Brick asks. 'What's the matter?'

V hesitates for a moment.

'I guess I just don't want to give Delaney the satisfaction of maneuvering us into bed.'

Brick sighs. He stares up at the flawless, wedding cake ceiling. In principle, he is in agreement. And now that the subject has been voiced, he cannot ignore it. At a deeper level, he wonders whether this had been her game all along—a sounding of waters, followed by plausible escape.

'Well, I wouldn't want you to lose your bet,' he quips.

She folds neatly off him. Curling her legs, she reaches for her purse. Brick sits up against the headboard. He watches the pulse of her cold cigarette. She turns her head, looking him over from behind a shoulder. He meets her gaze. She quickly exhales. A pennant of vapour engulfs her again.

'I suppose you had better get some sleep.'

'Good idea,' he agrees.

V rises lithely. Then slips on her shoes. Gathering her bag, she moves to the door, where she lingers. They exchange a brief look. But neither speaks. V leaves quietly. Brick sags back as soon as she is gone, utterly exhausted.

He is awakened moments later, by a distant pounding on the door. He fumbles for his phone, only to realize that hours have passed. Afternoon trundles across the wall. Livid gold stripes. The pounding intensifies. How long has this barrage been going on, he wonders? Brick drags himself up, through the light shafts. Squinting in the glare, he enters the lounge. There, he is confronted by an enormous drawing of the letter 'V'. It is rendered in bright blue lipstick, across the largest mirror. The graffiti frames the Oscar statuette neatly. The territoriality of it perplexes him. Especially in his hung-over state. And with all the loud banging. It must be an arcane reference to *something*, he ponders, staggering to the door. He is surprised to find Fortunato in the corridor. The dealer wears a long, black leather coat and mirrored sunglasses. In his hand is a switchblade. Fortunato grabs him by the collar and muscles him back into the room before he has a chance to speak. He waves the knife close to Brick's face. The action star stumbles.

'Listen, I don't have much cash,' Brick fences.

'Where is she?'

'Who?' Brick asks, confused.

Fortunato points the knife-tip to the enormous 'V'.

'You can come out now you star-fucking whore!' he calls.

'She isn't here...Are you her boyfriend? Listen, if you are, I can assure you...'

Fortunato turns his back on him. Stalking over to the mirror, he moves as though to smudge the lipstick. He is suddenly distracted—by the Oscar. Brick watches tentatively. Fortunato takes up the statuette, weighing it carefully in his hand.

'You're welcome to it,' Brick tells him. 'It means nothing to me.'

'I could never take another man's trophies,' Fortunato comments, without turning.

His eyes are riveted to the golden figure. Brick is now awake and adrenalized. He recognizes Fortunato.

'Hay, you're V's ex, aren't you? Fortunato, right?'

'She's the worst kind of sycophant,' Fortunato mutters, his eyes still glued to the award. 'Just your type, I imagine.'

'What do you mean by that?' Brick asks, irritated. 'And listen, what the hell are you waving that knife around for? Put it away now. Let's talk like men.'

'How are men supposed to talk?'

'Look, what do you want? If she isn't here, then I don't see...'

Fortunato takes off his mirrored sunglasses. He turns around and regards him squarely.

'Look at you. Playing hero for all these bourgeois swine. You're nothing but a sex tourist. Fucking another man's wife in the colonies.'

The statement knocks the wind out of Brick's sails. He looks away, sagging to a nearby sofa. There, he rubs at his temples.

'Don't tell me you're another one of those sentimental African-Americans,' Fortunato sneers. '- Coming here to re-colonize Africa under the pretense of 'getting back to your roots.'

'No. I'm an American. I hate it here.'

'Good.'

'Look, I didn't know you two were married. Maybe that's why she decided to leave before anything happened.'

'It doesn't matter. She'll fuck you sooner or later because you're famous. Because she 'loves all your films'. You won't have the integrity to refuse.'

'Look, if you're not going to stab me, why don't you just get the fuck out of here?'

'I think you're lying.'

'I told you, she isn't here!'

Fortunato holds up the Oscar statuette.

'I think this *does* mean a lot to you.'

Brick stares at him, furious and bewildered.

'Admit it,' Fortunato pushes. 'After all, you are the one who properly deserved it.'

Brick remains speechless. The stranger has him at a disadvantage. Fortunato replaces the award on the mantle. He begins to pace around.

'You know, I wasn't much in Lagos—by international standards. But I was something in the film world. More than she'd ever seen. You know these fucking Congolese, so upwardly mobile.'

'Actually, I don't know,' Brick murmurs quietly, taken aback by Fortunato's unexpected capacity for discrimination.

'I thought it was love,' Fortunato continues. 'But I was only a part of her education. She was just grooming herself for a better life. She's a wonderful student, you know. Just like a sponge. Put her in coloured water and in just a short time, she will have absorbed enough to blend in perfectly—as though she had always been that colour.'

'This has nothing to do with me.'

'Don't be such a coward. I don't think I could stomach cowardice from you, of all people. I think I would have to stab you in the heart if you showed me cowardice.'

'Why the fuck would you say a thing like that to me? You must be crazy, man...'

'I say it because you were *my* childhood hero. She doesn't even have enough of a personality to seduce her own heroes.'

'Jesus fucking Christ, what is it with this country? You would think people would just ask for an autograph, or something...'

'I wanted to kill Croeser when I heard that they were running around. But let's face it, it's crueler to let that old has-been live.'

'Keep talking like that and I might start to like you.'

'I'll gut you like a pig.'

Brick sighs, irritated.

'Well, would you mind if I drank a glass of water first?'

'Just one night with those two vampires and you've already relapsed. I can't believe how weak you are in person.'

'Hay, fuck you!' Brick snaps. 'I don't need to take this shit from you, you little prick.'

Fortunato strides threateningly forward. He slashes the blade in front of Brick's face. The actor falls back, glaring up at his oppressor. Fortunato grins. Seating himself across from Brick, he withdraws a glass bottle from his coat.

'The tap water is bad here,' he says. 'This is from the spring near Newlands forest.'

He tosses the bottle to Brick, who catches it gracefully, despite his state. The star uncaps the bottle and takes a swig. The water *does* taste different. It's sweetly harmonic. Almost creamy with mineral content. He could drink a barrel of it.

'The mountain is also a sponge,' Fortunato tells him. 'It filters the rain. That spring is the purified blood of the land.'

Ignoring Fortunato's arcane commentary, Brick drains the bottle completely. When he is done, he sets down the receptacle and sighs with satisfaction.

'Thanks,' he says.

'You make me sick.'

Brick looks up, only to find that he cannot properly defend himself. He too, makes himself sick. The dealer gets up. He snatches back the bottle and begins to pace. He picks up the Oscar again—he can't leave it alone.

'You had better directorial instincts than Croeser ever did,' he tells Brick. 'You could have been great. Croeser saw that and squashed you for it. Now look at you. Still eating his leftovers.'

'You talk as though you know me. You don't.'

'But I do know you. Everybody knows Brick Bryson.'

'Listen, from where I'm sitting, you're just another judgmental fan. Only, you have a knife.'

A fury clouds Fortunato's face.

'It's the lack of respect that makes me want to put this knife in you,' he snarls. 'I have told you already that we share a profession. What makes you think that fame gives you any more right to film-making than it does to me? You Americans are all the same—provincial! Like ants, you colonize and consume everything around you. You think you have the right to turn everything you see into your own personal property, simply by pissing on it? Sickening!'

Brick sighs.

'You know, you're right,' he admits. 'I apologize. But look at it from where I'm sitting. You barged in on me with a weapon. Don't expect me to be polite.'

Fortunato shakes his head in irritation. He sets the Oscar down on the table between them.

'I suppose a grown man should expect to be disappointed by the idols of his youth.'

The telephone begins to ring. Brick looks to Fortunato. He nods, signifying that Brick should go ahead and answer it. Croeser is on the other end. Brick tells him to wait a minute. Fortunato replaces his sunglasses and moves to the door. He hesitates for a moment before leaving.

'It's not too late to go home,' he says. 'These people will only drag you down.'

He leaves. Brick returns to the call. Croeser asks if he can make it to the set. Brick agrees. He hangs up and slumps slowly down.—until he is sitting on the floor. He is about to shower, when something catches his attention. The Oscar is at eye-level with him. It seems to stare in an accusatory manner.

Staff members eye Fortunato on his way out. He walks down the long, down-sloping drive. Onto the highway outside. A rusted, yellow Toyota Conquest is parked beneath a pine on the verge. He makes his way down to it. It's an unusual colour for that particular make. The grim, custardy shade always draws attention. No matter where it is parked. The tinted glass only adds to it. Yet, despite its dubious appearance, the garish junk is a formidable racing vehicle. Fortunato had driven it to the Transkei the previous year. There, he knew a skilled mechanic by the name of Don White. This man had a workshop in Umtata. He spruced up vehicles for stock car racing. Don specialized in Conquest's. This was because his daughter competed in one. He'd suggested the model. It was easy to hot-rod. Don performed a weight reduction first. He stripped the interior of everything unnecessary. This included carpeting and door panels. He replaced the glass with one-way Perspex. Then fitted lightweight racing rims and low-profile semi slicks on the wheels. He dropped the suspension with a set of adjustable coil-overs and upgraded the exhaust system. He did this by adding headers and a straight-through free flow exhaust. He installed a cold air induction kit and upgraded the software, removing all speed and rev limiters. Once he was done with these outer adjustments, Don zeroed in on the engine. He modified it, gas-flowing the head and changing the cams. Before balancing and blueprinting the motor. He also boosted the rig with turbos and an intercooler, installing kill switches for everything. The gear box was refitted with dog gears, which lent more power to the vehicle, even though they whined like screaming animals when properly unleashed. Fortunato downgraded the outside. He allowed rust to spread across the roof. Even chipping the paint manually in some places. He wanted the power of the car to remain disguised. Cars like this were called sleepers or rat rods—in the lingo of the stock car scene.

Afternoon boils on the skillet of town. But the temperature could drop unexpectedly. When the ocean breeze hit town, heat raises an icy mist. This happens far out to sea. On a clear day, you could see it coming. Like a wall. Coast and mountain make for erratic weather. Paradoxically, the sea is sometimes coldest during the heat. The temperature affects ice-melt tides. They wash the white sands of Camps Bay, Clifton and Llandudno. Hypothermic currents. The chilly water is numbing. Surreal, when experienced beneath a roasting African sun. This type of exaggerated duality manifests throughout the city. It is not uncommon for one side of the mountain to suffer rain and fog, while the other languishes beneath blue skies and sunshine.

Ziq chews a match-stick. On a street-corner near Greenmarket Square. He dresses in blatant denial of the heat. A smart, black suit beneath his ever-present coat. He also wears a white Sicilian hat. Lifted around breakfast time—from a hotel lobby. The heat is kind to him. As it is to reptiles. Ziq can loiter for hours, in the death-ray of an afternoon. Drinking espresso after espresso in a quiet show of defiance. He switches to his second match. The first is in splinters. Jaybird appears out of a nearby shop. His t-shirt bulges ridiculously. His face has a constipated expression. Ziq is convinced that the US accent is Jaybird's most valuable criminal asset. Everyone must assume he's a tourist. Ziq can't fathom what else it could be that forestalls shop-owners from shooting him on sight. Some queer turn of logic has compelled the American to forsake bathing—for the last three weeks. He is filthy. The heat only triples his animal stench. His clothes are matted with grease and neon paint. A large streak has been shaved, haphazardly, along the left side of his head. He signals to Ziq. They drift into the crowds. Then huddle beneath the eaves of the church on the square. Jaybird pulls a bullet shaped juicer from beneath his shirt. Ziq raises an eyebrow.

'It's not like you to steal something useful,' he remarks.

'I thought we could drop it off a bridge or burn it or something!' Jaybird snaps.

They meet Fortunato off Parliament street. In an alleyway, between the Company Gardens and Slave museum. Fortunato pops the Toyota's trunk. He withdraws a box of stolen iPhones. Fortunato is a big advocate of shooting movies on phones. Ziq was happy to supply some. 'Amateur film-making technology is in the hands of the people, yet so few produced films'—this was Fortunato's logic. In Ziq's opinion, the public was conditioned. To such a degree, they believed film-making could only occur within existent processes. Or at the whim of corporate interests. He was more than happy to assist Fortunato in these acts of cultural resistance. They made low-fi, guerrilla films that cost practically nothing. They used anything at their disposal to accomplish this aim.

Fortunato would upload the finished projects to view-sites. These could be viewed without charge. On Pan-African streaming networks. Fortunato had formed work relationships during his time in Nollywood. It was due to these platforms, and a small, die-hard fan base in Nigeria and Burkina Faso, that he was able to rack up a significant viewership during his exile.

The stolen phones have been charged using illegal electricity from the Pharm. Fortunato packs them. He hands one to Ziq for good measure. Despite the arsenal of devices, Fortunato goes on to prime a vintage, shoulder-mounted camera. He'd picked it up at a garage sale in Bellville and repaired it himself. The cumbersome machine uses only VHS cassettes and is problematic in many aspects. It does, however, provide a unique visual flavour. As well as functioning as a sort of psychological prop. Fortunato checks that the battery is firmly housed, before handing the heavy camera to Jaybird. Prepared, they set off into the Gardens.

It takes under twenty minutes to locate the 'chimps' (as Jaybird has dubbed them). A requirement for the shoot. The target is a young student couple. They are seated beside a fountain. Fortunato breaks away. He sets up phones in various, hidden locations. In this way, he is able to capture the area from various angles. When he has about five set up, he situates himself at a remove. He then cues his co-conspirators.

Cut in to: a hand-held shot of the fountain area. Museum is visible in the distance. Fortunato hovers outside the rose garden (barely visible on the tape grain). Ziq steps into foreground. Autofocus kicks in. Jaybird lines up on the couple. Zooms in tight. The shot jiggers (distance). He zooms back out to regain stability. Together, they approach the chimps. Wind blurs the mic. The couple have by now noticed their approach. Undisguised suspicion. Ziq calls out buoyantly:

'Greetings, earthlings!'

'Ahoy?' the male chimp captions hesitantly.

His female mate is shooting nervous glances. A volley of plastic arrows. Jaybird zooms into a pimple on the male's forehead.

'Sorry to trouble you folks,' Ziq banters conversationally. 'We're film students shooting a documentary on pickpockets in this area.'

'Pickpockets?' the male chimp replies—a distinct Stellenbosch twang.

He flicks his fringe photographically, attempting to stare down the lens.

'Yes, my good man,' Ziq continues, without breaking stride. 'The area is rife with the bastards. We have been commissioned by Delaney Croeser, the renowned director, to make a protest film. He's in town, shooting a movie, and wants to reach out to the community.'

They perk up immediately.

'We need to stand up for our rights here, don't we?' Ziq prattles on.

'All these… *township people*, stealing things, you know?'

'Hay, that's really *pro-active!*' the female chimp slogans, jumping on the bandwagon.

The male is still reeling. The possibility of an appearance in an actual Delaney Croeser film. He slicks back his hair. Best James Dean pout.

'Yes, yes,' Ziq intones solemnly. 'We all have to do our part in the fight against crime.'

'Yeah!' Jaybird shrieks—a little too enthusiastically.

Ziq turns to the male chimp. He fixes him in a your-country-needs-you kind of stare.

'We were hoping you could help us out,' he says gravely. 'We need a…stylish, young volunteer.'

'Sure,' the chimp answers, feigning a casual attitude.

A bead of excited perspiration leaves his gelled hairline. It travels down an oversized beard. The female chimp is grinning. She chop-sticks blue hair out of her face with tattooed fingers.

'What do I have to do,' the male chimp squints.

'Just go stand over there,' Ziq orders.

He points out a particularly ugly, overflowing trashcan. Someone has recently vomited down the side of it.

'I am going to walk past and pretend to pickpocket you,' Ziq continues. 'Ignore me. The camera will track my advance. Ignore that too. Especially—ignore the camera.'

The male chimp nods. Like a soldier briefed for an airstrike. His girlfriend, however, has begun to tone down her excitement. Too much positivity might lower her street-cred in the eyes of *the movie people*. She affects a disenchanted frown. She pretends to be distracted by a passing bird. She even makes a ridiculous little bird noise to press the illusion home. Jaybird zooms in lasciviously (and rather absurdly) on her knees.

'The camera will follow me as I walk off,' Ziq finishes. 'But take no notice whatsoever. Until I yell 'cut', understand?'

'Delaney Croeser is producing this, you say?' the male chimp checks, with just a flicker of desperation.

'It's his pet outreach project,' Ziq assures him.

Now the male is ready to jump through flaming hoops. His fifteen minutes have finally arrived and he is dressed for it. All those nights of mirror-swimming have paid off. The female, on the other hand, has cooled considerably.

'We're making a similar video at my tech, you know…' she begins, only to have her mate cut her off.

'I'm ready!' he announces.

'Ok!' Ziq declares.

He turns to his cameraman.

'Let's go retro on this bitch. Do it all Dogme-style. Copenhagen in the 90's. Get shaky and dramatic, 'f' every stop and check every gate. Compositional tension. And above all—*keep it real!*'

Jaybird cackles evilly.

'Yeah, sure boss.'

'Ok!' Ziq shouts, clapping his hands.

He turns on the chimps, giving his best 'Orson Welles on crack' impression.

'Get over to that fucking trashcan!' he commands.

The male chimp gives his hair a final once-over. He flips up his collar and shoots a double thumbs-up. He then trots over to the bin, pants dangling low on his hips. Stripy boxer's glint in the sun. At one point, he runs a little too fast and his pants almost slip off. Luckily, he is able to catch them. Throwing in a little gangster swagger to mask the close call. Ziq is shaking his head with the whole 'shooting fish in a barrel-ness' of it all. The female chimp is sulking. She sharpens her next question like a knife.

'Look, would you just fuck off while we are filming!' Jaybird unexpectedly snaps.

Shaken by the viciousness of an *actual verbal assault*, the female chimp cowers, deeply offended.

'Artists, you know…' Ziq apologizes absently.

'But, *I'm* an…' she begins to protest.

'CHECK THE FUCKING F-STOP GATE LIGHT SPEED!' Jaybird screeches.

The male throws an all-ready signal. Ziq politely elbows the female out of the way.

'Sorry Miss,' he winks.

She is about to protest when Ziq yells out in a commanding tone:

'When I say 'action', remember, take no notice of us!'

The male chimp throws another thumbs-up. The novelty is fading fast. Ziq shoots the lens a grin. Jaybird almost doubles over.

'Now, look here…' the female pipes in her most uppity tone.

'ACTION!' Ziq calls.

The word immediately pacifies the female chimp. The male looks away, suddenly self-conscious. Ziq strolls casually in his direction. Looking, for all the world, as though he were about to run him through with a rapier. Jaybird skulks in his wake. He swerves the camera this way and that. Maximum dramatic effect. The male chimp keeps glancing at them and then quickly away. Somewhere in all his rehearsals for celebrity he has forgotten what it means to behave *naturally*. Fear overcomes the chimp. He begins to mimic attitudes and stances. Characters he has seen in television shows and popular music videos. The female chimp woo-hoo's like a cheerleader. Ziq brushes violently past the male chimp. Then continues upon his way. Jaybird follows briskly. The male studies a tree. Pretending to be completely oblivious to the pair of reprobates that have practically knocked him over a vomit-soaked garbage bin. The VHS camera pans down. It reveals the male's leather wallet in Ziq's hand. They are laughing openly now, throwing glances over shoulders, quickening the pace. The camera swings back to reveal a confused and uncertain chimp. He diminishes rapidly. Patting down pockets. Looking around worriedly.

'Hey!' he squawks impotently.

The camera shakes crazily. Ziq and Jaybird begin to run. The female's shouts can be heard. The camera catches a glimpse of the male chimp. He clutches his pants with one hand, attempting to give chase. The thieves split up. Ziq dashes into a row of foliage. Jaybird hurtles past the café and into the street. The words 'LOW BATTERY' begin to flash in red, 8-bit numerals. Jaybird runs for a few solid minutes. Across busy roads and heat-baked plazas. He moves the camera back every now and then. Determined to document the event in its entirety. Re-entering Greenmarket Square, he finally slows. Panting raggedly. Ziq is laughing beneath the eaves of the church. The camera abruptly dies. The words 'PLEASE RECHARGE' flicker momentarily across the viewfinder.

They walk back up Long. In the direction of the Fin. With Jaybird, conversation had a tendency of drifting back towards 'the States'. Like most of the Americans Ziq had come into contact with, Jaybird was nostalgically patriotic. He did tear up an American flag once, but ruined the effect by wearing the remains as a ragged kimono. Pleading some form of statement. What was left of the flag was torn apart by the Pharm's Alsatian, one stormy Tuesday.

'You can say and do anything you like in the States. As long as you don't have a gun.'

This was Jaybird's credo.

'As long as you DO have a gun, you mean,' Ziq would habitually counter, leading to labyrinthine debates.

Jaybird often pestered Ziq about his reasons for leaving New York. He had been enrolled in a respectable musical academy. Classical piano on full scholarship.

'Being in America was like being trapped in a sitcom,' was Ziq's favourite complaint. 'I couldn't find the mute button.'

'But aren't you even the slightest bit patriotic toward your own armpit of a country?'

For Ziq, the question added water to long desiccated thoughts. He usually refused to answer. But now, as they walk, the question resurfaces. He begins to rant.

'I don't see how anyone, who doesn't believe in violence, can believe in the concept of countries.'

This piques Jaybird, but Ziq is almost unstoppably caffeinated.

'The basic definition of a country, are its borders. And these borders usually exist because of war, or some dispute. But there are no real borders. We got sold this whole idea of *countries* because of violence.'

'What about national character?'

'Culture and lifestyle? Programming. In this day and age, people live in boxes. They are disconnected from the land. They are only comfortable at a remove; water from pipes, packaged food—you know what I mean. Anyone who isn't disconnected is probably exploiting their environment, or doomed to exploitation by bigger fish. It doesn't really matter what country people live in! It's all one big, stupid moon-base full of zombies. You can do variations of all the same zombie things wherever you go. The illusion of reality is *maintained*...And who dictates it? People who want to sell you stuff. They dictate your lifestyle and then sell you what you need to fit in—in exchange for everything you have. Fuck's sake, all that money is just paper...'

'It's motherfucking denim!' Jaybird shouts.

'It's supposed to be a token for gold. But there is more credit in circulation than all the gold in the world. It doesn't even exist. Just like countries. It boils down to a handful of people with guns, communications monopolies and psychological know-how—People who want and have the means to achieve power.'

'Over fucking what?'

'Over the masses—over us, over resources, does it matter? At least the monarchies attempted to preserve arts and culture. Sure, they did it for supremely selfish reasons, but they managed to leave behind a legacy of craftsmanship. What do you think it meant to the common man, acquiring their ruling power? What does the common man want, after all? They want what they imagine all the *uncommon* people have. What they, themselves, have never experienced. And who educates them as to what is the latest, new, must-have *uncommon* thing? The people who sell. They *educate* them. They teach them to pursue things like fame—that need common people have of being recognized amongst their own faceless masses. All the comfort you can buy, home, home on the range. *And who is selling it to them*? Come on. The revolutions were just a marketing ploy. Now we are all in debt...'

Conversations like this usually ended with Jaybird burning something. In some perverse way, Ziq respects his pyromania. It is direct action. Something real in a world full of ambiguity and perpetual hesitation. But Jaybird is drifting further afield. Day by day, he consumes more mileage over extreme territories. One day he will run out of neurological gas. As much as Jaybird dwells in a kind of jolly denial of his own catastrophic potential, Ziq can see the flames on the horizon. They burn like a beacon in the desolation to come.

The pair sit at the Daly Deli. Espressos in the sun. Before the property values escalated (extortionately) in response to Africa-struck foreign buyers, the area had been something of a bohemian address. Jaybird's paint-smeared appearance is tolerated by the old establishment. As is Ziq's troubling paraphernalia. But a new waitress is hovering. She eyes both with undisguised suspicion. Adrian sets her at ease. He has worked the Deli since time immemorial. He never forgets a regular from the good old days. The owner of the Deli, Paul Daly, and his wife Theresa, live in the adjoining house with a pair of feisty Scorpio daughters, their collection of rabbits and Paul's mother Francois. Francois is a red-haired relic of bygone glamour. In her youth, she had been an opera singer in Paris. Now she bakes the Deli's cakes and questionable meat lasagna. She drifts from coffee shop to coffee shop in her spare time. She is fond of the only indoor table at the Deli. Ziq competes with her for it. Theirs is a silent, civil war—the kind only former musicians could wage. When Ziq and Jaybird arrive, Francois has the inside seat. She offers the ghost of a smug smile to the thieves, who courteously adjourn to the sidewalk. The café is relatively quiet. Other than Francois, Adrian, the kitchen staff and the new girl—Ziq and Jaybird share the place with five other people. The first is a young, troubled office type. He works on a laptop at a far table. Beneath a canvas umbrella. The second is a local resident; Volker Von Hase. Volker owns a colonial era mansion on the street. Volker, like Ziq, wears a suit despite staggering heat. He has been a patron of the Deli since it was conceived. He has lived on Brownlow most of his life. The house has been in his family for generations. His suit, in contrast to Ziq's thrift store variety, is grey serge. Purchased in Frankfurt, where he once worked. Volker is currently in finance. Though he has dipped into many worlds. The suit is accessorized with a Burgundy silk cravat, gold pin and a Mason's ring. Namibian by birth, Volker schooled in Bavaria. There is a suspicious lack of records detailing his family's relocation to Lüderitz from Germany. The move did, however, occur quite soon after the Second World War. A common enough story. There is a reptilian aspect to Volker's professionally barbered face. It seems at once to suck in sunlight, as well as reject it. Redness radiates from behind vintage Carrera sunglasses. It drains down drawn features. Collecting around a snowy collar. He sips black coffee. Screwing and unscrewing cigarettes into a pearl holder. He scribbles occasionally, while he does this. In a skin-bound diary, using his father's fountain pen. The remaining three patrons comprise a table of 'ponks'—a trio of teenage girls. They gobble marshmallow cake in the sun. 'Ponk', of course, derives from the popular Japanese band 'Pink-Ponk-Punk'. The act went viral a few years ago. Jaybird would describe the word 'Ponk' as contagious. He is obsessed with words like this. Words that infect and mutate. He is always on the lookout for the next catch-word or phrase. The one which, as he likes to put it, would 'neutralize the former'. The ponks arrange themselves—colourful human confectionary. One of them eyes Jaybird's shaved streak with appreciation. She also has several (albeit professionally barbered) streaks along the left side of her scalp. Jaybird is oblivious to her sideways glances and giggles. He swallows great gulps of black coffee. Blinking behind enormous spectacles. He plots great disasters. After a bit, the ponks pay their bill and rise. As they pass Jaybird's table, his admirer turns to him and announces:

'I like your hair, man!'

Jaybird jerks his head in terror.

'Your hair,' she fumbles. 'It's like, totally fad, man...'

Jaybird smashes his fist into the table. Crockery flies. Espresso cups shatter against the curb. Even Ziq is taken aback. He brushes coffee from his coat with a napkin. The girl has nimbly retreated. She stares at the maniac she has unwittingly provoked. Everybody is now paying close attention.

'Oo uckin ear!' Jaybird screams. 'Un fatchoo eenin! Un ear ooh eenin! Kyn in...'

The American disintegrates into an inexplicable outburst of tears. The ponks rescue their speechless compatriot. Then beat a hasty retreat. Ziq drags the wildly gesticulating Jaybird out onto the tarmac. An attempt to avoid further property damage. Jaybird is scrabbling desperately—for a bird mask that isn't there. Bereft of his disguise, he lurches down the street. They all watch him disappear into a hedge. Ziq sighs. He crosses over to Adrian, handing him several large bills to cover their tab and damages.

'Jason...is he alright?' Adrian asks.

'Paint fumes,' Ziq flusters.

'Those paint fumes are a killer,' Adrian winks, returning to the till with a crafty smile.

Volker observes Ziq's departure with a grimace. His distaste intensifies as Sulette drives past in her Mini Cooper. She parks outside her block. Volker watches her for a bit before returning to his notes. To him, Sulette represents a type—one of the new breed of bourgeois materialists. These riff-raff have invaded the sanctity of his street. Even the bohemians are preferable to him. At least he could buy their paintings and occasionally use them for sex. He simply has no use for upwardly mobile homemaker housewives and their little dogs. He finishes a sentence or two. Then studies what he has written. In his mind, the words ring over the antique street lamps, lemon and jacaranda trees like bells on Sunday. To him, they are not commentary. They are the voice of the street itself:

I've come to trust in suburbs—the prettier, the better. I don't like ugly suburbs. I mean, who does? For me, a pretty suburb has that feeling of blood, living blood, coursing through its veins. This kind of suburb does not exist in the past, no matter how old or pretty it is. Everyone is hiding the latest things and ideas behind all those old and pretty walls. They see these things on screens, in faraway parts of the world. They call these things to them and situate them in their reality. In this way, the pretty suburbs all begin to exist in a perpetually unfolding future. They are like the shores of a beach, with the water of the future always lapping at them, changing things.

Ah! My beautiful street. This car, this car, this car, that I hate—This dog, this dog, this dog that I hate—This girl… this girl, this girl, that I hate. I know this type of woman. I had a mother like her. She's new to the neighbourhood. She came with everything. Fully furnished, like her apartment. She came with everything. She will leave with nothing.

Volker looks it over a few times. Then crosses out the last line. It strikes a false note. He cannot foresee this woman's future. Dissatisfied, he signals to Adrian. After settling his bill, he leaves. At the furthest table, the man on the laptop is finishing off a paragraph of his own. An ad-bar blinks above the text field. It reads: ORACLE 24 HOUR PSYCHIC HOTLINE. ARE YOU IN NEED? DO YOU SUFFER? WHAT IS YOUR QUESTION? LET THE ORACLE ANSWER YOU. Her face is depicted above, floating. The man glances at it occasionally. With her penetrating eyes, she seems to peer directly into his mind. She might be able to help him. Her twitter feed is trending. After a few minutes, he finishes his email. Jennifer will respond later that week. In a dingy future. A forgettable hotel.

When Brick makes it to the limo, he is surprised to find only Greenie. A stack of papers awaits him.

'Where's V?' he asks.

He is anxious to discuss his recent experience with Fortunato. Greenie sighs. He shuffles through some colour-coded scripts and manifests.

'V actually isn't a member of the crew or production staff,' he reminds Brick. 'So, I'm not entirely certain where she is.'

'Too bad,' Brick grunts.

The car heads off. Greenie hands Brick a folder.

'What's this?' he asks Greenie.

'I have to brief you on a couple of things before we arrive on the set. Delaney would like you to handle a scene with Sasha today.'

'Handle?' Brick repeats, incredulously. 'Is that the word he used?'

Greenie nods patiently.

'He doesn't seriously expect me to direct a scene without any preparation or contract in place? I haven't even read the script yet!'

'There's a temporary work agreement in the file. It should cover this while head office drafts your contract.'

'This is complete insanity!'

Greenie sighs.

'The listed shots have been completed. And we've wrapped on the original schedule, which was structured around effects sequences. Most of the picture is going to be generated in post. Delaney wants to retake some of the dialogue today. So, see if you can give it all a spin and twist.'

'Why is the picture going over-schedule if you've already wrapped on the list?

'The dialogue is weak. Delilah has also backtracked on nudity. She was against it at the outset. But now, after some cajoling, she's willing to walk the plank. New scenes may need to be structured around this development.'

'Where's her agent?'

'Flew back to LA last month.'

'Because of Mo?'

'He talked Delilah into flying solo for a few weeks—under his supervision, of course. Studio is backing him because she will bring in the numbers. Polls are in Delaney's favour. At this point, I'm guessing that Luminstein will do anything to keep the ship afloat.'

'Why haven't they cut the rope, Greenie? Why is this oil leak still gushing?'

'Does it matter? The door is open for you here.'

'I want to know.'

'I can't get into it, Brick.'

'Let me guess, Delaney had you sign a gag order or something.'

'Something like that.'

'How much time do we have on the new schedule?'

'A month, maybe less. Impossible to say until your contract comes back. Delaney's list of retakes is solid. Just a matter of rewriting and getting the talent to swing it—that's your job, apparently. The main problem, aside from the fact that we have no script and are flying completely blind—is Sasha.'

'I take it he and Mo are still not on speaking terms?'

'Ever since Delilah's agent left town.'

'So, it's the wild west down south and there's an earthquake.'

'You better believe it. My advice is to just to do what you can with what we have, take the credit they offer. When the smoke has cleared, just walk away.'

'That your position?'

'It was, maybe two months ago,' Greenie sighs. 'Of course, now I'm just here for the booze.'

'Wish I could say the same,' Brick nods.

He begins to look over the folder. The set is in an area of white dunes called Atlantis. Atlantis is just outside of town. Security is tight due to the close proximity of 'dangerous areas'. The limo stops at a checkpoint. They transfer to a jeep. It rides them out to a carnival of hardware. The set boils like an ant nest in the whiteness. Brick notices that the driver is smiling. He tips his cap at the star. The cap is an old crew item dating from the original *Game Over* shoot. The kid is obviously a fan. Usually, Brick is generous these circumstances, but the situation has him feeling nervous and lackluster. He doesn't speak a word throughout the bumpy ride. A ferocious hangover is nagging at him. He watches the hypnotic trawl of sand from behind sunglasses, plotting script angles. They grind to a halt. Luther, the director of photography, comes out to greet them. Luther is an old friend. He and Brick have worked together on several occasions in the past, most notably on *Game Over*.

'Good to see you back on the range, mister spaceman,' the old Czech grins. 'What happened to the nose?'

'Don't ask,' Brick replies testily.

The old action star's presence is causing more than a few heads to turn. He can see that the set-up is minimal. Luther is using his usual two camera rig. The system makes editing easier—especially on the match-ups. Everybody appears to be doing what they can to make life easier, Brick notes. It's almost as though the crew is gearing itself instinctively toward damage control. Brick and Luther walk down, toward the camera mounts.

'Mo driving you up the wall as well?' Brick probes.

Luther laughs tactfully. Brick is getting sand in his loafers. He's irritated that he wasn't briefed about the working conditions. Everything feels rushed.

'Same old, same old,' Luther mumbles enigmatically.

'How's the crew handling the delays?' Brick asks, trying to gauge the on-set atmosphere.

'They've given everyone fat overtime bonus's and its summer!' Luther laughs. 'Anyway, you know how crews love Mo. They'll do this all season if he asks them to.'

Brick is flummoxed by the situation. He turns to Greenie.

'Where is he, anyway?'

'Delaney's working on Delilah at the moment,' Greenie coughs diplomatically.

'I'll bet he is.'

Luther runs him through the shot-list. Since it's a retake, everyone seems to be relatively relaxed about what they have to accomplish.

'How was Sasha the first-time round?' Brick asks. 'Original script looks like your standard ham and eggs to me.'

'That's green eggs and ham,' Greenie pipes up.

'With cheese,' Luther's assistant, a snarky little brat with a goatee, adds.

'You have some new dialogue we can try?' Luther asks Brick.

'Sure,' Brick grimaces. 'I wrote some in the car, on the way here. On the back of a cocktail napkin…'

'I'm sure you did!' Luther chuckles.

He twirls his mustache with a gloved hand. Since Brick could remember, Luther has been in the habit of wearing thin cloth gloves while he worked.

'So, where's the leading man?' Brick asks.

A runner manifests with coffee for everyone. She beams at Brick. Luther signals the goateed assistant.

'James, take Brick over to Sasha. Let him know we're ready.'

'What's our window?' Brick asks.

'Light will change in an hour and half,' Luther answers, disinterested.

The reaction confuses Brick. It's not in keeping with the pedantic work ethic he is familiar with from the seasoned director of photography. James hands Brick a soya latte. He signals toward the edge of the set.

'Let's get this over with, then,' Brick mutters.

He follows James into the dunes. They trudge for a few minutes. Up, down and around bone-white formations. Brick glances back at one point. They have already lost visual contact with the set. They could be lost in New Mexico, he thinks. Only the distant haze of empurpled mountain caps and a fruity trace of sewage on the wind, gives the place away. A uniformed figure with a machine gun resolves out of the blinding whiteness. Brick and his companion approach the security guard. The man nods to them in greeting.

'Where's he at?' James asks.

The guard raises his jaw. Shading his eyes, Brick is just able to make out the silhouette of a tall, caped figure. He stands at the crest of a high dune.

'There's some skellums about,' the security guard mentions in a thick Cape Flats brogue. 'I scoped them, smoking bottles on the beach. But I think it's safe now.'

'Skellums?' Brick frowns.

'Dodgy types,' James mentions, somewhat apologetically.

'Shouldn't you be up there with him, then?' Brick points out.

'He wants to be alone and he's got his sword,' the security guard shrugs.

'His sword!' Brick exclaims.

'Delaney insists that all the edged weapons are combat ready,' James explains.

'Typical,' Brick mutters.

'It's attention to detail,' James protests.

Brick notes how quickly James flies to the production's defense. It annoys him. Though, he realizes how critically this attitude must be maintained on-set. Particularly at this stage of the game.

'Don't worry,' the security guard assures Brick. 'He's had saber training.'

'He played that knight, remember?' James pipes up.

'He can chop someone's head off with that thing, if he wants to!' the guard laughs.

'Jesus,' Brick mutters.

He instructs James to wait with the guard, thinking it might be best to meet the star alone. Halfway up the steep dune, Brick stumbles. His shoes fill with sand. Some of the coloured pages in fly off like frightened birds. There's coffee on the sleeve of his cream-coloured jacket. Brick realizes how out of shape Paris has left him. Not wanting to litter any further in the sterility of the dunes, he retrieves his fallen cup. Then slogs the rest of the way to the top. By the time he reaches Sasha, he is out of breath and nursing a stitch. A bead of sweat leaves his jaw. Sasha leans majestically on his jeweled broadsword. He is staring out over the distant ocean. His heavy cape thrashes in the wind. The sound is unsettling. He sports the winged helm Croeser had stolen the night before. But there is nothing ironic about its appearance when Sasha wears it. It suits his profile perfectly. Even Brick is taken aback at how iconic the star looks—especially against such an unreal backdrop. Yet, despite the sense of creative inspiration Brick feels at seeing Sasha in full force, the young star's appearance leaves him jaded. The Hollywood machine has perfectly fabricated his new and improved upgrade. Then thoughtfully sent him along to play coach. Brick had assumed that Sasha had not noticed his approach. So, he is surprised when star addresses him without even turning his head.

'Did you know that this part of the country is the only landmass that didn't move with continental drift?' he asks above the wind.

'No,' Brick wheezes. 'I didn't know that.'

'It's stayed in exactly the same place since all the continents were joined,' Sasha announces. 'It's the navel chakra of the world!'

'Navel chakra. Right.'

Sasha turns on Brick with a winning smile. He extends a gauntlet.

'It's a fucking honour to meet you,' he says sincerely. 'Brick fucking Bryson. In the fucking flesh.'

Brick returns the handshake peaceably.

'Thanks, man. Good to meet you too.'

'What happened to your face?'

'Walked into a fridge—listen, Sasha, I've had a couple of ideas about the scene we're going to shoot today...'

'I wasn't aware that you were in this scene, Brick.'

'Well, I'm not, Sasha. I'm directing it. Has no-one spoken with you?'

Sasha's face freezes, without noticeably altering its expression. A subtle, yet powerful shift.

'So now, you're playing stooge to dirty old men,' he says. 'How far the mighty have fallen...'

Brick sighs. After the morning's drama, he is no mood for an argument.

'Are we going to do this or not? Like I said, I've had some ideas about how we can approach...'

Sasha cuts him off.

'Del Croeser is a fucking disease. I will not support him or any of his hired underlings. Sure, I'll show my face, kill some bad guys. That much is in my contract. This whole fiasco will gross in the upper mid-range no matter what happens now. So, I don't need to lift a finger—for you or anyone else.'

With that, Sasha pulls his sword from the glittering sand. He strides effortlessly down the slope. Brick can see James gesticulating. He is throwing his arms around, in a 'what's going on' gesture. Brick sighs again. He stuffs his note-scribbled pages in his pocket and navigates his way back down.

By the time they make it to the set, Sasha has already left with the wardrobe people. Luther has called for the crew to strike the set. Everyone is busy packing. The director of photography shrugs at Brick—another wasted day. Greenie takes a hit from a brass hip-flask, calls for the jeep. Back in the limo, Brick manages to gather his composure.

'Still no word from Mo?'

'He's not available at the moment,' Greenie fences. 'You want to go back to the hotel?'

'Maybe he's at the studio. Doesn't he review dailies there?'

'I doubt it. His schedule is all over the place.'

'What the hell is going on here, Greenie?'

'I wish I could talk about it, Brick.'

A text comes in on Greenie's phone.

'I've located V,' he informs Brick. 'We could swing by if you need to speak to her?'

Brick's phone begins to ring. He realizes that he hasn't looked at it for ages. Sal is on the line. He also has messages from Lisa-Marie and Alix to contend with. Brick pauses for a moment. He quickly replies to Greenie.

'Ok, let's do it. Just let me know the second you hear from Mo. I need to meet with him asap,' he says, before taking the call.

'Hi, Sal?'

'Brick, I woke up to an email from Lenny down at the studio, saying that you are demanding a co-directing credit? Fuck is going on down there?'

'It's no mistake. Mo made the offer.'

'It's not his to make, Brick. This is a production decision—as I'm sure you know. I don't know how crazy Luminstein is going to be about doling out major credits this late in the game.'

'Don't back down, Sal. No credit, no contract. If Luminstein can't make good on Mo's promise within two days, then I'm on the next plane out of this ashtray.'

Brick catches a nod and a thumbs-up from Greenie.

'So, my old prize tiger grew back his claws,' Sal laughs. 'Ok, fine. If you feel we have Croeser in a corner, I'll squeeze some balls and see what comes out. Good to hear you talking all John Wayne again.'

'Don't count your chickens, buddy. It isn't all peach flambé in the navel chakra.'

'The *what*?'

'Never mind, chat later.'

He hangs up.

'So, what's your plan with Styles?' Greenie asks.

'I don't think anything is going to turn him around.'

'Hey, you could write in a telepathy angle. We could use outtakes and static shots as fillers. Maybe hire a mimic to do a voice-over…'

'The really tragic thing is that it could actually work. Psychic conversations are part of the mythos, after all. Does it violate anything in Sasha's contract?'

'I'll have to check, but I think we are good. Performer contracts have been structured to allow a lot of leeway within FX sequences—Delaney's money area.'

'Ah, the bottom of the barrel! Whatever we do though, I have to meet with Delilah first. From where I'm standing it looks like some of pivotal the changes are going to be on her shoulders.'

'On her tits and ass, you mean,' Greenie scowls, handing him some more papers.

'We'll just see about that,' Brick replies decisively.

Directors (and their girls)

Summer twilights are protracted at the season's zenith. The night sneaks up on you like a mugger. One moment its cocktails at sunset. Then, before you know it, midnight has swung round. By the time the limo cruises the Camp's Bay strip, the sky is gloaming with unearthly, neon sea-rinds. Five-star lobbies twinkle beyond veils of palm. Beach-facing restaurants are livid with custom. Upon the dramatic rock formations at the end of the beach, a photo shoot is taking place. Key lights slick across reedy equipment stands. Ancient boulders frame the oiled bodies of three girls in swimwear. Even at this distance, Brick recognizes V's physical presence. Is it just his imagination, or is there a predatory aspect to her supple line? Hers is a body whose athleticism has been honed by trauma of a secret past. *Who, but Fortunato*, Brick's inner voice mused, *could know the troubled lands those coltish legs had stalked?* The desperate ambition of the locals bewilders the first-worlder in Brick. He can't get his head around the place—the great gulfs between superficiality and substance. All its feasts and famine.

Greenie asks the driver to park beneath a line of royal palms. Brick leaves the old hand at a sea-facing table. With an entrée and a couple of pineapple Mojito's. He heads down to the rocks. Finally gets a chance to remove his traumatized loafers. Rolling his trouser legs up, Brick tramps the water-chilled sand with pleasure. As he draws closer to the shoot, he notices that the models have been caricatured. They resemble a foreign stylist's vision of 'African savages'. Cavorting about with fake spears, animal hide armbands and cannibalistic face paint. They take turns to snarl at the camera. To Brick, the cartoonification strikes a somewhat forlorn note against the great silences of sea and mountain. Brick pauses at the edge of the proceedings. He catches V's eye. She signals back with a smile. The others recognize him. They begin to titter. V's expression falters against Brick's stony gaze. He quickly turns away, moving back to the waterline—before anyone takes the opportunity to introduce themselves.

The sideshow goes on for another half an hour or so. Brick observes the light's gradual disintegration. He makes mental notes as to its cinematic potential. He studies it's fade against the Twelve Apostle mountain range. The mountains stretch panoramically off, in the direction of Cape Point. V walks up to him. She looks serious. But her expression is ruined by the absurdity of its war paint.

'Your husband came to see me,' he tells her.

'My husband!' she exclaims. 'You mean Fortunato?'

He nods grimly. She begins to chuckle.

'No, we are not married,' she laughs. 'Well, I mean, technically we are. But it was to help him out with his visa problems. In reality, we broke up some time ago…'

'He doesn't seem think so.'

They drift along the water's edge, splashing feet against the icy foam.

'Ah, Fortunato,' she smiles. 'He is not a bad guy. Crazy, sure, but you know, that comes with talent.'

'It does?'

'Sometimes…'

'So, his films were good?'

'Yes, of course,' V replies. 'He was very young when he started—assisting on shoots, you know. But he always had his own projects on the side. He didn't have much to work with, in those days. But he planned everything very precisely. In this way, he was able to accomplish a lot.'

'Mo used to be like that.'

'Yes, I know. Delaney was a great influence on Fortunato's work ethic. He also ended up doing action pictures. He would create comic strips out of his shot lists, 'like Hitchcock', he used to tell people. He even composed his own soundtracks on synthesizers, operated the camera and so on. In his own way, he's a real auteur.'

'He did well in Lagos?'

'Nollywood can be kind to a talented and prolific guy like Fortunato. Everything was good, until some trouble started for him. He had to leave.'

'What kind of trouble?'

She looks away. He watches her remove her electric cigarette from her bag.

'Who knows?' she defers, chasing the blue glow with her breath. 'Political maybe. I am from Congo. It is very far from Nigeria—in so many ways…'

'I wouldn't mind seeing his work. Then I would have something to criticize him about—the next time we bump heads.'

'I'll make sure you get copies.'

'Thanks.'

'In the end, I was the only one there for him,' she confides after a moment's pause. 'But he is the ungrateful kind. He repaid me by falling in love—so irritating.'

'What happened?'

'I have a French passport, through my mother's side. We married—tried to get him one as well. The French government didn't recognize the union. So, he is here now. On refugee status. There are many like him. It's difficult for them to find work or a decent place to live.'

'He isn't involved with the film industry?'

'God, you Americans!' she laughs. 'So naïve! Film work? Here? He couldn't get work as a car guard. He is mostly selling cocaine now.'

'He's a drug dealer? Jesus...'

'It's not how you think. Sometimes, it's all a person can do to make a living. You are not in a position to judge. This may look like the first world sometimes, but it is a very different reality for most people.'

'But is Fortunato actually doing coke? It sure seemed like he had a monkey on his back...'

She laughs heartily.

'No,' she replies, amused. 'Fortunato is the only monkey on Fortunato's back.'

'Are you sure about that?'

'He is somewhat health obsessed. Though, I suspect that he is depressed. He was a great fan of yours, you know.'

'So he said.'

'So, the two of you had a good chat?'

'...At the point of a knife.'

'He is very dramatic.'

'I noticed.'

'How are things with Delaney?'

'Well, I just met Sasha Styles...'

'That boy—so hot.'

'He was pretty cold to me.'

'It will be difficult for you to persuade him to go along with Delaney's wishes. Sasha thinks his treatment of Delilah is reprehensible.'

'It is.'

'I agree. But as a result, Sasha will not operate in your favour. It is a failure on Delaney's part.'

'True.'

'Not to worry though, my dear. You are clever enough to work around them both.'

'I appreciate the vote of confidence.'

Brick's phone buzzes. He looks at it. Greenie has finally located Croeser.

'Listen, I'd better get going,' he tells V.

'Ok, good luck. I'll get some of Fortunato's videos over to you later.'

'I would appreciate that. Need a ride? I have the 'Croesermobile'' handy…'

She laughs and leans forward to kiss him. He hesitates at the last moment, still unsure of his ground. She retracts. Then loses a cattish chuckle, patting his cheek.

'I am cursed with sensitive men!' she laughs. 'Why can't I just find myself a nice, heartless savage?'

'You did, remember? He just prefers drugged-up teenage starlets.'

'Who doesn't these days?' she shrugs rhetorically. 'See you, spaceman.'

She turns on her heel and strides away. Brick watches her go. The fact that she refuses to look back, seems too deliberate a statement to him. He wonders if her pride is wounded by such an inconsequential slight. Somehow, the thought amuses him. He finds himself smiling all the way back to the car.

The limo heads up Brownlow. The Daly Deli is still open. It draws a crowd around dinnertime. But has now thinned out considerably. A couple share an intimate coffee. One of the locals pops in for takeaway ciabatta and a handful of overpriced avocados. Adrian is at the far table, legs crossed, smoking a Stuyvesant red. Brick watches the place slip past. He is considering stopping there for a bite to eat, when a top-of-the-line stills camera sails out of the night. It cracks the limo's windscreen. The vehicle swerves to a sharp halt. Brick and Greenie are tossed to one side. Both scramble for the windows, to get a look outside. The limo driver climbs out to inspect the windshield. They join him. The glass is spider-webbed. It needs replacing. Greenie retrieves the shattered camera from the tarmac. Brick notices him remove and deftly pocket the SD card. A scuffle is going on near the end of the street. Beneath some gloomy fruit trees. A suited man drags Despierre between a pair of Harley Davidson's. Brick recognizes the assailant. He is one of Mo's personal bodyguards. The show-room polish of the bikes carry a garish undertone of mid-life crises. The image of the surly bodyguard holding a French tabloid photographer in a stranglehold, between all that chrome, strikes Brick as somewhat comedic. Croeser comes out of a pomegranate lined passage. He doesn't see Desmond in the shadows. The paparazzi gets the director in a chokehold. Greenie is in the thick of it before Brick has time to register. He exchanges a glance with the limo driver, who has elected to avoid involvement—perhaps for legal reasons. By the time Brick crosses the street, Greenie has managed to prise the bodyguard off Despierre. Seeing this, Desmond relinquishes his grip. Croeser spins loose. The two red-faced enemies face off, panting.

'You'll be hearing from our solicitors,' Desmond barks.

'You're a fungal rash on the ass of society!' Croeser blusters, somewhat lyrically. 'Go peep in on someone else!'

Brick separates them.

'Look, calm down, the both of you!' he snaps.

Faces are appearing at windows. Sulette rushes to the gate. She resembles the excited pug at her heels. The dog is spluttering. It won't stop barking.

'You will pay for my camera,' Despierre tells Croeser.

The photographer levers himself up off the street, clutching at his knee. Greenie lends him a hand.

'Don't worry,' Greenie assures him. 'Your equipment will be replaced. Can I give you my card? We can always arrange an interview at a more suitable time...'

'Sure,' Desmond sneers. 'But we want to talk to Delilah, too.'

'Fuck you!' Croeser blasts.

Greenie is quick to cut in;

'We'll see what we can do,' he assures the reporters.

'Is it true that she has a drug problem?' Desmond asks.

'Now, listen...' Greenie says.

'Why isn't she talking to the Press?' the reporter barrels on. 'And where's her agent got to, eh?'

'Now, just a minute...'

'What about her twitter? What does she mean by—*every day I am underwater*? What are these fish glands she's always on about? Some New-Age superfood, or are they a code for some new party drug?'

'Come on, guys,' Brick interrupts. 'We all have our work to do. Let's be professional.'

'What about you, Brick?' Desmond snaps. 'Do you have a drug problem?'

'Actually, I have a great headline for you, Des,' Greenie smiles. 'How about; Film star stops tabloid journalist's assault on legendary director'. How's that sound?'

'Too wordy for my editor, sport,' Desmond grins acidly.

'Let's go,' Despierre says quietly.

'We can add breaking and entering!' Croeser shouts, still rubbing at his chafed throat.

'Get back in the house, Mo!' Brick commands.

He pulls the director aside. Despierre does the same with his aggravated partner. Sulette is now on the sidewalk, in fluffy slippers. Her pug is still barking its head off. She has it firmly in hand, despite gratuitous, false nails. Negotiating her way into the pomegranate passage, she keeps her eye firmly on Brick.

'I'm going to blow this open, Croeser,' Desmond shouts from his car. 'When I do, you're finished! You washed-up, old pedo!'

'Enough!' Brick calls, eyeing the faces in the windows.

Adrian comes over and offers to lend a hand. Brick is trying to get Croeser back into the passage before he starts yelling again. He finds his way blocked by the smiling figure of Sulette, who extends her hand in greeting.

'I'm Delaney's landlady, Sulette Labuschagne,' she announces.

'Hi,' Brick replies in irritation.

He shakes her hand nonetheless.

'*Game Over* was one of my best films, when I was a teen,' she grins lasciviously.

'Christ, not now,' Croeser growls, pushing past.

'Excuse my friend,' Brick mutters, following the director.

For a moment, he is certain she will follow them up. But the dog's barking fades. Brick finds himself following Croeser. They traverse a narrow flight of stairs, entering the upper apartment.

The deco lounge has strange angles. But Brick has the feeling that it gets good light during the day. A bay window faces Brownlow. A row of windows patterns the opposite wall. These look out through the tops of jacaranda trees, toward the mountain. At the height of their season, you could probably reach through and pick fat pomegranates with your hands. This is now impossible. Delilah has covered every window in the room with three to four layers of aquamarine lighting gel and blue cellophane. By day, the room is lit with an intense blue light. This effect is amplified by the tin foil she has plastered over the ceiling and walls. The sprawling room has also been stripped of furniture. Large pot plants colonize vacant areas. They lend the interior the muggy closeness of a tropical grotto. Crystals wands lie everywhere. For the most part, they are arranged in geometric patterns on cloth and silk. Four massive plasma screens dominate the area. The screens are always on, streaming everything from surveillance feeds, cartoons, nature footage, underground news, serials, pornography, live streams— virtually anything. Delilah's capacity for sensory intake has boosted considerably. Ever since she started eating fish glands. She feels as though she is finally getting a handle on what's going on in the world. She is capable of inter-relating seemingly discontinuous events with surprising ease. She discovers secret patterns and programming in everything. Even now, as voices come into focus in the hallway outside. She sits in a lotus position, scanning a constant stream of images. All she wears is a necklace of seashells. Her hair is wet with aloe. A savaged pawpaw lies at her feet, engorged by ants. A continuous lull of whale song emits from the quadraphonic sound system. The air is stratified with incense. Trill sleeps on the floor beside her like some giant pet. The creature is also naked, its face pillowed by a mountain of popcorn. Of course, Delilah won't touch popcorn now. She has recently learned that almost all the corn in South Africa is genetically modified. To what she considers an indigestible degree. She sees the alien corn as a kind of corporate coup; a Machiavellian takeover of a country's staple diet. A plot to reduce future resistance.

Croeser storms into the kitchen. He begins to furiously fix cocktails.

'That Whitechapel wharf rat is starting to give me piles!' he yells.

Brick watches him hurl Maraschino cherries into four goblets.

'No kidding,' the star mutters, eyeing the messy kitchen.

'We need to go down to his hotel, take him out to the dunes and dispense from good, old-fashioned frontier justice!'

'I think we have more pressing issues to deal with,' Greenie says, entering the room. 'Like Sasha, for example.'

'That little prick has it in for me,' Croeser sighs.

He hands rum coco's to both of them. Brick gives him a cold look.

'God damn it, Mo, you know I'm just out of the funny farm for this shit.'

'It's just a fucking cocktail, Brick,' Croeser protests. 'Anyway, it will help with your hangover.'

Brick takes it. Greenie observes the exchange with interest, fishing out his cherry.

'What's your plan for Sasha, then?' Brick asks, sipping at the drink.

'My plan?' Croeser explodes. 'What's *your* plan, buddy boy? You wanted to direct, didn't you? This is the shit a director deals with on a daily basis.'

'How am I supposed to write material for someone who won't perform?'

Croeser was right, Brick realizes. The rum is already soothing the clotty ache in his head.

'Write around him,' Croeser argues. 'I don't care! The narrative is flexible. You'll have a hundred ideas.'

'Maybe when I actually get time to read the script,' Brick mutters.

'Don't worry about time,' Croeser says. 'I know it looks like we are in dire straits, but it's all taken care of. Trust me. Greenie will supply you with everything you need to get up to speed.'

'It's all in the car,' Greenie reports. '...Which is out of commission, by the way.'

'Did I smash the windshield?' Croeser cackles.

'You sure did,' Greenie sighs, lifting his glass wearily as Croeser toasts.

'It's no problem,' Croeser says. 'I have a cherry red mustang out back. Take it.'

'Listen, Mo...' Brick begins.

'Just a second, buddy,' the director interrupts. 'Bikie! Get in here!'

His bodyguard clatters up the stairs. Croeser hands him a cocktail. He accepts it without expression.

'What's going on with the limo?' Croeser quizzes.

'Driver says it should be fixed up by morning,' the man answers, tasting his concoction.

'Great. Listen, get all of Greenie's shit out of there and put it in the Mustang.'

Croeser tosses him the keys.

'No problem, boss,' Bikie nods.

He takes a final swig before heading back down.

'We do have a serious problem with Sasha,' Greenie says. 'Bastard has a loophole written into his contract. He is obligated to adhere to the shooting script, but not to any changes made once principal photography has begun.'

'He knows you well,' Brick smiles at Croeser.

'Don't count on it,' the director winks back.

'What about what's already in the can?' Brick asks. 'Greenie tells me you've wrapped in the original schedule.'

'It's just no good,' Croeser says, shaking his head. 'I can use his parts. But it'll be shit! Fucker is clearly going through the motions and I can't write for him. I mean, we all know I can't fucking write, ok! I can fix what the hacks churn out, sure. But you know the system. They don't let the good writers work these days. Producers don't want writers. They want worker bees to run the numbers.'

'Then why get me in?' Brick asks.

'Because you're a star and we have history. You're the only way I can get a talented writer in—one who can also buck the system with me.'

'He's right,' Greenie agrees. 'Studio won't take narrative risks with a project of this scope. But at this stage of the game—in the situation we're in, there's a narrow window we can work with—purely in regards to your standing in the franchise, of course. You should grab it. Fan base will be all over you.'

'Look at the script, study the dailies,' Croeser tells Brick. 'Write whatever the hell you want and I'll make sure Luther shoots it. We'll find a way to deal with Sasha Styles.'

'Is Delilah around?' Brick asks. 'I need to touch base with her, see if I can work with her on this.'

Croeser hesitates for a second. He finishes his drink.

'Sure,' he tells Brick. 'She's in the other room. Why don't you go in and say hi while I chat to Greenie.'

'How do you think she is going to take this?' Brick asks.

'Oh, don't worry about Delilah,' Croeser laughs. 'She's as solid as a rock!'

Brick abandons his half-finished drink. He begins to hunt through the mazy apartment. When he finally finds Delilah, he pauses at the threshold, taken aback by her grotto. The young actress remains in her yoga position. She appears engrossed by the cacophony of visual information on the various screens. Brick approaches cautiously. He is wary of her nudity and the entire room in general. Slowly, she turns her head. When Delilah eventually recognizes him, it is as though she is looking out through a misted window. An award-winning smile blossoms across her face.

'What's the weather like on Mars?' she quotes, from one of his films.

'I could ask you the same thing.'

Squatting down to her eye-level, he asks:

'How you holding up there, soldier?'

'The sea is too cold...'

Her attention is already beginning to drift.

'I want a warm sea,' she murmurs.

Brick notices a saucer, spoon and a pack of clean syringes. His face darkens.

'Listen,' he says. 'I don't know if Mo's mentioned anything specific. But I'm apparently going to be doing rewrites and directing some of your scenes. I haven't had a chance to chat to your agent yet, though. Are you ok with that?'

'Sure, whatever,' she replies, distracted by something on one of the feeds.

'You look a little tired,' he mentions cautiously. 'Everything ok?'

She looks at him again.

'If you're referring to my new drug habits, then yeah—lol,' she smirks.

He nods diplomatically.

'Can you believe people actually say 'lol'?' she adds, looking away. 'It's an acronym, for fuck's sake...'

'Habits are like that. They seem silly at first. Next thing, you're saying them every day.'

This makes her laugh.

'That's just so fucking cute, Brick Bryson,' she smiles. 'What a superhero thing to say...'

'Any plans to cut down?'

'The fish glands hamper opioid addiction. So, I'm doing smack for research. It's safe for now. I'll drop it soon.'

'And these...fish glands?'

She fixes him in direct eye-contact.

'They heal you. You should try one.'

Meeting her gaze, Brick finds a familiar, Hollywood hardness there.

It's layered in deep beneath all the sugar crystals and fairy dust. But its presence is as solid as steel.

'Not right now,' he tells her. 'But, I appreciate the suggestion.'

His side-step makes her chuckle.

'Don't worry about me, Champion of Earth. I'm just peachy.'

And then seriously, almost as a professional courtesy, she adds:

'I never miss a call.'

Croeser comes in unexpectedly. He crouches behind Delilah. Smiling broadly, he puts his arms around her, squeezing her breasts. This amuses her. She snuggles against him. Brick observes their interplay in a detached manner.

'She's a piece of work, isn't she?' Croeser brags.

'Aren't we all?' she teases, tactfully sparing Brick the need to answer.

'What a little princess,' Croeser sighs, kissing the back of her neck.

'Princesses have magical kingdoms to run. I want to be free—in the sea....'

'I don't believe that for one minute, your Highness!' Croeser laughs.

'Have you tried swimming in the sea here, Brick?'

'Could I speak with you alone for a moment?' Brick asks the director quietly.

'Sure, sure, no problem. Let's go back to my study. I have some good Scotch there.'

They get up. On their way out, Delilah calls over her shoulder:

'Hope your nose grows back!'

Brick isn't quite sure whether she is joking or not.

Croeser leads him around the confusing apartment. Eventually, they emerge into a study. The work room is almost at direct odds with the chaos of the kitchen. It is neat and orderly. It reflects a paradoxical, somewhat scholarly side to Croeser's personality. Electronics are in the minority. Bookshelves line the walls, organized with plastic tabs. Aside from the hoard of old paperbacks, there is a predominance of pictorial reference. These include art books. As well as a substantial collection of graphic novels and comics. Brick recognizes the collection. He's explored it before. In better days. The room relaxes Brick. A long trestle table stands in the far corner. Balsa wood set miniatures have been constructed upon the surfaces. Wiry contraptions—Croeser's own design. They stand like alien invaders. Watching over tiny, wooden buildings. These machines allow their operators to plot camera moves throughout the miniatures, with great detail and efficiency. Easels stand to attention around this table. They hold design boards. Pinned stills and schematics of costumes and vehicles decorate their surfaces. A pair of surfboards obscure a wall. French doors open onto a little balcony, complete with a coffee table and some armchairs. A large desk dominates the corner opposite the trestle tables. This area is lit by a warm lamp. Upon the desk are many piles of paper, sketches and notebooks. Croeser's illegible handwriting covers everything. The most surprising feature for Brick, however, are the posters. Most depict the actor himself—from films the pair had collaborated on. One or two even advertise movies that Brick made before they had met. Croeser smiles when he catches Brick sizing them up.

'My superhero pal,' he announces proudly.

Brick had forgotten the nick-name.

'Check this out,' Croeser tells him.

He calls Brick's attention to the desk and opens up a veritable bible of sketches—all drawn by him. This singular amount of work covers everything in the project. From the smallest costume details to the broadest set designs. Brick is reminded just how staggering the volume of Croeser's output could be. Art directors and designers had always appreciated the career boost that a collaboration with Croeser awarded. Yet, not a single one has ever claimed to have enjoyed the experience. Croeser is notorious for micro-managing every aspect of his films— particularly the art department. Creatives have been known to leave his productions with the sense of being treated like chess pieces—or worse. Brick is the single exception in a long history of tyranny. Croeser has an undeniable affection for the star. Even now, it's hard for Brick to believe that he was allowed such creative freedoms. He admits taking it all for granted at the time. Now, looking at his old friend's creations and being in the presence of such tireless energy—Brick is reminded once again, of the awe he had once felt for Croeser.

'Well, it's good to see you working like this again,' Brick acknowledges.

He thumbs through a stack of structural diagrams. They detail one of the cycloramas. Croeser developed a passion for cycloramas after watching 'Rear Window'. Brick had been a fan of the writer, Cornell Woolrich. His story had provided the basis for the film. When they first met, Croeser compared Brick's dualistic onscreen presence to Jimmy Stewart's. He claimed that both actors had a paradoxical ability in common. They were able to bridge dark, obsessive qualities with an inviolate sense of inner virtue. This had been the pair's first talking point.

'Yeah,' Croeser growls.

He pulls out a wooden box of marijuana and a rolling kit.

'After I stopped the cocaine, it all just started to come back—the urge to draw. I just never seemed to be able to sit still for long enough when I was high.'

Brick discovers a series of sketches, tucked beneath a folder. They describe the interior of an anti-gravity chamber. The large area is dominated by strong, blue lighting. Robotic tentacles stretch from highly reflective walls. Diagrams of Delilah's character float through these weightless rooms. She is nude in every image. Sometimes, she is depicted in sexual congress. With machines or unearthly creatures. Brick has by now skimmed the location list thoroughly. He's also viewed photographs and sketches of all the sets. Despite this, he doesn't recall anything pertaining to this particular area. The sketches are complex. With many different chambers and FX areas. Much thought and planning has gone into them. There are notes and references to scenes that Brick is not aware of.

'What's all this, then?' he asks, perplexed.

Croeser looks up. He takes the series of drawings and closes their folder.

'It's nothing. Just a section I cut.'

'Pity. Looks promising.'

Croeser's shiftiness breaks Brick's reverie. The director's many personal flaws suddenly gleam through the nostalgia. Brick drifts away from the table. He looks up at a younger, caped image of himself. The poster is from their first film, *Weekends on Mars*. Croeser is working a mound of indica through a fancy grinder. He pauses for a moment. Then withdraws a cut-glass bottle of pricey Scotch. Brick watches him pour out a pair of drams. The director gets up and hands him one of the glasses. Brick raises the whiskey, but does not drink.

'You've got that little girl hooked on smack, you know?' Brick toasts. 'Proud of yourself?'

Croeser swallows his drink whole. He wordlessly pours another finger. Then returns to the desk to finish rolling.

'She's not as *little* as you might imagine. You'd be amazed the shit she's into…'

'I can't fault Sasha for judging you so harshly. How can you justify what you are doing? She's just a kid.'

Croeser sighs.

'Seriously, Brick,' he says 'It's just *method* shit to her. I mean… Ok, look. This is all very hush-hush at the moment, but—she's just been cast as the lead in a hot project about smack culture in 50's Tangier! I told her, you can't expect to fill those shoes without a little research. How else is she supposed to give a believable performance?'

'Why doesn't she try *acting*?'

'Ah, Brick,' Croeser laughs. 'Listen, the fish glands hold off addictive substances to a degree. If she stays light and cuts within a couple of months, she'll be fine.'

'That reporter is onto them. Shouldn't she just stop?'

'The glands aren't illegal. I don't think Desmond will chase that.

Anyway, he's not after her.'

'What the hell are those things, anyway?'

'Some psychedelic—similar to ayahuasca or iboga—or so I'm told.'

Brick is surprised.

'You haven't tried it?'

'Not now. That Jennifer girl and her cronies—they all use them. It's a girl thing. I don't want to rock the boat.'

'Well, Delilah offered one to me. And that cross-dresser of hers. He also looks like he's on them.'

'Trill's a girl, Brick. Don't you also have a daughter now?' Croeser chuckles.

'You know what I mean.'

'Look, I'll probably eat some after the shoot. You know I don't like to trip during filming.'

'Unfair enough. Sounds risky, though. Letting her bug out like that. What about V, does she use them as well?'

'She did a few times, sure. Her ex is the supplier. But, you know, these Africans, man—they're used to weird medicinal shit.'

'*These Africans?*' Brick laughs. 'You should hear yourself!'

'Hey, this is the original continent. Everything is upside-down and inside out. We're just tourists. These people live it.'

'*These people?*'

Brick pulls up a chair and sits down. Before he realizes it, he's taken a few exploratory sips of the Scotch. He raises his eyebrows. It really *is* the good stuff.

'I'm not sure I can work around Sasha,' he admits. 'He seems dead set against you.'

'But he idolizes the great Brick Bryson! I was sure you could bring him around…'

'You underestimate your ability to alienate people, Mo. Maybe if you get Delilah clean and sober and leave her the fuck alone. Maybe then Sasha would start to play ball.'

'It's her decision, Brick.'

'Is it?'

Croeser swings around. He pours another round. Brick hadn't even realized that his tumbler was empty.

'Stop worrying,' the director says. 'Let's smoke this reefer. You can worry later.'

'There's something else we need to talk about.'

'Go ahead.'

'According to the script, first time we see *Club Ded*, is when Andro gets debriefed. But from that point, the movie avoids going back there. It traipses around the whole mutant uprising on the planet's surface.

It details various power struggles. But we only see *Club Ded* one more time—towards the very end. When it gets destroyed by the ion-bomb. That's very little screen-time to justify a title.'

'Great title though.'

'Sure, sure.'

'Club Ded is pivotal—as a plot-point. Anyway, it's is a production decision. Whatever sells—you know the score.'

'But don't you think we need to get inside this place?'

Croeser shakes his head.

'Firstly,' the director points out. 'I don't want to shoot scenes in anti-gravity unless they are actually captured in anti-gravity. Usually they use that plane—the vomit comet, or whatever they call it. To simulate zero-g in a fast dive.'

'Right.'

'But, Club Ded, as you know from its description, is grandiose! It's a pleasure isle of the future! So, no. It would be too much for the rating and budget. I worked around it. So can you.'

Brick can't help but laugh.

'Fuck is so funny?' the director erupts.

'I've never knew you to turn down anything because it was too costly or overtly sexual.'

'Well I did!'

'Fine, fine.'

'Enough damned questions, Brick! I want to show you more designs. You haven't even seen the monsters! Also, I have these great, new reprints of vintage Italian comics and…'

By the time Brick makes it to the Mustang, he's smoked two hydroponic joints and is down a quarter of Scotch. Bikie has to drive him so Brick can hang onto the car. A large case of documents and dailies occupies the back seat. Brick goes through some notes, but is unable to process anything. After Bikie drops the load off in his room, Brick stares up at the blue lipstick V. His gaze eventually drifts to the statuette beneath. Finally, he recognizes the conjunction. It's another weird reference to *Two Weeks in Another Town*. Brick thought it all looked familiar. The mirror lipstick V was in Irwin Shaw's novel. But not in the movie. What kind of game were V and Croeser playing? Again, Brick gets the sense that Croeser has bugged the suite with fiber-optics. Surveillance, however, has never been an issue with the star. 'They can't put a camera in my head', was what he used to say. Of course, now, he isn't so sure. He touches base with his wife, sending a substantial message before quickly shutting his phone down. He can't face any more communications tonight. Particularly the fleshy photos Alix has sent through. The room is pulsating. It's an old, familiar feeling.

He tries sitting down. It only makes things worse. He needs a break from *Club Ded*, V, Croeser and the whole affair. He collapses across the bed with a copy of Walter Tevis's *The Colour of Money*. The writer always had a knack of inspiring Brick to action. He doesn't disappoint. As Brick skims the section detailing Fast Eddie Felson's preparations for his climactic nine-ball tournament at Lake Tahoe, Brick realizes what he has to do.

He goes into the kitchen, swallows a few bottles of water. The plastic tasting liquid is unsatisfying after Fortunato's spring elixir. But it does the trick. Brick then removes his abused bandage. The nose is still a swollen mess. He redresses it. Then asks reception if he can have access to an indoor pool. They tell him that there is one in the spa. But it is now closed. They must have been name-checking his room. Because they then go on to inform him that he would be welcome to make use of it. *The good old celebrity pass-card*, his inner voice winks. He thanks the girl at reception and orders some kombucha. They offer to deliver it directly to the spa. Changing into a track suit, he heads down. A porter is waiting with his drinks. He lets Brick in with a smile. Brick wonders whether his eyes are too red. It's been a while since he was high (*with the exception of last night!*). When asked if he'd like the sauna and hot tub activated, Brick shrugs.

'Why not?' he consents, feeling more and more like Fast Eddie with every passing moment.

It used to help Brick in the past—to spontaneously take on literary or filmic characters. The practice allows him to explore characterization. It also temporarily removes his personal insecurities. There's a perspective to it. He is able to view his issues through a stranger's eyes. He hasn't tried it for a while. But the old routines kick in smoothly. Brick decides that he needs Fast Eddie Felson's methodical hunger for victory now. He needs his relentlessness. Brick tosses the character around in his head. Swimming lap after lap in the salt water pool. In the novel, Felson had been at Caesar's Palace in Lake Tahoe, for a competition. He had worked out in the hotel gym between nine-ball matches. He swam lengths and relaxed in the whirlpool tub afterward. Brick had always been fond of Scorsese's adaptation. But the script changes bothered the writer in him. Cruise' character didn't exist in the book. The elegant Minnesota Fats had been written out. Brick felt that the picture ended up becoming something of a rehash of *The Hustler*. It had left him dissatisfied. He wonders if this is what Mo now expects by bringing him onboard like this—some sort of rehash. Brick isn't going to give it to him. He realizes that he has a chance to accomplish something no-one expects of him. He means to grab it with both hands. Come what may, Brick plans to win.

He swims till his body burns. A stitch comes and goes. When he has swum for over an hour, he dredges himself out. Then he sits in the sauna until 3am. He plans to force a few more half-hearted laps. But ends up in the hot tub with a cold kombucha. Despite the ordeal of the last few days, his head is exceptionally clear. He should be exhausted. Instead, he is energized. Brick knows what he has to do. Sal had emailed. He cautioned Brick not to begin work on the script until the contracts were out the way. Despite this, Brick is burning to start. He thanks the porter for the use of the spa. He leaves a generous tip and returns to his room. There, he starts to pore over the material.

He calls room service, ordering a pot of matcha with 'anything vegan, that isn't fried'. Time to be good, he decides. He finds TCM. *The King of Marvin Gardens* is halfway in. Rafelson suits his mood. So, he leaves the movie playing. The suite has a sea-facing balcony. He moves one of the lamps from the lounge to the outside table and piles papers to one side. Greenie had the good sense to pack in an extra Mac. He sets it up next to his. He has an idea to stream footage through the second machine, whilst perusing the script on his Air book. Croeser had also supplied him with a pair of studio headphones—so that he could monitor sound. The food and drink arrives. The outside lamp has already attracted a large moth and a couple of smaller, midge-like things. The moon glitters across the sea. Brick is starting to feel good about the situation. He would swim laps every day and maybe do some rock climbing. He and his wife have been vegan for over a decade. But he wasn't particularly health conscious about it. A lot of industry people followed similar diets. Though he felt that very few did so for ethical reasons. In his experience, most became vegan simply to prolong their careers. Lisa-Marie had been great about getting him back on track after rehab. He planned to stick with what she had shown him. Ordinarily it would have been toasted sandwiches and black coffee till dawn. But he was happy to put all of that behind him now and focus on streamlining his energy.

Brick dives right in. The overall pacing of the script is jagged, the character interaction lumpy. He wants to thin it out. Inject some wit and fun. He gets the idea that Sasha might come around to his way of thinking if he could make him look good—with some sterling one-liners. Brick proceeds chronologically. He skips the intro sequence. This details one of Croeser's over-extended signature tracking shots. Flicking through the thumbnails of a balletic, post John Woo action sequence, Brick arrives at the introduction of Sasha's character, *Jack Andro*. A holographic projection of the character is being debriefed. The action takes place in a spacious control-pod aboard *Club Ded*. Brick rigs the scene's dailies, loads up the script and sets to work. He is immediately sucked in and works well for an hour or so. At 4am, the phone starts ringing. The intrusion takes him by surprise. He saves his draft, rises and goes inside.

'Sorry to trouble you Mister Bryson,' comes the now familiar voice of the concierge. 'A young lady has dropped a package off for you at reception. She said that you would want it immediately.'

'What is it?'

'It's hard to tell, a book sized box, gift-wrapped in matte-black paper. Not too heavy.'

'Did she leave?'

'Straight away.'

'Ok, thanks. Send it up.'

Brick paces around till the box arrives. Inside are three DVD's and a small card with a lipstick V, this time in red. The covers amuse Brick. Two of them have a Rambo-esque motif. Rippling muscles, Ray-Bans, badly airbrushed machine guns and helicopters. All depicted against jungle sunsets. Their titles, both in blood red, read; *Fire at Dawn* and *Loose Connection*. The third is titled *Children of the Cow*. This has been printed in a lumo-green typeface. Its cover depicts a gang of Nigerian strongmen. All painted chalky white. With matching lumo-green fangs, they munch at the savaged carcass of a fallen cow. The tableau is set against the forlorn backdrop of a ruined village. Brick gets out his phone. He has several messages, including one from Lisa-Marie. He decides to read it later. He calls V, only to get an automated response. Her number is currently out of service. Perplexed, Brick picks one of the DVD's at random. He loads it and collapses across the couch.

The titles are a barrage of video effects. Slickly edited. The nimble cutting continues into the feature. The film has been shot on a wide array of substandard digital cameras. The image of a heavy-set soldier of fortune flickers—badly transferred playback. The character squats against a line of jungle undergrowth, dressed in olive fatigues. He clutches a machete with a metal hand. The prosthetic pivots at the end of a robotic arm. Although homemade, the arm is clearly well crafted (albeit out of stripped tin cans and bits of junk). Brick can find nothing hokey about its movement. Cheesy, arpeggiated synth lines throb. A Casio drumbeat. A fast cut to the label on the character's combat jacket. It reads: 'MACHETE MAN 2000'. A hot, oversaturated sun beats down on the character's square face. He glances from side to side with a predatory squint.

We cut to a POV—something moving through the jungle toward Machete Man 2000. Brick suspects that Fortunato taped the camera to the end of a pole. Using a wide-lens he must have run through the jungle, holding it out in front of him. The footage has been subtly accelerated. The effect, along with some fancy editing, is dizzying. Despite the low quality of the equipment, Brick senses a polished, technical style at work. He recognizes a homage to Wolfgang Peterson's *Das Boot*. There are also hat-tips to John McTiernan, Russell Mulcahy, Tony Scott, Renny Harlin and others. It reminds Brick of Mo. Croeser had refined that particular brand of 80's action, in the following decade. The picture is starting to excite the old action star. Its cleverly loaded, stylistic references to the summer blockbusters of his youth work a nostalgic magic.

Machete Man 2000 spins around. A form explodes from the foliage. The frame cuts back. Sound and image freeze on the leaping figure of a man. He is dressed in a terrifying suit of stitched crocodile skins. The camera zooms in, cued by a synthesized orchestra hit. A title: 'CROCODILE WITCH KILLER', scrolls. It moves, video game style across the character. Radioactive green lettering. The freeze frame is rhythmic and well-timed. It also blasts back into action at exactly the correct moment. The Casio line comes in hard. A fight scene follows. Again, the editing is agile, almost musical. The Foley work over-compressed and jagged. It's cheap kung fu sound. But it works because the timing is so perfect. Brick is starting to get the sense that Fortunato might be even more of a perfectionist than Croeser. Certainly, their styles are similar. Though Croeser is notorious for outsourcing. He had always had an army of technical wizards and an arsenal of hardware at his disposal. Fortunato, on the other hand, works on low quality gear and does everything himself. His signature is on every frame. From the well-timed slaps and grunts, to the unorthodox camera positioning and editing. There isn't much of a narrative—and none seemed forthcoming. But the relentless barrage of technical virtuosity more than makes up for a lack of storyline. The whole film looks set to be one endless, hallucinatory chase scene.

Machete Man 2000 raises his machete. He lets loose a canned scream. There is a fast zoom on the blade. Fortunato has hand-animated heavily pixelated twinkles along the blade. The character slashes at Crocodile Witch Killer. But misses each time. Scaly legs and arms wrap round Machete Man 2000 in double-speed.

We cut back. A panoramic overview of a sluggish, brown river. It wends its way through thick jungle. Soundtrack cuts to hissy, tape-compressed jungle noise. The shot is cleverly captured from above—probably from the underside of a cliff face. However, the positioning is careful. It suggests an aerial shot. In the near distance—an outcrop of greenery. Large, prehistoric (papier-mâché) birds circle on strings. They are accompanied by echoing shrieks. Lifted, no doubt, from open source birdcall catalogues. A pair of dummies, carefully dressed to resemble the characters, bursts from the outcrop. They fly as though fired from a cannon. The synth line kicks in again. A distant scream, heavy with reverb, comes out of the distance. They plummet to the river below. The camera cuts, to what Brick later considers as his favourite shot. Fortunato has reprised his 'running through the woods with a pole' act. Only this time in aerial fashion. The machete has been attached to a long wire. The opposite end of which, has been wound around the lens of a camera. Fortunato has secured another line to the back of the camera. After setting the focus to the length of the front wire, he threw both off the cliff. It must have taken luck and several attempts. But the camera eventually succeeded in tracking the blade for a few moments. The low-fi audacity of the shot causes Brick to laugh out loud.

The film cuts to a different stock—16mm this time. Bubbles boil and froth beneath sepia water. Crocodiles thrash. Most likely, it is footage stolen from a nature documentary. Ordinarily the insert would have been tacky. But, aligned with the general mash-up style, the addition evokes a sort of vintage MTV style. Brick likes it. The atmosphere is further enhanced by the absurd way in which this stock footage has been edited. There are about five distinct shots—some reversed. Others speeded up and manually zoomed. Sometimes, until the grain of the film itself is revealed. It is truly sordid film-making. But energetic, thoughtful and indisputably hand-crafted.

The narrative cuts to a shot of a raging river. There hasn't been a single static camera shot. Every little thing has movement. The dummy versions of Machete Man 2000 and Crocodile Witch killer flush down the white-water. The film pans up to a series of Jurassic rock formations. Then cuts to an unexpected a stop-motion sequence. Three weird, velociraptors laugh and jibe with one another. They point at the passing combatants, sporting ridiculous purple Mohawks and sunglasses. All wear expensive basketball high-tops. Each carries a bottle of Japanese beer. A fast cut to one of their labels reveals a sponsor. Canned American sitcom laughter blazes from the toothy snouts of the dinosaurs. The labour-intensive animation sequence does not last long however. It cuts sharply to a waterfall. Once again, Brick is treated to a lens-weighted camera being hurled into space. The vertiginous shot cuts back. A panoramic wide-angle that shows the dummies plummeting for many meters. The music collapses—an out of time drum solo, on a live-kit.

A secluded jungle pond. Nesting beneath an overhang of rock. The soundtrack reduces. A lone flute and various 'sloshing' FX. A busty girl in a bright blue bikini stands, lashed to a polystyrene statue of a screaming gorilla's head. It all rises majestically from the water. The image freezes. It zooms in on her and freezes. Another kung fu style orchestra hit. Sultry, tropical eyes fill the screen. The title 'LEOPARD

LOVER' scrolls. Hot-pink typeface. Lalo Schifrin string samples. The scene explodes back into action. The combatants erupt from the still water. Music kicks in after the drop. Once again, perfectly timed. Machete Man 2000 clutches the Gorilla statue's hand with his robotic arm. Leopard Lover swings her head in Machete Man 2000's direction. A mane of curls tosses in slow motion. Soft focus highlights all manner of twinkles in the water. In her eyes. And along the lines of copiously glossed lips. Machete Man 2000 lifts his sunglasses on a slow zoom. Their eyes connect. A fatal mistake. Crocodile Witch Killer detonates from the water. A fast cut of a stuffed crocodile's jaw. It snaps around the robotic arm. A bone-crunching sound effect. Machete Man 2000 screams. He is pulled beneath the surface of the water.

The frame reverts back to the 16mm stock footage. Micro-edited snatches. A hefty crocodile, swallowing meat.

Brick makes it through most of the video. He passes out cold, just as dawn lights the horizon. Some hours later, a nightmare awakens him sharply. He sits bolt upright. Straight into a knife of sunlight. He dreamed that he was being chased around the hotel suite by a vampire cow. With glowing green eyes and elongated snake fangs. A young Kirk Douglas was standing by the mirror. He was dressed as a porter and was cleaning up the lipstick. He used an unwieldy wad of tissue paper to accomplish this. He was shaking his head. Clearly unimpressed by Brick's terror. In the nightmare, the cow had a human voice. It was his son, begging Brick not to let him down.

II

Strangers in Paradise

Trillzone

Trill and Delilah haven't contacted Sulette. A week has passed. She's glimpsed them through her window. But neither stopped to say hi. Sulette thinks it's because she made a fool of herself at the party. Trill assures her she didn't. She can't believe it. She'd nagged everyone for extra fish glands until she'd gotten them. Her memories are hazy. In any event, she certainly *had* made a fool of herself with Brick Bryson. Maybe that's why Trill has been so quiet? Or has the creature been busy? She wishes Trill would call.

Sulette is craving the hyperreality of the glands. Without Trill to supply her, she has already relapsed into television serials, menthol cigarettes and post-lunch vodka tonics. She renames her pug Tupac. It irritates Malherbe no end. He works non-stop. She suspects that he is on dating sites. She's been spending a fair amount of time there herself, but mostly to stalk Trill. She reads that Trill specializes in 'interracial gang bangs'. Sulette likes this concept of 'race-play'. She always felt that black men were different—'more primal', as she liked to put it. Why would it be such a *thing* all over the internet if there wasn't a grain of truth to it? The thought preoccupies her. Sulette has never considered sex with a real life black man before. But now, fantasizing about Trill in parking lots has her listening to gangster rap, trying on her shortest skirts and checking out the bulge in her gardener's overalls. One night she becomes so desperate for attention that she heads down to Long Street on her own. It's Friday. Malherbe is out working on a commercial. She gets herself 'slutted up'. But without Trill to hold her hand, she only makes it a far as the Engen garage on Orange street. Club kids infest it on the weekends. It's the only place to get food after a certain time. Sulette sits, eating a chicken burger in high heels, trying to call Trill. The creature doesn't pick up. Of course, Sulette's friends are all worried. She doesn't attend movie nights with the wives anymore. She turns down invitations to barbeques and dog walks up the Shark Fin. Unforgivable transgressions in certain circles. Sulette has no regrets. It's all too bourgeois and boring after the fish glands. Tupac becomes fat and whiney. She's putting on a fair amount of weight herself. She wonders if, with a more substantial posterior, it would be easier to twerk? Inane fantasies consume her daily life. She goes down to Adult World one day and buys the biggest black dildo on offer. She had an idea that she would get herself accustomed to its monstrous size. Whilst watching interracial gang-bangs on the internet. Unfortunately, the clips she finds only make her laugh. Maybe she isn't looking in the right places? What did she know about online porn? In any event, the sex toy is simply too massive. She decides to use it as a doorstop, to frighten Malherbe. But then starts worrying about how the maid will lecture her. In the end, she gives it to her dog as a chew toy. It affords her no end of giggles, seeing little Tupac, fighting with the thing across the carpet. Sulette realizes that she is in desperate need of someone to play with. What kind of loser goes down rabbit holes alone?

Her adventures in the foreshore had got her thinking about her father, Henk de Villiers. She imagines him to be a denizen of such lowly places. She doesn't see him much. But slips him cash from time to time. They would usually meet at the bar of the Kimberly Hotel. She would buy him lunch and ceremoniously hand over an unmarked envelope. He would act surprised each time. Sulette never lingered. Her usual excuse was that she was late for an appointment.

Henk and Charlize had been a hit in the eighties. They had driven a cream Mercedes cabriolet across an ocean of merlot. She eventually managed to tone down her drinking. But he couldn't keep up with her— even when she was quitting. Henk had been a professional firefighter. After the navy, he worked the city's main station. Seasonal fires were a common occurrence in the foothills. Even the national flower wasn't able to germinate unless the entire plant, and the ground surrounding it, had been scorched to cinder. Henk came from a small desert town. He'd never really acclimatized to the city. He often talked about moving back to the Karoo. Though, he never got around to it. Perhaps he didn't want to ruin his happy image of youth. Charlize dumped him after a cruise on the Achille Lauro. She managed to keep almost everything they owned. Fifteen years later, after a string of bad luck, Henk rooms in a hostel downtown. 'Working on my navy memoirs' is what he tells people. Although Sulette had driven past his street many times, she'd never really had occasion to turn up it. Barrack Street is a sordid little tributary. One end leads to a big strip club. A road of bars. An old soup kitchen haunts the opposite end. It's the type of dingy borough where no-one ever complains about the noise. Where cars are sometimes stolen.

Henk comes out with a worried look. He has on a seaman's jersey and professorial spectacles. Sulette turns the gangster rap down. When he climbs in, she keeps her sunglasses on. The hostel is a real fleabag. It looks just like the movie set of a fleabag hostel. This is what she decides.

'Everything alright?' Henk asks.

The question catches her off-guard.

'Why wouldn't it be?'

'You've never come down here before.'

They used to speak Afrikaans when she was a child. For some reason, the relationship switched to English when Henk lost everything.

'I come down here sometimes,' she shrugs.

He still seems suspicious. She extracts an envelope and hands it over.

'What's this?' he asks, taking it automatically.

'You know what it is.'

He seems to hover on the verge of saying something. Then thinks better of it.

'For services rendered, eh?' he jibes.

'Sies, Papa.'

She studies the building. Seagulls fight over a scrap of bread. They lead her gaze to a new coffee place. Gentrification strikes Sulette as a form of civilization. The freshly painted décor, white cursive signage and tasteful graffiti. They all give her a great sense of relief. Especially when viewed against the surrounding desolation.

'It's not so bad out here,' she comments.

'It's not bad.'

'Real problems?' she adds, uncertainly.

'You can deal with a real problem,' comes his reflexive caption.

She smiles slightly, taking her cue.

'Soos a vuur?' she ventures.

Henk meets her eye and smiles.

'Just like a fire,' he grumbles with satisfaction.

A hobo crosses the window. A skinny figure trails in his wake. Tattoos give away the thin man's membership in a numbers gang. The hobo has a stick. He starts beating a wall for no reason. The gang member gently disarms him, shepherding him up the sloping street.

'We had this fire once,' Henk reminisces. '…In an old pub. Set to be a blazer. Pine trim, you know? But when we broke the top window, we saw. Wasn't so bad.'

'En toe wat het julle gedoen?'

He laughs.

'What did we do? We kept that fire going so we could take all the drink!'

'You've got to have your fun while you can,' Sulette smiles, parroting another of Henk's cherished nuggets of wisdom.

'You've got to have your fun while you can,' he repeats pleasurably.

A whiff of booze makes her turn away. Suddenly it's all a bit too much. She slides her designer sunglasses back on. He is accustomed to her signals, but savours the moment a little longer.

'You know, you always used to tell us that,' Sulette mutters. 'Where did it come from?'

It has never occurred to her to ask. Now she wishes she hadn't.

'From the navy.'

'From the ships?'

'Dis reg,' he grunts.

He gazes out again. But really, he is looking back through time.

'Sometimes on bad nights you'd come out on deck...'

He is about to build on this image. Then thinks better of it.

Sulette drives back, feeling miserable. She wonders what possessed her to go down there in the first place. The day passes in a funk. Eventually, she sees Croeser traipsing past the window. Bodyguard in tow. She is quick enough to take a photo for her growing collection. Delilah isn't with them. Has the star been tripping upstairs all day? Malherbe arrives around seven. She throws some Woolworths chicken in the oven and leaves him watching a cooking program with Tupac. She takes a long bath. Halfway through, Malherbe knocks on the door. He has to go oversee some problem at work. She grunts. He thanks her for the chicken. She lies in the bath for perhaps an hour longer, looking at dating sites on her phone. After a while she gives in and tries Trill again. This time her call is answered.

'Liefie! I keep thinking of you in all those hotel rooms. Are you in one right now?'

'No, I'm not working now. How you feeling?'

'I'm fine, why?'

'Maybe you had too much fun—at the party.'

'Are you kidding? I haven't had so much fun since I was a teenager.'

'I don't think you should have so much fun.'

'You've got to have your fun while you can.'

'Funny spelled backwards—is *enough*.'

She hesitates for a moment.

'I think I want to try it,' she says.

'...What do you mean?'

'I want to go into a hotel room and be with some black men for money.'

'But you don't need money?'

'I need fun.'

'I don't know. It's dangerous. Why only black guys? Men are all the same, you know...'

She ignores the question.

'What about ones who like to watch? I mean, you have a dick, don't you? We could put on a show...'

Trill makes a negative sound.

'I don't really do that kind of thing.'

Sulette splashes the water in irritation.

'You don't know what it's like for me!' she complains. 'It's all fucking potato salads, TV and dogs! You don't understand how many people in the suburbs have dogs. I need to have some fun, please help me! I mean, isn't that what you *do*?'

'I don't know...'

'I'll pay you a finder's fee.'

Trill starts to say something, stops, then with resignation, finally answers;

'I know someone.'

Sulette gets excited.

'I knew you would!' she squeals.

'He makes a beach in his lounge,' Trill explains. 'All he wants is a real girl, in a bikini or a swimming costume, I don't know. You can lie on a towel, or something. Maybe make a sandcastle. I don't know.'

'That's it?' she frowns, perplexed.

'Sex is too real for some people. They make a kind of bubble. They go inside this bubble and they make a nest there. They don't want anything outside of their bubble to come inside.'

'So, he wouldn't touch me at all?'

'No. Because that would mean you went in there and popped his bubble. He just wants to see this beach, you know...like in a movie, but real.'

'When can I do it?'

'I can phone him maybe tomorrow...maybe even later?'

'Do it now!' she says excitedly

'Ok.'

'Can you bring some magic pills!'

'I don't know if...I mean I have to ask...'

'*Please!*' she yells.

'Ok.'

'Will you come with me?'

'I'll take you. It's nearby.'

'Call me later!' she splashes. 'I have to think of a beach outfit now—love you!'

She hangs up, thrilled.

Volker Von Hase first saw Trill on Kloof Street. The creature had walked up from the city. It wanted to buy weed—from a car guard in the area. Volker was exiting a restaurant. Quite by chance, he noticed Trill happening by. The creature looked sick. It was coughing thickly. Its chest was heavily congested. Volker waited, observing the drug buy. He decided to trail the androgyne into town. Trill rarely picks up punters on the street these days. Now, the creature prefers to find clients online. Despite the change, it still follows old patrol routes. Habitually hunting up and down Long, on a dreary autopilot.

Trill knew a lot of people on the street. Volker was stopping constantly. On a lonely stretch, bridging upper Long and Greenmarket square, Volker eventually cornered the coughing hooker. He propositioned the wraith, suggesting they meet later—on the steps of a gallery in the square. Trill asked for a down payment, in case Volker didn't turn up. The stranger surprised Trill with a couple of R200 bills. He took the creature's number and left. R400 was a generous amount to give on faith. And there was something slightly disturbing about Volker. Trill couldn't put a finger on his off-key. The creature went into a seven eleven and shared some fries with a drug dealer. Afterward, Trill decided to keep the appointment. It shoplifted two red apples and ate them on the way to Greenmarket square. Somehow the fruit triggered another coughing fit. Its lungs were definitely congested. Trill detoured into an alleyway to vomit. But after dry retching for a minute or two, gave up.

It took the long way around. Cutting down to Adderley, where it passed through deserted taxi ranks. It stopped to smoke a joint with a security guard. They chatted in Xhosa. The guard asked for oral. But Trill was in a hurry and coughing too much. Unfortunately, the police had raided the city's main marijuana supplier a few days ago. Hydro was the only weed on the street. Trill had never been a fan of genetically modified strains. The buds were often coated in pesticide, which caused throat and sinus problems. The modified plants also delivered unnatural highs. These lapsed all too easily into acute paranoia. Trill and the security guard shared the opinion that long-term use of modified marijuana evoked schizoid symptoms. Both had noticed these effects in chronic users. They discuss the subject at some length, as they did each time they met. They arrived at their usual conclusion: the influx of hydro was a conspiracy, perhaps one of military origin. Something to do with corporate cabals and large-scale social destabilization, at the hands of 'foreign' powers. It was a theory well fueled by smoke. The guard groped Trill while they talked conspiracy. The creature indulged the armed guard, kissing him deeply after each exhalation of smoke. By the time Trill made it down to Greenmarket square, the weed was reacting heavily with its morning micro-dose. This often remained active well past midnight.

The creature took up an elevated position. Beneath the pillared entrance of the gallery. Some time went by. It tried to vomit again. To clear its lungs. Volker didn't appear. Trill was on the verge of abandoning the roost. Then a heavy man stopped by. He stood at the foot of the stairs in a Friday the Thirteenth hockey mask. Trill ignored him. But after a few minutes of being stared at, decided to move. The creature scampered down the steps, fleeing across the square. It was heading toward a late-night Ethiopian dive. There were still customers at its outside tables. The figure followed. Trill stopped halfway. The figure stopped too, about twenty meters distant. Trill realized its phone had been ringing for some time. Usually, the creature carried the device in its underwear. Often, its outfits were too sheer, or lacked pockets. Volker was on the line. He told Trill to stay put. Then hung up. Trill saw the masked man lift his own phone and nod imperceptibly. He then marched forward across the cobblestones. Trill started to get a sour feeling. But tempered the urge to flee when the masked man held up yet another R200 bill. Trill took the money. The man punched the creature in the stomach. It wasn't a hard blow. But Trill hadn't expected it. The hooker fell to the cobbles in shock. It tried to bolt. A futile exercise. The man already had Trill by the hair. He dragged his struggling prey to a shadowy region. Behind the public toilets. All of a sudden, Trill noticed the distant silhouette of Volker. His suited figure was cut against the stain-glass of the church. The masked assailant flung Trill against a stone wall. He then flipped up his victim's miniskirt to complete the rape. After a few thrusts, Trill realized that the man was holding back. He didn't want to cause any serious damage. He was putting on a show. A moment came when it was possible to flee. Trill decided to stay put and watch the narrative play out. The creature could sense the rapist working in simpatico with its submission. There was a game on here. Trill was certain that, under different circumstances, the man would kill without hesitation. The assault came to an abrupt end. The burly man pulled out, mashing his member down the prostitute's throat before ejaculating. Trill experienced the usual moment of panic for breath. But within moments, the man was striding away. Trill pulled itself off the dirty stones. Leaning against a tree, it coughed up a residue of ejaculate. The action finally triggered the vomit reaction Trill had been waiting for. It threw up a few pints of bright blue gel. Breathing clearly for the first time all day, it retched up more of the vivid substance—directly from its lungs. Volker was standing nearby, watching. He handed Trill another bank note. Then extended an invitation to join him at one of the Ethiopian places. Trill accepted warily. Volker stayed quiet throughout two cups of black coffee. Trill gobbled plate after plate of injira—which, resembled soft, warm hand towels. At some point, Volker started to speak about the beach in his lounge. He asked the creature if it knew any 'nice girls'. Trill was about to suggest a couple of streetwalkers. But quickly realized that Volker would be unsatisfied with them. The man wanted something off a billboard. Someone fresh, clean and suburban. A working girl wouldn't fulfill his 'casting call'. Trill asked what was to be expected. Volker shrugged. He just wanted to look at her. For some reason, Trill believed him. The creature promised that it would call when it located the right person.

Sulette had begun to dream of the hotel rooms in which Trill worked. The dreams were recurrent. Always the same. Sometimes the 'room' was large and convoluted. With endless passages and cul-de-sacs. At other times, it was cramped and claustrophobic. Yet, no matter its size or shape, the 'room-realm' was always recognizable—by its inner-city dinginess. It was an ambiance that frightened Sulette. Her well-to-do, suburban upbringing feared it. Yet, when she was in the dream, the transient griminess became oddly soothing. She would gaze deeply into its formations of dust. And out across stained wall-scapes, through naked, spotted bulbs to accumulations of insect bodies. A kind of beauty was resonant there. In many ways the room, echoed the void. The nothingness that the fish glands had shown her, hidden behind the veil of everyday reality. The room was a place sacred to that nihilistic atmosphere.

Then one day, the dream changed. Sulette found a mannequin in the room. The dummy resembled her. But was different in many aspects. In one way, it had the kind of body she had always aspired toward—one that was chic, yet somehow wanton. She saw strength in its allure as a sexual trophy. For her, the mannequin was a sketch of an ideal. One that, at a deep level, she wished to embody. She would sit for what felt like years. Simply staring at the thing. One day she asked it the name of the hotel. The mannequin withdrew a phone. It showed Sulette an album of photos. Each captured a detail of the dismal room-universe. In both macro and microscopic detail. The album was titled: *Trillzone*.

Trill hits Brownlow around midnight. It finds Sulette in a skimpy neon swimming costume, straw hat and gold ankle bracelet. The housewife also has a fancy dolphin-print towel, suntan lotion and a plastic lobster (stolen from a seafood restaurant). Trill offers her a fish gland. Sulette is unsatisfied. She does not stop nagging until she gets three. Which she promptly swallows, before Trill has a chance to stop her. The prostitute reminds Sulette about the finder's fee she offered. She seems to draw a blank. Rummaging around she eventually hands over fifty rand. Trill stares at the note for a few moments. Then wordlessly pockets it. Sulette is very excited. She cycles through various swimming costumes, modeling them for Trill until the drugs kick in. Secretly, she is procrastinating. In the hopes that the creature might invite her upstairs. But Trill simply sits in the lounge, waiting moodily. At one point, it requests food. She finds the creature a banana. By the time they make it outside, Sulette is as high as a kite. She laughs outrageously. Trill notices a neighbor watching from a high window. It guides her up the street. Sulette asks Trill repeatedly: 'Does she need to drive?'. She does not seem to understand that the house is close. She is shocked to find herself outside its gates. She keeps repeating the phrase 'But, this is *my* street!'

'Can you manage?' Trill asks. 'Three glands is a lot!'

Sulette insists that they enter the house. She screams at the top of her lungs. She wants to go to the beach. Staggering, clutching onto Trill's arm for support. She attempts to climb out of the coat the creature pulled around her. Her eyes have already dilated to black holes. Trill had consulted with Volker about entry. The homeowner related careful instructions. Trill rings the buzzer three times. The gates open quietly. The creature drags Sulette up a long circular drive, toward an enclosed entrance. It pokes through a colonnade of potted kumquat trees. There's a guard. In a shed across the street. He observes their progress. The house is kidney-red. A fatty, cream trim, rimes the edges. The front door is unlocked—just as Volker said it would be. The creature had originally planned to leave Sulette at the door. But the housewife nags for Trill accompany her inside. The guard in the shed has begun to take an interest in the shouting. Trill quickly bundles Sulette inside.

The creature insists that she be quiet. To listen for the sound of breaking surf. Realizing that she has transgressed into another realm, and being competitive about games, Sulette obeys.

They stand in a yawning entrance hall. Everywhere are rugs, antiques and ornate portraiture. Although the lights have been extinguished, moonlight spills in.

'Somewhere in this house is a beach,' Trill whispers urgently.

Sulette nods excitedly. Her dilated eyes catch the wan light like an animal's.

'I can't come with you,' Trill instructs her. 'That's the game.'

She nods again. Trill strips the coat from her. A sudden inrush of air goose-pebbles her exposed flesh. In the gloom, her paleness and neon swimsuit gleam. Trill puts a finger to its lips. It kisses her, vanishing backwards into the darkness. In a split-second, the creature is gone. Along with her coat. Sulette blinks a few times. She can't quite believe how Trill just vanished like that. She looks around. Has she always been alone in here, she wonders? She begins to explore the house barefoot. It is a trove of wonders. Huge clocks come and go like ships. Tapestries seethe with secrets. Statues observe her walking by. In a wide passage, she finds a conch shell. She lifts it from its setting and places it to her ear. Inside it, she can hear the sea. But when she drops the shell, the sound of the sea continues. So, there is a beach in this house, Sulette thinks. She begins to hunt here and there. Following the noise. At one point, she pauses beneath a forlorn skylight. Its aperture throws a bluish halo of moonlight across an indoor koi pond. Despite the opulence of the house, she finds herself back in the hotel room of her dreams. Everything carries the comforting dinginess of her dream hotel. A smile of wonder creeps across her face.

'Trillzone…' she whispers out loud.

The sound of her voice is unreal to her. Is it possible to dream while still awake, she wonders? *Is* she awake? The beach is closer now. She can even smell its salt tang in the air. She realizes, with a start, that the mannequin must also be in somewhere in the house. She looks around, puzzled. Where could it be? Has it been following her? Was it stopping every now and then to disguise itself as a statue—like a character in a children's story? Sulette wavers. She passes through a veil of moonlight. Turning a corner, she finds herself in a glass ceilinged conservatory. Beyond looms the lush darkness of a garden. Sulette pads between sofas. She crosses a cold hearth. Then stops dead, sensing movement. Easing back on the balls of her feet, she realizes: she has found the mannequin. Questing toward it, she enters a moonlit bathroom. Her reflection dances in a floor length mirror. There, smiling in the glass, like a porcelain Victorian doll, is the dummy from her dreams.

Trill flees across the lounge. It drops behind a bookcase and waits there. Eventually, Sulette staggers off. The creature tosses her coat aside, feeling irritable. Volker had invited Trill to make use of the house while they were 'at the beach'. But Trill has no inclination toward games. Especially with a sadist like Von Hase. It has a sense, however, that Sulette will be unmolested. After all, she is a 'real girl', and of similar social standing. Trill is niggled. Sulette promised so much, but paid so little. Now the creature is hungry. One banana is unsatisfactory. Another reason to be annoyed. Trill decides to find the kitchen before leaving. Feeling somewhat paranoid, Trill quietly unlatches a large window in one of the lounges. It plans to use this as an emergency escape route, should things go awry. The creature has a suspicion that the front door has locked automatically. In any case, Trill is not the sort to take risks. Everything is calculated. Once the window is ajar, the creature ventures deeper into the house.

It's easy enough to avoid Sulette. Her noise gives away her position. Trill locates the kitchen quickly enough in the dark. It's at the far end of the ground floor. Careful to not to make any noise, Trill opens one of several well stocked fridges. It withdraws a fistful of cold bacon. Delilah wouldn't have approved of the meat. But as the star is so fond of saying; she and Trill hearken from different regions of fairyland. Delilah is a mermaid princess. Trill is a denizen of caves, dungeons and dragon lairs—a keeper and giver of secrets. And sometimes, treasure. Trill deliberates. Stopping by Delilah's sanctuary is an option. But the creature is in no mood for Croeser. Or any fish related shenanigans, for that matter. Town is buzzing. Trill wants to dance. The creature stuffs chilly handfuls of meat into its mouth. It gobbles until it is sated. Then it drinks an entire bottle of pomegranate presse. Trill is setting down the empty vessel, when it gets a feeling. Someone is watching. Of course, there were cameras. But this sense was different. Trill freezes. It looks around, preparing to flee. A row of masks lines the wall of a sunken dining area. Some belong to statues, ensconced by niches. One of the masks slips out of place. Trill recognizes the man from the square. The masked rapist is dressed in combat fatigues. In his hand is a toothed, hunting knife. Trill reacts instantaneously, darting back through the house. The mask closes the distance with heavy footfalls. Trill veers into a lounge. The man splits, cutting down the central passage. Clearly, he has an idea to cut his prey off at another entrance. But Trill is well versed in the mindset of predators. The creature bounds across a sofa. It pivots a toe-tip lightly against a lintel, launching itself through the open window. The exit is soundless. Trill hits the moist grass running. It cuts cleanly toward the tangled edge of the garden, scampering quickly up a tree. The creature drops over the fence, from one of the overhanging branches. Somehow, it had managed to snag a couple of guavas along the way. It proceeded to devour these. The guard fails to notice the elfin, mini-skirted figure. Trill manifests out of the dark, skirting the pavement line toward the Deli. By the time the masked man has opened the door to inspect the front, Trill is streets away. After swallowing the guavas, the creature digs in its underwear for kumquats. Trill doubles its stride. There was still enough time to make the free entrance curfew to one of the hip hop clubs.

The Beach in the Basement

Volker's beach is not much of a beach. But it did the trick. He has not visited a real beach for decades, despite living so close to the sea. His mother had drowned at the beach, when he was still very young. She had been in her late thirties around the time of her death. The only images the child saw of her were the ones that his father kept around the house. Volker's senior had been a successful industrialist. He was a heavy and competitive man, whose primary passion, apart from his wife and the maintenance of substantial personal wealth, was game hunting. He had always treated Volker's mother as a kind of doll. His attitude was made clear by the pictures he chose to display of her. She had beauty. Perhaps it was the only reason he wed her. Certainly, he was pedantic about her wardrobe. He dictated her day to day activities. In exchange for her loss of freedom, Volker's mother received a life of wealth and leisure. This was their unspoken understanding. Volker was fifteen when his mother drowned. He did not immediately understand that the ornamental function she fulfilled came with a price. The youth grew up, surrounded by pictures of his mother. In them, she wore swimming costumes or bikinis. Nothing else. Often, she would be posing unattainably. Along a vivid shoreline. Smiling perfectly against the sun.

Despite his mother's many enchanting qualities, her loss did not particularly affect Volker. His mother had detested him. Not as a son, or even a human being—but merely as the result of a pregnancy that had permanently altered her appearance. It was a subtle change. But one that had affected the balance of power in her marriage. Of course, it would be absurd to suggest that she lost her beauty after childbirth. Yet in her eyes, she never fully recovered what she regarded as her essential self. After the birth of Volker, she experienced, with great bitterness, the loss of her own childhood. She had grown up spoiled and pampered. But it was a condition of youth. These wells dried up as soon as she became a mother herself. The magnitude of this grief scarred her deeply. Volker's mother had been a popular girl. One that was unused to functioning without a support structure, or in a subservient role. Her body had always mirrored her youthful temperament. In fact, she did not appear to age at all—until she gave birth. Unwilling to lay the blame upon her husband, to whom she felt inextricably bound, she reflected it all inward. After all, her gratuitous lifestyle depended upon his satisfaction with her appearance and manner. Luxury was paramount to Volker's mother's wellbeing. To her mind, it was a state that was absolutely necessary to continual survival. She did not dare trifle with its inner workings. So, without any other course in which to direct itself, the suppressed anger and humiliation, channeled itself toward her offspring.

From the start, she was icy to the child. Volker was raised in an atmosphere that punished any outward display of emotion. She refused to care for him at all. These duties fell primarily to the manservant—a Bavarian ex-soldier. There was also a maid. This elderly woman did all the cooking and spoke very little English. Volker's mother would not tolerate a nanny or wet nurse. This was due to the fact, that in the period following her pregnancy, her husband had begun to see other women. Younger women. This sort of thing had not occurred prior to the pregnancy. Volker's mother blamed it on her swollen belly. To her mind, her son had stolen her youth. And since her husband's tastes ran to nubile bodies, she came to blame the child for stealing his affections as well. She would torment the Volker when the mood took her. Often the boy would find himself locked in his room. He would sometimes remain incarcerated there for days at a time. With barely any food or water. He learned to treat these periods as a kind of endurance training. In the end, he excelled in surviving them. Sometimes he would break out of the window and pick fruit to sustain himself. Once he even resorted to eating insects. Even so, these torments were not the worst of it. Sometimes, after drinking, his mother would order him to strip. She would then dress him in some of her under-things. The manservant would be forced to witness her actions. Invariably, Volker's father would be away on during these occasions. His mother's state of mind would thusly be aggravated, by visions of her husband in the arms of prettier, younger girls. She would beat the boy senseless after applying make-up to his face. Sometimes she would molest him rectally, using the pearl handle of her grandmother's hairbrush. The trauma was compounded. In the days to come, when the woman was overcome by guilt, she would invariably call for a doctor. The physician would examine the boy thoroughly. This was always accomplished under the close supervision of his mother. Afraid that Volker might reveal her mistreatment, she would glare at him while the doctor inspected his wounds. Her story always followed the same lines. She had caught the boy playing with himself and intervened. The manservant, under threat of losing his position, would invariably provide an alibi. Once he was even called to do so, directly to Volker's father. Who had received a concerned note from the doctor. His father had beaten Volker then too. He felt great shame at the possibility of having a self-abusive homosexual for a son. Of course, any show of emotion from young Volker was rewarded only by increased beatings and punishment.

Later in life, Volker entered the service of the Austrian military. He discovered that he slotted quite comfortably into the regimental lifestyle. Of course, his childhood had only primed him for the rigours of military life. He wanted to pursue an officer's post. But his father insisted that he quit and undergo specialized training. Training that would one day enable him to take over the family interests. These included, amongst other things, management of various mining franchises, in Namibia and the Congo. Volker was later to discover that the decision had a deeper root. His father was uncomfortable with his son being in close quarters with other soldiers. One of the tactics he used to help combat the growth of Volker's possible homosexuality, was to ply the young boy with pornography. When Volker turned fourteen, his father treated him. He made his first visit to an elite strip club. From then on, the visits continued semi-regularly. At his father's behest. When Volker turned sixteen, he was taken to a brothel. One of the first impressions of this initiatory rite, was of how closely the girl's bikinis resembled the ones that his mother wore—in the photos around the house. Volker's burgeoning desire was stultified by rage. Often, at crucial moments in love play, he would become paralyzed. His mind would plunge into cavities of excruciating shame. He began to harbour secret desires. He wanted to tie one of these women up. He wanted to torture this victim until they begged for clemency. Volker fantasized greatly about this. All through his teens. When he was old enough, he began to experiment with vulnerable sex workers. Though none of them truly satisfied his desires. After all, they were not well bred, pathologically vain debutantes. The spirits of many of these girls had already been broken—and he had no desire to torture an already broken thing.

He wasn't sure exactly how the image of the beach came to mean so much to him. Certainly, it had to do with the photographs of his mother. But the affair went deeper. She was so buoyant and carefree in the photos. He barely recognized this phantasm as his mother. In fact, the woman in the photographs barely seemed human. Rather, she embodied something mythical and impossibly distant. The photographs represented a kind of ideal world. And the woman within, a totem of that realm. One that might conceivably be summoned, through ritual evocation. Volker saw watered down versions of similar wraiths. In the sex clubs his father exposed him to. They disappointed him. The atmosphere had been stripped from these ghosts. Along with everything else. He had a kind of sympathy for these women. To him, they had the character of prisoners. Their work reminded him of when he had been locked in his room as a boy. There, he had felt simultaneously trapped and exposed. Locked up and subject to invasive authority figures. Every surface in the sex-trade became, for Volker, a candy-coat. One that had been plastered over infirm substance. For Volker, to whom atmosphere was key, this limited universe was simply not enough. He craved the heights of a more rarefied atmosphere. To his mind, atmosphere itself was a language. One that he hoped he could use—to summon a very particular spirit. The images of the beach represented Volker's perfect atmospheric realm. Yet, he was unable to approach this sphere materially. To do so, he felt, would transmute the dream instantly—into the drossiness of reality. The vision would crumble in his hands. Like a construction of ash. He might never recover it. Volker feared this Heisenbergian destruction above all else. The dream of the beach would have to be stalked cautiously. Then watered, as one watered a garden. Only in this manner, could its verdant soil be coaxed to bear fruit—within whose flesh, could be mined the seed of deeper visions. Volker followed his paradisiacal visions up into the attic. There, he began to sift methodically through the accumulation of many lifetime's. Somewhere, within the flotsam and jetsam of his family memorabilia, he knew he would discover something. Some kind of magical key to his imagined realm. Volker's persistence was eventually rewarded. After a week of digging, he discovered, at the bottom of a trunk, a dusty box of slides.

Slide shows had been a fixture of Volker's youth. The memories of every childhood holiday had been transmuted into a lightshow. The family would roast meat and gossip. Against the muted glow of their collected images. When Volker discovered the slides at the bottom of the trunk, he dug up the old machine and serviced it himself. His father had shown him how. When he was young. Volker distrusted electronics. But he had always been handy with machines. He rigged the device in a cavernous basement. This place had been converted to a billiards room in the twenties. But quickly fallen into disuse. The chamber was accessible, via a narrow case of stone stairs. Adjoined to it, was the arched entrance to a wine cellar. At some point, Volker had attempted to convert part of this area into a dungeon. He even purchased a wide range of fetishistic equipment toward this purpose. Unfortunately, without the correct sort of girl to animate the space, the gear soon gathered cobwebs. Volker ended up covering the instruments with canvas. Once he strangled a neighbour's dog in there.

Without the billiards table, the basement lounge became quite stagey. It was already a somewhat theatrical space. Volker stripped the paintings from the farthest wall. He rigged the projector at the opposite end. When the machine was switched on, it filled the rambling space with a dull whirr. He liked the sound. It reminded him of school holidays. The machine was old, but of good workmanship. Volker was able to adjust the beam so that the projection took up the entire wall and some of the ceiling. All the while maintaining perfect clarity. When Volker was satisfied with the technical aspects, he began to sort through the slides. Volker was unused to weeping. He had always done so quietly and in secret. Even in the sanctuary of his lair, he felt as though he may be punished. Nevertheless, the impact of the images was undeniable. They were all from various beach holidays. And the selection had been refined over the years. It was clearly a kind of treasure that his father had hidden away. Most of the photos showed his mother in various stages of undress. But these pictures had less of an impact for Volker, than those which showed the beach itself. Volker was finally able to excavate deeper—into the structure of the dream zone that had haunted him since childhood. Every image seemed to hold a thousand secrets. Even an otherwise drab image of a palm tree against barren dunes was enough to fill him with wild emotion. He took to sitting for long hours, meditating upon a single image. When he was younger, he had wished that he could paint. He was desperate to express the fascination he had with certain atmospheres. The slides seemed to perform the same function. The worlds that they tapped, however, had a far more potent and direct effect upon him. Volker had finally migrated beyond the framed pictures of his youth. He felt that he had come as close as he could, to actually existing within the mystical zone that the images described. At certain moments Volker felt as though he were wholly and consciously present within a dream.

The effect began to lessen with over-use. He experimented with outside effects and set up a sound system. He spent weeks tracking down recordings of coastal sounds. At first, he went for high-definition field recordings. Later, he found that the clean sound jarred with the dreaminess of the old film stock. In the end, Volker discovered a vinyl in a record shop opposite the old Theosophical society headquarters. The record contained various coastal recordings. It had been produced in the sixties. The cover carried a lurid, colour-saturated image of palm trees. The entire B-side was devoted to a single track; Pacific surf lapping against a placid shoreline. When Volker listened to it, the soundtrack seemed almost *too* perfect. He immediately purchased the disc. And an old record player to go along with it. The mysterious crackling of the worn vinyl and the rich sound that only vintage analog equipment could generate, somehow completed his magic-lantern images. Even so, Volker decided to take his obsession further. He ordered his manservant to fetch sacks of beach sand. During the course of a week, he spread the grains over the old carpets of the basement. He sculpted sand with a trowel, creating a facsimile of wind-driven dunes. Volker then strategically placed buckets of seawater around the room. These infused the air with a sympathetic scent. He left strict instructions to have the brine refreshed on a weekly basis. The basement became a kind of Aladdin's cave—a dream temple, dedicated to a vision. Yet, despite these great lengths, a final piece of his jigsaw was still missing. For a while, it was possible to pretend that his theater of worship was complete. Soon it became apparent, that he had merely set a stage. It was an arena, ripe for evocation. To finish his grand work, Volker would need a host. A woman capable of channeling the exact spirit required. This would finally animate his cave of dreams.

Volker receives a telephonic alert. It's the front buzzer. He opens the house with a two-button combination. Then he switches off his phone. Even though he is able to reroute numerous camera feeds to his handheld device, he prefers a first-hand impression. He's set up a high-backed chair in the darkest corner of the basement. He is comfortable. Beside him is a side-table, complete with gentian schnapps and a bucket of ice. Sliced limes, a couple of remote-controls, cigarettes and a flip-top ashtray complete the repast. He is well into his second drink and chain-smoking when his guests arrive. An air-vent just above his head soundlessly catches his exhalations. He couldn't bear to have the smoke pollute the saline tang of his carefully orchestrated 'sea air'. Volker likes to think that he has every detail covered. But he is apprehensive about the girl. He expects to be disappointed. The only other woman he had brought down to the beach was a Russian stripper. He had picked her up in club near Barrack Street. She had been ejected from the house within a quarter of an hour. She had laughed out loud at his 'beach'. He had found the girl attractive. But her attitude had completely devastated his intricately arranged atmosphere. She even approached his chair on one occasions. After being specifically ordered not to. The Russian didn't seem capable of grasping the concept of this snow-globe world he had invented. Or the remove it required, to work its magic. So, despite the excitement that a potential new dream-girl evoked, Volker has fully prepared himself to be let-down. Nevertheless, the slide he has chosen for the evening is one of his favourites. It shows a calm stretch of white sand. This vanishes, in a declining perspective. The sea-line is azure. Nearby palms glow in the sunlight. In the distance, a lush fringe of emerald vegetation broods. The sky is free from cloud. The image fills the basement with the artificial gleam of paradise.

Volker can hear them moving around the house. He wonders whether his manservant has secured the ladyboy. He turns the volume of the vinyl up a few notches. The sound would disseminate further now. Throughout the floors above. He waits patiently, sipping at his liqueur. Finally, he discerns a tell-tale shuffle of feet. In the drawing room above.

His pulse becomes unsteady. He adjusts his silk tie. Someone begins to descend the staircase. He hears a sharp intake of breath. The visitor is stunned by what she sees. He glimpses the shadowy figure, but forces himself not to look directly. He wants to wait. Until she has entered the light. He wants to savour his first impression fully. It happens within a few moments. Of course, when Volker recognizes Sulette, he is stunned. At first, he is completely and hideously enraged. How could someone he loathed be in violation of his most private sanctum? However, within the space of a moment, his brain decodes the root of his hatred. He has detested the woman for one reason only. She reminds him of his mother. His rage transmutes instantly. Almost alchemically, into sharp desire. The sensation bewilders him. As does the strange intervention of fate. For truly, in her swimming costume, the woman does indeed resemble the wraith from his photographs. Not only in character, but now also in appearance. Volker can tell that she is drugged. She exudes a powerful sexual charge. Here is someone who is in love. Perhaps even in lust—with herself. He watches her smile luridly. Harshly illuminated, she sways with her back to him—staring out at a false horizon. The projection cuts her clean shadow into the image. It hardly matters. She is as engrossed in the false reality of the beach as he is. She does not even attempt to look for him. She is besotted with the magic-lantern show. Volker swallows his drink. He can hardly believe it. His hand is shaking. His eyes ache. Tears invade his vision. Yet, this is an exception. Most of his emotional changes are internalized. From without, with the exception of slightly moist eyes, Volker maintains the seamless demeanour of a lizard on a rock.

Sulette sinks to her knees. She cups a handful of sand to her face, breathing in its aroma. A seagull shrieks in the distance. She can hear the lazy lap of freeze-frame waves. The 'sunlight' feels so real. She begins to regret not having brought suntan lotion. She gives a small laugh. Then lies down slowly. She wishes she had remembered a towel. The air smells so fresh by the sea. Within a few minutes she is up again and staggering toward the wall. Her shadows reels in toward her. She feels as though it is being drawn, via suction, to her navel. Eventually her cheek, belly and breasts press against the coolness of the wall. The pesky shadow finally vanishes. Shrinking and absorbing back into her. She turns into the light and looks down at her body. The livid hues of the beach are imprinted, upon her slopes and curves. She has become the seascape itself. She can sense, within her blood flow, the ebb of great tides. Her bones harbour millions of small, shelled creatures. Waves of sensory input crash against the reef of her mind. She desperately wants to submerge. In warm tropical water. Yet, remains trapped. In some inter-dimensional glass coffin, outside of time. It is a strange cage. One, which separates her from the tropical universe burning, just beyond the meniscus of her bubble.

Volker watches her for an hour or so, utterly entranced. Her absorption into the illusion is so complete—so believable. It draws him even deeper than he has ever gone before. A blizzard of emotion is awakened. The tears have not stopped. They seep thickly from his inner being, falling and catching in his collar. When he can stand it no longer, he unbuttons his jacket and releases the snap on his grandfather's SS-issue shoulder holster. He lights a cigarette. Then, instead of the holster-standard Mauser, Volker draws a tranquilizer pistol. He slowly lines it up on the sylph-like figure. When he feels ready, he fires. A feathered dart enters one of her thighs. She shudders and falls limp. Volker sits, racked by violent, completely soundless sobbing.

The manservant lives in a small garden cottage. It has easy access to the house. He goes there after receiving his orders. He replaces his toothed knife in a collection of military blades. Removing his horror movie mask, he stores it inside his jacket. Then rinses his face. He re-enters the house, pulling on latex gloves. It is well after three am. His master has retired to his bedroom. This is located on the highest floor. The old-fashioned bay window of Volker's bedroom, looks out through the branches of a pear tree. The manservant notes that his light is still on. While Volker was at the beach, the manservant had waited upstairs. He had hoped the creature would show up for its friend. He had occupied himself by cracking hazelnuts. He took these from a burlap sack, stored in the old, farm-style larder. After laboriously placing the cracked shells in a bowl, he would transfer the nuts to a large jam-jar. Later that week, he planned to mass-produce Alpine muesli for the dwindling house store. It was a task he liked to get done properly. He had just managed to fill three jars when his new instructions came through.

The manservant goes down into the basement. The beach is still burning brightly. He stands for a moment, regarding the fallen figure of the girl. He then kneels to read her pulse. He checks her breath and has a look at her pupils. Satisfied, he switches off the record player and slide projector. He activates a rack of powerful, overhead lights. The chamber is immediately flooded with harsh illumination. The manservant dumps the girl on the stairs for a moment. Then he spends about forty minutes reshaping the sand. Inside one of the seawater buckets are some live crayfish. Purchased only this morning. In another are some crabs he caught himself. He has an idea to cook them for his master's lunch over the next few days. One of the dishes he is planning is a kind of crab broth with lemongrass. He has just learned the recipe and wants to practice it. Of course, he'll roast the crayfish alive. When he is done with the sand, he tidies up. He turns off the lights and slings the girl over one of his broad shoulders.

The house has four cars. Each is housed in a separate garage. There is a new edition burgundy Daimler. This is followed by the obligatory German ex-pat, vintage-model Mercedes. In cream. There is also an off-road jeep and a large, black van. The manservant lays the girl in the back of the van. Then drives down to the city. Long street is still buzzing. It has transgressed into the dangerous volatility that sometimes arrives after two am. People are screaming on the road. Cars jostle unnervingly. Someone is being attacked in the alleyway connecting to the Company Gardens. Uniformed security guards converge upon the assailant. They descend like a swarm of white blood cells. The manservant keeps a look out for Trill. But the creature is nowhere to be found. The manservant drives down Loop, which runs parallel to Long, heading for the foreshore. When he reaches Strand street, he turns in the direction of the Waterfront. There, he takes the off-ramp heading to Sea Point. Just before the lane merges onto the main highway, he pulls over. A line of concrete blockades seals the entrance to the unfinished overpass. Now he is high above the ground, framed against tall, downtown bank buildings. High arc lights illuminate the highway at intervals. Grey halos of crisp light. These do not extend across the unfinished section however. This extends into darkness. There is still some traffic. Late night party people, cruising between town and the Sea Point strip. The manservant parks beside one of the concrete blockades. He removes a Glock from the glove compartment. Checking that the handgun is loaded, he releases the safety and tucks it into an inside pocket. A smaller, tributary road runs alongside the overpass. This is separated from the larger highway by a meter-wide gulf. The drop is bridged by concrete crash barriers. The long schism looks down, upon a world of trash and barbed wire. The world below the highway supports. This secondary road is also unfinished. Some tents and shelters have sprung up at the severed end. Shabby constructions of plastic flutter dismally in the heavy sea breeze. The wide overpass is barren of habitation. It lies desolate, all the way out to its jagged stump. Such is its reputation that even the transients will not lodge upon it. The manservant puts on his mask before exiting his vehicle. He engages the alarm. With his handgun within easy reach, he carries the girl out. Onto the broken road.

The masked manservant keeps to the edge. He stays in shadow. At some point, he gets the sense that he has been spotted by the tent people. Nevertheless, he continues right to the end. The unfinished flyover terminates in a grisly concrete stump. It juts, in silhouette. Over the barren roofing of an automotive enterprise and some fenced in lots.

Outside a four-way crossing. High, corporate blocks soar beyond. A wide, trash-caked ledge extends below the surface of the broken tarmac. This area is shot through with rusty metal wire and corroded support grids. The manservant finds a spot relatively free of detritus. There, he unceremoniously offloads Sulette, face-down in the garbage. Satisfied, he begins his return trek. Some shadowy figures have already congregated around the van. They are trying to break in. The manservant has been waiting for this. He wants to test out his latest, homemade security feature. Smiling behind his mask, he presses a remote. A powerful electric current hurls two figures from the van. The third is standing away from the vehicle. Recoiling, he flees. Leaping the divide between highways. The masked man stops to kick the prone figures. When he has broken a bone or two, he returns to Brownlow. There, he sets about finishing up the last hazelnut jar.

White Knights

A gang of preteen street kids finds Sulette in the morning. They are in the habit of using the ledge as a perch. There, they douse plastic shopping bags with glue, petrol and whatever other solvents they have managed to scrounge throughout the night. They stuff their faces into these packets. Inhaling the fumes to get high. This often left their lips and cheeks abscessed. Many had missing teeth. The street kids stand, studying Sulette. She has lain in the same position all night. On her belly, compressed against the lip of the unfinished road. She is streaked with grime.

'Lady?' one of the kid's ventures.

He prods her foot with his toe. After some deliberation, the gang decide to jump the highway gap. They fetch the Captain. The Captain hails from the winelands, where he had laboured as a farm hand since the age of six. After a bad experience, he ended up in Pollsmoor correctional facility. There, he found Jesus (amongst other things). When the Captain was finally released, he had nothing to show for himself except amateur tattoos and a couple of scars. One misfortune followed another. Eventually, the Captain found himself out on the street. He isn't a bad sort, though. Over the years, he has built a solid, Christian reputation around the highway people. The gang find him passed out in a homemade plastic shack, just inside the crash barrier. They have to drag him out to the edge. The Captain's hangovers are no laughing matter. Methylated spirits are his tipple, though, he prefers Old Brown sherry when he can get it. Years of dedication to this formidable toxin, have reduced him to the state of a Dickensian caricature. His skin carries a greenish tint. He is losing his sight. He would filter the meth's through slices of stale white bread and drink the purple fluid neat. He sobers up fast enough when he gets a look at Sulette, however. For ten minutes straight, the Captain paces the barrier edge. Swearing at the top of his lungs. A couple of the other transients hear him and come running. There had been some drama the previous night. Men had been electrocuted and assaulted, whilst unconscious. One of these vagabonds lies in a lean-to closer to the verge, nursing a shattered rib. The other has been pushed in the general direction of

Somerset hospital, in a stolen shopping cart. The Captain had taken a look at him before getting sauced. He thought the man was bleeding internally. He doubted that he would survive the day. The incident had created tension amongst the highway folk. But now, seeing Sulette, the community becomes enraged. The Captain issues orders. They ferry Sulette to the Captain's shack, where they lie her down across some filthy blankets. The Captain dispatches the fastest street kid to fetch the sack-cloth wearing Rastafarian, from his nest beneath the highways. This man is a member of an old cult. They believe that black lions still roam the mountain. Some wear only rough Hessian. Most walk barefoot and possess extensive knowledge of indigenous herbal remedies. The Rastafari was the one the highway people turned to, when one of their number fell seriously ill. While they waited, the Captain pulled out his bible. He began to implore Jesus at the top of his lungs. Jesus must have been listening, because Sulette woke up almost immediately. Aside from its psychogenic alkaloids, the fish glands showed many other tonic effects. In some respects, they were not unlike strong ginseng or winter cherry. Muscle performance, tissue regeneration and flexibility became vastly improved. One rarely awoke with a hangover. The glands even mediated the negative effects of other substances. Nevertheless, the tranquilizer dart had been potent enough to knock Sulette out cold. She is still blurry around the edges. This, of course does not prevent her from screaming 'rape', as soon as she registers her whereabouts. The children take flight like frightened birds. But the Captain is shouting 'Hallelujah' at the top of his lungs. Sulette pushes past. She erupts from the shack with such force, that she collapses one of its walls. Stricken by her surroundings and state of undress, she panics. She runs toward the verge, where she spies a flow of morning traffic. Some of the kids keep pace, begging her to stop. They are afraid she will fall and injure herself. The Captain is also in hot pursuit. His malnourished old paunch swings pendulously with each stride. The rest of the tent people stay put. Everyone is watching the drama unfold. None want to be involved at this stage. Sulette makes it to the shoulder with the concerned mob at her heels. She starts waving frantically. A car stops almost immediately. A couple of corporate-looking fellows dash chivalrously out. Sulette runs, crying, into their arms. She jabbers in Afrikaans, explaining how they had all been trying to rape her in a tent. The street kids quickly change direction. They flit down holes and jump highways like mice. Another car pulls over. The Captain is not as fast as the kids. The men catch him, kicking him to the ground. Some of the vagrants rush to his rescue. A couple manage to prise the would-be rescuers off. They attempt to explain the situation. Sulette begs the drivers to take her home. Someone offers to call the police. Sulette stops him. She doesn't want to explain her new drug habit to the law. In the end, they put her in the back and drop her off on Brownlow.

On the way, Sulette manages to borrow one of her white knight's phones. She calls Charlize in tears. Luckily, her mother is nearby. She is able to collect Sulette on short notice. Mother and daughter have a bit of a row in the car. Charlize is simply stunned at Sulette's appearance. She insists that they contact the police so that they can press charges against the vagrants who tried to rape her. Sulette, by now thoroughly confused, changes tack. She admits that he isn't sure who did what. When Charlize demands to know what really happened, Sulette starts bawling. She invents a barely credible story about her drink being spiked at a Camp's bay party. By now, Charlize is at wits end. Well versed in her daughter's dramatic, self-aggrandizing temperament, she simply gives up. She cannot quite believe how awful Sulette smells and how filthy she is. She takes comfort in the fact that her wayward daughter is at least safe. She uses her spare key to let the girl into her own flat. Before she leaves, she extracts a promise. Sulette must tell her the truth, at a more convenient time. Charlize then drives to a nearby automotive service and has her car thoroughly deodorized.

Sulette takes a three-hour bath. She tries desperately to recall the events of the night before. After some thought, she arrives at a conclusion. The man at 'the beach' must have drugged her. How she woke up in a shack on the side of the highway, is still something of a mystery. She examines her genitalia thoroughly and comes to the conclusion that she was not raped. She is furious at Trill for leaving her in the hands of a madman. Still, she is hesitant to discontinue her only real link to Delilah. She tries to call the creature. Its phone rings unanswered. In the end, after bathing, she takes three Nurofen capsules and devours a bucket of cookie dough ice cream. She passes out in her fluffy bathrobe, watching reruns of the Kardashian's. When Malherbe gets home, he demands to know where she spent the night. By now she has the story all worked out and has begged Charlize to remain silent. She tells her husband she was out partying with Trill. She was afraid to come back so late, so she had stayed over at the creatures 'apartment'. He seems to buy it. Then lectures her about not leaving her phone behind, the next time she decides to 'go large'. By morning, her life has already reverted back to its original inertia.

Another day slides past. Sulette is starting to remember the beach episode with a kind of fondness. Despite being conflicted about lost time and the circumstances of her rude awakening, the episode is simply too exciting to sweep under a rug. Whatever blame existed, fell toward Trill and the vagrants on the bridge. After all, how could she detest a man he hardly knew? This is her argument. The reality, of course, is that Sulette always judges a person's character by the quality of their house. And the man at 'the beach' has *such* a fine one. She walks past his gates a few times, hoping to call attention to herself. But the place always seems impenetrable and deserted. She catches herself admiring its size. It really *is* splendidly maintained vintage architecture. 'A real part of history', she nods knowingly to herself. How she wishes she lived there! She debates ringing the bell and schmoozing her way back. Quickly, she realizes that the owner would logically expect her to be angry with him. Perhaps she *should* be angry? Whatever events had transpired to cause her to wake up in a tent surrounded by *poor people*—they almost certainly had to have been the homeowner's doing. Yet still, what a beautiful house...Surely there must be some way for her to return? Sulette becomes very conflicted. She had been abysmally high in the weird, little basement beach. The owner was also sitting in the dark. She had no way to recognize him now. This doesn't pose too much of a problem for girl like Sulette, however. Raised on Lindsey Lohan films, Sulette knew very well how to 'get her Nancy Drew on'. For one thing, she could always interrogate Adrian. He knew the names, history and dietary specifications of almost every homeowner on the street. And if that line of questioning failed, she could simply call up an estate agent friend and make some casual enquiries about a certain historical landmark...

She starts with daily sweeps of the Deli. She boosts her already considerable cleavage. If the man is at the Deli when she passes, then her breasts, she reckoned, should provide a good offensive line. Sulette has always firmly believed that every man on the planet would love nothing more than to fondle her breasts. They were her pride and joy. She loved to boast that their larger than average size was, as she would put it; 'completely natural'. If a man were ever to say to her that her breasts meant little or nothing to him, she would immediately assume that he was either gay or lying. In fact, she was so vain about them, that she relied heavily on her décolletage in petty, day to day power struggles. 'You'll never guess the discounts my twins have gotten me over the years!' was one of her favourite boasts.

As luck would have it, Volker *is* at his usual table. He is scribbling in a notebook. Sulette spots him from a distance and takes refuge behind a lamp post. She checks her make-up. She practices an angry expression. Eventually, Stanislavsky-like, she is able to allow the sensation of anger to rise and engulf her completely. When she feels that that the rage has achieved believable levels, she storms over to his table. She seats herself directly across from him. Naturally, he is taken aback. But recovers his stride more or less instantaneously.

'Could I offer you something to drink?' he ventures.

She raises her sunglasses, fixing him in her best glare. It seems to have little or no effect. Dark glasses disguise his eyes. The reptilian face does not betray a hint of emotion. She takes the opportunity to get a good look. As irritated as she is by his undeniable ugliness and bad skin, she is equally impressed by his attire. She can tell at first glance: here is a man accustomed to finery. No wonder he is interested in her, she thinks proudly. Outwardly however, she continues to radiate outrage and hostility (whilst simultaneously squeezing up her cleavage).

'You left me to die on the side of the highway! I could have been raped!'

Volker leans forward imperceptibly.

'I rather wish you had been,' is his candid reply.

Sulette is bewildered. She goggles in shock, unsure of how to proceed. Whilst incapacitated, he smoothly retracts a card and offers it to her.

'Should you wish to return, I would be more than happy to accommodate you,' he smiles thinly.

She stares at the card for a moment. Then smashes her palm dramatically against the table. One or two of the other customers look up sharply.

'Fuck you, you...you pervert!' Sulette exclaims imperiously, making sure that everyone at the café can hear her.

She storms back up the road, counting her steps carefully. At some point, she would have to go back for the card. It is the only way to secure a return to (what she has recently begun to refer to as) 'one the best and biggest mansions in the neighbourhood'. It's too much of a risk to simply walk off. She might not be able to approach him again. Her idea is that the 'storming off' would convey the outrage that she is obligated to feel. She wants to leave the right impression. Her strategy then, is to publicly embarrass him with an outburst, before feigning reconsideration. Her return would also then suggest to the Deli's clientele and staff, that she is romantically involved with the elegantly attired (hideously wealthy) man at the deck table. She slows down around the fifth white traffic line (a fair enough distance) and pauses for a moment for effect. She does not turn. This is to make certain that her posterior is displayed to best effect. She then whirls, nose in the air and returns to the table. She is somewhat nonplussed to find him smiling. Her irritation only increases when the waiter delivers her a gratuitous, red velvet cupcake. He had ordered it for her in absentia. Clearly, he was expecting a return.

'Alright,' she declares haughtily. 'I'll accept your invitation. But I don't want to be drugged and wake up on the side of the highway.'

'I *will* drug you,' he insists.

Then leaning forward, offers a compromise:

'But…I'll make sure that you don't get left on the side of the road.

She mulls this over for a moment. Then she also leans forward.

'*If* I choose to return to your house, I'm going to need some more of those pills. The trannie knows where to get them.'

He smiles graciously, once again proffering his card.

'Make a list of all your requirements,' he tells her. 'I will be happy to fulfill them.'

Sulette returns his smile, snapping up the card. She is enjoying their conspiratorial familiarity and his generous offer of gifts. It is the style, to which she is accustomed. She rises in stately fashion, feeling victorious.

'I'll be in touch,' Sulette says primly.

She turns and walks off. Then hesitates again, returning one last time to the table. Volker observes her snatch up the heavily iced cupcake. She eats it all up before she is even halfway home.

A few days later, Sulette is thrilled to return to the magical mansion. She is even more excited to finally have her own personal supply of fish glands. As well as a brand-new wardrobe of designer beach apparel, jewelry, a couple of hats and matching footwear. She goes through the motions at 'the beach'. She barely notices being shot in the thigh. However, when she wakes up on the side of the highway at dawn, wearing nothing but a bikini and a Swarovski ankle bracelet, she is furious. This time the street kids steer clear of her. Though one does wave from the crash barrier in a friendly way.

'Hi Missus!' the vagabond calls. 'You back, hey!'

Nonplussed, Sulette drags herself toward the gridlocked flow of morning traffic. With the intention of flagging down the nearest white knight. As it turns out, they are not in short supply.

Deer Park

The Oracle looks beyond the horizon. Silence permeates her temple room. The chamber is set upon a high crag. It has the airy dimensions of a ballroom. The Oracle lies, belly down, across a metallic stone, which has been placed in the center of the room. She is dressed in long white robes. Her hair is wound with linen. The silver monolith upon which she lies, is in fact a valuable meteorite. The object is many millions of years older than the earth. It had been recovered from the Arctic Circle. Now, it has been cut and polished, in such a fashion so as to help boost the Oracle's powers. She lies, propped on her elbows. Palms, stomach and thighs flat against the highly polished surface. There is a suggestion of the Sphinx in her positioning—like that dark painting by Von Stuck. Perhaps similarities start to manifest of their own accord, in those who live so wholly by the Sphinx's code. Whatever the case, something inhuman appears to animate the woman. Her chamber is floored with white marble. The smooth, curvature of spotless walls perforate with long openings. They give out onto the broad sweep of the Atlantic. Young girls busy themselves along the edge. They move barefoot. In uncanny silence. All dressed in white. One of the corners of the meteorite seems out of kilter with rest of the room, however. It is troubled by tiny movements, not dissimilar to the girls, except rendered in miniature. A stream of ants is exploring the creviced surfaces of the asteroid. They too are building networks into the unknown.

Ziq drifts in a swarm. People move frenetically. Up and down streets. Taken together, humanity at times appears to him to constitute a single, harmonic mass. He imagines them as a single waveform, moving into the future at high speed. Ziq drifts with and against their current, a mote upon a great and shifting surface. He senses each individual, caught up in various microcosms of need and bondage. He feels magnetically repulsed by them. Yet, the sense of separation is illusory. No matter his remove, Ziq is forced to recognize that he is still exists as one of their number. He wishes that he could communicate something of himself to them. But a wall of glass seems to exist between. He slides off this barrier. Invisible, rarely seen. Reflected thusly, the great surge only propels him further out. Caught in their orbit, he skirts the rushing edge of limbo surrounding mankind. He is a minor satellite against such immensity —a micro-asteroid. Skating precariously above the hurtling wreckage of an entire species. In this way, it is easy for Ziq to maintain the aloofness of a pilgrim. He is of the outer reaches. Perpetually watchful of re-entry. The wallets dry by morning. The washing line drops into shadow. Light reveals cows, tumbling in the pasture beyond. One of the animals has graffiti spray-painted along its starved flank. The indecency numbs Ziq. Moments like this could stop a person eating meat. He gets to work. Taking down the pink wallets. Dropping them into a tin pail. They are conveyed to a rickety table. Ziq dryly refers to this as 'the processing plant'. Every morning he wakes up, puts on a suit and tie. Then goes to work. He filters the city through his apparatus. Until it emerges, processed and ready for consumption. Starlings flit through the light. He prepares his work-space. Derelicts and chickens stagger. A goat dozes in the rusted hulk of a car. The goat's name, when it is in the trunk, is 'Television'. Morning traffic haunts the background noise. The city is dominating its distances. Within the confines of his 'office', Ziq feels at one with the march of industry. He sidesteps the scattered trash piles and leavings of night creatures. He sweeps furiously. A radio garbles from a shack.

While he is working, Ziq is a model of methodic repetition, He arranges a wad of manila envelopes. Then a shoe box and current telephone book on the table top. The box is full of zip-lock bank bags. They carry labels like: 'SNAKESKIN WALLET', 'SEQUIN SNAP PURSE 1' or 'BLACK LEATHER CARD HOLDER'. Each bag houses the contents of the item listed. Ziq systematically swaps these items around, repacking the bags at random. Once he has completed this laborious task, he selects a pink item from the washing line and matches it with its bank bag. He then places the items into their now mismatched receptacle. Gradually, he empties the washing line and bank bags.

When the process is finally complete, he packs the pink items into individual envelopes. As he does, he refers to small slips of paper tacked to the desk. They list a description of each item. Corresponding to the labels on the bank bags. Beside each bulleted pink item, he has written an address or a name. Some of the items have the word 'UNKNOWN' listed instead of details. Ziq occasionally consults the phone book in reference to this list. He addresses each of the manila envelopes. Substituting random postal information for those marked 'UNKNOWN'. After a while, he has a neat stack of A4 envelopes, all ready for postage. Ziq places them in a large brown paper packet. He glues fresh, blank labels onto the bank bags. The bags are layered with labels. Their history could be read like the trunk of a tree.

When Ziq has processed the batch, he hefts up a pail of fresh, unpainted wallets and purses. He transfers their contents to the bank bags. He scribbles a brief description of each item upon fresh slips of paper. Then on blank bag labels. Ziq prioritizes ID cards and other contact information. He lists these details beside the article's description. When he is finished, he replaces the bank bags in the box. The empty wallets and purses go in the pail. Ziq hoists the bucket to the washing line. He levers open a tin of the lurid pink paint. Dunking the items, one by one, he transfers them to the washing line when they are completely pink. The freshly coloured items accumulate as morning turns toward noon. They pattern the grass below with splotches. Once Ziq has readied the next day's workload, he clears the table and leaves. The brown paper bag of envelopes goes with him.

Suburbs fan out from the city. Ziq likes to tell people that they have been 'corrupted by inertia'. For some, the description is too broad. For Ziq, it is precise. To his mind, these places clump together. A single, nebulous waste. Bleached of colour, they rust in their sockets. While the march of progress spreads further and further afield. Even at their deepest points of stagnation, 'progress' sifts through the suburbs. Like the fanfare of a distant battle. Ziq is put in mind of a Titan, abandoning useless, degenerate children. He used to be in the habit of calculating the waste these sick offspring generate. Now he considers it a futile exercise. Always too many hopeless details with these lists. Reefs are dying. Microplastics disperse. Fukushima is leaking. The ice caps melt, yielding mercury fields, methane sinks and vague threats of apocalypse. Unexplored forests are being pulped hourly. For animal feed and fast food cartons. Yet, despite the production effort, this packaging is transferred almost immediately to waste disposal units. They are pulped. Their remains explore the ocean. Ziq has to ration out his crises. Too much is at stake. Sometimes, he imagines a pudgy, mustachioed man. This man stirs. In a house. Somewhere in Ziq's image of the suburban wasteland. The man has just disposed of a fast food carton. Ziq can picture it clearly. In his vision, the man has just awoken. He prepares for the rush-hour commute to an office. Morning sets a metallic sheen. Small lawns and high fences. He leaves his house. He checks the post, carrying some mail indoors. In a dingy kitchen, he flips through the correspondence. All the morning miracles are contained within this kitchen. Cheap toasters popping. Breakfast television and an obligatory aroma of coffee. The images replicate a million times over. Breakfast routines cycle through identical boxy households. Every morning. To Ziq, the scenes are as repetitive as cancer. After all, what is cancer but a disease of repetition? This is his reasoning. An excess of similarity—

uncontrollable repetition. Cancerous cells become malignant in response to themselves. Ziq cripples himself with these thoughts. He focuses instead on the man in his kitchen. Ziq imagines him going through his mail. A lap-dog yaps next door. A manila envelope stands out from a rash of bills and brochures. 'TO WHOM IT MAY CONCERN'. Opening the envelope, the man is stunned to discover his missing wallet—now painted pink. He curses out loud when he finds someone else's credit cards and personal detritus. Eventually he discovers a small slip of paper. It seems out of place. The paper has been folded neatly around a minute object. Un-wrapping it, he discovers a shiny pink pill. The slip carries a message. It reads: THE END. Ziq imagines the man becoming silent. An elemental force has come and put its eye to his tiny world. He bursts back out onto his lawn, expecting to find the culprit. All he sees is humanity. Set permanently into the tablet of nature. A galaxy of badly knitted bones. The man, one star in billions. This galaxy pulses in a great void. Ziq imagines him staying silent about the suicide pill. He feels that the man will keep it safe. In a secret place. Taking it out in troubled moments. Those private moments. The ones people tell their gods about.

Ziq takes his place in post-office queues. He watches envelopes fly from him like homing pigeons. The glands are coated in basement labs just outside of town. Pharmaceutical cowboys run clandestine trade out of these holes, aping trade specs and catering to party scenes the world over. They too have their homing pigeons of the apocalypse. It had been Ziq's idea to coat the glands to industry standards. To manufacture 'suicide pills'. Most of what Ziq takes from his daily harvest goes toward their production. Fortunato prefers the glands in their natural state. He admits, however, that the shell aids preservation. The lab boys enjoy Ziq's concepts. They give him a discount for his audacity. They like to joke about how many suicide pills he has sent out, when he makes his pick-up each week. Ziq laughs with them. But a bone of desperation protrudes from his smile. The 'processing plant' has, after all, become his sole activity. It has taken on the patina of a *grand plan*. Somewhere along the line Ziq has become that lone gunman. The maniac with an End-Is-Nigh signpost. He doesn't like to discuss it. He passes Jaybird a few pills every week for kicks. He himself has never taken one. He is told that the effect of the psychedelic is to open one up to the truth of things. The effect has been described to him various times. Fortunato's suggestion is that the glands allow access to a spirit world. All Ziq can do is imagine the consequences of his actions. For all Ziq knows, the majority of his pills are disseminating in sewer systems. Devoured by doomed rats. He cannot measure the breadth of his work. Despite this, he feels that he is somehow helping—those lost in the land of the blind. His view is undoubtedly solipsistic, yet (he believes) one-eyed. Ziq inhabits his post-offices like a phantom. He has become a regular in some. The employees assume that he works for a nearby firm. Certainly, he dresses the part. Sometimes, he lingers outside these establishments. Observing pregnant postboxes and their subversive content. He wonders constantly—What effects do his actions really have? As he stands on a traffic-smeared corner, watching a postal pick-up—Jennifer's unmolested purse balances on one of his open palms.

Ziq kills time downtown. He consumes a cheap falafel at the Oriental Bazaar. He watches the code and flow of the inner-city. He drinks take-out espresso. Jennifer's vinyl clutch is on the table—a dueling pistol. He swallows a substantial amount of coffee before removing the medical aid card. Glancing at the photo for a moment, he flips it over. An address is printed on the back:

APARTMENT 13, TOWER THREE, THE THREE TOWERS, DEER PARK, 8001.

The road to Deer Park runs through leafy boroughs. Large houses seclude, in groves of oak and beech. The road climbs beyond, into the windy perimeters of the mountain. The winds grow fiercer as the escarpment ascends. The city-facing side of the mountain presents a hollowed curvature. This directs the air. It concentrates the velocity throughout Deer Park. Before blasting it in the direction of Devil's Peak and Skeleton Gorge. Fires are a real hazard here. Household evacuations a seasonal tradition. The neighbourhoods peter out into woodland, which collars the rise. Indigenous flora thrives between the alien pines. Ziq occasionally harvests their cones for kernels. The pinecones resemble hand grenades. They yield rich, fatty nibs. Their egginess is quite unlike the dry, overpriced flecks traded in health stores. Ziq extracts the kernels by placing the cones near a fire. The heat causes them to bloom prematurely. They release chocolatey capsules, which could then be cracked with a stone or a hammer. In the upper reaches, above these towering trees, cable car lines quiver. The spoor of some fantastic spider. A solitary road rings the berg, housing the cable station. Its surrounding greenery sounds lower, inventing grottoes around prehistoric springs. These founts are said to possess healing qualities. A signpost announces Deer Park. Near a trail, leading to the fabled waters. It frames against a dark tableau of trees, just beyond the road. Just in front of these first vestiges of forest, stands the silvery semi-circle of Deer Park Cafe. On the opposite side of the road is a barrier. This fences off areas designated as parkland. Some large houses and antique apartment blocks shoulder this mantle. Further afield, behind these structures, and towering over the billowing foliage surrounding them, lie the monolithic Three Towers. If one discounts the structures upon the mountain summit, then these towers constitute the highest man-made points of the city. The builders had taken advantage of height restrictions. They had constructed the base legally, whilst allowing the towers to rise over the permitted mark. They have been a source of controversy ever since. The towers soar into a sea of winds. Their sound-proof windows flash against monumental rock faces. Raptors roost in their satellite arrays. They were constructed in the seventies. Black metal, and smoked glass. The geometric apron of concrete, upon which the towers rest, enclose rambling parking lots. These areas are disproportionately large. Winds gust within them. They are lit by batteries of white neon. It is a well-known fact that the architect responsible for the design had committed suicide by leaping off one of his towers. A Finnish author had penned the story of the architect. A slim volume, entitled 'The Windswept'. It had done relatively well in Scandinavia. But only a hand-full had even heard of the book in its hometown. The majority of the city's population abstained from the abstract or aesthetically challenging. Books were either chewing gum or unexplored wastelands. To be crossed in convoy. You could perhaps blame the wind, blowing thoughts around like wildfire. Maybe it was just the tepid preoccupation media towns have with themselves. It's hard to settle into anything when the rooms are mirrored—and the wind is howling fit to wake the dead.

Ziq ventures up into the woody reaches of Deer Park. It's a chilly Friday's midnight. A full moon churns the sky with milk. Heavy winds sweep the trees. They have travelled in from the outer darkness, bringing with them the tang of Antarctica. Ziq slips through a rift in the security fence. He'd cut it earlier that day. After walking the perimeter, scouting for a vulnerable area. His pliers are secreted nearby, in case he has further need of them. Ziq enters the sprawling concrete lots. He uses an app on one of his phones—to scan for and avoid CCTV cameras. At several points, the lots divide. They angulate, inventing sudden drops. To dark inlets of underbrush. Walkways connect these various levels. They span gulfs, knitting the parking areas into a coherent whole. Ziq crosses the cat paths, searching for an access to the third tower. Security guards crisscross the complex. They wear black combat uniforms and carry automatic weapons in alpine gloves. They are good looking too. Selected for their appearance. Ziq hopes it was a choice made at the expense of ability. Though he isn't too concerned about being caught. Ziq has spent a lifetime sneaking around other people's properties. He has never once been spotted, let alone apprehended. He'd grown up in a township on the East Coast—a place called Chesterville. Just outside Pinetown. In those days Ziq would never have stolen anything.

He simply enjoyed sneaking around the large gardens of the affluent suburb adjoining his township. Later, when he started playing piano professionally, he would be invited into the sorts of houses whose fences he was so expert in jumping. It seemed a natural progression at the time. He'd met Fortunato in one of those houses. But that was all so long ago. He and Fortunato are different people now.

A guard passes quite close to him at one point. Ziq watches from the shadows. The security detail irritates his delicate sensibilities. He distastefully notes that the guards are all same height and build. They might as well be clones in a movie. Cultured in basement vats. Bred for this purpose alone. It disturbs Ziq that some cocaine-addled marketing division went to the trouble of casting security guards, simply to satisfy a decor scheme. He wonders how handy they are with their weapons…

The lobby of the third tower is easy to locate. A large, marble floored area. Well-lit and protected from the outside world, by a cube of fortified glass. The interior is presently deserted. Peopled only by glossy leaved plants. Black marble also skirts the stairs and elevator area. The dark stonework lends the lobby an oddly Egyptian flavour. It puts Ziq in mind of a grand tomb. A large engraving is mounted upon the wall. 'TOWER THREE', in minimalist font. Completing the funerary atmosphere. A similarly minimal intercom system presents an electronic eye and talk-point. Ziq avoids this. He withdraws the envelope containing Jennifer's purse. He has addressed it. Just outside the door is as good a place as any to leave it. He realizes, to his acute embarrassment, that he is more nervous than he has been in years. Anxiety brims behind his every action. After a moment of doubt, he buzzes number 13. He is ready to drop the purse and flee, when he realizes he wants to hear her voice. The notion is reckless. He is amazed that he is indulging it. He buzzes again, only to realize that the apartment is probably deserted. Logic compels him to drop the envelope and disappear. But the moon is full and he is feeling adventurous. He pockets the envelope and vacates the area. Crossing back into the echoing vaults, he locates 3-13's parking bay. Empty. He reconnoiters and discovers that the lift and stairs are under construction. Gaping holes hint at mechanical upgrades. A notice has been posted. It informs tenants to use the main lobby entrance as the only access point. The glass of the lobby is partially visible from Ziq's vantage point. It can be glimpsed beyond one of the upper level's cat paths, which looks down upon the cars. Ziq thinks for a moment. Returning to Jennifer's parking bay, he squats at the wall end. He then removes a pair of smart phones from his coat. Both have been fully charged. Usually the previous owners would block the phones as soon as they realized theirs had been stolen. Ziq, however, had a friend who could extract all the personal information to a hard drive.

Before unlocking and resetting the devices. The hard drive had become a treasure trove over the years. But Ziq rarely explored it. This was due to his aversion to computers (which reminded him a little too much of pianos). One of the phones is loaded with data. The other is dry. He turns on the empty phone's Wi-Fi, selecting the strongest available network. He then begins to run a code, overriding the password. He is online within a couple of minutes. He sets up a video-call between the two phones, and for a moment, the speaker systems feedback. A whooping, bird-like sound emits stereoscopically from the machines. It echoes eerily down the long concrete. The tones elasticate. As he draws the devices apart. Eventually, when they are far enough away from one another, the sound dwindles to nothing. Ziq rises cautiously. He takes a look around. No machine-gun clones have heard the music of the smart phones. He gets back to work. Rigging the network-connected phone into a shadowy niche so that it faces the bay, he deactivates its screen. Checking the other device, he finds a clear, transmitted video image of himself and the parking bay.

Ziq painstakingly retraces his steps. Back to the hole in the fence. He steals into the billowing darkness, taking the fence-cutter with him. Circling the perimeter, he stops when he is adjacent to the lobby entrance of Tower Three. There, he makes another incision in the security perimeter. The lobby is obscured by trees. So, he stashes the cutting implement and moves to higher ground. Eventually, he is able to locate an elevated vantage point. It allows unobstructed observation of the lobby. He removes the video-engaged phone and sets it carefully against a stone. He does what he can to dampen the screen glare. So that it won't be noticed. Once he has muffled the light sufficiently with a handkerchief, Ziq finds that he is able to monitor the parking bay from a seated position. He removes a third phone and activates its camera. His plan is to use this device to zoom in on the lobby. This way, he can closely observe the comings and goings. At this distance, it is impossible to distinguish faces. After satisfactorily testing the zoom a few times, he switches the phone off. To conserve battery power. Finally, he settles back into the foliage. Preparing for an indefinite wait.

An hour passes. The wind drops completely. A hush descends upon the woods. It crystallizes into an immense silence. Even the hubbub of the city becomes distant. Existing at a subliminal level. Beetles begin to communicate across the distances. The whole forest is teeming with the full moon. The vibration enters Ziq. It seems to settle the anxieties fermenting in his mind. He finds himself relaxed and alert. He is content to wait in the forest for the whole night if necessary. He'd wanted to come here the whole week without completely realizing it. Now that he is finally where he feels he is supposed to be, everything seems to slot into place. He gnaws at a breakaway globe of raw ginger, savouring the burn. Time passes. He changes position several times. He stretches his limbs, making tiny turns into the surrounding trees. The following hour finds him ensconced comfortably upon a mound of pine needles. Ziq gazes dreamily at the faraway security guards. Their perambulations remind him of ants on a cake. Suddenly, he becomes aware of a sound. From somewhere behind him. Sitting up, he tunes his ears to the clarified silence of the trees. Whatever it is, it is drawing closer. Ziq turns his head. He peers into the weave of the wood. A faint glow. Growing steadily stronger. He rises and changes position, gazing intently from a nearby tree. The glow does not emanate from a single source. The radiance appears to be split into chains. These travel, caterpillar-like through the darkness. Ziq realizes that the sound is the quiet, uniform shuffle of many feet. Moving across dried pine needles and leaves. The dim radiance drifts closer. Then it begins to veer. Ziq observes a procession, winding over a gradual rise. It passes at a distance, wending its way deeper into the forest. He decides to get a closer look. Drawing up, he sneaks alongside the procession. Moving from tree to tree. There appears to be no obvious similarity between members of the caravan. Apart from the candles, the only thing that appears to unify the pilgrims is their lack of speech. They shuffle in absolute silence. Ziq is mystified. He is about to follow them into the trees when a faint glare catches his eye. Headlights graze the side of the tower behind him. Ziq hurries back toward his vantage point. The car has already entered the parking lots. The sound of its distant engine transfers to his pocket. He pulls out the phone. Just in time to see a yellow convertible pull into the parking bay. The S2000 parks haphazardly. Three girls spill out. The driver is clearly Jennifer. The second girl, exiting the passenger bucket is dressed rather outrageously. Especially in contrast to Jennifer's standard black cocktail and heels. She sports a black, ninja-ish Niqab. It hides her face, leaving only her eyes visible. The hooded designer garment runs long, like a cloak. It flickers open at points, revealing a black strappy costume underneath. Calf-length white athletic socks and costly split-toe trainers complete this ensemble. The third passenger is definitely not an Oracle girl. With her glitzy horn-rims, she has the air of a fashion week veteran. Her clothes are from all the latest lines. But they seem thrown together. When viewed in relation to her companions, she appears somehow garish and lackluster at the same time. She operates a handheld device, staggering out of the sleek car. Ziq, clips in earphones so that he can listen in on their low-fidelity conversation.

'But why?' the fashion victim howls in a heavy Italian accent. 'Why you wear a burqa if you are not Muslim? Why!'

'I've told you already that this is a niqab!' Chloe laughs. 'Burqa's

cover everything—like in that bar… on Tatooine.'
    'But why this thing! Why!'
    'I'm taking it back to 2013!'
    But WHY!'
    'It's uber-goth!'
    'Health goth!'
    'Health goth is so fucking over, man…'
    'What clothing label!'
    'Phantomlovely.'
    'Ah! Yes, I know Phantomlovely. Of course, so good! But they are
not Islamic?'
    'No, they are gothic!'
    'But why a burqa! This is NOT 2013! You are NOT Islamic!' the
woman protests, failing to grasp the concept.
    Clearly, they are all intoxicated. Their voices fade as they move away.
All of a sudden, a weird light catches Ziq's eye. He looks up sharply.
Two objects dart out of the night. They resemble tiny, glowing UFO's.
He watches them fly—above the road leading to the third tower. They
continue for a distance, before splitting up. One circumnavigates the
tower. The other swoops into the parking lot. Ziq watches it light up
gloomy interiors. The object appears on his phone. It zooms past the
S2000, in hot pursuit of the girls. Blinding flashes strobe sporadically
from both objects, briefly illuminating the area around them. The
harsh bursts of bluish-white illumination occur at random intervals. Ziq
cannot anticipate them. Each time they flare, they leave freeze-frames
across his retina. Drones. He tracks the one that is spiraling around
the building. It ascends, eventually coming to a stationary position.
Outside a high, lightless window. Ziq tallies the floors. He comes to the
conclusion that the window most likely belongs to Jennifer. Despite
the unfolding drama, he finds himself hesitating. The procession in the
woods has struck a note of mystery. Under any other circumstances,
Ziq would have followed them to the end of the line. He casts his gaze
back to the forest. The glow of candles is already fading. The procession
swallows back, into the silences of the prehistoric landscape. Ziq realizes
that he is at a kind of crossroads. Predestination saturates the moment,
awaiting a response. Down at the tower, three figures travel across
concrete pathways. They move toward the lobby. The second drone is
trailing them. It dive-bombs constantly, contorting shadows against a
barrage of stroboscopic glare. Jennifer is pulling ahead, eager to get
indoors. Her hair flashes in the white blasts. Ziq is able to track and
zoom in on her facial expression. She appears furious, swiping uselessly
at the drone strikes. The sight of her doing this hooks him. He moves
down to the fence, casting one last backward glance at the vanishing

candles. Passing through the trees, he slips through the fence. Back into the windy lots.

Two bottles of premium vodka haven't slowed the journalist. She, Jennifer and the Chloe are catastrophically coked. High on suicide pills. The journalist stepped off the plane from Milan with knives in her voice. Pretty soon there were wounds. Again, Jennifer wishes that Anita could have joined them. She would have loved to watch Anita handle this bitch. But Anita's been sneaking off for too many nights. Jennifer is starting to run ragged. Anita has many pots bubbling on the side. Some of which were, in Jennifer's opinion, 'calling the kettle black'. Anita's latest shady scheme was something she called 'Operation: Miss Lonelyhearts'. A few months ago, Team Omega had been on Response. Anita had recognized an email from the 'Helpless' stack. She dubbed the sender 'Miss Lonelyhearts', even though he was clearly male—it was a sort of homage to Nathaniel West, of whom she was a fan. Miss Lonelyhearts became a kind of joke between the girls. But his origins remained a mystery. A week or so later, it came to Anita. She had the sort of bulldog mentality that refused to relinquish its hold. Often, she would remember the most inconsequential details, lest they should be of some benefit later on. In this case she was to be rewarded far beyond her expectations. She recalled the email from her shipping days in Namibia. She'd had to deal with a lot of private cargo contractors. There were many wealthy individuals. Moving antiques or artwork around the world. Often under the tax radar. When Anita first dealt with Miss Lonelyhearts, he was trying to illegally ship a Grecian temple. Stone by stone, to a private estate in New England. He was obsessed with the Goddess Diana and anything written by Robert Graves. Hence his interest in Oracle Inc. Anita saw an opportunity. She began to investigate the Oracle realty along the coast. Having worked this division, she knew that there were prime properties. Including luxury mansions. Simply lying vacant, waiting for resale. It was nothing for her to stagger the availability and secure the keys for one of these. She spent a bit furnishing the place. To bring out its more 'Oracular' qualities. She bought a few togas and religious antiques. She did some reading. Then she contacted Miss Lonelyhearts. She informed him that Oracle Inc. offered a special service to select clients—An *empathic, ceremonial* service. Weekend getaways inspired by John Fowles, etc. She had a professional photographer take 'tasteful' portraits of her. In front of suitably mythological sea-views (in revealing robes). Miss Lonelyhearts took the bait. Anita found herself charging twenty thousand pounds for a weekend of 'intensively Oracular counseling'. She and the lonely billionaire hit it off. He told her she was under-charging and schooled her a bit in the history of temple courtesans. He then gifted her with a client list of other lonely (and incredibly wealthy) history enthusiasts. Before Anita knew what had hit her, she had cleared a cool million in sterling. Tax-free and secure in an account in the Cayman Islands. She had to keep it under wraps of course. She needed to maintain her job. To avoid any unwanted attention from the authorities. Of course, she wanted to cut her bestie in on the action. But Jennifer wasn't too keen on selling her body, no matter the price tag. V smelled a rat. But Anita knew enough to buy her silence. She and Jennifer would receive regular envelopes of cash when Anita abandoned them to Eye-Detail. Despite this, the pressure reached a strenuous threshold. Especially after V vanished without a trace.

No-one has heard from V. Emails bounce back. Even her phone is disabled. She had sent out a group message, informing everyone that she was leaving town. That was all. They had to replace her with Chloe. Jennifer and Anita both liked her. Still, it left a gap and changed all their routines. Now Jennifer hobbles away from the journalist and her drones. She hides her eyes from the perpetual light storm. Chloe has been laughing for almost an hour straight. Her hands are fisted to white knuckles. She's coiled tight enough to explode. The journalist pulls up the rear of this Punch and Judy show. She monitors the drones from her handheld. The flash-work ignites areas disproportionate to their casings. The journalist is just as offensive as her drones—perhaps even more so. She's an unstoppable farce. A Minotaur in designer spectacles. She's fishing with heavy hooks and there's already blood in the water.

'I am supposed to interview this Oracle!' She shouts in a heavy accent. 'I have questions about the future! I want my future!'

She ups the drone's still-capture rate. The blinding assault intensifies. Some guards stop to watch from a distant balustrade.

'Where the fuck we are!' the journalist protests in broken English.

At this point they are blatantly ignoring her. Politeness died in a puddle of its own vomit, three wine bars and one restaurant ago. Jennifer and Chloe are running on fumes. The moon is rising. It bloats nauseatingly over Signal Hill. Jennifer thinks it looks like a severed head.

'You bitches think you can palm me off with *snacks!*' the reporter shouts, through a heavy red smile. 'You have no idea the pull my peoples we have! We pay big monies for interview! I want the future! I want it now! You hear?'

Chloe laughs outrageously at this tirade. In her drugged state, Jennifer visualizes Chloe's laughter as a solid thing, tumbling down to the city. It sounds just like breaking glass.

'Fuck the future!' the journalist begins to yell, over and over again.

Chloe's laughter intensifies as the lobby comes into view. Jennifer struggles for a full three minutes to get her thumb into the scanner. The drone, sensing that she is interacting with another machine, drops low. It plagues her with close-ups. A staccato hurricane of photography stuns her. At some point Jennifer becomes aggressive. She slaps at the thing with her jacket, provoking a shouting match. The reporter argues belligerently. Her drones are not to be interfered with. They almost come to blows. But the Chloe is quick to intervene, still giggling hysterically. From inside the sound-proofed lobby, their battle would appear comical—a mute squabble of vultures for guts. Jennifer finally bypasses the security lock. They spill heavily across the funereal interior. The din of their raised voices breaks into focus. Chloe does her best to push the glass slab shut before the drone has a chance to enter. But the machine is too nimble.

'Fucking bitches!' the journalist rages. 'Fuck the future! We signed papers! Where the fuck are your offices! I only go to the top—straight to the top!'

'Like shit!' Chloe guffaws.

Her kohl-heavy eyes are tearing behind the black veil. She smears them with henna-patterned fingers. The journalist takes a mad swipe. But Chloe catches her wrist in a playful judo grip. She twists the woman around, causing her squeal furiously. Jennifer slams the elevator control repeatedly. The scuffle behind her escalates. The pair careen into a row of plants. Ceramic urns crack. Soil streaks the marble tiles. The drone drops. It circles the fighting pair in the manner of a predatory bird, blasting them with light. By now, Ziq is moving in the shadows of the lot below. He is able to observe the Chloe and the journalist. They crash repeatedly into the shock-proof glass. A series of dull thuds—but everything else is muted. The drone's lightshow stammers. The glare filters down to his level. Shafts, dimly illuminate the sunken parking bay. Ziq observes a twisted face overhead. It pushes against the glass before careening off again. He moves a better vantage point, unable to see Jennifer. After some realignment, he finds her again. The remaining girls struggle against a marble pillar. The spectacled one breaks free for a moment. She tries to tear at the veil of her oppressor, but cannot quite reach. The lack of sound lends the scene a farcical aspect. Ziq cannot help but smile at the veiled girl's mastery of her opponent. His line of sight runs through an angular chink. Created by an overlap of walkways. When they move toward the elevator, they vanish. Ziq abandons his position. He trots over to Jennifer's car. He cannot quite believe his luck. Not only has she left the top down. She has also forgotten the keys in the ignition. He is so pleased that he doesn't register a whirring sound until it is too late. The remaining drone drops abruptly down, lighting up the gloomy sub-level. Ziq freezes, caught off-guard. The machine jets directly toward him, settling to a dead hover. A brilliant sequence of light momentarily blinds him. Audible camera shuttering. Ziq realizes that his image has been captured. He curses, ducks, but the drone has already left. Through a pink-blue retinal flare, he sees it zoom down a concrete tunnel. Lighting up walls as it recedes. Ziq's tranquil spell in the forest compromised him. Made him careless. Nevertheless, he is still loath to turn his back on the car. In fact, it almost seems to beckon him to it.

Jennifer topples into the glassy elevator. She slides down a mirror-surface. Till she slumps to the floor. There, she tightens her fingers in her hair. An attempt to calibrate the roar in her head. The fighting rages unabated outside. The doors begin to close. She muscles them open.

'I can't hold it together forever!' she shrieks.

Chloe grins. The veil has finally fallen. She grabs the journalist by her couture collar and heaves her into the elevator. Unbelievably, the drone follows them in.

Ziq slides into the driver's bucket seat. Sinking low into the racing upholstery. He remains still for a few moments, listening. When he feels secure, he turns the ignition. The car purrs to life. Deep and satisfying. Definitely a custom job. He pokes around until he has located the hood control. Once the roof is down, he shuts off the engine. Then waits for a full minute, stealing glances across the dash. As he waits, he relaxes again. His mind is telling him to worry about the clones and drones. But being in her car affords him an inexplicable sense of security. Like he's been in there before. He quests a hand along the side of Jennifer's seat, feeling its latent warmth. The realization that he is soaking up her residual body heat chills him unexpectedly. It's a feeling he thought long purged from his system. This sudden manifestation bewilders him into dreamy abstraction. He sniffs deeply. Cigarettes and perfume. The smell of her hair is dense at such close proximity. It clings to the dark leather beside his face. His behavior catches him by surprise. He begins to feel uneasy with himself. He opens the cubbyhole. Several dozen fortune cookies spill noisily out. Onto the seat and floor. He regards them with puzzlement. He realizes that the floor is already covered with fortune cookies. Many are smashed within their packaging.

Inside the elevator, things have calmed a notch. The drone has gone into some mode reserved for enclosed spaces. It hovers unobtrusively. Near the roof of the (thankfully) high-ceilinged lift. Every now and then it takes a snap. The flash is still offensive, especially due to the fact that the walls are mirrored. But the elevator is brightly lit. This diffuses the shock value somewhat. The journalist nurses a bloody lip. The drone gets several close-ups in rapid succession. She stares hatefully up at Chloe, who is taller. The drone-controlling device dangles. From her wrist on a catch-chain. It displays live-feeds from both drones. If they hadn't been engaged in combat, they might have all seen Ziq outside Jennifer's car. Chloe leans against the mirrors. She smirks at her pigeon-toed trainers. Jennifer puts her spinning head against the cool glass. She winces each time the flash ignites.

'That drone is giving me fucking epilepsy,' she mutters.

The journalist contemptuously spits blood against a mirror.

'It is hot, new art form,' She states haughtily. 'Drones take random images, record sound, all day, all night.'

She extracts a vivid white handkerchief. Daubs at her injured mouth, before barreling on mercilessly. They are all too high and drunk to realize that no-one has pressed any buttons. They are going nowhere.

'My team develop hot new fractal VR technique. It fucks with you. It's art. It fucks with you! One drone left eye, one drone right. Fucks you hard, baby! We debut show at Biennale—right on the edge. Right on the fucking edge! I shop it to magazine to replace photographers, do a deal, co-sign with gallerists. That's originality!'

She spits more blood, talking more to her reflection than the others. She expands on her concept. Her speech becomes more eloquent. But sounds rehearsed. Her face is disconnected to what she is saying. It becomes obvious that she has given this same speech. In a hundred different elevators, from Dallas to Taipei. And as she does so again, her gimmick strobes on high. It collects more snatches of their lives. Some great, electronic mosquito.

'Drones are also programmed fly tandem to capture 3-D in stereo-flight path alignment! Beat that! They are synched like that. I find best programmers. Best! Next, we plan fire lasers, create holograms. Real-time! Real-time bitches! You just wait! All shows downloadable from magazine archives for VR interface. This why we make you sign release before arrival. In four months, I go LA for talk about movie deal...'

Jennifer unexpectedly snags her handheld device, snapping its leash. The journalist bursts into a volley of Italian curses. She launches herself bodily at Jennifer. But is pulled short by Chloe, who pins her spectacled face against bloody glass. Chloe is still chortling hysterically. The journalist's expression distorts with rage. The drone begins to shutter stills madly. Jennifer fiddles with the device.

'Fuck art is what I say,' she mumbles, trying to figure out the drone's controls.

The journalist thrashes. She screams her lungs out in the boxy space.

'How do you manually override...' Jennifer thinks out loud.

The journalist unexpectedly breaks loose. She elbows Chloe's forehead viciously. The perpetual laughter cuts short. Chloe flags down, stunned. The journalist is on her in a second. They flail like about.

Ringed fists rain down into the veil. Jennifer side-steps the chaos, thoroughly engrossed. Within a moment, Chloe has regained control. She unceremoniously back-hands the Italian and checks herself for damage. Her opponent reels. Blood traces down her throat. Somehow, in the light, it matches her waxy lipstick perfectly. Chloe discovers a growing bruise on her otherwise flawless temple. Some blood in her hair. Her merry face grows dark with fury. She rips the journalist's spectacles off. Then proceeds to crush her face into the nearest reflective surface. A feline yawl escapes torn lips. The Italian's face is smashed repeatedly against the cold glass.

'You broke my smile now, you cunt!' Chloe barks.

'I don't see how this photographic technique is so fucking original,' Jennifer mentions absently.

She flicks a tab. The drone begins to spin. It moves faster and faster, wobbling dangerously. Jennifer studies it drunkenly.

'Worst ceiling fan…ever,' she announces, impressed.

The drone is now spinning so fast that it's losing its center of gravity. It nicks violently against the glass. Some chips fly off, catching in Jennifer's hair.

'I'll have your heads on sticks in New York!' the journalist slurs. 'Give me my fucking future!'

Her cheekbone sounds another meaty thud. This time the glass shows a hairline fracture. Chloe decides enough is enough. She stands reeling, fingers tangled in her opponent's hair. There is a moment of heavy breathing. The drone has slowed to an acceptable velocity. Of its own accord. Some fail-safe, Jennifer reckons. Chloe's fingers tighten and loosen around hanks of treated hair. She seems confused by the damage she has wrought. Her reflection distracts her. She begins to laugh again

'My fucking lip!' the journalist wails. 'Too much dollars I pay for my fucking lip!'

'Too much is not enough!' Chloe giggles.

'You want some homemade Botox?' Jennifer sneers.

'Get a nano-bot hot job next time,' Chloe grins. 'Lasts longer.'

'Suck my dick!' the journalist hisses.

She struggles, pinned helplessly beneath a bloody trainer—which not so long ago was spotless.

Jennifer finally gets the hang of the controls. She also remembers to activate the lift.

As Ziq is heading back to the tree line, he spots the drone he encountered. It zigzags through the night air. For a moment, it loops groggily. As though confused. Then all of a sudden, it jerks into a fixed trajectory. Heading back toward the tower at full speed. A guard signals to his colleagues. They all watch as the drone accelerates straight into a wall. Somehow Ziq is expecting an explosion. The drone disappoints. Crashing into fragments. It looks like some broken child's toy as it falls. By the time the guards arrive at the wreckage, Ziq is long gone.

The three girls stagger down long black corridors. The remaining drone trails behind them—some sort of dog.

'Do you have any idea how many neuroses are caused by the magazines you whore for?' Jennifer rants.

'Who do you think pays for my lips!' the journalist responds acidly.

'Not your gallerist, that's for sure!' Chloe laughs.

Another skirmish breaks out, captured in rapid-fire snapshots.

Some weeks later, in Milan, an editor will attempt to make chronological sense of their evening. The archive will include stills. A shiny bathroom, tiled in black marble. The camera must have been damaged at some point—perhaps when Chloe kicked it. The focus is off on the remaining images. A crack shows on the lens. The editor glimpses mirrors sliced with cocaine. Bare legs in a bath. Porcelain splashed with blood. The soundtrack is all screaming and verbal abuse. Chloe's right knee is grazed with blood. That's about the only thing that is certain after they enter the apartment. At one point, the drone is forced out of a panoramic window. The machine manages to document its fall and lopsided recovery. The outside of the lobby is once again described. Then the parking area. The machine reroutes, passing the S2000. It must have paused to recapture the car because there are some very clear photographs of a vinyl clutch purse. Placed neatly. On the driver's seat.

Blue Fire

The future is closer now. Events form like mist on a mirror. In the future, Jennifer will apply make-up before this mirror. She will stand on the black marble of her bathroom—just as she has always done. The enclosed sanctuary of the bathroom, perhaps all bathrooms, presents a sort of timeless continuum for her. The future may as well be the past. Or the present... Looking through panoramic window walls, she sometimes imagines that the geometry of the city is mirrored in the cubic faces of the mountain. She is at a great height. The apartment is usually kept dark. In the future, this hasn't changed. The heavy, black drapes are open. But the glass is set to a high factor auto-tint. Colour mutes in the darkness within. Contours soften. Frosted glass partitions blur the rooms further. The carpet swallows sound, diminishing echoes, deadening space. An atmosphere of sleep pervades. When Jennifer paints her eyelids, she does so with surgical precision. Now her entire body is covered with matte blue paint. Ziq sits on the edge of the bath. He observes blue limbs, moving beneath an open kimono. The colour strikes a discordant note in the dim apartment. Earlier that day, security had gotten in touch. She was reminded of the night the Italian journalist visited. A drone had captured footage of an intruder outside her car. Now, she was shown the images. Asked if she could identify the culprit. It gave her a kind of déjà vu—in reverse...

'What did you tell them?' Ziq asks.

'That you live with me.'

'I didn't live with you then.'

'I suppose that was the day it started.'

'I came to return your purse.'

She smiles strangely, remembering.

'It was like a *sign*, finding it in the car.'

He watches her line her eyes. Even more blue paint. Her natural skin tone is close to being eradicated. As though her entire body is cast from plastic.

'It was just there on my driver's. Immediately, I thought of the writing at the bottom of the pool. Isn't that strange?'

He doesn't reply. She pauses, studying his reflection.

'I thought it was spirits.'

He digests this.

'In a way it was, I suppose,' he answers eventually.

She finishes off her eyes, drops the kimono and studies herself critically. The blue is just a base-coat. Highlights and detailing will be added later. By professionals.

'Is the tone even?' she asks, running blue hands under warm water.

The paint is untroubled by the gush. It coats as smoothly as vinyl. The mirror begins to mist. It smudges her face.

'You don't have to go to that house anymore,' he pleads quietly.

Unreadable emotions travel beneath the blue of her face. Her hands remain frozen in the hot gush—pristine as stuffed birds. She is staring at them intensely, seeing something terrible. Something only she can see.

'It's not a house,' she replies, without shifting her gaze.

'It isn't?'

'It was once. It isn't anymore.'

'What is it then?'

'It's a realm.'

'It is?'

'It's not even in this country.'

'I see.'

'No, you don't. You couldn't possibly. Not yet.'

'There's hope?'

'You would have to leave this world.'

'The realm is off-world?'

'It exists outside of space and time—like those continuums you read about in science fiction.'

'What do you call this place?'

'We call it Club Ded, of course. Just like the film.'

A recurring dream has been plaguing Jennifer for some time. Like the continuum she described, it also exists independently. Outside time and space. When it comes to the dream, it doesn't matter whether Jennifer is in the past or the future. The dream is always the same. It is a vision of her own death. The portent fouls her precious waters. Keeps her awake in the satellite feeds. Stops her from eating. Slowly fills her future with poison. At some point in this contaminated future, she will pluck up enough courage to approach the Oracle about it. The Oracle will respond with a vision. She will speak to Jennifer in a room full of flamingoes. Her voice will be low and sonorous, teeming with miracles. In the days following, Jennifer will tally the Oracle's telling against the warning in her dream. Yet, as much as the premonition of death terrifies her, it fascinates her too. She picks at it like a scab. She gets lost in the solving of the mystery. Re-arranging its details. Like furniture in a dark room. She does this until the dream feels more like a memory of events past, than a precognition. The Oracle's interpretation of the vision, on the other hand, is more akin to an event that is always in the process of happening. As she explains it, the dream will loop continuously. In the realm of possibility. It would continue thusly. Until it has gathered enough momentum to break through into reality. The Oracle's suggestion is to attack the mechanisms of its becoming. To derail it from eventuality. Jennifer understands that to give the premonition of her death attention, or even fear, only adds to its strength. But in the manner of a moth to a flame, she persistently self-sabotages herself by dwelling on it. Her obsessive morbidity fills her with self-loathing. The dream describes a kind of fire. So, she tries to negate it with water. She cannot die by fire when she is underwater, she reasons. She eats suicide pills to luxuriate and amplify these sub-aquatic sensations. Yet, each evasion only fans the flame by lending the fire credence. With each night, her anxiety grows. Still, she cannot bring herself to voice the source of it. Let alone to anyone else. The demon remains within her. A ghost glow, or perhaps the embryonic manifestation of her own future ghost. Speeding recklessly toward her.

In the dream Jennifer is flying. She travels round the mountain in an upright position, suspended. She wears a black swimming costume. Below her it is night. Above, however, the sky appears alive with twilight colour. For some reason, none of this radiance reaches the ground, which seems to exist in another sphere entirely. Its rocks are deep with shadow. The city clotted. Webby, insubstantial lighting. Jennifer travels at an increasing velocity, circumnavigating the mountain again and again. At some point, over the cable station road, her acceleration reaches the point where it becomes uncontrollable. Tiny sparks flicker in front of her eyes. As though she were re-entering the atmosphere of a planet. She panics. Starts to lose control of her flight. The sparks ignite. Things fall apart. She is hurled into a burning spin. The mountain converts to inky liquid. Its tsunami crashes down upon her tiny, whirling form. Jennifer finds herself encapsulated by a bubble—a cosm of warm, blue water. Except that somehow, the water isn't water. It is blue fire. She lifts her hands in the bath-like, glittery medium. The fluidic current prompts her to wash her hands. As though with soap in a sink. As she rubs them against one another, the flesh comes clean off her burning bones. She realizes that this is happening with the rest of her body as well. Usually at this point, panic overwhelms her. She awakens, drenched in sweat, clawing at herself. Sometimes she screams. But only when she is alone.

It was V who had first introduced Jennifer and Anita to the suicide pills.

She would pick up a supply from Fortunato every Thursday afternoon, along with their weekly weed and cocaine. The girls had suppliers for everything except the glands before V came along. But the quality of Fortunato's merchandise swayed even the indomitable Anita. After V disappeared, Jennifer decided to contact him directly. She wanted to replenish the dwindling supply and initiate a new trade relationship. She was also worried and wanted to try get some information about V. Jennifer had met Fortunato a few times with V. She had his number. When she calls, the first thing he asks, is if she or Anita have seen V. Apparently, he is also concerned. Jennifer explains that she is in the dark as to her whereabouts. She explained why she is calling. He tells her that he would be happy to help her out. They arrange to meet in Observatory, later that afternoon.

Obz had once been a colourful neighbourhood. There is a strong student contingency, due to its proximity to the University. The main street is filled with the usual bookshops, live music venues and New Age restaurants native to this type of area. At one time, an annual Mardi Gras occurred down the main road. Now rampant crime and misery have reduced the place to a fallout shelter. The buzz remains to some degree. It festers in bars and pool halls. Even so, the place has starved to a shadow of its former self.

Jennifer drives through the grimy Industrial districts lying between town and Observatory. The last area is a place called Salt River. Previously, it had been something of a no-go zone, littered with crack dens and dingy corner shops. Imaginative graffiti diseases it's alleyways, describing visions of urban narcosis. The decay is still there, but the area is undergoing something of a gentrification renaissance. Glitzy galleries have moved into the wreckage. They peddle overpriced student drivel and interior decoration dressed up as fine art. A weekly market has also colonized an old biscuit mill. Spruced up to a fine polish, the market caters to the bourgeoisie every Saturday. Young, up and coming corporate couples inject finance into a starved flank of the city, lugging babies, protected from the outside world by sturdy fences. V used to enjoy doing lunch there when the market was buzzy, but neither Jennifer nor Anita could stand the place.

Fortunato had told her to meet him outside an old cinema at the deserted end of Obz's main road. It was a lush old deco building called the Bijou. It had lain abandoned for years but was being resuscitated for some sinister media-related purpose. Jennifer was surprised to find that Fortunato also drove a yellow car, though his looked as though it had been foraged out of a junkyard. She was surprised that it was even roadworthy. Somehow, she imagined that a former movie director turned drug dealer would be driving a fancy BMW. He is in the driver's seat on a call, but hangs up when she parks alongside. He is out and looking her car up and down by the time she greets him. She gets out as well. They shake hands, somewhat awkwardly. He has on a pair of impenetrable mirrored sunglasses. They make it difficult for Jennifer to gauge his mood. He hands her a package wrapped in brown paper.

'This is the coke and weed,' he tells her.

'What about the suicide pills?' she asks.

'They will only be ready tomorrow. Myself, I eat them raw—you want those?'

'I've never tried them like that,' she frowns.

He reaches under his driver's seat and lugs out a cooler bag filled with icepacks. From between some rope-bound bottles, he extracts a plastic bag filled with brine. Bloody little organs float around the pinkish seawater, collecting like frogspawn near the surface.

'You eat them like *that*?' she asks, disgusted.

'It's no different to sushi.'

'I'll wait till tomorrow, thanks.'

'It's no problem—I'll send the guy who makes the pills round to wherever you are.'

'Cool.'

He replaces the cooler box, eyeing her car.

'Nice machine,' he comments.

'Thanks.'

He goes around the front of her vehicle and drops to a squat, glancing underneath.

'You've had her tuned?'

'I have actually,' she replies.

They've never really had a proper conversation before. Jennifer recognizes something familiar about his voice, though she is unable to put a finger on it.

'Who worked on it?' he asks.

'Some guy called Cookie out in Bellville. I got a good deal.'

Fortunato frowns.

'I know Cookie. He's not a good guy.'

The comment irritates Jennifer. She takes pride in her car.

'I think he did a good job,' she replies.

'We should race sometime and find out,' he offers.

'What car would you use?'

He removes his sunglasses and grins, indicating the Toyota. She raises an eyebrow.

'You want to race me in that piece of shit?'

'I'll show you something,' he says.

She watches as he opens his driver's. He reaches under the seat to unlock the hood. Jennifer notes that he's had the interior stripped out and installed Reccaro bucket seats. She follows him to the front and takes a look at the engine.

'Jesus fucking Christ,' is all she can muster.

'We should race sometime,' he smirks.

Again, something in the way he speaks, strikes a recognizable chord. She looks over the smoothly curved, well maintained hardware, accepting that she is out of her depth.

'This is insane,' she says. 'I mean, I've had mine boosted too—but my work is nothing like yours…'

'Let me have a look.'

'Sure.'

She pops the bonnet of her car. He fetches a grimy little laptop and some cables out the back of the Conquest, locking it behind him.

'What's that for?' she asks.

'I want to run your engine through mapping software,' he explains.

'Won't we need to go for a ride for it to work?'

'Correct,' he answers, climbing into her passenger seat.

She shrugs and climbs in. He uses his RO plug to interface his PC with the car's ECU. He asks her to rev the car so that he can check the fuel/air mix ratios and boost sensors.

'What?' she asks, fascinated.

'I need to check whether she runs lean or rich,' he answers.

Jennifer isn't quite sure what he means, but allows Fortunato to continue without further interruption.

'Why did you choose an S2000?' he asks, exploring her engine through the readings.

'I saw it in that movie. The chick was driving a pink one.'

'The S2000 has a Vtec motor—legendary. It's also the fastest naturally aspirated 2.0-liter engine in the world—revs to 110000 revs per minute.'

'Cool.'

'Convertibles are death traps for racing though. They flip. There are also weight distribution issues.'

'I'm a long way from racing at that level. I diced with friends when I was at Uni in Durban—down at Blue Lagoon and Makro in Springfield. Those guys from Phoenix know how to hot-rod.'

This makes him laugh.

'I know what you mean,' he chuckles.

Suddenly she realizes what is so familiar about his voice. She is about to say something when she sees that he is frowning at something on the screen.

'What is it?' she asks.

174

'Let's take a drive,' he says quietly.

She edges the S2000 back down the street, angling hard for Salt River. There, she gets onto the highway.

'Tell me,' he asks. 'Did he do the internals? I need to know what we can push the car up to.'

'I'm not sure, to be honest.'

'What kind of work did you want done?'

'I just told him I wanted it boosted.'

'Ok. Have you done a high bar boost yet?'

'How high?'

'1 bar up to 2.5?'

'No, highest I've boosted is 0.5. I haven't had a chance to push them at all—been too busy at work. I wanted to get out to the Karoo to do a test sometime. They have those long, flat roads...'

He glances at her with a grim expression. He tells her to rev the engine low again, watching the gauges dance. She is weaving expertly between cars, slowing for cameras. Twin rest stops approach on either side of the fenced-off freeway. Beyond, loom the colourless shack-lands of Langa.

'So, who put you in touch with Cookie?' he asks.

'Anita. Someone she knew recommended him. He did some work for her once—minor stuff. They hate each other now.'

'What happened.'

'I don't know. Anita is always mixed up in shady shit.'

'I heard she's a racist.'

'V tell you that?'

'She told me how she was being treated.'

'I won't lie. She's...abrasive.'

'She feels that she is somehow superior.'

'I suppose.'

'And you?'

'Oh, I think we're all equally worthless.'

They are approaching Century City. The rollercoaster shows up like a skeleton against an asphalt sky. He asks her to turn off and park on one of the monolithic parking verges, where he climbs out to inspect the engine. She follows him and watches him study the set-up. Again, his face becomes dark.

'What is it?' she asks.

'Look, there's a downside to the high revs on an S2000—if you tune them too much, or do shoddy work.'

'Like?'

He sighs.

'Ok, let me explain. Normally when you boost a car, there are a lot of things you have to change, so that the nitrous oxide system is supported. First you upgrade to Wisco forged pistons, then, you ceramic-coat all other moving parts and the cylinder head, including the valves. This is the usual practice for high heat application. It helps with compression too—you follow?'

'Ok.'

'You also have to change the bearings and do ARP bolts. Cookie took a short cut by only doing the bearings, bolts and stud kit. The con-rods have not been coated for heat and the pistons haven't been replaced.'

'What does that mean?'

'The engine will fail under a big boost. The heat will not be contained. It will create an explosion in the engine block that will set the fuel and nitro lines on fire. This will spread instantly to the tanks. If you kick that turbo anywhere beyond 1.5 bars, your car will become a fireball.'

Jennifer becomes very pale.

'What's the matter?' he asks. 'Are you ok?'

Without warning, she leans over and vomits. He reacts instantly, taking her by the shoulders to support her weight. When he pulls her up, he sees that she has begun to cry. He gets her into the passenger side of her car, passing her a serviette from one of his pockets. She stares wildly out of the windscreen—her eyes turn a blinding blue against their reddened whites. The highway slurs endlessly beyond the concrete barrier. The full revelation of her dream is unraveling right in front of her. He unplugs and begins to pack up his laptop. She looks down at her hands. They are still intact. When his machine is secured, Fortunato pulls a small green bottle from his coat and hands it to her.

'Drink,' he commands.

'What is it?' she asks.

She is a little steadier now, swabbing around her mouth with the tissue he handed her.

'Herbs,' he explains.

She opens it. The contents smell bitter and give off acrid fumes.

'Fuck that,' she retorts.

'Trust me,' he insists.

She gives in and swallows some. The potion makes her want to retch, but within moments, her stomach settles. She begins to feel calm and lucid. Impressed, she takes another swallow.

'That's enough,' he cautions, reclaiming the bottle.

She sits for a moment, getting her bearings. Then she tells him about the dream. He listens without moving. When she is finished, he maintains his stillness for a few more minutes.

'It is because you have been swimming,' he eventually tells her.

'What?' she asks, exasperated.

176

'You have been swimming with the fish. It has decided to show you your death. This is a warning you must heed.'

He glances out of the window, thinking it over for a moment.

'Actually, it's Ziq,' he tells her. 'He is the one who brought you to this vision. He manufactures the pills. I think that you both have things to say to one another.'

'What things?'

'I don't know.'

'Is he the one that I'm meeting tomorrow?'

'Yes.'

She sits, staring at her hands. They seem pale and shaky to her— ineffective mechanisms.

'What have these fish glands done to me?' she whispers.

'They have probably saved your life,' he replies with great seriousness.

She turns sideways, finding her own face in his impenetrable sunglasses.'

'You're not really from Nigeria.' she states blankly.

He snaps his head away, taken aback. After a few moments, he removes his sunglasses and looks at her again. His eyes glisten with vitality, but Jennifer gets the impression that he is troubled and tired.

'You have an accent,' she explains.

'I noticed that it had started to creep back,' he replies quietly.

'So, you're South African?'

He grunts unintelligibly.

'I'm originally from Chesterville,' he admits. '- Grew up around Durban.'

'Zulu?'

'Of course.'

'So, you moved north and burned your bridges.'

'Yes.'

'Why'd you come back?'

He shakes his head and laughs.

'I can't believe I'm talking about this. I suppose you feel the same about your dream.'

'You got that right.'

'This is what the fish does. In a way, it's like a turbo boost for the human. It sees where the future is tangled and it brings you to the knot. Then it forces you to deal with it.'

'So, stop evading my question and deal with it,' she smiles weakly.

A shadow of amusement crosses his face.

'Look, ok, I admit it,' he says 'I hate this fucking country. I've always hated it.'

'Why?'

'Chesterville, Pinetown, Durban—nothing interesting, not for me. I didn't want university. I didn't want school. I didn't want nationalist fuckery. I just wanted to watch films. Then I wanted to make them. You couldn't do that then. Not in this country. You still can't. Government film funding changes scripts to suit their agendas. It's all shit here—middle-class, corporate, bourgeois, political.'

'So, you ran away to Nigeria.'

'I think I liked Nigerian culture too much then. I didn't really like the films at first—but the literature was good. I liked that it was so far away. So, I went.'

'How did you get into film making over there?'

'It doesn't matter how. The fact is that I did. It was all working. I burned my passport—some stupid statement. I was very arrogant then. Burned my ID too, my whole past. It was all good. Then this fucking place reached out across the whole of Africa and dragged me back.'

'What happened.'

'The xenophobic riots happened. There were those that knew my real past. Maybe they felt they that they needed to retaliate for what had been done. They had lost people here. They didn't like me. They accused me of various sympathies. I mean, look, no-one would have believed them if it came out. I had protection. In the end, they threatened to hurt V. We had to leave.'

'You left for her?'

'No—for both of us.'

'It sounds like she could have left on her own.'

'We were married. Wherever she went, I went.'

'Why don't you get a new SA passport? Why are you living like this?' Fortunato shows her a smile.

'I destroyed all my papers. They don't believe that I was born here and I can't prove it.'

'Biometrics?'

'I need a lawyer to pursue an appeal. It's not as easy as it sounds—especially in my situation. Until then, they are content to believe that I *am* Nigerian. It's ironic, I suppose…'

'I'm sorry that V abandoned you after everything.'

'She was following her own fish. I respect that.'

'Do you think she's ok?'

'I can't say.'

'You still love her.'

Fortunato sighs.

'She is free now. Does it matter how I feel?'

Jennifer looks out of the window for a while. Then she spontaneously slaps him on the back. A show of support. Taken aback, he chuckles.

It is Written

The Roxy had been a popular cinema in the fifties. It comprised an intestinal, subterranean space near the city hall. For a while it was a popular venue. But falling sales forced its closure, sometime in the late sixties. By the mid-seventies it was floating face-down in the makings of an inner-city slum. To make things worse the Roxy had submerged entirely. For ten years it drowned on a ruptured municipal drainage line. Degrading slowly in the murk of the city. Later, when urban reclamation projects found it sitting on prime property, in a newly developing district, surveyors started assessing the damage. The premises were drained. Stripped to concrete. A club owner bought the place for more than it was worth. Then set to work restoring it to a smidgeon of its former glory. By the end of the nineties it was launched. A dingy live venue under the name of 'The Basement'. It took some years for the place to gather steam. But when it did, it became a landmark. A cocktail bar was added. The interior underwent several radical, cosmetic reconstructions. The antiquated, velvet draped cinema facade remained however, becoming a familiar fixture. The Basement had a popular jazz night, hosted live bands and enjoyed raucous dance floors over the weekend. All the same, the Ethiopian restaurant across the road was showing a larger profit margin. This was due to the massive overheads required to run the club. The Basement closed its doors right after the millennium. It lay, gathering dust for several years. Nostalgia about The Basement's golden era grew over time. It was remembered fondly. There was always talk of re-opening. A luxury supermarket chain ended up buying the space and incorporating it into their headquarters across the road. The marketers plan was to create a venue that traded on the reputation of the legendary club. After some wangling, they managed to acquire the original name. A crude, private-sector clone of the famous club was born. During the day, it would function as a cafeteria for employees and the general public. Trading only in supermarket produce, which had been dressed up by culinary spin doctors. By night it would operate as a live music venue. Hosting bands promoted by an affiliated energy drink, which also operated a recording studio in town. A brand new red velvet curtain was hoisted, emblazoned with beverage branding. All in all, it was a tidy bit of corporate franchising. Jaybird had been threatening to burn it to the ground for ages.

Anita, Jennifer and Chloe have a new ritual. They inaugurate the Eye-Detail sessions with Bloody Marys at the Basement. This started when Anita, in a bizarre show of solidarity/nostalgia or both, declared Quan's a no-go zone without 'the '3rd Girl'. Now they book a regular booth near the Basement's dancefloor. The booth has a curtained entrance. It allows them to do lines in privacy. Anita and Jennifer are all in black. But Chloe is still switchboard white. Just clocked out of Control. Pulling double. Jennifer wonders where she finds the energy. Jennifer also started out at Control. She knows the system like an ex. Blackbirds used to swap her out on weekends. It was then that Jennifer discovered a taste for the night. She worked switchboard with Chloe. In fact, Chloe was the first girlfriend she made at Oracle. They used to take luxurious smoke breaks in the observation lounge. Regular space-station buddies. Silvery dust glitters on Chloe's cheekbones. Even in switchboard white, she can't resist a bit of a twist. Jennifer usually enjoys talking outfits with her. But tonight, she is silent and apprehensive. They have just swallowed their last suicide pills. The corners are beginning to fill—with a ghost of bluest water. All night Jennifer's been on edge. That 'something is going to happen' pensiveness. The twinge of a future thread.

Ziq wrestles a bottle of petrol from the bird-masked Jaybird. He had taken every precaution to disguise his destination. But the pyromaniac was quick to scent a conspiracy. He'd followed Ziq discreetly. Ziq was lucky to spot him and act, before any damage was done. Now they struggle. Beneath barred windows. Tepid house music, bubbling from deep ventilation shafts. It oozes out onto the street. The can skitters onto the sidewalk. It lollops pungent blue fluid across the paving. Jaybird squirms loose. He squawks and shrieks in fury. Scooping up the can, he flaps into the night. Ziq rushes to the opposite end of the alley. He is just in time to see Jaybird vanish. Around a dark corner. Ziq collapses against a wall. He catches his breath. The opposite end of the alley connects to a cramped, but well-lit street. Abuzz with foot-traffic. Ziq is about to head in that direction. An iron door swings open just beside him. He catches it on reflex. Red light bathes the walls of the passage. A broad, dark man in a white t-shirt and sunglasses exits. He carries a cashbox and a sub-machine gun. Nodding briefly to Ziq, he crosses down the dark side of the alleyway, leaving him holding the door. Ziq peers around the edge. After a moment's consideration, he passes through.

A system of antiquated corridors unfurls. Blurry music. It focuses in volume, the deeper he penetrates. Ziq is in the habit of walking through doors that fate makes available. For him, it's a path being pointed out. As a result, Ziq has seen the hidden faces of many, otherwise pedestrian structures. The backstage quality tends to bring into question the nature of the perceivable world. Is the sky a façade, disguising celestial mechanics? The hidden areas leave him ruminating. Often, his curiosity will draw him inexorably to such areas. He finds himself spending more and more time in forbidden territory. As a result, the city is infinitely larger for him than it is for the average citizen. He has tasted its high hairs and cauldron of guts. Of course, one who chooses to exist in such a manner becomes acutely aware of restrictions. But there is a recklessness to his constant questing toward the abstract. And every so often, he is rewarded with strange fruit.

Ziq cracks a fire-door. Despite the lackluster beats, the crowd is frenzied. Bodies writhe beneath strobe-chatter. A stench of up-market cologne. Ziq swims through a mangle of limbs. He locates the line of curtained bar booths. Then proceeds to search for the appropriate number. He walks loosely, eyeing transactions. But when he finds the face of Jennifer, his mechanism freezes. He drifts toward her. Carried by inertia alone. She is also staring. Anita snaps her head up—a moment of psychic alertness. Her mind calculates the exchange in a heartbeat. She stops dead in conversation with the Chloe. An outsider has transgressed into her circle. Chloe frowns. She follows Anita's eyes. Ziq places a bag of pink pills neatly on the table top. Jennifer finds herself rising clumsily to greet him. In her haste, she knocks over a glass of wine. The ruby fluid topples across her hands. She looks down, finding them red. The gland-enhanced shock of seeing this, breaks the moment like a smoke ring. Reminded of her dream, she reaches reflexively for Ziq. Anita's eyes follow the movement like a hunting cat. Vulnerability follows. Anita turns to drug-induced glass. Parts of her shatter. They discharge pieces this way and that. Jennifer's fingers leave a smudge on Ziq's coat. The mark seems to fascinate him. A synchronous recognition. Clutching his arm, she balances herself. She finds herself smiling. An undisguised expression of relief. This smile somehow transfers to his face. Jennifer looks to the blackbirds. She utters something—lost to the club noise. Gesticulating, she waves toward a distant lavatory. She appears to be oblivious to the intensity of Anita's gaze. Her hand still clings to Ziq, refusing to relinquish contact. She gets a hold of herself. Motions for him to wait. Then she is gone, winging down the aisle, leaving him mute and unmoored. She has to clean her hands, before this goes any further. She can't stand this reminder of her dream. It makes her anxious. In her haste to re-establish reality, she finds herself fleeing the very thing she has been seeking. Ziq watches Jennifer enter, then leave his sphere. Realizing he is being scrutinized, he snaps from his reverie. The pale smile on his face dries when he sees Anita. He backs down the aisle. She glares after him. Fleeing into the crowd, he searches for Jennifer. She is already gone.

Jennifer fights her way to the bathroom. The exertion intensifies the effects of the psychedelic. She pushes open a heavy door. Slipping fish-like, down a flight of stairs. The club noise fades against the sharp click of heels. Here, the walls are soft and furry. A white door gleams. At the end of a dark shaft. She smiles as she descends, secure in this snug little reef. There is an otherworldly atmosphere about this bathroom. Warm water gushes over her hands and wrists. The wine pales, sluices away. But just as she is sure the redness has purged, it resurfaces again. Collecting in her the lines of her palms. She frowns. Looking up, she sees that her nose is bleeding. She paws at her face. It only reddens her hands further. The dream suddenly begins to feel more palpable. Is she asleep? Is this place an extension of the nightmare? Phantoms rise all around her. The redness cuts vividly down her throat. The glass begins to mist. Now she is on other side of the looking glass. Anita finds her later. Wailing uncontrollably in one of the toilet stalls.

Ziq will tell Jennifer that he looked for her. He will tell her this as she applies blue make-up. In a misted mirror of the future. She is preparing herself for Club Ded. He explains how he loitered for hours. In an underground warren of rooms and corridors. His words cloak the desperation of her own memories. Their activities cover the past in a mist. She doesn't dare to disturb the fragility of this veil. Despite her discovery of the dream's antidote—the power of prophecy has not faded.

'I thought I'd never find you again,' he admits.

She recalls fleeing. Red-hazed reefs. Stubbing her cigarette out in the pale light of the future, she folds down to him. Her blue face pushes into the slope of his throat. It does not smudge. She feels cool and plastic against his skin. The contact momentarily erases the dream. He traces fingers along her back. Ziq had paced the streets for hours. After leaving the Basement. Before it occurred to him to return—to Deer Park. He waited there. Till dawn began to bruise. Anita, meanwhile, had caught Jennifer. In safety-nets of logic, cyclical inebriation. She had not mentioned the coated figure or questioned her hysteria. Instead, she plunged them deeper into the flesh of the night. Dawn found Jennifer ragged. A nightmarish trip. All night, she could not tell where she began, where the dream ended. The indestructible Chloe, sensing discord, had attuned herself to it. She took charge of Anita. Who by then, lay curled across the backseat of the VISION NEXT like a fallen bird. Ziq spotted Jennifer, stumbling barefoot across raw concrete.

Her face was caked with blood. Shoes dangling. A ruthless exhaustion. Halfway across the lot, some instinct caused her to lift her eyes. She sighted him, slowed. Chloe observed. Saw them both. Recognizing their emotional undercurrent, she drove off quickly. Before Anita could open her eyes and annihilate everything. The pair stood against the dawn. Staring across a cold divide.

Steam occludes the checker tile bathroom. It fogs metal, mirrors, feelings. Ziq lowers Jennifer, fully clothed, into warm water. The blood falls away like scales. She lies underwater for a long time. When she finally surfaces—it is into a different stratum. Another existence. Mist rifts the room. He is in the corner, waiting. Awe-struck to find himself at the crown of the tower, with the princess. It should have been so obvious. Yet still—he is a train derailed. He finds that he can operate without track. Another miracle—or part of the same? She gazes. Mute fascination, unsure of his existence. She is amazed that he should manifest in her private world. She accepts it without question. Part of a greater spell perhaps. He, in turn, meets her gaze with reflexive guardedness—seeing a new world. For the first time. From a staggering height.

The Rivers of Pheeling

Jennifer floats in the rich, loose currents of the sea. Golden hair spools. Through the crystalline chaos of a rock pool. Refraction. Quartz crusted boulders. She shifts position. A muscular ebb pulls her through space. She rolls lower, beneath the frosted surge. Flicking herself out of reach of the rocks—with an inbred assurance of aquatic forces. Water is certainly her natural habitat. Its bright, mineral iciness penetrates directly to her core. Warms her savagely against the world. The grain of the fluid is buoyant with salt. Fanned by sun, flagged with kelp. Shafts of luminosity dance through the swells. They illuminate another figure in the surge. Ziq swims into focus. He hovers beside her. She reaches out and touches his cheek in a moment of stillness. Then the ebb topples. It detonates a wreath of bubbles. Kinetic forces swirl them energetically apart.

Seagulls mewl and scrape down a bone of sand. Dunes elongate to wilderness. On either side, chalked in by the brushing of a glassy sea. A lonely cottage on a rise. Jennifer had stayed here once. When she was a child. Her parents had rented the cottage for two weeks in October, when the flowers came out. Although her sister was with her, puberty had already opened a gulf between them. Her elder sibling was more interested in the magazines she'd brought along than in any exploration of the surrounds. Jennifer spent most of her time at the cottage alone. Wandering the alien reaches of a prehistoric coast. She passed the days swimming. Sprawling rock pools, meandering caves. At night, silvery crescents of phosphorescence. A ruthless glint of stars. Jennifer would take her sleeping bag down to the beach to count the waves. She remembered hating the cottage, nagging each day to be taken home. Eventually, when they left, she began to miss it. For years, that desolate place haunted her. It made tiny, potent guest appearances in dream. Of course, Jennifer promised herself that she would return—and later in life, when she found herself living within a day's drive, she was quick to mark it out. It would be one of the first things she would do. But like so many vows, she left the cottage lying. Shelved clumsily, beside insubstantial intentions. It slowly reduced. To a hollow, memory shell.

The cottage's accessibility stripped it of its magic. So, she forgot it. The way a child forgets fairies. Now, suddenly, it had returned in full force. She was shocked that the place still held such resonance for her. Still, she wasn't certain what it was in her pickpocket that had made her recall the cottage with such potency. A memory of that beach came back to her. While she floated in the tub that first night, studying his face. The vision surfaced from nowhere, demanding reality. Jennifer slept like the dead the following day. He dozed on a couch. Waking her wordlessly with tea or food. She consumed in silence. They watched each other. Words seemed to have died abruptly. They left neither holes, nor traces, in the skin of their interaction. Silences were potent. Crisscrossed with vitality and meaning. She called in sick. Two more days passed. He played nurse, cooking soups, watching television, sleeping. Nothing was really discussed. She needed nursing. He wordlessly supplied it. She dug up her laptop on the third day. Tried to locate the cottage in reality. She discovered that it was still there, moonlighting as a holiday chalet. Miraculously, it was available for rental. Jennifer made a reservation for that very night. Somewhere along the line, time had stopped. She dressed quickly, packed a tog bag and lent Ziq a track suit. Within an hour they were on the road.

Jennifer didn't realize how disorienting it would be to leave the city. Like severing an umbilicus. Entire quadrants of weight disintegrated. Sloughing off into the slipstream. She had forgotten how pleasurable it was to drive a sports car down an endless road. Suddenly, she felt in command of the recurrent prophecy. The car's fatal flaw was within her control—and for the first time, so was her dream. Ziq sat very quietly in the passenger crash-couch. Penniless and serene. A pleasing numbness had entered his mind over the last few days. His thoughts had atrophied. They became unnecessary and therefore disposable. He discovered himself in a world of slow, sustained action. He diced and stewed vegetables. He filled baths. Sat speechless for long periods of time. He became fascinated by the movements of her cigarette smoke. In the tomb-like stillness of the apartment, the smoke coiled with all the muscularity of solidified emotion. It was like watching thought emerge in physical form. Directly from the ether. He felt inexplicably secure within the scope of her breath. All notions of paranoid flight petrified when she met his gaze. He realized that he had been accepted. As a naturally occurring facet of this slow, contained world of hers. It became immensely pleasurable to sink into this vacuole of slow-time with her. He nursed her with the meticulous attention to detail that he afforded his wallet-processing procedures. She absorbed it like a hungry plant, unearthed suddenly into sun and water. They drove then, in this barely acknowledged state of euphoria. Toward the clean image of Jennifer's memory. Passing inland, they navigated orchard country. Moving in the general direction of an outlying mountain range. These peaks would eventually give way to desert. Turning north at some point, they started up the coast—toward Namibia. Obligated to detour, to collect keys, they arrived at a small farm. A rickety iron gate barred the entrance to a dirt road. At the end, a homestead, surrounded by crumpled orange trees. Cats roamed the surrounding fields. A child stared suspiciously out of a bush. His grandmother emerged, dressed in a stained apron. She eyed the couple with pastoral distrust. Accepting a down-payment, she handed over the keys. The highway turned away from the highland. It curved back, toward the sea.

Her disorientation was reinforced by the appearance of the cottage. Jennifer felt as though she had circumnavigated time. With just one, tiny little trick-step. His presence was the final jigsaw piece—she saw that now. This stranger was the one thing missing from those two weeks in her youth. He cemented the place into reality. In one fell swoop, without even knowing it, the everlasting mystery had been solved. He solves mysteries, she thought. He solves them without even knowing. Ziq sensed that the place was sacred to her the moment they arrived. In fact, she did not mention its importance until much later. But he had known it from the moment he had seen the cottage. Its winter of memory grown ripe, in the silence of her eyes. Some additions had been made. Modern conveniences. A fresh pair of tacky curtains. Otherwise, the cottage lay unchanged. A defiant coast of the past, resurrected afresh, from the ocean of time.

They lie in a wooden bedroom. Overlooking the beach. Salt and sun have bleached the outer timber to a shell-like whiteness. A pea-green stool stands in the corner. As though it has stood there for centuries. Ziq reclines in white linen, her arms slung around his shoulders. Jennifer's eyes flicker behind their lids. He realizes that she is dreaming and lies still. Their warmth collects in pockets—at interlocked joints. Where her hair blankets his arm. In the palms of unmoving hands. The air is growing frigid. Their exposed flesh chills quickly. Ziq studies a faded painting of a shipwreck. He listens to the creak of wood. The distant crash of the sea. Seagulls patrol mournfully. The birds utter plaintive calls—shards against infinity. His eyes are clear, focused. He realizes, in a distant sort of way, that he hasn't had coffee for a week. Jennifer wakes abruptly, craning her head up. Her hair withdraws from his arm like a cat. For a moment, she is unsure which point in time she has awakened at.

'I'm still here...?' she mumbles—a little girl's voice.

He draws her head back to his breast. She slips under within moments. He observes the pilgrimage of a lone ant, travelling across

186

the featureless landscape of the ceiling. The blurry sea heaves slowly. Tuning itself in turns, toward the frequencies of twilight.

Ziq stands some distance up the beach. The wind muffles against Jennifer's ears, numbing them. She scrubs herself with a rough towel. Her teeth chatter in the icy scrape of wind. Sunlight cuts diamond-white across the surf. She looks across at him, blurry in the distance, pulling apart salt-encrusted hair. The sun sets in a ribbon of glass.

The bathroom is pitch pine. A low ceiling shifts in candle light. Jennifer is in an old iron tub. The candle is set on the edge. It illuminates the water vividly. Steam moves against the grain of stillness. It dissipates in the wheezes of wind, which creep through the boards. Ziq sits against the wall, a cup of tea forgotten beside him. Both have been motionless for some time now, travelling back-roads of thought.

'What work do you do?' he asks, out of nowhere.

She straightens gradually. Drawing an arm about her knees, to warm them.

'I help people,' she states, creating little whirlpools with her hands. She watches them. Then breaks them.

'Well, that's how it started at least,' she sighs. 'Helping people.'

She eases back slowly, into the heat.

'I don't know what I do anymore,' she admits blankly.

He feels for his tea, inspecting it against the light.

'Sometimes, I become certain that I don't exist,' he says quietly. 'Days go by, weeks sometimes. I become sure.'

He plucks a leaf from his cup. Turns it between thumb and forefinger, while he talks.

'Some years ago, I decided to methodize joy.'

She turns her head quizzically.

'Because joyful moments sometimes seem to last forever.' he adds, almost nostalgically.

'The method I formulated became foolproof to me. I refined it so that it could be performed anywhere and at any time. Although I've never had the conviction to devote myself to it completely.'

'Why?'

'Because, to do so, I would have to follow this method to the exclusion of all else. Instead, I began to use it as a device—to pull myself out of dark moments.'

'Take me through it.'

He gathers his thoughts.

'To put the method into action, you first have to force yourself to stop—your thoughts, your actions. Everything must stop so that you can engage the entirety of your senses in a thorough scan of your immediate surroundings.'

'Ok.'

'During the course of this scan, you will be certain to detect something, anything, which is at the very least, even remotely, *heavenly*. This is subjective. It could be anything -the smell of something baking, a glowing cloud formation, a sensation of warmth on a cold night, a butterfly's wing, anything. Whatever the case, you must have faith enough to believe that there will always be some little sign of paradise, in every sphere, and that it will be detectable—if the intent to seek it out is true.'

'I believe that.'

'Now, once this heavenly thing is isolated, the idea is to move towards it. When it is reached, one should once again *stop*, and repeat the entire process. I call this method *hitchhiking to heaven*.'

'There are difficulties,' she murmurs seriously. 'What if the summit of Mount Fuji is the apex of your immediate heaven, what then?'

'Of course, there are fantastic difficulties involved in such simple processes,' he smiles wryly. 'If I devoted my life to it, I'd be able to eventually formulate some sort of 'karmic barometer'—based on the circumstances surrounding each initial scan. Then, the austerities required to reach the heavenly object. Maybe one day I'll write a book about it. Future paleontologists can find it frozen beside me, in a glacier, near the Arctic Circle.'

'Narcissist,' she teases.

'Is there an echo in here?' he fences playfully.

'Did you ever make a serious attempt?'

'I started with stone's throws. When I quit New York. Tried to shed my life like a skin. I wanted to join as many dots as possible into the wild blue yonder. Within two weeks I was standing on a white sanded beach, looking out over an eternity of turquoise…'

He stops, staring into the memory.

'But I closed my eyes in the postcard of it,' He admits. 'Next thing, I was asleep.'

Later, he expanded on this. Telling her it was the physical inaccessibility of the landscape that lent his sapphire paradise the veneer of a postcard. He believed humanity had weakened itself, by isolating itself from nature. Bodies could no longer integrate with the reality of paradise. Its rocky heights had become too high. It's seas too cold. Ziq sounded bitter. He described how the routines of society had stripped the mythological from humanity's carcass. He saw people as soft, pliant and utterly dependent. Centuries of programming had, in his eyes, manufactured prisoners of comfort. Time-victims, scattered about the earth, in futuristic anthills. These hives were governed by, what he described as, 'attention-magnets'. The media, various 'isms', all manipulating awareness. It was an expansion that carried the cost of the natural world. He called it *terminal-reality*. Cities orbited these vortices of nihilistic consumption. Space-stations in a void. They housed human insect-colonies, lost in psychological space. Citizens lived shoulder to shoulder. Light-years apart in almost every other regard. It was a desolate vision.

'A city can be a whirlpool of time,' she replied. '…Paradise a thing stolen at birth.'

The comment gave Ziq pause. Because for him, it encapsulated the tragedy of his 'stranger in paradise' routine. From his existential perspective, it was the stranger, alone, who saw the beautiful trick of paradise. Ziq's stranger was an outsider with perspective. He might recognize paradise—cut clean as a fruit. But he also understood that he could never eat of its flesh. Ziq's stranger, by virtue of his own nature, would remain forever—a stranger to Paradise. This stranger was a citizen of another, perhaps crueler world. Paradise recognized this. For Ziq, it was this unspoken and abstract exile that left him unfulfilled on white sanded beaches. It stranded him in eternities of colour and light. While everyone else frolicked in gutters of 'self-manufactured bliss'. He was reminded of those billboards in the subway. Those windows, where some strange god of faces had leaned down. Promising island water to buoy his aching body. Tropical sunshine to warm rain-grimed skin. It was this unthinkable revelation. The realization that *Paradise* had been sold to him. Just as it had been to everyone else.

Jennifer leads him into shining rock pools. She fords grottoes and cold caves. They lollop with the swell of an Antarctic tide. Cowls of stone fold them in. The forms collapse down the coast, fidgeting with pockets of shadow. Jennifer gleams with vitality in these waters. Ziq is entranced by her underwater self. It glides somewhere above everything else that she is. In its movement, he can discern all her childhood dreams. Bottled and preserved. In the privacy of her submarine universe. Jennifer beams like a little girl. She shows him old haunts. All her secret hidey-holes. Together, they discover kaleidoscopic channels of anemone and the great separations of the sea. He feels her chilled limbs against his own. Pebbled with the cold of the caves. Milky surf cargoes glassy froth into the recesses of these caverns. They pick their way along the bones of this strand. Gulls carry on the long winds—scraps of white, funneling out to sea. Following the surge. Ziq watches them dip along the horizon. Jennifer navigates a labyrinth of tidal pools, somewhere below. Sunlight cuts shadows out of the day. They kiss for the first time. Tentatively, amongst the fallen, broken boulders. Their contact is nerve-racked. The touch of newly grown flesh. Even here in Eden, it's like tending a wound. Softness haunts their interactions thereafter. A fingerprint of bliss, mined from the bedrock of inertia. Lying on flat monoliths, they stare at one another. He traces her one of her cheekbones in disbelief. Externally, she is quiet. Immobile and languid. Her entire being has been concentrated in her eyes, which shiver and shout.

Long ago, Jennifer became convinced that lines of fate ran through her being like threads in the weave of a carpet. The lines transited her, similarly to strata in a mineral. Just as she imagined they did, to every other living being. The weaving of these lines was, to Jennifer's mind, an organic and natural process. The resulting patterning shifted and transposed according to her choices and the varying course of her life. She posited that the patterns created were subject to her will and sensitivity. This theory was strengthened by her observation of the Oracle's teachings. It was a personal attunement to, what she liked to describe as, the 'world of spirits'. This was a sphere that fascinated Jennifer no end—one which could be enhanced by narcotics. It was a ghostly zone. In which Jennifer had sighted the far shore of the unknown, and sampled, first-hand, it's sub-zero fruit. By forcing herself to remain aware of the thread-lines, she was able to glimpse emergent 'pattern possibilities'. Also, the flexibility of steering—toward a nexus of her choice. The threads themselves were abstract, four-dimensional. Some suggested sequential events, unfolding like vertebrae. A domino-play of cause and effect. Others were comprised of what she could only describe as *feeling*. These threads could not be sensed by rational radar. Or by the flickering tail-ends of events or actions. They existed, rather, as a resonance of *atmosphere*. The resonances would collect and branch. In filaments and nodes of varying intensity. Throughout the matrix of past, present and future. The Oracle described them as rivers of feeling, but Jennifer preferred to call them rivers of *pheeling*. The Oracle told her once; that by using sensitivity and attention as a rudder, a person could effectively travel these rivers. By isolating a specific atmosphere from the kaleidoscope of threads. Then focusing on its signature 'pheeling', one could map its course throughout the fabric of time. Once isolated, an individual could tap the river's current. Manifesting situations, life developments and even people, unique to that current of *pheeling*. The rivers ran in streams. Plunged in event cascades. Sometimes they formed atmosphere-pools, where time seemed to splay out forever. In other instances, the rivers expanded beyond their scope. They grew sluggish, stagnant. Depthless, spiritual mangroves. Psychic swamplands, which the Oracle warned, were difficult to escape. A river-traveler was cautioned against entering such all-encompassing regions. Jennifer was fascinated. She made a serious attempt to refine her sensitivities at one point. She was committed to developing, within her, the secret arts of empathic navigation. She sought to plumb rivers stretching out on all sides. But, despite her best efforts, an onslaught of daily life painted her into perpetual corners. The lotus eating of sensory consumption numbed her. It layered dead time over her passing life. Impermeable scars. One day she realized that she had lost contact with the rivers flowing through her. She understood this, yet did nothing to remedy the situation. Life flowed by, crystallizing around her like time-sugar. It was fate which eventually jolted her back—into the intimacy of a fresh current. The writing in the deep end. The lion cabinet. The re-appearance of a missing purse. All these chaotic clicks of co-incidence guided her slowly, out of the dead calm of inertia. She began to drink at this River of Pheeling with a quiet greed. Slaking her thirst at its fount of written and unwritten memory. It was a waterway, encapsulated by this asteroid-figure. Marked by his appearance into her world. Here was a living mystery, who was at once familiar and still a stranger. Now she languished dutifully in this new course. She began to follow its stream into a sphere of light. Writing her future as though it were a thing already written.

He is cooking in the cottage's kitchenette. Night had closed over the world like an eyelid. Through the window, he can see rivulets of moonlight. They squirrel across the shoreline. Fat tubes of paint. Black clouds occasionally swallow the moon. They make an inky sphere of the world. She is curled quietly. At a wooden table, reading a yellow paperback. Smoking to the sizzle of the pan. They ran out of food on the third day and were forced to drive to a derelict farm stall near the highway. He discovered that, with the exception of the fish glands, she didn't consume animal products. She didn't even touch honey. Even her cosmetics were untainted. He himself had not eaten meat for years. But dairy seemed such a large step. She had told him that her vegan diet was primarily due to Anita. It was the first time Jennifer had mentioned her name. He immediately sensed a cavern of secrets. She spoke of Anita in an off-hand manner. It somehow demarcated territory that was off-limits to him. Anita was 'statistics-girl', she explained. A hundred facts a second. She had once told Jennifer that it took, on average, two thousand five hundred liters of water to produce one kilogram of factory meat. She quoted the National Audubon Society, the Worldwatch Institute, the Sierra Club and the Union of Concerned Scientists. She spoke about dust particulate pollution, the greenhouse effect and argued convincingly about how the meat industry was the leading contributor of carbon emissions. Anita argued that if only half the arable land used to grow feed for cattle were re-farmed to produce food, there would be no worldwide starvation problem. She saw eating animal produce as an indulgence the human species simply could not afford. She called fast-food slogans the epitaphs of mankind. Anita had no moral scruples about the consumption of animals. She consumed fish glands because they served her purposes. Her decision to stop eating meat was clinical and calculated. Her little contribution to the ship of fools. Ziq cooked a kind of beetroot stew that night. Jennifer did not mention Anita after that. But she had already entered into the air like a premonition.

Later, Jennifer checks the time on her phone and forgets to turn it off. It rings while he is cooking. They both look up, startled by this intrusion into their cocoon. Jennifer shoots Ziq a pensive glance. She pads barefoot into the gloom, retrieving her phone. She gives Ziq a final glance, then passes out onto the veranda. She answers the call when she is well out of an earshot.

'What's up?'

Anita is on a crowded landing. Mirrored walls and palms. She wears a black, tailored silk suit and high Nazi boots. Her nostrils are pink with cocaine. Music pounds. It's crowded.

'Hey! Where've you been?' Anita chatters.

She ducks into a corner to get some privacy.

'Are you in town? Control says you called in sick.'

Jennifer hesitates.

'I needed to run away.'

'Shame, babe,' Anita coo's. 'You want me to come by with dumplings?'

'I'm not at home.'

Anita's smile fades. Her eyes grow liquid. They dart about. Her mind strives to recall some detail she might have overlooked.

'Where are you?'

'I'll be back the day after tomorrow, probably,' Jennifer replies, vaguely.

She drifts clumsily to the shore, waiting for a reply.

'I'll see you then?' she asks Anita.

Still, there is no reply. Jennifer waits, her feet bathed in an icy lap. Tinny club-noise barges rudely against her ear.

'Anita?'

Anita is against a polished mirror. Her smile has been completely erased. It leaves a porcelain doll's face in its wake. She stands, a mantis amongst the ferns. Doubled by reflections.

'I miss you,' she whispers suddenly.

Jennifer squats into the freezing fans of water. They swallow her ankles, making her numb. She sways against their movement, feeling her feet whiten in the dark.

'I'll see you the day after tomorrow,' she repeats thickly.

'Is there someone there with you...' Anita begins, only to realize that the call has been cut.

She quickly slips her phone into an inside pocket. Lights a fresh cigarette. A tiny, jagged tear leaves her eye. Someone calls from across the room. She smiles and waves, palming away the droplet, cutting back in. Ziq stands beside the window of the kitchenette. He observes Jennifer's silhouette. From this distance, and in such moon-swallowed darkness, she is no more than a swatch of shadow. Somewhere, the rhythm of the sea has been broken. The food is burning.

The drive back is monotonous. She wears sunglasses most of the way. He is quiet, attempting to listen to an old field recording of gamelans. The subtlety is lost in the roar of the highway. Coppery sounds peer out occasionally, like dishes in a sink. At some point she turns to him.

'I wish we could have stayed longer,' she offers.

He turns his gaze from the flux and collapse of distant coastlines. He's unconvinced. She smiles weakly behind her dark glasses, turning back to the road.

They stop at a filling station in apple country. Orchards multiply. Out toward a tattered horizon. Jennifer enters the tuck shop. She buys mineral water. He waits in the car. She watches him through dirty windows, clutching plastic squeeze-bottles. Somehow, it makes her apprehensive to be away from his thoughts. He is engrossed by a view. She pays and returns to the car. The attendant takes her credit card. She clambers into the driver's seat. Wordlessly hands him a bottle.

'Thanks,' he mumbles.

She takes a swig, then looks squarely at him.

'Where are you staying tonight?'

He's been afraid of this question. A lurking specter of illusion. The dream-like purity of their interaction seems, by its very essence, to demand a rude awakening.

'It depends,' he shrugs.

She takes another swig—then, after a moment:

'Why don't you just stay at my place?'

She watches him think.

'I have to work,' she adds. 'But I'll be back later.'

He turns around to face her. A ghost of a smile warms his face. It reflects onto hers.

The coastal regions drift away. Swallowed by tiny towns and outcrops of rock. The highway becomes weighed down. By industrial areas, fruit packing warehouses and rusty, train-track townships. By dusk, suburbs claim the windows. By night, it is the city.

Bubble Free

Jennifer stares vacantly out of the backseat window. Three battered boxes of fortune cookies secured by her manicured hands. They get them at a warehouse now. Her make-up is immaculate. Hair freshly treated. The look in her eyes doesn't match her ensemble. Since she rejoined the team, Jennifer's dreaminess has disarmed their routine. Anita watches her from the rearview mirror. All night, the pair have been polite and affectionate. Beneath the skin however, a bone lies dislodged and in urgent need of attention. Conversely, Jennifer hasn't been in the mood to deal with Anita. The unspoken desperation of their situation repulses her. The Response-Room comes and goes—a highway mirage. At one point, they share a joke behind a cigarette. Jennifer has, for a moment, the feeling that Anita might let things lie. But even then, her stomach is telling her something different.

Anita pilots them across concrete wastelands. It's uncharacteristic. Chloe has unofficially taken over the driving since V disappeared. Now Chloe pops vitamin boosters in the passenger seat—LED encrusted shoes up on the dash. Jennifer watches the windows. She's not quite there, seeing ahead to the bed that she will share. The image warms her.

Anita stops unexpectedly in Camps Bay, breaking Jennifer's reverie. Chloe cracks her door. Lingers for a moment, half-in, half-out. She shoots Anita a loaded glance.

'Later,' she murmurs cryptically.

Anita pulls off the curb before Jennifer has a chance to climb in front.

'Coffee?' she asks.

'Actually, I need to get home,' Jennifer replies casually.

'Somebody waiting?' Anita smiles.

Jennifer hesitates. She catches Anita's eye in the rear-view.

'Look, I'm sorry I haven't been round...' she begins.

'It's fine, really,' Anita responds—a little too quickly.

She flashes the sort of smile you see on air hostesses. It's not at all the smile that will do. But Jennifer is prepared to accept it after the night's accumulation of tension. Anita changes lanes. A familiar, business-like tone enters her voice.

'Listen,' she mentions. 'There's something work-related I need to talk to you about. Are you sure you don't have time for a quick drink?'

Jennifer glances about uncomfortably. She checks the time on her phone. Eventually she relents.

'Where do you want to go?'

Anita surprises Jennifer with a sly grin, knifing the car unexpectedly down an off-ramp.

Ziq has been cooking something semi-lavish, hopping between pots. It's been so long since he's taken pleasure in cooking. The watch-like perfection of Jennifer's well stocked kitchen pleases some aspect of his former self. It reminds him of New York, he realizes—the pleasures of small restaurants. That life seems a century away. Yet, part of it has resuscitated, here in her kitchen. Ziq keeps an eye on the oven. Steamers billow. A television mumbles in the background. Domestic bliss, he thinks facetiously. His phone beeps. He glances at the intrusion pointedly. Then sets down some costly utensil, whose purpose he is still trying to fathom. A message from Jennifer reads:

DELAYD—BACK LATA X.

Ziq sets the phone down. He stares at all the bubbling pots.

They used to go to the Lexington for cocktails, in summer. The smoking lounge is all kidney coloured leather and gold highlights. A hundred cows died to furnish that room. Cigars fog the bar. A lost American digs through foreign papers with a vaguely hunted air. Anita and Jennifer take a booth beside some large windows overlooking the waterfront area. A soya macchiato hovers at Jennifer's hand. Anita nurses her second cognac, rambling on about logistics. Eventually she comes to her point:

'I've been lying to you.'

'Let me guess,' Jennifer sighs. 'You got tired of fleecing billionaires and got mixed up in something even shadier, which you then hid, in order to protect me.'

'You know me well, babe,' Anita smirks.

'…Except that you're telling me now. What—don't I deserve to be protected anymore?'

'It's not like that.'

'Maybe it is. Your timing for the big reveal couldn't be more perfect, wouldn't you say?'

'No, really…'

'Anyway, I don't want to know. I don't want to be involved. Just take me home, please.'

'Look, it wasn't my idea to involve you!'

Jennifer frowns.

'What do you mean? Whose idea was it?'

Anita glances around in paranoid fashion. She leans in over the table and speaks in a whisper.

'Ever wonder why Club Ded stays in production, even though it's tanking like a bitch?'

'Fuck sake, Anita! Who isn't wondering about that. What does that have to do with anything?'

Anita leans back heavily and lights another cigarette—her fifth since they arrived.

'Hitting those sticks pretty heavy, wouldn't you say?' Jennifer mentions.

Anita meets her gaze, but a fidgety anxiety clouds her eyes.

'Listen, Jen, before we go any further, there's something I need to tell you.'

'What?' Jennifer sighs.

'It's not that easy.'

'Why?'

'Because, right now—we are under surveillance.'

Jennifer blinks several times in non-comprehension. She looks around the near-empty establishment in disbelief.

'Right now?' Jennifer asks, incredulous.

'Yes.'

Knowing Anita well enough to realize that she is being serious, Jennifer leans over the low table.

'Are we in danger?' she whispers.

Anita meets her gaze for a moment. Her eyes are jittery with cocaine. She fumbles for her purse and extracts a neatly folded paper.

'Jen, this is going to sound ridiculous, but before I continue—I am going to need you to read what is on this paper—out loud.'

'Why?'

'It will act as a legal statement. It will be valid, since you are aware that you are being recorded.'

'What is it?'

'It's a non-disclosure agreement.'

Jennifer shakes her head.

'Enough cloak and dagger, Anita. Tell me what's going on now or I walk.'

Anita falters. She looks out across the dark waters, unable to meet Jennifer's gaze.

'You're not in danger, Jen,' she eventually admits. 'But I might be...'

'Oh Annie,' Jennifer murmurs.

She reaches out a hand to brush her friend's knee. Anita turns her head sharply, surprised by this sudden physical contact.

'Look, if you just read this…' Anita begins.

'I'm not reading anything!' Jennifer explodes. 'Tell me what the fuck is going on!'

'Not here.'

'Ok, where, then?'

'I suppose there is one place we can talk…'

Jennifer immediately begins to gathers her things.

'Let's go,' she snaps.

Anita signals for the tab. Something about the way she does it, makes Jennifer suspect that this was her plan all along.

They drive back toward Camps Bay, threading through the rickety neon signage of Seapoint. Chinese diners flash upside down in the wet street. Jennifer wonders how Anita managed to talk her into missing dinner.

'Are you honestly trying to tell me that people are listening in on us—now?' Jennifer scoffs.

'It's not like we are shielded,' is Anita's only response.

Jennifer looks sidelong at her. For some reason, it suddenly comes to her how many nights and days they have spent together. She begins to feel concerned.

'How much coke have you done?' Jennifer asks quietly.

'This is serious.'

'Why did you bring up the movie?'

'We need to get where we are going before I can explain.'

'Where *are* we going?' Jennifer laughs.

'Club Ded. We're going to Club Ded.'

They pass beyond Camps Bay and Brick's hotel. Skirting the dark foothills of the Twelve Apostle mountain range, they strike out in the direction of Cape Point. Where the two oceans merge. In a shadowy area, beneath towering rocks, Jennifer spots a glowing blue cube. The object suspends on an elevated spur of rock. Positioned on the side of the road, it overlooks the ocean. As Anita approaches, an armed guard shifts in silhouette. A mechanism recognizes the vehicle. One of the walls unravels along a seam. They drive into the cube. The car tilts down on a ramp, descending below the road level. A small but spacious parking area reveals itself. It's deserted. A space designed to accommodate at least four large vehicles. Red stripes neatly demarcate their areas. Anita parks within and kills the engine. At the top of the ramp, the cube reseals, cutting off all outside sound.

'Don't happen to have your passport?' Anita asks.

'Why would I?'

'ID?'

'Sure.'

'That should do—I have certain privileges.'

'Fuck are you on about?'

Anita thumbs a control affixed to her keys. Machinery responds with a subdued hum. The floor splits along the red line encircling the car. An elevator platform is revealed. Jennifer is caught by surprise when they begin to sink into the floor. Strips of lighting activate along the inside of the shaft.

'We'll be at the border soon,' Anita tells her. 'Surveillance is prohibited beyond that point.'

'Look...'

'There it goes.'

A thick, red line slips past. It has been emblazoned along the circumference of the wall in red enamel. Just as Jennifer is about to protest, the shaft ahead turns to glass. The elevator slips beneath the cowl of rock supporting the cube, A gigantic ocean vista dominates the view below. As the conveyance slips down the ragged line of a cliff, Jennifer cranes her head out of the window, trying to get a better look at the shoreline.

'Go on,' Anita prompts. 'It's safe.'

Jennifer pops her door. Gingerly cusping the front of the car, she stands in the narrow space between glass and bumper. Far below, on a rocky strand, she sees a compound of domes and interconnecting tubes. Beach dunes crescent the front. The back extends into a cavernous breach. The lighting scheme is overwhelmingly blue. Cool strip-glow encircles the architecture, filling the windows with water patterns. These frequencies play out onto surf and rock.

'I didn't even know there was a beach down here.'

Anita lights yet another cigarette. This time, however, she smokes contemplatively. She seems more relaxed.

'What is all this?' Jennifer asks, indicating the structures below.

'Club Ded.'

'Explain.'

Anita exhales smoke, gathering her thoughts.

'As you know, I brokered the land rentals for set building. I mean, at that time Croeser was locked up between production realities and his own grand vision...'

'I didn't know you dealt with him directly—didn't V beat you to that?' Jennifer quips.

'I lied.'

'I thought you two hated each other.'

'Maybe at first—later we cultivated that image.'

'Why?'

'Deflection.'

'Go on.'

'Let's rewind. Croeser had been developing Club Ded for over a decade. It was supposed to be a stand-alone film—totally divorced from the franchise. Not many people know that. There was only one problem.'

'What's that?'

'In the original script, Club Ded is an orbital pleasure isle—a kind of space station dedicated to hedonism. The original plot centered about sixty percent of the action there, while the rest took place on the planet below.'

'Ok.'

'Of course, Croeser, being the perfectionist that he is, wanted to shoot all Club Ded's sequences in actual zero gravity.'

'They capture zero-g in those nose-diving planes, right?'

'Oh, that wasn't good enough for Croeser. As real as the antigravity in those aircraft gets, their interiors are cramped. Simply not conducive to what he had in mind.'

'You're not going to tell me he's been shooting in outer space on the weekends?'

'The idea was tossed around.'

'Come on. The overheads would blitz costs.'

'Croeser had a trump—private investment from the Saudis. These crazy fuckers started talking about existent orbital platforms and modular add-ons to space hotels already under construction.'

'How'd that pan out?'

'Initially, everyone was excited, of course. Money was pouring in. Croeser's investors bought him a more powerful role in production. Even if they were able to capture ten to twenty percent of the shoot in an authentic anti-gravity back-lot, the powers that be were prepared to toe the line. At the very least, the film would set a production precedent. There was even talk of some marketing gimmick involving a co-production between the US, SA, KSA and free space. Complete bullshit, of course. But it looked good on paper…'

As they sink, Jennifer watches the blue tinged domes rise up to meet them. It isn't long until they are engulfed by chromium arches. The glass reverts to concrete. Jennifer climbs back into the car.

'I take it none of this space shit worked out?' she comments.

'It took a couple of months to sink in.'

'But Croeser wouldn't let go of his ace?'

'He had another idea to keep the Saudis in…'

Anita punctuates her cliffhanger by starting up the VISION NEXT. The platform comes to rest before a pair of hanger doors. They are in the process of opening. The car glides down the sloping tunnel beyond. It enters an expansive parking area, dotted here and there with luxury automobiles.

'What is Club Ded, exactly?' Jennifer frowns.

She eyes a nearby Lamborghini.

'I was just getting to that,' Anita comes back.

She parks in a deserted corner and kills the engine.

'Croeser had a crazy idea to sell the Saudi's on a second, secret Club Ded,' She explains. 'This film would be shot in tandem with the existent movie—completely up to spec with the original.'

Anita pulls out her kit. She prepares a line while she speaks.

'Croeser's plan was to shoot the secret picture with select members of his crew. His selling point was that it would have no rules and no rating—anything would go. The biggest hook, of course, was that Delilah would star in both.'

'Fuck.'

'So, he got her on smack, made her pliable. Of course, when I turned them onto the glands—the fish became Delilah's focus. By the time they started shooting, she was swimming twenty-four seven.'

'When did this go down?'

'About eight months ago.'

'Are you saying she's been doing glands all this time?'

'The legals are off the scale. Croeser managed to blind-side her representation and the producers. Still, they were playing a dangerous game. Their shenanigans placed the entire project in jeopardy. The insider crew shot some naughty weekends, mostly in beach houses I found for them. Croeser had ambitious plans for the unseen film, but without proper backing, it was deteriorating into a high-end sex tape.'

'Delilah went that far?'

'Oh, don't believe the hype—little miss Ariel crawled straight out of some degenerate LA rabbit hole. She made her chops long before she hit mermaid-ville. Course to Delilah, porn is some kind of fucked up, tantric spiritualism...'

'And you, Anita?' Jennifer asks coldly. 'What is it to you?'

'Retail.'

'Of course. How could I forget? So, I'm guessing that at some point during filming, you had some brainwave to expedite earnings?'

Anita smiles self-consciously. It's a strange and tender thing to see, but reminds Jennifer of their uncomfortable personal gridlock.

'You know me so well,' Anita admits.

She touches Jennifer's leg.

'What the fuck did you do?' Jennifer demands.

Anita gets a faraway look. She seems to disassociate. Like she did in the Lexington. Finally, she replies.

'Miss Lonelyhearts and I were hitting our stride. He was in on all the gossip, of course…'

'Of course.'

Anita does a line. She offers the compact to Jennifer, who refuses curtly.

'He mentioned this city-state he had set up in the nineties, somewhere in Eastern Europe. Friends of his used it to traffic out of the USSR.'

'What were they trafficking?'

'Does it matter?'

'At this point, I suppose not…'

'You'd be surprised how easy it is to set up a miniature, private country that is subject to its own laws and governance.'

'I'm sure anything is easy—if you have the cash and connections.'

'He gave me an idea. I remembered this particular compound. It had been on our list for years—abandoned. The original elevator mechanism dislodged, you see. There was a rock fall. It fell into the sea. No-one knew what to do with the place. It was going to be a marine sanctuary, but sea access was ruined by the avalanche. Since then, the property remained red-zoned.'

'Any other incidents with the rocks?'

'Nothing. Miss Lonelyhearts pulled some strings. We set the place up under diplomatic protection.'

'A realm?'

'A monarchy, to be precise—one that came with its own justice system, constitution and governance. We were able to offer Croeser unique co-production and a distribution deal.'

'How do you distribute an unrated, antigravity fuck-fest?'

'Through a billionaire old-boys network! Lonelyhearts loved the idea of a Hollywood blockbuster with no rules and he had friends who loved it too. His grapevine is pure peaches and platinum. Distro is miniscule in comparison to global numbers, but the projected earnings double the studio's best estimates.'

The coke has energized Anita. She behaves as though confined, playing with her door handle. Jennifer, however, isn't ready to leave.

'Surely it's illegal?' she asks.

'Not here. Not in the realm. That's what our co-production deal offered: complete, lawless creative freedom. I mean, the second picture will never go public. You have to understand that right off. It's targeted to tiny market of uber-wealthy freaks.'

'And production went in for this lunacy?'

'Not officially. But on the back-end, the secret movie was green-lighted with all the frills. Of course, that was when the real problems began…'

'Croeser?'

'I'm telling you, as soon as I threw him the bone, he became my bitch. What film director is going to turn down total creative freedom and unlimited funds?'

'So, where's the problem? It all sounds perfect.'

'Croeser started to focus almost exclusively on the unseen picture. The official version went to the dogs. Of course, the studio made sure that he was contractually obligated to deliver a sellable release—to justify the risk. Everyone needed a legal earner that looked good on paper. You can understand that. Back-end returns wouldn't make it through tax. We all needed a show to bury proceeds in.'

'So Croeser calls in Brick Bryson.'

'A calculated risk—fan response alone will revitalize the picture.'

'I heard he has real talent.'

'He's a washed up drunk. But maybe he's hungry. We believe that he can bring in the wagon.'

'So, you're a movie producer now as well?'

'Hardly. Though, I have sway.'

'Come up in the world, haven't you?'

Anita finally opens her door.

'Let me show you how far.'

Jennifer sighs, relents, follows her out. They cross the lot, approaching another glowing cube. A lurid sign: 'Customs'. Anita invites Jennifer to go ahead. A portal irises open. Passing through a magnetic tunnel, they emerge at a check point. A single desk dominates the space. A uniformed official looks up sharply. Gas-masked guards man the entrance. They wear riot gear, hefting Japanese stun-rifles. Everyone salutes when Anita crosses the threshold. Jennifer is impressed. The customs official signals.

'Passport?'

'She only has her ID,' Anita intervenes.

'I'm sure that we can accommodate, majesty.'

'*Majesty?*' Jennifer sneers.

Met by frosty stares, she surrenders her ID. Three uniformed valets enter while the official processes her document. One ferries a tall, fairy crown. Set on a rich purple cushion. The second valet transports a fur-trimmed cape. The third an emerald-tipped silver scepter. They dress their queen. Jennifer watches. The spectacle disturbs her. When they are done, Anita beckons. The pair pass through another electric gateway, entering unexpectedly into a sushi restaurant.

'You've got to be kidding,' Jennifer mutters.

The establishment has only one table. Set with thimble-cups and porcelain chopsticks. A chef nods, already preparing their repast.

'Sit,' Anita commands.

Her vestments lend her a somewhat imperious tone. It amuses Jennifer. She glimpses a tank of blue and yellow fish. The function of the eatery suddenly reveals itself.

'I'm not getting high Anita, forget it.'

'It's the law.'

'So, you're the fucking queen. Change the law.'

'Sit. Let me explain.'

Jennifer reluctantly joins her at the table.

'You know how these suicide pills have changed things,' Anita says. 'They've transformed our lives.'

Jennifer can't stop staring at her Disney villain crown.

'Ok, I agree with that,' she admits.

'Don't you see what I've done? I've built a temple to them. This is the real thing, Jen. For years we thought we were saving the world—all those death letters and cookies. But the fish really do represent the divine. You see that, don't you? Maybe they can really make a difference—Certainly more than some third-eyed psycho on a Bitcoin pillar. You have to see this with me. You have to see what I've done. It's so special—You have to!'

Jennifer chews her lip. Behind the counter, the sushi chef smiles. He flips blades with consummate skill.

'I can't believe I am actually listening to this shit,' she flusters.

'Yes, you can,' Anita presses, taking her hand.

Somewhere along the line, she has managed to draw on arm-length velvet gloves. It's all a bit much.

'Can't I just wait in the car?' Jennifer pleads.

'I'll make you wait for hours,' Anita grins playfully.

'Oh, fuck it,' Jennifer moans.

As though on cue, the chef arrives with two plates and a ceramic pot of tea. The plates have been dressed neatly with their psychedelic maki. Herby paste laces them.

'So, Fortunato is in on this?' Jennifer asks, staring at her food.

'Oh him,' Anita sighs. 'No, Croeser had the trannie steal some fish. We cultivated them.'

'What? How'd she manage that?'

'*He* knows where the breeding tanks are—managed to slip some fry past the gate.'

'What about the medicinal plants to accompany the dosage? You can't just fuck around with this shit, Anita.'

'Oh, Trill is a cunning little monkey—Knows exactly where Fortunato stashes the aquaponics. What you think is in the secret sauce?'

Jennifer stares down at the gourmet edition of her suicide pills.

'He's a good guy, Anita. It's not fair to cut him out. He found these things and bred them. If anyone was responsible for spreading the gospel, as it were—its Fortunato.'

'He doesn't even have a passport!'

Jennifer glares at her.

'Ok, look we'll throw him some cash.'

'That's not the point. I mean, if anyone is going to understand what you are doing here, it's him…'

'Oh, please. This is a unique market and I cornered it. That's all there is to it.'

'I thought it was a sacred mission.'

'…say's the Oracle Inc. employee.'

'Don't be a bitch.'

'I said we would throw him some cash. Now eat.'

'I'm not eating.'

But even as the words leave her mouth, Jennifer knows that, within moments, she will.

The fish tastes bitter. But the herbs help. Jennifer realizes that she has never taken the glands raw. Usually the effects take an hour to manifest. But ten minutes in and she is already feeling a buzz. Anita snorts a couple more lines. She is talking non-stop.

'…So, we got the tank system for the marine sanctuary up and running. The idea was to shoot the zero-g scenes underwater. It gave Croeser flexibility. He could script a more complex narrative. But Delilah started taking strain. Not only was she working on psychedelics—now she was being asked to do it all underwater.'

'She walked?'

'She threatened—Croeser had to keep it under the counter. If word got out, the project would dissolve. Then various military organizations tuned in.'

'The fuck?'

'It's big budget Hollywood, Jen. Defense interests are always in the mix.'

'I didn't realize…'

'There's this new thing called Google.'

'Funny.'

'Commercial movies are a perfect testing ground.'

'For what?'

'For tech, for everything…Budgets can be merged easily. Everything siphons through an established base—get the picture?'

'Ja, ok.'

'Various powers were quick to set up consulates in the Queendom.'

'Queendom, now is it?'

204

'…US interests had been pushing from day one, but Croeser was holding out for creative insulation. When Delilah started getting antsy, they zeroed in on the bubble problem…'

'The bubble problem?'

'Bubbles Jen, fucking bubbles! When you are shooting underwater and trying to make it look like anti-grav, there's going to be bubbles—a fuck-ton of bubbles.'

'But that's ridiculous.'

'No. That's a time consuming, multi-million dollar problem! You know how long it takes to remove bubbles in post?'

'Makes sense, I suppose.'

'So, their affiliates had this crystal—originally developed in Denmark. It's some organic cobalt compound—can store vast amounts of oxygen. Originally, they wanted to release the oxygen through heat application, in combination with various trace metals. Military refined the process. The material was adapted to be photosensitive. Now breathable air can be released with light. A delivery device was also constructed so oxygen could be harvested directly from prepared water. It gives the mouthpiece an indefinite yield.'

'Fuck you say!'

'I thought you would like that.'

'So, the cast is breathing underwater? I can't believe it. That's fucking fab!'

As the words leave her mouth, Jennifer realizes that she is experiencing a little too much euphoria at the concept. Not that breathing underwater doesn't excite her.

'You should try it,' Anita smiles slyly.

Jennifer stands up in shock. Light trails holographically after her.

Drowner

Staggering down half-lit corridors. Walls shimmer with aquatic dissonance. Channels gutter the mazy passages. Their flow of crystal water interrupts Jennifer's balance. A detail of gas-masked guards flanks them. On either side. Originally, Jennifer had considered this chaperoning a queenly extravagance. Distant screams force her to reconsider.

'Have to stop at the bank,' Anita informs her.

They detour down a sloping ramp. Signage illuminates the bottom region. A medical glow. Mall-friendly tellers orbit behind bullet-proof glass. Jennifer collapses, vomiting sushi into the running water. Blue and yellow fish dart through the flow, avoiding the chewed up remains of their brethren. Anita withdraws sack after sack of pure gold coins. She kneels down to show Jennifer one. Her profile frescoes the money. The guards take the sacks on belt-riven hooks. Jennifer touches Anita's coin-face.

'That's not chocolate,' she finally manages.

As she is assisted to her feet, the screams grow louder. They enter a space littered with half-destroyed sex robots. Nubile limbs invent abstract patterns. Some twitch. A ginger haired man crouches in the half-dark. All he wears is a pair of designer running shoes. An aluminium baseball bat is clutched to his chest. He sobs uncontrollably. Jennifer recognizes him from television. He's an Olympic athlete. The guards switch to stun. The man's head lights up with laser tracers. Anita dances forward, trying to provoke him. If anything, the athlete is terrified by her antics. He squats in his own excrement, howling like a baby. Jennifer takes the opportunity to lie down on the tiles. Her ear flattens against the cool, ceramic surface. A flash of light catches her eye. The head of a sex doll is lies nearby. Also on its side. Its neck has been cleft, raggedly. Black fluid spurts from internal piping, puddling the area. A sensor in the face registers Jennifer's presence. A silvery eye begins to wink repeatedly. Sleek lips auto-gloss. They mouth words. Anita tires of her teasing. She signals to the guards. Soft, cold robot fingers find Jennifer's hand. She experiences a phobic shudder. The disembodied hand links fingers with her. A plastic thumb traces circles along her palm. It's not unpleasant.

As she is hauled up by a guard, Jennifer holds fast to the friendly hand. Despite her best efforts, she loses her grip along the way. The hand scuttles off. She is surprised to hear herself calling for it.

The interior is riddled with a bewildering array of ornamental water features. The ceilings and walls are diseased by shifting reflections. Minimalist white furniture cascades geometrically. Blue light dominates. Jennifer is full of helium. She floats through these rooms. She is reminded of aquariums. Where all the fish disappear overnight—due to a single, thoughtless predatory addition. Anita is in her element. She shows off her realm with grand gestures. At one point, they enter a space crowded with men. Jennifer is surprised (or perhaps unsurprised) to discover Chloe tending bar. In one of the sunken lounges. She wants to approach her. But some unspoken protocol prevents them from exchanging more than a quick nod. Maybe it's the glands, Jennifer reasons. She suspects that it's more a case of her being in the Queen's company. Chloe is hired help tonight. This is Anita's world. Her rules. Jennifer nervously eyes the patrons, unsure of her role. The Queen moves amongst them, accepting kisses and expensive gifts. She palms these offerings onto her security detail, who log and stow them. Trill is also present. The creature is comatose, sprawled across a minty couch in a black bikini. Jennifer notices that Trill's skin is uniformly slick. Some kind of blue, gelatinous coating. The gleaming gel encases the creature's face. Leaks in tentacles from its nose and mouth, collecting across the tiles. Jennifer is about to investigate, when Anita pulls her into the company of men.

For a while its chaos. But within twenty minutes, the place has emptied. Jennifer finds herself cornered against the bar. A couple of tuxedoed men won't leave her alone. Behind them, Chloe constructs an endless succession of fancy drinks and narcotics. Earlier, she'd the presence of mind to pass something to Jennifer. A rice cracker—buttered heavily with herbal paste. This temporarily muted the effect of the glands. Jennifer is able to recover her state of mind for a moment. Anita has gone in the other direction. She's lost her top, is giggling hysterically. Her crown is on the bar. Robe and scepter thrown across a nearby chair. A brand-new diamond choker bisects her throat. At the rate she is going, it will be ruined before the hour is through. The longer the girls tarry, the closer the men hem them in. A dance of predatory birds. The shorter tuxedo calls himself Squee. He sports a well-groomed flabbiness. And, although magnificently drunk, manages to remain erudite. His friend, Bex, is a little more disturbing. Bex is absurdly tall. Perhaps seven foot five. He wears a West African mask. All night, he's failed to utter anything more coherent than grunts and gurgles. None of the girls have seen his face. At one point, Jennifer attempts to quiz Anita. She wants to know how a character like Bex managed to pass customs. Anita brushes the question off. According to Squee, Bex is an expert free-climber and spelunker. Certainly, his enormous frame suggests a dedication to the conquest of nature's most inaccessible places. The third player is Saud. He sits aside, observing. He has not consumed anything more intoxicating than clove cigarettes and civet coffee. His suited valet accompanies him, at a remove. The taciturn man wears impenetrable sunglasses, carries a bulky briefcase. Does not speak. Another Oracle girl appeared at one point. Moving in the night. An old man pursued her. Jennifer watched her flee to a glowing pool. Their laughter still drifts through the bracing air.

'Bex and I used to throw liquid nitrogen parties in Montevideo,' Squee confides. 'You get a load of the stuff and drop animals in.'

'Oh my God, that's disgusting!' Anita ejaculates.

Squee blows smoke across her breasts. Saud smiles appreciatively. Jennifer finds herself humoring the men against her will. It's a kind of preprogrammed geisha reflex. Triggered and spurred on by Anita's ruthless competition for attention. Jennifer's irritation is growing. It smashes against the expanding narcotic.

'You see,' Squee explains. 'The trick with a liquid nitrogen party is to hold it at a great height. Top of a cliff or something. Because then you see... you can drop the beasts off the end! They shatter like glass. Extraordinary thing...'

Bex begins to laugh. The first remotely human noise Jennifer has heard him has utter. It does little to soften him. Jennifer watches the wooden mask jerk. Up and down.

'You gentlemen are to be commended for your creativity!' Saud chuckles. 'I have seen many unbelievable things done to a sheep. But never have I seen one shattered like a porcelain ornament!'

'The animals were Bex's idea,' Squee admits. 'I just wanted to freeze automobile parts and flowers. Never thought to drop a sheep in there...'

He trails off, gazing myopically at Anita's pale breasts. Abruptly, he drains his champagne, setting a Montecristo between his teeth.

'Of course, it's simply a matter of quantity isn't it,' he mutters.

Bex lets out a deafening shriek. He jerks his limbs about, 'playing savage'. Anita responds. Uncontrollable laughter.

'Quantity really is everything these days,' Saud agrees, politely applauding Bex's antics. One of his manicured hands fondles Jennifer's hair. The physical contact shocks her from her cocoon of introspection. She freezes. The Arab's hand migrates down her side. It settles at her hip. Somehow, Anita's protocols still immobilize her. She looks to her friend for support. But she is oblivious. Anita has now joined Bex. Jennifer watches her kick off her heels, mount a table. Bex smashes something else. Saud sidles closer. His smell of mint and roses comes sharply into focus.

'Are you an actress, my dear?'

Jennifer motions to Anita. She waves her away.

'I'm not an actress,' Jennifer complains.

Saud's thumb explores her navel. Squee is observing closely. Somehow, Anita comes to her senses. She approaches, removes the Arab's hand from Jennifer's stomach.

'Jennifer is not here to play,' she scolds. 'She is my very, very special guest...'

'Of course,' Saud bows.

He smiles pungently at Jennifer. She raises a glass in a kind of ceasefire.

'Well at least it is possible to observe the observer observing...' Squee rambles.

He takes a belt of whiskey. Then smiles viciously.

'Why don't you get your skirt off so we can observe you better,' he leers up at Jennifer.

This catapults Bex into another frenzy. A globe of coldness opens somewhere in Jennifer's stomach. A drop too much of power play— suddenly she is lost in the wild wood. Fear allows the glands to reassert. All the colours fizz and shift. Jennifer is about to say something. Squee hurls his tumbler against a wall. It explodes. Jennifer flinches. Fragments snag her hair. She catches Chloe's worried eye. Saud applauds the breakage. He is studying Jennifer as one might study a pinned insect. Jennifer forces another polite smile. She grabs Anita's arm. But Anita is doubled over with uncontrollable laughter. She falls to her knees.

'Can I talk to you, Annie?' Jennifer stammers through a forced and broken smile.

Anita chokes. She emits a series of guttural, hyena-like coughs before doubling over. Squee shows a wide, wet smile. The men have tuned into Jennifer's discomfort, sensing opportunity.

'I'm sure that whatever you have to say, you can say in front of us, my dear,' Saud reassures her.

'We know how to keep secrets, down here in Clubby Deddy,' Squee nods, red-faced.

Bex suddenly staggers. He trips over a coffee table. Smashing it under patent leather shoes. Jennifer observes with escalating panic. Chloe also watches. Clearly plotting something. The Arab gently takes Jennifer's arm.

'I would really like to see you act,' he tells her. 'I think you have ability.'

'I have to leave,' Jennifer replies.

'You do have a certain cinematic appeal,' Squee murmurs. 'It's a spot-lit sort of charm. Like a snowball in the oven...'

Jennifer sidles out of Saud's grasp. She attempts to drag Anita up. The men watch, offering no assistance. Bex, his attention by now diverted, lurches off again. Unbuckling his trousers, he emits more shrieks and ape-like grunts. He hefts Trill's slippery body around. But the creature slides from his grasp, like a heavy fish. It cracks head and limb against edged surfaces. Slipping across the floor.

'I would be more than willing to finance your acting career,' Saud continues.

Anita appears to surface. She comes back to the bar, red-eyed, grinning. The mention of money adds a bitter patina to her mirth. Neutralizes her back to her machine-like self.

'It's true,' Squee agrees, lending support to the proposition. 'I've known Fazil, or whatever his name is, for years. His word is as good as gold.'

'He certainly is good as gold...' Anita slurs.

She hooks an arm around Jennifer, attempting to launch her bodily at the men. Squee flicks one of Anita's nipples while she is distracted. The queen cackles, overbalances, pulls Jennifer down to the floor with her.

'I have to go,' Jennifer sobs, struggling up again.

'Perhaps we could arrange a little screen test?' the Arab suggests. 'I could compensate you in advance.'

He gestures. The valet produces an envelope.

'Ten thousand pounds,' the Arab announces. 'I'm told you Oracle ladies prefer sterling.'

He winks at Squee, who sniggers at Jennifer's numbed expression. The shock of money reminds her of a freshly picked flower. Something that remains fresh and bright—even though it has been severed permanently from its body. Bex penetrates Trill from behind. But the creature begins to slide. Mollusc-like, along the slab-like couch, leaving blue, sticky trails. Eventually, at the apex of particularly savage thrust, Bex loses traction. Trill slithers loose. It slides a couple of meters across the floor, slamming head first into a wall. A thin trickle of blood exits the creature's hair. The fluid travels throughout the gel in a tendril. The impact has finally awakened it. Trill lifts its head, cat-like. It spews translucent blue jelly down its front. Anita nuzzles at Jennifer's cheek with a moist nose.

'Croeser thinks you're a dead ringer for Delilah from the back...'

Jennifer can't seem to pull her eyes from the envelope.

'Take it,' Anita hisses.

'I don't quite understand what it is that you...' she fumbles.

'It's really quite simple,' Saud explains, as though to a child. 'I am offering you this small token in return for a screen test—something that will probably benefit you greatly in the long run.'

'When is this even supposed to happen?' Jennifer protests weakly.

'It could happen right now.'

Anita slides her tongue into Jennifer's mouth. The sensation reflexively shuts her eyes. There in the dark, Jennifer's fingers close around the envelope.

Now they are back in the long, white corridors. Men in riot gear flank them. Physical movement has diminished the effects of the herb paste. Jennifer is falling back to the blue zone. Trill leads the way. Marching like a zombie. Leaking gel everywhere. Jennifer is confused. How is the creature breathing? It sucks gel back and forth—from its lungs. Coughing up an excess every now and then. Gruesome gurgles. The group pass several checkpoints. Eventually, they emerge into a large laboratory space. Machinery hums everywhere. White coated technicians move amongst the hardware. Jennifer collapses against a console. Dizzy spells. She notices Croeser and his white-gloved DOP, Luther. They study dailies. A wall of screens. Man-size glass pods line the walls. Each is filled to capacity with translucent blue gel. Trill makes for the nearest pod, is accosted by technicians. They activate a small, rubberized metal brace. Insert it into Trill's open mouth. Light flares brightly behind the creature's teeth. Its head is illuminated redly from within.

'He's doing the oxygen business now,' Anita informs Jennifer.

Croeser notices the girls. Smiling broadly, he makes his way over. The technicians assist Trill up a ladder—to a hatch in the crown of the pod. The airlock opens with a hiss of hydraulics. Within moments, the creature is in the gel capsule. It floats in suspension, relaxing its posture. Like some sort of monstrous frog, Jennifer watches the creature flex its jaw. She realizes it's sucking the glutinous substance into its lungs. The mouth-brace flares on each intake. Its light fades with each breath. Until a steady threshold of oxygenation is achieved. Jennifer becomes aware of large hands. They reach under her skirt, grasping each of her buttocks firmly. She feels them being spread and winces.

'I'm so glad you could join us,' Croeser smiles.

Jennifer tries to struggle. But her muscles are weak, non-responsive. She drapes heavily across the hardware. Croeser moves his hands up to her breasts.

'Dead ringer,' Anita slurs.

Croeser shoots her an irritated look.

'Thanks for delivering.'

'Thank you, *your highness!*' Anita shouts at the top of her lungs.

Everyone in the room looks up. Croeser releases Jennifer. He flushes red with fury. Then strides back to the wall of screens. Luther observes their exchange with an amused expression. One of the technicians takes Jennifer's arm. He wears latex gloves, with the air of a medical student. Security tags announce some kind of military clearance.

'How do you feel?' he asks Jennifer—a modulated Bostonian twang. He inspects her corneas with a pencil torch.

Jennifer has trouble vocalizing. They get her onto what looks like a dentist couch. They begin strapping her down.

'It's quite normal to panic first-time round,' the technician informs her.

Everything he says has the quality of being rehearsed. As though he were reading off a tele-prompt. Anita attempts to massage Jennifer's shoulders. She knocks a tray of delicate instruments to the floor. The technicians ignore her, recovering their goods without comment. Once Jennifer has been completely secured, one of the technicians taps for a vein. An IV is inserted. Jennifer barely registers it.

'You might feel a little sting,' the Bostonian informs Jennifer blankly. 'We are giving you an electrolyte booster. It assists in the oxygenation process. Nod if you understand.'

Jennifer is past nodding. She stares up at the technician with dilated pupils. The man looks to Anita.

'You sure about this?' he asks.

'Just fucking do her,' Anita slurs.

Another technician produces papers, which Anita manages to sign. A table of hardware and insulated piping is wheeled to the couch. The technicians get Jennifer's limp mouth open. They insert one of the rubberized braces. As her teeth make contact with the bite-ring, the device lights up.

'Now, this next part might seem a little disturbing,' the technician prattles on. 'But you will you be in no physical danger. You have my assurance.'

'Hurry it up,' Anita complains.

The technician glances at her, but continues his patter.

'We have to flood your lungs with carrier fluid. The device in your mouth will trigger a timed slow-release oxygenation process within the medium. You may experience panic, feel that you are drowning etcetera—this is all quite normal. The important thing to remember is that you are perfectly safe.'

Jennifer drools, blinking away tears. The man signals his colleague, who preps a large, bubble helmet. The headpiece is linked, via a complex plumbing system, to tanks and an operating console. They slip the fishbowl over Jennifer's head. Careful to keep her hair from snagging in the pressure seal. Automated locks click green. The seal is secure. Jennifer's ears pop lightly as the interior pressurizes. A machine starts to chug, removing the air incrementally. She experiences something like bathwater beneath her chin. The body temperature gel inches pleasantly up her throat. Beyond the glass of her helmet—an array of faces, observing her closely. When the gel spills into her mouth, she begins to struggle. When it covers her nose, she panics. Somebody injects her thigh.

'It's just a light muscle relaxant,' the technician's voice explains her blandly, via radio earpiece. 'We can't give you too much. It can interfere with intercostals and diaphragmatic action.'

Jennifer flusters, chokes. Eventually the gel blurs over her eyes and she drowns.

Jennifer wakes up in crystalline water. She hangs suspended. In the center of a long, smooth-walled white tank. The area is illuminated by strips of cool blue. The layout of the tank is similar to the halls and corridors of the compound. It confuses her. Snatches of blue glare travel across her naked body. She realizes she is moving slightly—shifting in a barely perceptible flow. Fascinated, she raises water-paled hands. Strangely, they are perfectly un-blurred. As though she were wearing goggles. Her eyes feel strange. She must have been fitted with contact lenses. She is breathing lightly, reflexively. But her lungs are congested. They feel as though they are full of phlegm. Despite this Jennifer isn't at all short of breath. She puts her fingers in her mouth. Finds a metal device.

'Do you see the hole?' Anita's voice comes suddenly into her left ear.

Jennifer spins in shock. Only to realize that she is wearing some kind of glass earplug.

'Do you see the hole?' Anita repeats.

Jennifer looks around, hair swirling. She eventually spots the entrance. A shaft, far below. In the floor of the tank.

'Do you see the hole?'

Jennifer nods slowly.

'Go into the hole.'

Jennifer flips lightly. She fins downward with slow, strong strokes. Somehow, being underwater makes the psychedelic effect of the glands more natural. In fact, the narcotic seems to only enhance her subaqueous awareness and capability. Catching a glint of movement, Jennifer stops abruptly. A long, mirrored window stripes the mid-point of the tank's right wall. Jennifer swims slowly toward it. Eventually, she makes out the silhouettes of a camera crew. They track her as she floats.

'Go into the hole,' Anita repeats.

Confused, Jennifer obeys. The tunnel quickly becomes claustrophobic. She feels as though she should be panicking. Being trapped underwater like this. Eventually, however, the tunnel loops into another tank. This area is massive. Brightly illuminated by racks of lighting. When Jennifer's eyes adjust, she sees that she is somehow floating above an impossibly vast, mechanical city.

'It's just a cyclorama,' Anita sighs. '…A set. Here's Croeser.'

The microphone rustles as Anita switches channels.

'Hi Jennifer! Delaney Croeser here. Nod for me if you are feeling ok.'

Jennifer processes this. She nods slowly.

'Great. Now listen, honey. The cameras are positioned directly behind you—around the shaft you entered from. No, don't look! Good. Ok, now, do you think you could you swim slowly toward the city, without turning back? We just want to shoot a test from the back.'

Jennifer nods slowly.

'Thing is,' Croeser continues. 'I want you to imagine that you are in an air-filled room. I know that sounds confusing, but what I mean is— can you propel yourself forward without using any kind of recognizable stroke? The Queen here tells me that you're a wonderful swimmer…'

Jennifer nods slowly, entranced by the images of vast machines below her. As though reading her mind, Croeser says:

'It's a visual trick honey—the city set is in fact not below you, but directly ahead.'

Once again, Jennifer nods.

'Alright then, sweetheart—action!'

Jennifer begins to fan her hips and shoulders, traveling forward slowly.

In the control room, Luther checks her progress through several camera positions. Satisfied, he turns and gives Croeser a nod.

'Think she could fill in the gaps?' Croeser asks.

'I can make it work,' Luther replies.

Croeser turns to Anita, who has collapsed drunkenly across a couch.

'Thank you, *your highness*,' he says with a little bow.

Anita is still topless. Her face is a mess. Somehow, the crown manages to stay on her head.

'Don't hurt her, asshole,' Anita sneers.

Croeser smiles accommodatingly.

'I don't think you need any help with that one,' he replies curtly, returning to the screens before Anita has a chance to retaliate.

The Early Bird Catches the Worm

Brick's alarm wakes him at 4am. He's still naked. Somehow, he'd ended up video-calling Alix. One thing led to another. It couldn't have been more than two hours ago. *She could still be awake,* the inner voice smirks. Flicking on the bedside lamp, Brick reaches for a print-out of his screenplay changes. Suddenly he remembers the bottle of Scotch. It lies shattered on the floor. He'd forgotten about that. The room is heady with the smell of spilled whiskey. He's still a little tipsy. A couple gallons of water will take care of that. Pulling on a jacket, he readies himself for his conference call with Luminstein, Croeser and Sal Stark. They are on LA time to suit Luminstein's schedule. Hopefully no-one will ask him to stand up during the conversation. Sal comes up first on the four-way split. The conversation has been tabled as a 'meet and greet', so Brick expects to get between two to three minutes to confirm his credit. Croeser pops up with a long white terrace behind him. Shane Luminstein's face is younger than Brick expected. *Fresh out of the shark infested custard.* Sal introduces them briefly.

'Hi Shane.'

'Actually, we've met,' Luminstein grins toothily. 'My husband Carl knows your Lisa-Marie from that crystal healing center in Santa Monica. We bumped into you guys at the Farmer's Market, about a year and a half ago.'

Brick see's where he's going and decides to nip it in the bud.

'Let me guess—I was blind drunk.'

Luminstein blinks but doesn't drop the smile.

'I hate to say it, but…' he begins.

'You try being directed by Delaney Croeser and not turning to drink,' Brick cuts in suavely.

Luminstein skips a beat. Croeser comes in hard with a belly laugh.

'Damn, buddy,' the director chortles.

Luminstein decides to drop the pleasantries.

'So, Brick, we understand that you have an issue about a co-directing credit?'

'Why don't you take this one, Mo?' Brick replies curtly.

Croeser falters. Clearly, he had been expecting to watch the conversation play out from the sidelines.

'Shane, I've already sent you a memo. I have an idea as to how we can structure the contract. I think you'll find everything still tilts in our favour.'

'And I can expect this paperwork later today?' Sal interjects, still smirking at Brick's joke.

'Sure,' Luminstein nods.

He checks his mail off-screen.

'Ok, I see the memo,' the producer confirms.

He scans through it quickly.

'Right,' he nods 'Ok, I see. So, we are 'go' on this, Delaney?'

Croeser nods. Luminstein shines out a reassuring, somewhat robotic smile.

'Then it's all systems go, guys,' he confirms. 'We'll send the paperwork over asap.'

Somehow Brick expected more of a fight. Sal is impressed.

'Just a formality, but I'm thinking of popping over to give everything a once-over,' Luminstein adds unexpectedly.

'When?' Croeser frowns, clearly taken by surprise.

'I'll be there in two days.'

'Suit yourself,' the director gruffs.

'Let's talk on safari. Brick. When last did you see a lion in the wild?'

Now Brick is frowning.

'I don't think I've ever seen a lion, Shane,' he replies warily.

'There's a worst time for everything,' Luminstein winks—cutting off.

'Wasn't that one of your lines from Game Over?' Sal asks.

Croeser shakes his head in annoyance.

'I'll call you later, Brick,' He says.

Brick is about to ask him something, but Croeser has already gone.

'Well that went well,' Sal shrugs.

'Too well.'

'Hey, don't kick a gift horse in the teeth—mister co-director of a major studio picture. This is a big score, no matter which way the boat rocks.'

'We'll see.'

'So, what are you going to wear on safari? We need some publicity stills of you and *Gimme Mo…*'

Brick groans.

Croeser deactivates his pad in irritation.

'Another fucking safari,' he mutters.

The director glances out at the cold, dark sea. Blue light oils the water. A sulphuric stench of spawning kelp. Black, tentacular masses, rotting along the beach. Somehow, they suit the place. Replacing his device, Croeser crosses the wide terrace. He re-enters Club Ded through a different set of doors. Beyond the glass is a large, dim chamber. Dominated by a circular bed. Croeser can just make out Jennifer. She is on her knees and elbows. Throwing up clumps of bright blue jelly. Saud and Anita are also present. Unclothed and bickering. In the half-dark. Saud is attempting to pull on a white toweling bathrobe. He is complaining, a blue-gel slap mark on his face. Croeser exits quickly. The movement distracts Anita. Saud takes the opportunity to scoop his gold cigarette case and decamp to the terrace. Anita checks on Jennifer. Then follows him out. She finds Saud smoking at the edge. Wiping gel from his beard with the edge of his collar. Dawn pales the sky behind the mountain. She activates some floor-level illumination. The whole area lights up like a spaceship, irritating Saud further.

'You have no idea what you are doing, do you?' he snaps. 'What kind of brothel are you running here?'

'It is *not* a brothel, you patriarchal cunt,' Anita snaps.

Saud blinks a few times, absorbing the remark. Remembering his manners, he offers the open case to her.

'Cigarette?'

For a moment, it looks as though she is going to punch him. But she accepts one and allows him to light it. She leans against the chilly wall, winding a goose-fleshed arm around her bare midriff. She looks exhausted. Bloodless in the blue light.

'I apologize,' Saud says. 'Of course, this is not a brothel.'

The smoke causes Anita to cough up a mouthful of gel. She spits it over the edge. Saud observes in distaste.

'Perhaps that's the charm of this place,' he muses. 'There are no rules. It's just a place—a place outside of things.'

'Look, I'm also sorry—for my friend's behavior.'

It's a business-like apology. The board-room tone amuses him.

'Clearly you have not had enough practice being a queen. A queen has no need of apologies.'

She looks away, annoyed at the rebuke.

'In fact,' Saud smiles. 'An apology under these circumstances might imply a service unfulfilled...'

'Now listen...'

'All I am suggesting—as a friend, is that you consider the reality of your situation.'

Now he too becomes serious.

'You have had your fun, Anita. And I've certainly supported your wonderful reign. But make no mistake—this is a fairy palace. It will turn to smoke.'

She stares at him for a moment, hesitating.
'Get out now,' he re-iterates. 'While you still can.'
'This is *my* house,' she declares firmly.
As she marches off, Saud begins to laugh.

Dawn finds a chink in the drapes. A television mumbles. Ziq wakens.
Peering slowly about, on the couch. He switches off the television.
Jennifer's apartment is silent. Apparently deserted. Confused, he rises.
Shuffles down a nearby corridor. The fall of morning light bleaches the
bathroom. Somehow, it enhances the coldness of the tiles. Ziq runs
the faucet. He begins to sluice water over his hands and face. Glancing
up into the mirror, he realizes that Jennifer is lying, still clothed, in a
tub full of water. He spins, his heart stammering with shock. The bath
has long since cooled. Its water encapsulates her like glass. Ziq calms
quickly in the sterile atmosphere. Stillness reasserts itself. He blinks in
incomprehension, wiping his face on the back of his hand. Jennifer's
eyes are half-lidded. She gazes at the taps in a dazed fashion. Ziq leans
back against the sink, trying to make sense of the situation. The water
has flattened the darkness of her clothes and shoes. It lends her a two-
dimensional quality. When she finally turns to face him, he notices that
something else is out of place. A black leather satchel is beside the bath.
Unzipping it, he finds crisp pound notes. Dense bundles. Reaching in,
he fingers a handful of the cash, bewildered. Her face remains mask-
like. Even though she has begun to cry. Ziq sits on the edge of the bath,
listening to her. The sound fills the room. Vague snatches of a recent
dream come to him. After a while he gets up and leaves the bathroom.
He takes his coat from a hook and checks that all the phones are in his
pockets. He then exits the apartment, closing the door quietly behind
him. When Jennifer hears the soft click, she heaves a long, reptilian sob
across the surface of the water. Slipping her head under, she accidentally
inhales. Comes up choking.

By midday, Jennifer Beckett seems vague to Ziq. She is like the
dream he was trying to recall. The week-end feels like it had happened
weeks, even months ago. He is certain that he won't see her again. He
doesn't think about it. He can't quite locate the apparatus required to
form an opinion. That part of him is cauterized—by the black bag. To
Ziq, such a large amount of money could only signify catastrophe. He
avoids town. Sticking to the fringe. He picks pockets compulsively. The
world empties like a sink. Even Jaybird seems to have vanished. Ziq
goes through the motions of his processing-plant. But abandons it all
half-way. Wandering up towards the Deli, he drifts listlessly through
pretty suburbs, gazing up at the Shark Fin. The sun sluices lightly down.
Through blooming Jacarandas, hypnotizing him. The street appears

oddly familiar. Remembering a jasmine bush, he now recalls. Jaybird had brought him here a week or two ago. The memory refreshes his sense of direction. He drifts to the end of the street. A large 'FOR SALE' sign has been planted. The house advertised is a pretty gingerbread thing. Neat hedgerows and a lemon tree. Shoulder-high razor-wire packages it neatly. Glancing to and fro, Ziq scales a brick wall. Vaulting the wire, he slips around the back of the house. The sound of a radio seeps from next door. A ginger cat watches nervously. He finds a partially jimmied window and slides it up. The window's burglar-guard has been unscrewed. It lies on the floor of the room within. Slipping in, he secures the window behind him. The house is bare. Empty rooms lead into one another, producing unnatural acoustics. Ziq finds Jaybird in the lounge. He is curled in a filthy sleeping bag, snoring. Hundreds of bird statuettes and figurines have been mounted throughout the lounge. They watch the door like sentinels. Some of the birds are stuffed toys. Others porcelain trinkets. There are also cheap wooden carvings. The kind tourist-vendors sell on the side of the road. More birds cover the floor, radiating out from Jaybird's sleeping body. Like a stain. Their eyes fixate on anyone entering the room. Just as he must have intended. The scene awakens a despondency Ziq had all but forgotten. He picks his way soundlessly through the birds. A medical journal lies open. Along with the half-eaten remains of a cheap meat pie. The journal shows a high-resolution photograph of a tapeworm. A hand-written note reads:

THE EARLY BIRD CATCHES THE WORM

Some loose foolscap pages in disarray. Ziq squats down, collects them. They detail a cinema storyboard. Etched jaggedly. In blue ballpoint. Cartoons describe a giant Godzilla-esque version of Jaybird. This monster is setting fire to the mountain. Using a monolithic cigarette lighter. Ziq flips through the drawings with a growing sense of heaviness. A bee is trapped somewhere in the room. He can hear it buzzing around. Knocking its head against the panes. Eventually Ziq sets down the storyboards. He leaves without a sound.

The glands have changed everything. 'Trillzone' blossoms into a kind of transcendental reality. For Sulette, it has become nothing less than a dark paradise. Of course, if questioned, she would be hard pressed to explain. Especially how she came to associate the dreary atmosphere of cheap hotel rooms with the concept of 'paradise'. She would probably answer, quite naturally—that it was because she had mined such monumental seams of freedom and pleasure there. Of course, she would still be avoiding the question. If pressed, she would describe her excursions into Trillzone as 'dank' or 'ghetto'. She would do this without really delving into why these descriptions and images titillated her so in the first place. Of course, at this stage of the game, she no longer feels the need to question or explain herself. There would be no more standing on the outside looking in. Sulette is living the dream.

Volker didn't abandon her on the side of the highway again. But the next time they played 'beach', he was cruel enough to have her deposited on the street outside her apartment. A passer-by found her at dawn. She was lying on her stomach. Dressed only in a hooded, hiking jacket. Once helped to her gate, she began to shout. About how sand was made up of the remains of tiny sea creatures. People watched from windows. The Christian on the second floor descended. She carried a fistful of Panado and a single, crimson apple. Sulette had by then discovered a vuvuzela. This was one of those plastic trumpets left over from the soccer World Cup. It was loud and could only produce a single note. She was blasting Malherbe with it every chance she got. He was as mortified as a suburban husband could be. To him, his wife's behavior was genuinely disturbing. A German student showed up from next door. Dressed in a black cowl and grinning at everything. Sulette assumed she was a lesbian and tried to have sex with her. It ended in a cartoonish chase through the apartment. Cushions were hurled at the Christian. Tables overturned. Malherbe eventually lost his cool. Sulette had blown the trumpet into his ear one too many times. He smacked her across the face. She started bawling. The pug was intensely confused. After Malherbe cleared out the neighbours, he sat Sulette down. They were in the kitchen. He started issuing all sorts of ultimatums. She pulled on sunglasses and sat it out. The walls were pulsing like the aorta of a dying heart. Somehow, she had managed to paint the bottom half of her face red with lipstick. She claimed that she was supporting the Transylvanian soccer team. She had been screaming 'Go Transylvania!' at the top of her lungs every few minutes. Until Malherbe slapped her. The German student documented most of it on her phone. Malherbe's chastising brought Sulette down to earth for a moment. He threatened to throw her out (even though it was her own apartment). Sulette suspected that Charlize would side with him in any case. She sat stroking the dog while Malherbe paced. He was burning down like a fuse. When he finally disappeared to sneak a cigarette or three, Sulette popped another suicide pill. She went and found the German girl. On the student's suggestion, they spontaneously visited a photographer down the road. Unlike the student, the photographer actually was a lesbian. She was also German. And covered in tattoos. She had only recently declared herself gay. Though, for her this meant, attempting to predatorily seduce every young female with a heartbeat. The trio did an impromptu shoot—very arty. With Sulette waving the trumpet around and screaming about vampire goalkeepers. Of course, she was naked. She quickly became bored, however. Especially when the Germans started poring excitedly over the images. Sulette drank half a bottle of vodka and found a mirrored walk-in closet. She curled up inside, falling into a deathly slumber. When she surfaced around noon the next day, her husband was more or less out of her life. She was free to cavort with millionaires. Consequences be damned. She surprised herself by quitting her anti-depressants. That very day. Sulette had originally begun a short course of medication at her mother's insistence. She'd been suffering anxiety attacks. She claimed that they were caused by the stress of university. By the time she stopped, she had been on them for eight years. Without ever really knowing why.

Sulette realizes that the antidepressants had affected the potency of the psychedelic. Previously, she'd been swallowing large numbers of the pink pills. Now, one or two is sufficient to her needs. Volker is conflicted. Sulette is enjoying herself a little too much at his expense. The idea was to make her suffer—to break her. All of a sudden, the realization that he has involved himself in a sexual liaison with one of his neighbours, strikes him. How irredeemably bourgeois. Where was his precious moral compass now, he wondered? He reaches an impasse one Friday night. They are in a cheap hotel somewhere on the foreshore. His manservant is playing sentry downstairs. The location is one more breach of protocol on a rapidly growing list. Volker detests such places. He regrets being talked into moving the action from his house. He paces the grimy room, getting angrier by the minute. Sulette is half conscious on the bed. He tries to wake her. All she can do is giggle incoherently about interracial porn. In a fit of rage, he calls Trill. The creature is not immediately available. But rings back in an hour. The lapsed time has allowed Volker to cement his decision. He asks Trill to find him three to four large, clean, 'blacks'. He leaves the address of the hotel. Trill shows up in half an hour with a pair of heavy-set men. Both carry Nigerian passports and recent blood work. Volker asks if they are in the habit of carrying test results around with them. Trill explains that the men are 'professional breeders'. Cleanliness is part of their service. Volker instructs his manservant to pay them generously. Trill takes a finder's fee and leaves. The men are very pleased with Sulette. She is awake enough to cry out in shock at the sight of them. But too inebriated to protest any further. They have their way with her, taking care not to cause any physical damage. When they are done, Volker injects Sulette—knocking her out cold. Volker's manservant arrives and asks him where he should dump her this time. He surprises himself. He orders the man to take her back home and put her in his mother's bed.

Sulette sleeps in for most of the day. She aches when she awakens. Though not unpleasantly. A Rubicon has been crossed. Volker comes in later, expecting her to find her broken. Instead, she is ecstatic.

'Next time we have to charge!' she cackles. 'No-one rides for free!'

Trill is not too pleased about being asked to pimp Sulette at Volker's behest. Nevertheless, the money is good. Volker is particular. He wants someone who would take things too far—but not too far. He wants Sulette scared. Perhaps a little roughed up. But not damaged. Trill knows just the man—a middle-aged African American expat who keeps a flat in Seapoint. The man is a violent individual. But possesses a fear of authority. Trill describes him as 'uniquely American'. The creature explains that the man would definitely be rough with Sulette. But certainly not enough to land her in the hospital or incur legal proceedings. He would also enjoy terrorizing her. A meeting is arranged. Sulette puts on her skimpiest 'ghetto slut' ensemble. She is delivered to the American's door by Volker's man. The next day, everyone is surprised to find Sulette tweeting pictures of her new 'squeeze'. Somehow the man's gangland tattoos and heavy physique are neutralized by her phone's bad flash. With his weak smile and arm around her shoulders, he takes on the patina of yet another jaded sex tourist. She even has a shot of him handing her a couple of hundreds for 'services rendered'. Comments pile up, complimenting her on her 'shoot'. She is smug about it all. And very, very satisfied with how her life is turning out. Of course, everything changes a couple of weeks later when she discovers that she is pregnant.

Croeser calls Brick towards afternoon. He wants to meet for a drink in the hotel bar and brief him about Luminstein's visit. Brick is keen to talk about the rewrites, but the director is only remotely interested. When they get together, Croeser is distant and preoccupied. Predictably, he splits the upcoming safari into factions. Insisting that Brick remain 'wary about shifty producers and remember who's side he is on'. Brick takes it in his stride. He reassures Croeser.

'You're knocking back those Johnny Walker's,' Croeser mentions with a smile.

Brick hesitates.

'Only a couple.'

'Glad you're back on form, old man. Any action?'

'I'm married now, Mo.'

'Don't be coy, I know you're holding.'

Brick laughs. For some reason, he ends up showing Croeser a couple of the snaps Alix sent. Croeser is impressed.

'Bring her along,' he suggests.

'Are you crazy?'

'It's a joyride—Luminstein wants to go to some canned hunting place. It's legal, but shady. No word is going to get out about this week-end.'

'So, it's kind of a lost week-end?'

'You got it.'

'I don't know. Who are you bringing?'

'I'm flying solo, partner. I want to bag me a lion.'

'You aren't seriously going to shoot a lion?'

'We all are—it's part of the bonding experience. Shane will insist that you join in.'

'I'm not shooting anything. I'm vegan.'

'So is he, remember? These places are a nightmare for those animals, Brick. They keep them chained up and starved until it's time for them to die. We'd be doing them a favour.'

'You can't be serious.'

'Bring the girl, trust me—it will be wild. Anyway, you'll need a break before getting stuck in. Think of it. A hut out in the bush, champagne breakfast in bed with what's her name...Don't tell me you don't need a break.'

'I'm not shooting anything.'

Croeser chuckles. Greenie joins them. Unlike Croeser he is excited by the rewrites. He promises to get a copy over to Sasha and put in a good word for Brick. They all seem confident that the dialogue will have a positive impact on the star.

Later, Brick mulls over Croeser's proposition. He is swimming laps. When he is done, he hydrates thoroughly and downs a couple of kombuchas. The whiskey helped him back into the saddle with the writing. There's no doubt about that. Nevertheless, Brick has made the decision to shelve it. He has to fly straight from now. Africa has had its exotic impact. He allowed the experience—who wouldn't? Now, it's down to business. Still, why not a little latitude? It would help. He needs his mojo. Alix is within the bounds of his agreement with Lisa-Marie. It's not like he's going to run off with the girl. It's a lost weekend. Anyway, Africa might be a good experience for someone her age. They were fooling around on video every night already—why not get a little taste? He swims back and forth. Burning down toward a decision already made.

Alix dances around her shabby little room. She jumps on her bed. She flashes her breasts to the camera. Afterward, Brick sits down and writes a long message to his wife. He tells Lisa-Marie that he is going on safari. He fills her in on the gossip and politics. He considers mentioning Alix, but in the end, doesn't. After all, it's been so long since he's been out on his own. The couple had a thing about talking, when apart. They didn't like it. They preferred writing letters. 'Phone conversations are so limited', Lisa-Marie used to complain. 'Sometimes you just want to be quiet with a person'. If everyone in the Middle-Ages could wait until they were reunited, then so could they. This was the reasoning. Brick feels that the method had helped them both to grow as human beings. Maybe that was just his excuse. Regardless, there has been more than one occasion when Brick found himself grateful for the arrangement. This was one of those times.

Luminstein arrives on a Thursday morning. Croeser invites Brick along, to pick up the producer in his limo. Alix is landing in the evening. *It's going to be an airport kind of day,* comes Brick's inner voice. Shane Luminstein looks even younger in the flesh. 'Raw vegan' is his reaction to compliments. He has a straight-edge fringe of Malibu blonde hair, wears steel rimmed spectacles and is tall. To Brick, he looks like a Beverly Hills tennis coach. Naturally, they are at the same hotel. Luminstein is all smiles about the rewrites. He tells him that the studio is 'behind him all the way'. Greenie and Sasha join them for brunch. Delilah is conspicuously absent. Sasha is gracious with everyone, including Croeser. He winks cryptically at Brick at one point, causing the older actor to frown. Luminstein brings up the rewrites. Sasha is smooth as silk.

'Love what you've done with the script—Behind it all the way.'

Greenie looks positive. Brick is feeling the heat. Croeser doesn't smile once during the meal. In fact, he barely speaks. They finish early. Luminstein needs to get some sleep. The producer has been travelling for over twenty-four hours. As it stands, the plan is to depart for the lion hunt at dawn. Brick manages to corner Sasha on his way out.

'Seriously—are we going to give it a go?'

Sasha meets his gaze with mannequin blankness.

'Sorry about what happened on the dunes, Brick. Pressure, you understand.'

'Can we meet for a drink—have a chat?'

'I thought you didn't drink anymore,' Sasha winks, slipping down a nearby stairwell.

Greenie passes them on his way out.

'Oy vey!' he shrugs.

'Right,' Brick mutters.

He drives the red Mustang down to Camps Bay and takes a long walk on the beach, killing time. Passing some familiar boulders, he is reminded of V. He starts to think about her disappearance, going through various scenarios. He doesn't get very far. Soon, it's time to leave for the airport.

Alix passes customs in denim hot pants and a bikini top. She doesn't have much in the way of luggage—just a backpack. Her hair is in long, thin braids. She tells him that she thought it would suit her Africa trip. 'We've got to stop meeting like this,' Brick quips.

She doesn't waste any time getting her tongue in his mouth. He is in sunglasses and paranoid about the press. They drive out to Llandudno and manage to have sex on the beach. Afterwards he takes her clothes shopping. They eat dinner in some quiet Ethiopian place and spend the rest of the night in his suite. He makes her walk ahead of him in the public areas of the hotel. She tells him that she understands. They shouldn't be seen together. She is lapping it up. Probably the fanciest hotel she's ever stayed in, Brick reckons (*somewhat paternally*, the old inner voice chuckles). Despite his reservations about the situation (and his character), it feels good having a scantily clad girl around. *Brick Bryson rides again?* He politely wills his inner voice to jump off a cliff. The sex drops him down a hole of sleep. Waking at four am to use the bathroom, he notices a text from his wife. It begins:

'*Had a dream about that girl we saw in the airport…*'

Gloomily, he switches his phone off. Sometimes psychic connections could be irritating. The wake-up call is due in less than an hour. They squeeze in another round or two before it comes.

Luminstein is polite about Alix. Croeser is in his element. He chats her up, riding his hand along her bare thigh. Alix isn't offended. She lets him know what a big fan she is—'especially of the early films'. Too late, Brick realizes how inappropriate her presence could turn out to be. He decides that he shouldn't make important decisions while he is under the influence. It strengthens his resolve to quit. Just a little dabbling and he's already skirting hot water. It's not worth the trouble. This is his conclusion. They take the limo to the airport. Luminstein has a Cessna waiting. They fly to Johannesburg, drinking cocktails at high altitude. Brick sticks with juice. He looks out of the window and see's mostly dry earth beyond Cape Town. Somehow, he had been expecting jungle. Instead, it's mountains and desert. He might as well be flying to Vegas from LAX. During the flight, Alix divides her time diplomatically, between actor and director. Brick can see that she is hedging her bets. She has all her luggage and is completely mobile. Luminstein chats indirectly about the Club Ded. Croeser shows him some stills on his phone. Otherwise, the conversation is pretty banal. Brick gets the impression that they are all sick of talking about the film. When they disembark, the air is sharp and metallic.

'High altitude,' Croeser mentions to Brick.

They are met by two large men. One is balding, perhaps in his early fifties. The other is younger, with a dour look. Both have the look of soldiers. Brick's suspicion is confirmed when Luminstein introduces them as ex-IDF friends of his. They pile into a couple of range rovers and begin to drive in the direction of Pretoria. Luminstein takes the lead with his friends. Croeser, Alix and Brick follow. Brick is depressed by what he glimpses through the bullet-proof glass. Vast, colourless malls. Urban decay and security zones. The opposing poles of squalor and opulence dominate everything. Brick is beginning to understand this polarity as a kind of national characteristic. He falls asleep against the window. When he wakes, they are past Pretoria and moving through the veld. The rover traces thin, dirt roads, between parched grass and barbed wire. Alix sleeps with her head on Brick's lap, her feet on Croeser's. The director is idly toying with one of her toes. He appears distracted, staring out of the window. The light shines headache-gold against the windscreen dust. It makes Brick squint. He takes a swig of warm bottled water.

'How long?' Brick asks.

'Hour and a half, I reckon,' Croeser replies.

'Did she sell you a screenplay?'

'She tried.'

'Cute.'

'Very.'

'What else you talk about?'

'How in love with Africa she is.'

'Of course,' Brick comments sarcastically, eyeing the barren slopes of sun-dead grass.

'I told her she should get a job at this place we're going,' Croeser says. 'They want cute girls to handle the cubs'

'Aren't you supposed to leave wild animals alone?'

'Of course. That's how you test whether it's a sanctuary or a canned hunting place. On a real conservation farm, you don't get near the lions. Here, they over-breed the females. They take the cubs away—get them used to humans, show them who's boss.'

'Why?'

'So, tourists like us can go on wilderness walks with friendly lions— play with cute cubs that have been hand reared by cute girls. Of course, when the cubs are old enough, people like us jet in. We pay a couple grand to shoot them. Hang their heads in our kitchens.'

'And this is legal?'

'Sure. Sometimes, the farmers will spin some yarn about the dead lion feeding a tribe. Give it all a moral edge. Like these people eat lions every day. Now, that's bad writing, let me tell you…'

'Why are we here? What is all of this, Mo?'

'Are you kidding? This is show business…'

Sunset is as primordial it gets. The light turns crimson. It vibrates against a mesh of pure black silhouettes. Unlimbered of the weight of the sun, the air comes to life, Brick gazes into the rich skyline. It really is something, he thinks to himself. A distant smell of roasting meat comes to him, like a memory. Alix convinces him to share a cold beer. In the end, he doesn't regret it. It really makes the moment. Their chalet is thatched. The walls are mud. Everything else is luxuriously modern. She spots the floor tub and starts filling it. He stands on the veranda naked, facing the night. Now that he's here, the raw energy hits him in the gut. The ancient darkness is vivid with sound.

'Look at you, mister iconic,' she calls from hot, frothy water.

He turns, flattered.

'You can't see yourself, can you?' she sings gaily. 'Like a statue.'

He wanders back in.

'You're pretty statuesque, yourself.'

'I guess. Maybe you're not a statue. Maybe you're an idol, like in a temple...'

'Hay, don't let's Africanize me just because we're in Africa.'

'I was thinking more Greek. You have that.'

'That?'

'That Heroic thing.'

'Africans don't?'

'You know what I mean.'

'I'm just kidding.'

He turns and sits.

'Croeser mention this lion situation?'

Her eyes light up.

'You will do it? You will kill one?'

'You'd like that?' he asks, perplexed.

'Sure, sure! It's sexy, *n'est-ce pas*? Saint George!'

'It's barbarism.'

'It's sexy! Hemingway!'

'I couldn't.'

'Scared?'

'I don't believe in killing.'

'You don't believe in it. But you would do it.'

He considers for a moment.

'I don't believe I would.'

'Even if your life depends on it?'

'I guess. I wouldn't like it, though. It would be automatic.'

'Being an American born and bred, it was in my bones to kill.'

'Luke Rinehart?'

'Yes—Dice Man.'

'You read?'

'Sure.'

'My kid doesn't read.'

'You always bring him up. I remind you of him?'

'Similar age.'

'Pedo.'

'I thought I was heroic,' he laughs.

'Heroes have dark sides.'

'Why?'

'A hero must kill.'

'Nonsense.'

'Technically...'

'Anyway. I'm not a real hero. I'm just a stand-in...'

'Do it for me.'

'What?'

'Shoot this lion.'

'Forget it.'

'It will be good for your work.'

'I doubt that.'

'Delaney thinks so.'

'No.'

'I will love you long time!' she sings.

'And you won't if I don't?'

'Maybe I will love someone else long time...'

'Croeser?'

'Why not?'

'You find him attractive?'

'I like younger guys. Let's be honest. But you are famous and have this hot, old guy thing....'

'Hot, old guy. Great.'

'...And Delaney, he is fun you know—Crazy. Old and ugly, I guess, but I mean who cares when you are crazy...'

'I'll show you crazy, babe.'

'Show me, show me...'

'You would seriously get turned on by me killing a lion?'

'Look at where the fuck we are! Look at this wonderful place! Look at you. It's the perfect thing to do here. Slay the beast! So Primal...'

'This is not a movie.'

'Well, it sure looks like one...'

Brick wakes before dawn. He goes out and breathes the chill air. He's craving another beer, but settles for bottled water. Within an hour, they are all awake and packed into an oversized chamo-print rover. A big, red-skinned farmer called Oosthuizen joins them. He seems to be in charge. One of his rangers drives. Oosthuizen sells the resort while they traverse a narrow track. He's friendly, but his eyes are blank. He talks about how guests can pet cubs, go for walks with friendly lions— everything Croeser talked about earlier. Luminstein is courteous and friendly. His soldier friends observe quietly. They carry heavy 303 rifles. Croeser does as well. Brick had refused the weapon allocated to him. After a while, the conversation deadens. The landscape has somehow managed to become even more desolate. One or two trees break the slopes. Otherwise, the area is featureless. Out of nowhere, they reach a high security fence. It is manned by another khaki ranger. Like the driver, this man is local. Both appear permanently unimpressed. The ranger allows them through. Brick glances back and sees him securing the gate firmly behind them.

'Hard to believe this all is legal,' he announces.

Oosthuizen regards him without expression. Luminstein manages a cryptic smile.

'This place is called Aluta?' Brick asks Oosthuizen.

'Yes.'

'What does that mean?'

'The struggle continues.'

'You've got to be kidding,' Brick mutters.

A semi-transparent cube appears in the emptiness. As they draw closer, it resolves into a large cage. A pair of lion's circle weakly within. The animals are shackled at the neck—to a concrete post. The driver parks nearby and they exit the vehicle. Alix dances right up to the cage, filming the lions on her phone.

'No cameras!' Oosthuizen calls out abruptly.

Chastised, Alix replaces her phone.

Brick corners the driver while everyone is drifting down to the animals.

'What happens to the lions afterward?' he asks.

The man gives a large, dead-eyed smile.

'My village is starving,' he chuckles. 'You kind visitors will give us plenty to eat.'

'You're a disgrace,' Brick mutters.

Turning away, he passes the younger ex-IDF man, who is heading back to the car. Brick watches him raise his rifle to the driver's head. Quietly, he disarms the confused ranger. Brick turns in time to see the soldier's partner striking Oosthuizen across the face. The farmer's head turns. But the big man doesn't fall. When Brick reaches the group, Oosthuizen is looking grimly down the barrel of the rifle. Some blood spills down his craggy jaw. Croeser has his arms around Alix. He is being protective. But the girl seems invigorated by the turn of events.

Luminstein takes Brick aside.

'What's going on here, Shane?'

'My friends are with an independent anti-poaching unit.'

'You work with these guys?'

'Kind of. Oosthuizen is involved in a poaching operation.'

'They're running it out of the farm?'

'We've had our eye on the lion situation for a while, of course. But we haven't had any leverage until now.'

'That's why we're here?'

'We needed access. High profile movie people are all-access. I mean, everyone knows Brick Bryson.'

'I see.'

'You didn't think that we were really going to…'

'No, of course not.'

They hear a dull thud. Turning, Brick see's Oosthuizen go down one knee. He spits out a tooth. The driver looks panicky. But no-one is threatening him.

'What's going to happen?' Brick asks.

'We'll close this place down. The law might not follow up on our evidence. So, we want them to know that we have other means of applying pressure.'

'Violence?'

'I'm against violence,' Luminstein smiles politely.

Behind them, his colleague manages to break one of the farmer's wrists. The lions watch, unimpressed.

When they get back, Alix disappears with Croeser. Brick quietly packs his things. He pays one of the tour operators to take him back to Johannesburg. He's back in his hotel suite before the others even realize he's gone.

III

Weekends on Mars

Psychopomp

Jennifer calls in sick. For some reason, the nightmare is back. She sits in her car. She knows where nightmare keeps its nest now. Regardless, the prophecy has lost none of its potency. She reminds herself to get hold of Fortunato. She needs to source a good body shop and pluck the cancer out. For some reason, she procrastinates. Traumatized and invigorated in equal measure by her debut at Club Ded, she limps back to her hotel swimming pools. Yet, despite the comfort of old routines, the pools cannot compare to the subaqueous miracle garden of Club Ded. It's the kind of place that irreparably contaminates all other sanctuaries. Jennifer aches to return. But can't allow Anita her victory. The thought that this victory extends over Ziq, numbs her. Her memories of their time together have petrified so quickly. In no time at all, they are as brittle as seashells. Sometimes she finds herself placing too much pressure on them. They crumble. Their white, powdery remains dissolve quickly. Against all the potentialities of the drowning house. Her cocaine intake triples. What use are suicide pills when she has tasted the bottom of the ocean? The fish is calling to her all the time now. As though from the bottom of a well. She has breathed with it. She has turned slow somersaults in its huge, blue world. It's really just a matter of time before she goes back.

Anita phones in tears. She begs Jennifer to visit her at her flat. She claims to be suffering some sort of minor coke crash. Jennifer's apartment feels dark and empty. Especially now that she is alone again. She drives to Anita on autopilot. As though there had never been any other choice. They watch television. They eat dark chocolate. Anita falls asleep on her lap and some part of Jennifer forgives her. She feels as though she has been placed under an enchantment. Ever since Anita showed her how to breathe underwater. It is a spell which renders the waking world foggy and forgettable. Anita doesn't mention Club Ded. Instead she is self-piteous and morose. Constantly offering Jennifer tea and staring heavily at the television. Later, Jennifer awakens in her arms. She stares at the doll-like face, sleeping in the half-dark. It feels as though they are both refugees. Caught behind enemy lines. Avoiding the subject of their various, war torn countries. A hard, translucent substance is caking over reality. It fixes Jennifer in its glass. She imagines a fly landing on wet varnish. Becoming a part of its landscape. She eats. She walks. She sleeps. Everything is mechanical. One day her nose doesn't bleed. She finds herself picking at a finger with a scissors until the blood rises. Pale relief follows the bleed. She uses a razor the next day—calm and tiny, mechanical cuts.

One day, when driving to the laundry, she sees Ziq on the sidewalk. She almost crashes the car. The encounter forces a crack in the shell around her. She tails him morbidly. The sight of him makes her want to sleep. She pulls over when he spots her. He approaches warily. Her hair is wet. Her eyes purplish. She looks older than he remembers. They stare at one another. Frozen against a backdrop of commuters. After a spell, he climbs in. Without a word, they turn into the morning traffic.

Jennifer takes him to Deer Park Café. The establishment is quiet at that time of day. Cinematic windows survey alien pines. She nurses a mug of tea. Staring into its red depth. Her skin is waxy. Her hands cling loosely to things. They remind him of a squid he had once seen in a fisherman's trolley. Despite their lack of speech and movement, the pair remain deeply engaged. Sunlight dapples the dark rime of Ziq's espresso cup. He'd been watching it, trying to read it. Now he watches her.

'Come home with me,' she whispers.

He meets her gaze. But is deflected by its intensity. Looking back to his cup, he feels uncertain.

'What happened?' he asks.

Her face closes—a hastily drawn curtain.

'I can't talk about it.'

He nods.

'Is it always like this? Your work?'

She understands he is trying to be delicate. The duffle bag torments him.

'No. Not always. Sometimes, but not like this...'

'Why don't you stop?'

She hesitates, frowns. Her eyes flush. He is surprised to see how close to tears she is.

'I can't stop.'

He nods slowly.

'I think I'm in love with you,' he murmurs.

She smiles painfully. Reaching across the table, she takes one of his hands. He does not look up. Instead he continues the painterly study of his stained cup.

'I think you just want to escape,' she admits.

He withdraws his hand.

'Come,' she insists.

Cameras activate. Tactical light sources paint the massive underwater cyclorama. They blot out everything but a blue edge. Jennifer glides from shot to shot. It's like dancing. She was always good with choreography. The glands make the routines seamless. The routines make the days seamless. The days make the nights dreamless. Spectators smoke behind mirrored glass. Croeser is in there, somewhere. His voice is in her ear. They want her painted blue in every shot, 'for grading'. How many hours has she been living underwater, she asks herself? How many days?

Coming down from the fish, Jennifer lies exhausted across one of the many roofs of the compound. Cliffs soar majestically. But she is captivated by the sea. If it weren't for the salt, she could live down there. She can't stop dwelling on this concept. She wonders whether it is dawn or sunset. Cocaine has her in crystal quagmires. She feels cold. She doesn't have any clothes on. She begins to vomit blue gel. A machine falls out of her mouth, skittering off the edge. Drones make low passes. They have cameras. Even now, someone is compiling a shot list. Anita lies against her thigh. She smokes a black cigarette. Downstairs, the cleaning has begun. Jennifer can hear the industrial vacuum pumps compete with the breakers.

'We were supposed to be saving the world,' she sighs.

Anita's smoky exhalations are somehow amplified by the dawn/sunset.

'The world doesn't need us,' she replies.

Jennifer thinks about this in the days to come. She thinks about it when she is sitting in the backs of long, black cars. She watches the night through moving windows. Lighted windows describe a code. One that she fears she will never break. Distant petrol stations come and go. Research-stations in a tundra. She hears the night people. Sees them frozen in their dim, little worlds. But she is not there. That is the past. Or is it a future still unwritten? It is written, she thinks. These days, everything is blue. Even that is written.

'Time is doing its own fucking thing…' Jennifer slurs, to no one in particular.

'They send us their rotten dreams,' Anita complains.

She smokes cigarettes in rooms as still as tombs. Are they in a room, Jennifer wonders? She remembers that time they were up on the roof. Or is that happening now?

'We dig through these dreams, looking for pearls.'

Anita is playing a deeper game. Jennifer can sense it. What is she really after in Club Ded?

The blackbird routine is just a cover story now. Jennifer asks why they still do it. Anita mumbles something about tax. Team Omega fast-forward through a universe of cheap hotel rooms. They sort through the voices of the cities. The dingy rooms cluster. Like all the traumas the trio expose within them.

'We're like ants living off a corpse,' Anita's tells her. 'There's nothing left to save.'

Jennifer does a line. Her head snaps up in a shiny bathroom. Bass bins rattle all the mirrors with their throb. She grips the edge of a chrome sink. Someone starts smashing mercilessly against the door.

Ziq turns on a street corner. He struggles to hold his ground. The wind sucks at him like a drain. Water patterns tattoo the buildings. He notices Jennifer across the road. She wears a smart black cocktail dress. Her skin is painted blue. Her hair moves, as though in an underwater current. He notices that she is floating loosely above the sidewalk, dappled by a shifting light. She smiles, posing for a snapshot. The current intensifies, rocking her. He begins to approach, wading across the dim street. She does not notice. Her back is suddenly turned. A phone is ringing, somewhere in the distance. Brushing past Jennifer, he continues walking. His stride is light and lithe. She dwindles in the background. She blurs, staggers and falls. He looks down at his hand. He is holding one of her vital organs—maybe her heart. He screams. No sound comes. The phone sucks in jaggedly. It rings loud and close. He awakens to the noise, drenched with sweat in her empty apartment. It's almost 4am. Pawing an arm from the damp sheet, he takes the call.

'Hello?'

There is a long pause. Somehow, he can discern the grain of her breath.

'I only work when I'm underwater...' Jennifer repeats.

A girl laughs somewhere outside. There comes a muted splash, followed by the distant tinkle of water and incoherent conversation. A circular bed occupies the center of the chamber. Figures snake heavily across its sheets. They slide in and out of darkness. A broken helmet reveals Anita. She makes no sound as she moves. Jennifer crawls to an area of floor somewhere between the bed and the window-wall. Her hair is mussed, her bikini torn. She props herself against the wall. A phone-plug catches glare in its glass.

'All these broken cookies. Not enough dough...' She slurs.

The bedroom door opens abruptly. Sasha Styles steals in. His footfalls are cat-weighted. He is smiling. Jennifer observes blankly. He is making faces in the dark. Playful, feline faces as he kneels between her loose legs. She watches him like a snake. Does she look like Delilah now? He leans in close and kisses her. For a moment, she doesn't move. He carves into her like a hot spoon. She opens her mouth. Eyes swallowing closed. Pale arms shuffle around a burrowing neck. The glass phone-plug drops to the carpet. She slides onto her back. He begins to undress her. Slippery, tearing movements. He is a man on an unstable boat. Struggling with a stunned marlin. The blue light washes down on them. It shines dimly. Through the soft, white forest of the carpet. Into the hole of the phone-plug. It even manages to find its way into the dim room beyond. Where Ziq slouches in the darkness of a sheet twisted bed. He holds the receiver to his ear for a few minutes. Listening to the flutter and collapse of enormously small sounds. After a while, he hangs up.

Ziq is in front of the mumbling television. He's been like this for hours now. A grey dawn filters weakly. Through chinked drapes. He hears a jingle of keys and is suddenly awake. Rising quickly, he pads to the front door and opens it. Jennifer nearly falls over, her key still in the lock. She looks up at him and laughs. He can smell liquor on her. Her skin is still blue. A black duffle bag loiters beside a high heel. Slowly, the intoxicated giggles wind down.

'I'll run you a bath,' he says.

He goes back in. She follows jerkily, dragging the duffle bag, grinning to herself.

They lie in bed, cradling one another loosely. Mid-morning shines obstinately through drawn curtains. Jennifer watches the sunny patches, half-dead. Ziq is staring up at the ceiling. The back of a hand across his forehead. A thought enters his mind. It moves slowly at first, gathering weight. Like a dewdrop at the end of a leaf.

'We've never had sex,' he murmurs.

She gazes into the oppressive light. Red flecked eyes.

'I suppose we never will,' is all she can muster.

Something on the ceiling has him riveted.

'I can live with that,' he tells her.

Her bloodless face glows in the little intrusions of light. She closes her eyes very tenderly. Shrinking closer to him. They hold each other against the onset of afternoon. The sun repositions its stripes. Across them in the half-dark.

Last night's make-up films Jennifer's unwashed face. It's blackbird make-up this time. No blue skin on her. The sea pounds against barnacled concrete. This material has been manufactured into car-sized, geometric forms. They lie atop one another. Gigantic pollen motes, creating a sea wall. Icy morning glare pierces crusted eyelids. She awakens to the stench of kelp. A dog-like wind is nuzzling her face. She is crisp with salt. Opening her eyes, she is temporarily blinded by bleakness. Face-down on sea-washed concrete. She'd cut her hair the night before. Now it frames her face. A black Cleopatra bob. Identical to Anita's. The concrete landing is soiled at the edges. Vagrants and seagulls. Vaguely oblong, it crests the top of a pier support. Duplicate areas span the industrial pier. At intervals, separated by unprotected gulfs of cold water. Rusty ladders connect the landings to the main thoroughfare above. This cargo dock runs for about half a kilometer to her left. Terminating offshore. Jennifer lifts her head off the wet concrete. The pain is excruciating. The gloomy underbelly of the pier's superstructure yawns. It cuts off the sky. She breathes in a lungful of briny air. Then turns onto her left side. Her ear submerges in a deep puddle of seawater. She's so used to being below water these days. She barely notices that she is drenched. Rusted rungs extend above. She gets the feeling that she fell. Maybe in the night. She can't feel her fingers. Morning begins its break. Across the grey lilt of the sea. It scrapes away at the pier's desolate underside, revealing it. Miraculously, Jennifer discovers that she is still wearing her new needle heels. The remnants of a shattered vodka bottle. Glistening beside bare thighs. Some shards are imbedded in the flesh. But there is no pain. The sea has cleansed her wounds. A small, sleek handbag teeters on the brink. Attached to her scuffed wrist by a slender chain. She reels it in while seagulls circle. They are debating whether or not to harass her. When she is done, she pulls the glass from her legs. Eventually she manages to drag herself to a sitting position. Leaning her spine against the concrete, she inspects herself for further damage. One of her calves is grazed, badly. Ligature marks show through at her left wrist and ankle. Rope or hand cuffs? It's hard to tell at this stage. Her bone of her right hip feels bruised. She sits for a few minutes. Staring out across the leaden waste. Shuffling around in her purse, she extracts a black cigarette. Then her phone. Thirteen missed calls. She almost drops the device when it rings. The number makes her hesitate. Eventually the ringing stops. Her cigarette is down to the hilt when it starts again. Reluctantly, she answers.

'Hi.'

The deadpan tone shocks Ziq. He crosses a street in the inner city. He's been pacing since dawn. Now, finally, he slows to a standstill. After so many attempts, he has been calling out of habit. He wasn't expecting her to answer.

'I've been trying to call you for three days,' he blurts.

Even though he is concerned, the words sound desperate. Jennifer is pensive, quiet. She fingers one of her needle heels. A slow and repetitive movement.

'I cut my hair.'

The comment does little to ease his anxiety. A commotion erupts in the background. He turns. A masked Jaybird bursts out of a shop with a fully clothed mannequin. Its legs smash against passing obstacles. He tears past Ziq at terrific speed. The shop girl shouts. A security guard detaches from his niche. Ziq hesitates for a split second before plunging headlong into the morning traffic. He and Jaybird weave between the cars. They vanish beneath a bridge. The call cuts out. Jennifer closes her eyes in irritation. She lights another cigarette with prehistoric slowness. She's feeling the impact of the sea in her bones. Eventually she rises. Mounts the ladder. The pier above is deserted. Her car stands at an oblique angle. Front end mangled into a security barrier. Scraps of metal project over the drop. The bumper is some distance away. It has the look of a chewed and discarded rib. The bonnet is crumpled. Almost like tissue paper, discarded after weeping. The passenger door hangs on a hinge. This open door lends the yellow car the inescapable impression of a hornet. A damaged wing-part. The windscreen is cobwebbed. A heavy, inorganic immobility permeates the scene. Jennifer makes it to the top, surveys the damage. She is beginning to remember. The empty pier had seemed as good a place as any to take the car into the red zone. Despite her best efforts, she crashed before it could fireball.

'It must be a sign,' she mutters to herself.

Jennifer's face is clean. Devoid of make-up. Her new hair has been brushed. It gleams—the shiny black helmet of a storm trooper. Morning light comes through bay windows. It paints her gold. She's in a white toweling robe. An ornate hotel suite, overlooking the ocean. She is preparing to read a letter out loud. The Oracle sits on the opposite side of the room. A young girl attends her. This girl also has silvery hair. Just like the Oracle. Helpers flit through the room without a sound, arranging things. Anita reclines on a divan, Chloe opposite. Breakfast glistens. There is an inexplicable tension to Jennifer's delivery.

'I have a recurring dream...' she begins.

Breakfast ends an hour after the last letter. The blackbirds shed their white robes in an antechamber. They do a few lines. Then shuttle back to black. Riding the elevator down to the lobby. These days, it is hard to tell Anita and Jennifer apart. They complicate things further by wearing matching outfits. In the lobby, the concierge signals Anita, but calls out Jennifer's name.

'For you,' he says, holding up a receiver.

Jennifer shoots Anita a puzzled look. This was an unexpected development. Anita joins her at the phone, listening in.

'Yes?' Jennifer answers.

The Oracle's silver-haired attendant replies.

'Could you come back up? The Oracle would like to see you.'

Jennifer hesitates. Anita's eyes flicker from side to side, scrutinizing her reaction.

'I'll be right up,' Jennifer answers, returning the handset.

Anita watches her closely. They rejoin Chloe.

'What's going on?' she asks.

'She wants to see me,' Jennifer explains.

'Do you think it's about Club Ded?' Anita whispers anxiously.

'Fuck should I know, Anita?' Jennifer mutters, suddenly edgy.

'We'll wait at the bar,' Chloe suggests, attempting to maintain a sense of decorum.

'No,' Jennifer sighs. 'It's alright, just go, I'll call you later.'

'No fucking way Jen!' Anita snaps.

She is barely managing to contain herself.

'I need to know what's going on,' she pleads.

'You've had too much powder, girlfriend,' Jennifer sneers.

'You do seem a little paranoid,' Chloe offers diplomatically.

Anita glares at Jennifer in wretched fury. There is an absurdity to their mirror-image antagonism of one another.

'Fine,' Anita concedes.

She turns on her heel, stalks over to the revolving doors. Chloe meets Jennifer's eye for a second before following. A premonition of some kind passes between them.

'Call me!' Anita shouts from the door.

Her desperation is showing. Jennifer waves them off, heading back to the elevator. Chloe withdraws, Anita nudging and questioning her all the way.

Jennifer knows why the Oracle is summoning her back. Anita could never have guessed and wouldn't understand, even if she did. As the elevator doors close, she feels an enormous surge of release. With the passage of each floor, a tiny amount of ballast is removed. Staring at the passing numbers in a kind of trance, she realizes. Everything has already changed—perhaps forever. She has crossed over—to another River of Pheeling. The silver haired girl admits her without a word. She guides Jennifer through ornate rooms. Flutes play. But Jennifer cannot be sure where the sound is coming from. There is a smell of frankincense. The attendant knocks three times on a set of double doors. She signals for Jennifer to enter. Before scampering around a corner. Jennifer passes into a sunken bedchamber. A flock of flamingoes mills in the room. They turn their heads neurotically. Make tiny clicking noises at the sight of her. Jennifer is stunned. The Oracle is moving amongst the flamingoes. Jennifer doesn't spot her at first. Her ash pink robe blends almost perfectly with their plumage. She's been watching Jennifer. Feeding one of the heads a handful of insects. The old woman beckons. Jennifer closes the doors, moving down amongst the skittish birds. Their eyes strike her as reptilian. They avoid her tactfully, yet with a type of reserved panic. The Oracle smiles at Jennifer's expression of wonder.

She strokes the neck of a nearby bird

'Do you know what a psychopomp is?' she asks.

'A bird that carries messages, to and from the land of the dead,' Jennifer answers.

'Sometimes messages. Sometimes souls.'

The Oracle reaches under a wing, scratching some secret place.

'Psychopomps are always travelling, always in transit.' she continues. 'Limbo is their home. Messages their refuge.'

She fixes Jennifer in her gaze. Jennifer freezes beneath the sheer physicality of it. She begins to wilt to the richly patterned carpet. Birds bump against her. Like boats. Confused, she feels the pressure of tears. The Oracle is suddenly beside her, on the floor. She comes out of a bustle of feathers, taking one of her wrists. Her quartz-like eyes tune directly to Jennifer's.

'The recurring dream—It was yours.'

Jennifer nods. The tears spill down her face. The Oracle releases her. She topples back awkwardly. Then she is being summoned, from across the chamber. A circular bed, enclosed within drapery. The Oracle's voice comes from behind the curtain. Jennifer moves through the birds, drawing back the drape. The Oracle is seated on the edge. Her back turned to Jennifer. Jennifer sits beside her. Flamingo coloured fingernails trace talon-tips across Jennifer's whitened knuckles. The Oracle's eyes become distant.

'I had a vision while you were speaking.' She explains.

Jennifer becomes anxious. The Oracle's gaze drifts, to some undefined point in mid-air—an area. Her hands find Jennifer's face. Roughened fingers. They scrape. Claw-tips protrude against the bone of the skull. Jennifer begins to weep uncontrollably beneath the onslaught of The Oracle's presence.

'I'm drowning,' she heaves.

Her head sinks into the folds of The Oracle's robes. The birds preen themselves. Flexing their wings, in unexpected flashes of colour.

Ziq and Jaybird sit in the cobbled lanes of the old Malay quarter. Looking down over the city. A dirty sunset invades every street. It rimes city blocks. The yolk of some unspeakable cosmic accident. Exposure mummifies the seated pair. It lends them the aspect of statues from a fallen civilization. The great, immovable force of humanity—raw and naked in the heat. Tenements sink in a rift. Smokestacks describe the horns of behemoths. Between their stacks, rivers of traffic coagulate. Lava-like, against the rubble of progress. All of Ziq's aesthetic sensibilities wither in this prismic light. He has been walking the city for days now. Without pause. He is sleepless and starved. Jaybird, in contrast, is sprightly. He only steals mannequins these days. He hoists a freshly pilfered specimen against the nuclear glare. It wears a designer rubber dress. He peels it off and tries it on.

'I just can't understand,' Ziq says, completing some long and potentially incomprehensible train of thought.

'I'll never understand fashion,' Jaybird banters conversationally.

He writhes. Half in, half out of the garment.

'I've got to stop stealing,' Ziq sighs.

'Who is this bitch!' Jaybird barks, highly offended.

Ziq crosses the parking lot of the Three Towers. The night sways trees in its wind. He stops for a moment, staring into the woods. The clones recognize him now. He greets them in passing. They respond with sour nods. Feeling rebellious, Ziq turns toward a security guard and closes the distance. The guard tracks his approach suspiciously. He unlimbers his machine gun. Ziq stops right in front of him, unsure of his motivation.

'I was up in those woods one day,' he starts. 'I saw candles.'

The guard eyes him warily.

'Know anything about it?' Ziq asks.

'No English,' the guard grumbles.

Ziq stares uselessly at him for a moment. He tries Xhosa, but the guard doesn't understand. Ziq retreats. He gives a backward glance when he reaches the tower entrance. The guard remains in place, watching him. Ziq keys in the code. The glass doors unseal. An inrush of air. He reaches reflexively into the postbox. Surprisingly, there is an envelope addressed to him. It's exactly kind of cheap, manila envelope he uses in his processing-plant. Paranoia erupts. He weighs the envelope in his hand. Riding the elevator, he becomes confused and panicky. He enters the dark apartment, guts the package with a steak knife. Inside is a tiny USB in a featureless case. He crosses the lounge, inserting the device into the viewing system. The blue glow of the long screen illuminates the chamber harshly. A single video file. The media loads. An image of the lounge appears onscreen. The image has been captured from the on top of the television. By daylight. The inverted placement creates a peculiar mirror-like effect, when viewed from that location. Clicking shuffles through the speakers. Ziq steps away from the television. Just as Jennifer steps away from the camera. The synchronicity is not lost on him. He follows it. They both sit on the same couch. At the same time. Facing one another across the looking glass. Jennifer looks into the camera for a long time before speaking. It is almost as though she is trying to discern him across the divide. Her new hair disturbs him. He can't shake the sense that he is meeting some evil twin. Something sent to torment him

'Hey,' she finally says,

Her voice is bass-heavy in the quadraphonic relay. He watches, distraught, almost returning her greeting.

'The Oracle is taking me to Kyoto for a while. Then on to Greece.'

She pauses. Her behaviour appears exhausted, pre-programmed.

'They have an office at Delphi,' she smirks.

He smiles vacantly. Clearly, she anticipated his amusement.

'It's corny I know. Mostly industrial districts there now...'

She trails off, gazing down, finding it difficult to speak. Emotion resonates off her image.

'I can't process. I need to leave.'

She sits up jerkily. A pixelated tear slices out of her.

'You don't know. I mean I haven't seen you in so long now. I'm sorry. I'm so sorry.'

Her head sinks down to her knees. He imagines a doll, warping under heat. Her hair buckles just like plastic. Ragged breath glistens in the stereo field.

'I almost drowned last week. They pulled me out of a pool.'

He rises, fatigued.

'Maybe you love me. I don't know how. I'm so...disgusting. I'm so disgusting. I'm just so terribly...I look at myself and I want to die. I don't deserve your love. I don't deserve anything.'

He starts to break things in the kitchen—a cup at first, almost accidentally.

'I look at you loving me sometimes and I just think, how stupid can he be to love a thing like me...'

Her face is grainy with hair.

'I really hate you sometimes,' she hisses.

She gathers herself, swabbing at her face with a loose wrist.

'I'm so sorry,' she sobs. 'I'm really...I'm just so sorry.'

She looks directly into the camera. Composing herself.

'There's a bag of cash in the bedroom. The lease runs till the end of next year. Stay if you want. It's all paid for. I just...'

She trails off again, staring at the camera. A bird calls from her side of the screen. She gets up abruptly and approaches the camera. The screen flickers with white noise. It goes black. Then reverts to neutral blue. He peers out of the wrecked kitchen, teary eyed. The lounge is filled with blue light.

'Action'

Brick awakes to the sound of a phone ringing. Again, the room stinks of Scotch. Another broken bottle. Had he broken this one on purpose? His phone is on the dresser. It's Greenie.

'Look sharp, Brick. Sasha is in your hotel for a meeting. You could catch him in the bar.'

'What's the point, he's just going to freeze me out again,' Brick groans.

'Are you alright?'

'I'm fine. Did the great white hunters get back in yet?'

'Yesterday. Croeser's disappeared though. No-one can raise him.'

'Even Luminstein?'

'Ah, he does this. Look, you have to try with Sasha. If we can reshoot dialogue for even four scenes this week we could be in the ballpark.'

'I've been through the script and footage a few times. We'll need a miracle to make this shit-bird fly. It's a fucking mess and no-one wants to play ball.'

'So, you're just going to give up?'

Brick sighs. He eyes the broken bottles on the floor. There is a golden puddle of whiskey, the exact shape of Italy. He catches a glimpse of himself in the mirror. He looks like a wino. He turns his cheek this way and that. *Not a bad character look*, the old inner voice nods in support. Maybe for a Tennessee Williams play, he argues internally.

'You still there?' Greenie asks.

Brick sighs.

'Ok, I'll give it a try.'

'Good man,' Greenie says.

He hangs up. Brick's head is throbbing. He's still wearing his suit from the night before. It's also stained with drink. One of the sleeves is torn. He can't remember how. He wonders how quickly he could get himself cleaned up. He knows the moves. But somehow just can't get it into gear. Something has shifted. He realizes instinctively that he has to flow with it. It is either that or drown. He calls Sasha. It rings for a while. Eventually, the star picks up.

'Listen, Brick…' Sasha begins, irritated.

'Shut up and listen, Sasha. I'm not calling to try talk you into anything. I'm past that. Come up to my room for a minute. I want to show you something.'

'What?' Sasha mutters incredulously. 'If you think, I'm going to...'

'Do it or don't do it. I don't give a fuck.'

Brick hangs up unceremoniously. He goes into the kitchen and drinks a pint of water. He drinks another. He is half way through the third when there is a knock at the door. Brick opens it. Sasha is there, looking annoyed. His expression shifts to subtle shock when he registers the state that Brick is in.

'Come in,' Brick tells him.

He walks off in the direction of the bedroom, without bothering to wait for a response. Sasha hesitates, but follows him in warily. He eyes the mess, the stench, the giant lipstick V, the editing machines, the piles of paper and the solitary Academy Award.

'Fucking hell, man...' is all he can muster.

He enters the bedroom. Brick is standing barefoot, in a spray of broken glass.

'Look,' Brick grins, pointing at the floor.

'What?'

Brick chuckles.

'Looks exactly like Italy, don't you think?'

Sasha flounders. He folds his arms.

'You brought me up here for this?' he asks, bewildered.

Brick shoots him a glance. He drags himself over to the bed, where he sits down heavily.

'Listen,' he tells Sasha. 'Fuck Croeser, ok. I'm not doing this for him. I never was. I...I *need* this. I'm good at it. And I think that if you help me, then maybe, just maybe I can pull it off.'

Sasha regards him for a few moments. He rubs his jaw with a circular motion. Clearly, he has been taken off guard.

'That's it?' he asks quietly.

'Yeah, that's it, buddy,' Brick sighs. 'That's my whole spiel. Take it or leave it.'

Sasha stands dead still for a moment. Then he moves to the window and opens it. A gust of brisk sea air floods the room. Brick closes his eyes, refreshed. When he opens them, Sasha is regarding him evenly. His mask has slipped a little. Brick can see the kid from the skids made good, buried under all that hero-ice.

'Can you get sober?' he asks Brick.

'I don't need it when I'm working.'

'You don't need it, period.'

'I know. I'm getting there.'

Sasha sighs. He runs his hands through his hair and leans against the wall.

'Croeser's never said a bad word about you, you know. Not once,' Sasha tells him. 'You're probably the only one...'

'We have a fucked-up connection,' Brick admits. 'I don't understand it. He gave me my biggest breaks. You don't forget stuff like that.'

Sasha springs lightly off the wall. He crosses over to the phone and picks it up.

'Hi. Could you send up house-cleaning? ...Thanks.'

He hangs up and lingers for a moment.

'Tell Greenie to send me the schedule,' he says eventually.

Brick looks up at him.

'You'll do it?'

'I'll do it,' Sasha confirms.

'Thanks, man. I appreciate it.'

Sasha breaks into a grin.

'Brick fucking Bryson,' he laughs, heading for the door.

Greenie pushes for a last-minute schedule, starting the next day. The permits are still valid and the crew has been on standby for weeks. Technically, they still have a week left on the deadline negotiated in the wake of the conference call. Luther calls Brick to confirm. With Sasha in the ring, it's all systems go. The next day they are all back in the dunes. Brick shows up early. This time he makes time to chat with the kid in the 'GAME OVER' cap. He's finally removed the bandage from his face. The nose is discoloured and bruised. But it feels good to have it out. He feels like he can finally face the world on equal terms. He and Luther sit in matching canvas chairs, under a parasol. Together, they watch the set go up, eating coconut ice-cream sticks in all-terrain, mirrored sunglasses.

'How did you talk him round?' Luther finally asks.

'I appealed to his heroic side. Look, what really matters is whether we can retake the shot-list before the week-end.'

'I've looked over your revisions. If Sasha plays ball—it's no problem. I always plan for last minute retakes with Delaney.'

'Any word from him?'

Luther shrugs.

'Your guess is as good as mine'

Sasha shows up on time and they get to it. As Brick hoped, his script's fresh injection of wit and post-modern comedy, lend the scenes a real edge. Sasha's working it. The rewrites are tailor-made for him— and he knows it. Now that he's not rebelling, he expands the script instinctively. Even Luther is grinning in victory. Brick's overhaul and subtle, actor-driven direction expose previously hidden aspects of Sasha's charm—elements Croeser had always railed against, out of a sense of personal competition. Unshackled in this way, Sasha shows a glimpse of what could be achieved during the week. It is the sort of quality that seasoned film-makers recognize instantly—the sound of cash registers. The x-factor that will undoubtedly fill seats. Luther, Greenie and the crew all see it. And they respond in kind.

They manage to get everything and strike early. The mood is buoyant for the first time in months.

'Anything you need, Brick,' Sasha announces.

He makes a point of doing this in front of the crew. To boost morale. Greenie is over the moon. In the Mustang on the way back to the hotel, Brick gets a call from Shane Luminstein, who is already back in LA.

'Brick, this is a little awkward, but I can't get in touch with Delaney. Any leads?'

Now Brick is suspicious. If Luminstein can't raise him, almost anything could have happened.

'Sorry Shane, I was hoping you could tell me.'

'I've got a detective on retainer down there. Guy by the name of Wilbur Struik. He'll be in touch.'

'No problem.'

'Greenie tells me things went really well today.'

'I think we did some good work.'

'Story is you directed the character-driven scenes in GAME OVER. People say Delaney stuck mostly to the art and action, even though he scooped the credit.'

'It was a team effort,' Brick replies, diplomatically.

'Modest, eh? Listen, get through the week and we'll change the face of it, Brick. You have a lot of support here.'

'Good to know, Shane. I'll be in touch.'

When Brick gets back to the hotel, the concierge tells him that he's had numerous calls from a Sulette Labuschagne. For a moment, Brick doesn't recognize the name. When he finally remembers who she is, he expects that it must be news about Croeser. She answers on the first ring.

'Mr. Bryson! How wonderful! How are you?'

'Hi Mrs. Labuschagne…'

'Sulette, please.'

'Right, of course. Sulette. Is Delaney alright?'

'Oh, I couldn't say. I've moved out of my block. I'm currently staying in a big mansion on the same street. Maybe you've seen it, it has…'

'Forgive me for interrupting, Sulette, but I have someone with me,' Brick lies, hoping to get her to cut to the chase. 'What seems to be the problem?'

'Well, alright then,' Sulette huffs, a little put out. 'It's Delilah. She's...
well, she hasn't been doing so well—or so she told me. She shouted at
me from the window when I walked past. She said for me to call you at
the hotel and tell you to come over right away.'

'She can't call herself?'

Sulette sighs.

'She's swimming deep,' she confides.

'She's *what*?' Brick frowns.

The woman is beginning to exasperate him.

'With the fish...' Sulette whispers.

'Look, I really don't follow...'

'I think you should just get down here, Brick...You don't mind if I
call you that, do you?'

Brick grunts.

'You'll see when you get here,' she says. 'Just call me when you are at
the apartment and I'll let you in.'

'Can't I just ring the bell?'

'She's in no state.'

Brick is finally starting to get the picture. Delilah has become reclusive
to the point of being chemically dependent on Croeser. Without him
around to modulate her intake, she might have gone off the rails. Brick
is starting to worry. It isn't like Mo to abandon someone like Delilah.
Abduct her maybe. But certainly not leave her isolated like that.

'I'll be right over,' he tells Sulette.

Brick calls Greenie, who is in Camps Bay eating dinner.

'Something's come up,' he explains. 'I need to pick you up right
away'

'Delaney?'

'Not quite...'

Almost as an afterthought, Brick calls Luminstein to fill him in. The
producer hesitates a moment when he hears the news, deliberating. For
a second, Brick thinks he's been cut off.

'When do you think you'll get there?' Luminstein eventually asks.

'I can be there within half an hour,' Brick says.

'Make it an hour.'

Brick is perplexed. The suggestion strikes him as off-key.

'Surely, if the girl is in trouble...' he starts.

'Legals, Brick. Her agent has to be in the loop. There are a lot of
factors in play.'

'Ok, fine,' Brick relents reluctantly. 'Any word on Delaney?'

He felt it was a token, touch-base question. A couple of hours have
passed. Maybe the producer or his detective had some luck tracking
him down.

'Don't worry about it,' Lumistein answers cryptically.

He hangs up. Brick frowns. What did he mean by that? Had he located Mo? Brick stews on it all the way to Camps Bay. Greenie is waiting on the sidewalk, under a royal palm. He's chewing on a grilled crayfish that he's snatched off a plate.

'Better eat that thing sitting down,' Brick tells him.

'I thought this was an emergency?' Greenie protests.

Brick explains Luminstein's angle. It perplexes Greenie further.

'This doesn't strike me as particularly kosher, Brick,' he splutters through a mouthful of shellfish.

'Tell me about it.'

All the same, they sit down for twenty minutes or so.

By the time they reach Brownlow, it is already dark.

'Now we have to call Miss happy housemaker for the keys,' Brick sighs.

'No need. I had copies cut.'

'Greenie, you're a good man in a bad situation.'

'My basic job description,' Greenie nods, climbing out.

They go up the side stairs and enter the apartment. The first thing that hits them is the smell—rotting meat and chemicals. The place is a mess. A jungle of toppled pot plants and UV light. Thawed seafood lies decomposing in the kitchen sink and all over the floors. The sound of many, discordant televisions jangles the air.

'Christ,' Brick mutters.

They search the rooms. But the place appears deserted. Eventually Brick goes into the bathroom, where he nearly has a heart attack.

'Greenie! Get in here!'

Delilah is in a full tub of water. The labels on several, empty 25 gallon tanks, suggest that the water is from Fortunato's spring. Delilah lies beneath the glassy surface in a wetsuit. Her eyes are closed, as though asleep. Greenie barrels in and freezes, taking it all in.

'How long do you think she's been dead?' Brick asks quietly.

'She's not dead,' Greenie mutters.

'What? Listen, Greenie, she's obviously been under there for some time…'

'She's asleep.'

He pushes past Brick and takes her gently by the shoulders.

'Come on, honey. Wake up now,' he coos.

Brick is mortified.

'Greenie, come on, man. She's gone…'

Delilah opens her eyes. Brick stumbles back in shock. Her mouth goes wide. Fat tendrils of blue gel snake out of her. They invade the crystalline water. A small machine-brace emerges from between her teeth. Brick runs out as Delilah sits up. A loud splash and the sound of vomiting follows him down the hall. *This is too much!*—the old inner voice is howling. Zombies? *Mermaid fucking zombies!*

'Africa…' Brick mumbles theatrically to himself.

His hands are shaking. Greenie comes in with Delilah. He's wrapped her in a towel and puts her on a couch. She is shivering, staring at Brick with glassy, red edged blue eyes.

'Jesus H Christ,' Brick keeps repeating.

'Calm down,' Greenie tells Brick. 'I know it seems unbelievable, but there's a scientific explanation for all this!'

Realizing that Greenie is perfectly ok with the fact that Delilah was just asleep underwater, Brick sits down heavily on the floor.

'I need a drink,' he declares.

'You don't,' Delilah gurgles through a mouthful of blue slime.

Brick looks at her in horror before escaping to the kitchen. He pours himself a finger of rum and downs it. Fortified, he returns to the lounge. Delilah is speaking slowly. But her limbs are shaking uncontrollably.

'I can't control it…' she drools. 'The fucking smack comedown on the glands…I keep flipping out, man.'

'We've got to get her out of here,' Greenie tells Brick.

Brick nods, pulling it together. He kneels before Delilah and takes her by the arms.

'How you doing there, sweetheart? What do you say we ditch this clamshell?'

Delilah starts crying.

'There's fucking giant sharks out there!' she shrieks. 'In the fucking sky!'

'Calm down, now. It's ok. We got you.'

She seems to snap out of it. She settles into temporary lucidity. As though waking from a deep sleep. She looks at Brick, desperate to communicate something before losing it again.

'Champion of Earth?'

'Yes?'

'You have to go to Fortunato, now, this instant. It's, like, super important. Understand?'

'Let's take care of you first…'

'No! You have to go to him right now!'

Suddenly she becomes distracted by something in the corner of the room. Her eyes focus on a nightmarish vision only apparent to her. She begins to scream uncontrollably.

'Delilah!' Brick yells, shaking her.

Abruptly, as though a switch has been thrown, she passes out. They manage to catch her before she sags to the floor. Brick looks up at

Greenie. They muscle her onto the couch.

'This is some Edgar Allan Poe shit right here, Greenie.'

'Quoth the raven; Nevermore,' Greenie mumbles, his brow speckled with perspiration.

'Let's get her the fuck out of here, before she bakes a cake.'

'Roger that. But where do we stash her? We can't take her to Delaney's official residence—Desmond and his foreign legion flunkey will have it taped up. We show up with "Ariel" here and its Shakespeare time...'

'Doesn't she have a payroll place?'

'Not secure. Press has it staked out—official rags and mags too. Teenybopper press. It would be even worse. I vote we get her to your suite. Find her some, I don't know, *tennis clothes* and radio for back up.'

'Her agent?'

'Yes. I know Jean, she's a gem. She knows what to do with little mermaids whose tails have turned to sushi...'

'Sounds like a plan. But, once we've got her secured, I want to know what's going on.'

Greenie nods miserably.

'I'm serious. Fuck the gag order.'

'Ok, Brick. Ok.'

As their luck would have it, there is a black-tie event starting at the hotel. Brick remembers a notice about it when he left. The lobby is inundated with arriving guests.

'Too many people,' he concludes, circling the lot.

'Go to the basement parking.'

They drive down a ramp and find a quiet corner, near the elevator atrium. They've swaddled Delilah in a huge Disney-print bathrobe. Luckily it has a hood. Once her face is hidden, Brick takes her in his arms. Greenie reconnoiters. When the coast is clear, they enter the mirror-paneled elevator and go up. A couple get in for two floors, but pay them no heed. When they are gone, Greenie turns to Brick.

'So, what's the plan?' he asks.

'Kidnap the girl, demand a billion from insurance and live out our days marlin fishing in St Kitts?'

'I'm partial to Tobago myself.'

'Good beaches.'

'Aren't you vegan, though?'

'Marlin conservation then.'

They make their way down the corridor towards Bricks suite.

'Keycard, left trouser pocket,' Brick tells him.

Greenie scrabbles for it, glancing around nervously. As soon as they are in, he raids the minibar for a pair of double Scotches. The room is looking neater. As per instruction, the 'V' is still on the mirror. Brick heads for the bedroom with Delilah. Greenie follows with the drinks. He freezes halfway, for a moment, when he catches sight of the Oscar. Brick dumps Delilah across the bed and takes his Scotch. They almost drink immediately, but end up floundering for a moment to perform a hasty 'cheers'.

'Well, so far so good. What now?' Greenie puffs.

'I'm going to make some calls. You're going to get her out of that wetsuit.'

Greenie looks appalled.

'If she wakes up and screams 'rape', I'm moving to France.'

'What's in France?'

'A lot of people who don't speak English…' Greenie mutters, crossing over to the bed.

Brick goes out into the hall. He's only had a few sips of his Scotch. Reminded of his promise to Sasha, he abandons the drink and checks his phone. Sal has been trying to ring. Brick calls back.

'Sal—what's up?'

'I was about to ask you the same thing. Haven't you heard?'

Sal has his business-tone on. It's rare enough to make Brick worry.

'Have they found Mo?'

'Have they…what?' Sal asks, confused. 'Where did he go?'

'No-one seems to know.'

'It's probably related to what I have to tell you: They've cut funding. Whoever was bankrolling this fiasco has jumped ship.'

'Trouble in paradise?'

'I'm guessing you have the rest of the week to bring in the boat. After that the production is shutting down—for real.'

'Did Luminstein tell you?'

'Internal memo—my guy at the production house leaked it to me. It was circulated yesterday.'

Brick collapses onto the couch.

'Heavy…'

'Something must have happened down there. Something big. I was hoping you would know?'

'Not a clue,' Brick sighs. 'I did speak to Luminstein though. Wonder why he didn't mention it.'

'He probably figured it's better to keep the boat on course. Word is you did a good job with Sasha. If this gets out now, it will turn into a cluster-fuck….'

'How long can you keep something like this in a bottle, though?'

'I'm guessing they will make an announcement by Saturday, maybe Sunday.'

'What do you advise?'

'Do everything you can in the next few days to leave your mark. We don't want them scarpering out of the credit.'

'Can they?'

'There are some loopholes, not many. All fair. One states that Croeser can fire you—if you are drunk or incompetent, but that's hardly likely since he asked you aboard. It looks like a simple safety clause. The problem now is the time-squeeze. If you don't get enough done in the next few days to merit the credit—there's not much we can do, capisce?'

'Yeah, I follow…'

A piercing shriek emits from the bedroom. Brick's heart skips a beat.

'Fuck was that?' Sal asks. 'You got a cat in there or something?'

'Listen, I have to call you back,' Brick says, hanging up.

By the time he's reached the bedroom, Delilah is stable. Greenie is helping her peel off the wetsuit.

'At least she didn't scream rape!' Greenie grins confidently.

Delilah eventually wriggles out of the garment. She crawls weakly under the covers.

'How do you feel?' Brick asks her

'It comes in waves,' she groans. 'Before I go under again, I have to tell you something…'

'Shoot,' Brick says.

'Drop whatever you're doing and call Fortunato. Right now. He has something very important to show you.'

'Listen, honey, there's a lot going on now…'

'Don't patronize me,' she snaps. 'You don't know half of what's going on.'

'She's right about that,' Greenie agrees.

'It's too much for me to explain,' she insists. 'Just do as I say.'

'Give me his number,' Greenie asks, pulling out his phone.

She recites the number from memory. Her eyes are unfocused and lined with red. She is having difficulty keeping them open.

'I'm going to sleep now,' she slurs. 'I might not wake up for a bit… Fortunato will know what to do. Don't worry…It'll be ok…'

She turns over and passes out unceremoniously.

'Greenie, there's something I need to tell you.'

Greenie looks over his shoulder nervously. Brick quickly relates the new information.

'Christ on a stick,' Greenie mutters. 'What, is it a super-moon today? What's next!'

'So, what do you think?'

'Who knows what will happen now. I've got to get back and rearrange the schedules—see how much we can scrape out of the time we have left.'

'Can you get more time?'

'I can double certain slots, get in some overtime contingencies…I'll have to see.'

'What will you say to make it fly?'

'I'll make up something. Luckily, everyone is behind you. I think we can pull it off. You might lose any hope of influencing the edit, though.'

'You honestly think I'd have had any sway with that?'

'With Croeser on your six, you might have. He has final cut.'

'With a big franchise picture like this? How did he manage that?'

'He was controlling the money.'

'What! How?'

'It's a long story, and quite frankly, we don't have the time. I have to get my ass in gear if we're going to pull this off.'

'Fuck that, Greenie. You're going to precis things for me right now, as best you can.'

Greenie sighs.

'First, I need another drink,' he declares.

Greenie gets up and re-enters the lounge area, where he pours himself a stiff one. Brick declines the offer of a top-up. Instead, he goes into the kitchenette and gets the espresso machine going. It's going to be a long night. When he's done, he joins Greenie in the lounge with an Americano. Greenie's slouched on the edge of a sofa, staring miserably at the Academy award.

'Christ, it's just like that movie,' he mutters.

'Two weeks in another town?'

'That's the one.'

Brick sits down and Greenie concisely brings him up to speed on the secret film. When he's finished, Brick is left stunned.

'Audacious, isn't it?' Greenie admits, with admiration.

'Mo, you… crazy fucker,' Brick says, shaking his head.

A thought strikes him.

'Maybe he's in trouble with the money guys…or even the military. If there are defense contractors involved, anything could have happened. He could be dead at the bottom of the Atlantic, for all we know.'

'Call Fortunato,' Greenie tells Brick.

'Look, Delilah's clearly delirious. We have more important fish to fry here…'

'Don't underestimate her,' Greenie says. 'Delilah may play with seashells on the seashore, but the little mermaid has her finger on the pulse. I've watched her manoeuver since day one. She has an instinct for power play. If Delilah Lex says something's important—then, you better believe it's important.'

'Let's call him right now,' Brick nods.

Greenie dials and hands his phone over to Brick. Fortunato picks up after a few rings.

'I don't recognize this number,' he answers suspiciously.

'Fortunato, it's Brick.'

'Brick Bryson?'

'Yeah. Look, Delilah told me to call. She said that it's urgent—that you have something to show me.'

Fortunato digests this. Brick can hear music in the background.

'Fortunato?'

'Tell me, is she alright?' Fortunato asks.

'She's not doing very well.'

'Alright. The day has come, I suppose. Meet me at Club Lido on lower Long.'

'When?'

'When do you think? Right now.'

Fortunato hangs up.

'That guy really rubs me up the wrong way,' Brick tells Greenie, handing back the phone.

'I'm calling a cab,' Greenie decides.

'I'll drop you. I need to meet this guy now.'

Brick downs his coffee and prepares to leave. All of a sudden, he hesitates.

'Think its ok to leave her alone?' he asks Greenie.

'We found her asleep underwater, Brick! I mean if she was ok then, I really don't know what ok is, by Delilah Lex's standards…'

'I guess she has everything she needs.'

'Just get back as soon as you can. We can't trust anyone else to mind her now.'

The Mermaid's World

Club Lido turns out to be a dingy, Nigerian dance-club. It roosts at the end of a sinister alleyway, in the foreshore. It seems buzzy enough. Dancehall pumps out of the neon lined door. Brick eyes the unfriendly bouncers. He parks the Mustang just outside the door. As he exits, one of the men approaches.

'No parking!' he barks.

Brick is about to find somewhere else, when the man's expression shifts. He takes Brick by the shoulder. Ushering him toward the people at the door. Everyone begins to grin, slapping him on the back. He is allowed in free of charge. Bewildered, Brick enters the club. He spots Fortunato almost immediately.

'Let's go,' Fortunato shouts over the music.

Brick nods and follows him back out. The bouncers seem disappointed that Brick is leaving so soon. Someone has already brought him a complimentary cocktail and asked for an autograph. Fortunato smooths it out. Brick can't understand the language they are speaking. Eventually, Fortunato turns to him.

'Ford Mustang mk2 1972. With 5.4L Windsor motor. Iconic.'

'It's Delaney's,' Brick replies. 'I'm not much into cars, myself.'

Fortunato snorts.

'Well, you guys do have a lot in common,' Brick grins.

Fortunato glares.

'Are fucking with me?' he hisses.

Brick is bewildered.

'Why would you think that?'

'I will not tolerate any insults regarding my wife!' Fortunato snaps.

Brick sighs.

'Look, I didn't mean that. I meant as a film-maker—I watched a couple of your films. That's some good work.'

Fortunato considers this. Reverts to neutral.

'Leave the Mustang,' he tells Brick. 'It will be safe here.'

Brick is doubtful. But nods all the same. He follows Fortunato onto Long Street. It's a buzzy night. The pavements are alive with foot-traffic. When they pass the Parliamentary courts, the concentration of nightclubs intensifies. Fortunato leads the way down a dodgy alleyway. At the end, they find Fortunato's custard car. It is parked alongside the Company Gardens. When the doors open, Brick is taken aback by the stripped-down interior.

'It's like a helicopter!' he exclaims.

Fortunato seems vaguely amused by this. But does not comment. They drive parallel to Long, back towards the foreshore. Fortunato cuts past the train terminal and takes the turn-off to Salt River. Brick notes the urban deterioration with some apprehension. Fortunato turns off the main road, entering a sullen poverty row. Although the streets are deserted, they hold a kind of wary pregnancy. The car comes to a halt outside a derelict furniture shop. One of the doors has been removed. The hole in the wall is guarded by a heavily tattooed man in a glittery pink zoot suit, complete with top hat and tails. The man's face is painted a vivid yellow.

'What's with the cosplay?' Brick asks.

'It's his carnival suit,' Fortunato explains.

He reaches under the seat and withdraws a package.

'When its carnival, they go in the streets, play in brass bands.'

'Like Rio?'

'Stay here. I'll be back.'

'Listen, Fortunato…'

'Just a minute,' Fortunato interrupts.

He exits and approaches the hole in the wall, carrying the package. The guard allows him to enter and then turns his head to the car. Brick avoids his gaze. Fortunato is back in under two minutes. He gets them onto the main road, turning in the direction of Observatory. He takes the highway off-ramp leading back to the sea. Brick recognizes the large industrial districts he had passed on the way to the studio screening. Fortunato, however, does not take the highway. He crosses a bridge, entering a no-man's land beside the harbour. Huge cranes drift past. A small city of shipping containers. Fortunato parks beneath another grim little bridge, overlooking the entrance to a deserted loading dock. When the car stops, Brick realizes how quiet the area is. It feels dangerous.

'What are we doing, Fortunato?'

'I just have to drop this off. Then we can get down to it. Ok?'

Brick nods irritably. Fortunato gets out. Brick watches him go through a hole in a barbed wire fence. He passes alongside a wall of shipping crates, slipping down an unseen crack. Brick looks around warily. He nearly gets a heart attack when the back door opens. Looking back sharply, he sees Trill slither in. The creature is in tiny denim hot pants and a crop top. It wears thin flip flops. *Beach clothes*—Brick's inner voice notes? *Here?*

'Hi there,' Brick says.

Trill smiles shyly, pulling out a cheap phone. Brick studies the elfin figure in the rear view. He decides to try something.

'You know, I saw Delilah today,' Brick fishes.

Trill looks up and blinks a few times.

'She has a plan,' the creature replies cryptically.

'A plan?' Brick repeats, confused.

'A secret plan.'

Trill returns to its text message. Brick watches.

'Can you tell me more about this secret plan?' he asks.

Trill pauses.

'Well, you know Daddy Del has this world?'

'Daddy Del... you mean Croeser?'

'He has this world,' Trill repeats. 'Daddy Del is king of this world.'

Brick is unsure where the creature is going, but nods, signaling that it should continue.

'But, he was never really in charge of this world....'

'He wasn't?'

'No.'

'Who was?'

'The Queen.'

'Who is the Queen?'

'It doesn't matter who she is now.'

'Why?'

'It doesn't matter.'

Brick tries another tack.

'What *does* matter?' he asks.

'The world is what matters,' Trill answers childishly, as though it were obvious.

'Who has the world now?'

'The Queen gave Delilah the world.'

Brick nods. Despite the fact that he is completely lost, he senses that there is a kernel of vital importance being communicated.

'So, is Delilah the Queen now?' he ventures.

'No.'

'If she has the world, then isn't she the Queen?'

'She cannot be Queen.'

'Why?'

'Dilly doesn't make rules. She breaks rules.'

'What *is* Delilah, then?'

'A mermaid.'

'What will she do with the world now?'

'This is why you have been summoned here, Champion of Earth.'

Trill returns to its phone. Brick sits in silence, digesting.

'Hey, you know my son's going in for surgery,' Brick mentions conversationally.

Trill glances up, distracted.

'He sick?'

'No, nothing like that. It's for...you know.'

Trill looks completely blank.

'Sex change,' Brick admits, finally managing to get it out.

Trill sneers like a feral cat.

'I would never let someone cut me up,' it hisses.

Brick is thoroughly confused.

'I thought you guys...'

Trill is texting again.

'Never mind,' Brick sighs.

After a few moments, Fortunato re-emerges from the shadows.

They head in the direction of the airport, but turn off into the townships along the way. Enormous mesh-enclosed pedestrian bridges span the grim, trash-swept highway. Brick looks out at the improvised shacks and public housing blocks.

'Where are we now?' he asks.

'This is Langa,' Fortunato tells him.

They navigate the remains of a decayed, overgrown suburb. The neighbourhood is wedged between a miserable government estate and the onset of a great shanty town. The shanties strike Brick as a testament to human ingenuity. The population has constructed housing out of anything at hand. Up close, the scape defies his post-apocalyptic expectations. The magpie instinct to hoard and nest, has manifested a cubist wonderland—out of pure need. Brick is impressed, but keeps his tourist sentiments to himself. It's almost as though Fortunato can read his thoughts.

'Visually arresting, don't you think?' he asks.

Trill is watching them in the rearview like a benign, pet snake.

'It's quite wonderful,' Brick admits.

They pull up to a rambling house, surrounded by barbed wire. Fortunato gets out and pulls a chain, running through a dislocated storm gutter. A thin gun slit slides open in one of the fortified windows. As soon as the watcher gets an eyeball on the car, someone starts to hand crank a metal shutter open. A spacious garage, full of automobile parts and mechanic workspaces is revealed.

'My shop,' Fortunato says. 'I make some extra cash tuning.'

They park. Trill hops out and winds down the heavy shutter. They lock the chain in place with a deadbolt. The house is even more labyrinthine inside. Dingy passages lead to sparse rooms. They enter a large, dim lounge. All the furniture has been pushed against the walls. A dilapidated television hangs from the ceiling. A colour-scrubbed edition of *Rambo III* plays through a rift of marijuana. The sound has been turned down. Three massive men sprawl on couches, spread around the room. They all hold flashlights, which they train at separate areas of the tarnished linoleum floor, walls and ceiling. With their free hands, they balance antiquated, brassy opera glasses to their faces. These are trained on the illuminated quadrants of the floor. A bong is travelling around the room. French hip hop leaks from another room. Trill detaches from them. The creature curls up on one of the men's laps, reaching inside his shorts. Fortunato is about to move off, when Brick gives him a 'what's all this' look. Fortunato hesitates for a moment before going over to a chest of drawers. He removes a flashlight and a pair of opera glasses. He hands the glasses to Brick. Fortunato shines his light at a spot on the floor, indicating that Brick train his glasses on that area. Through the magnifying lenses, Brick observes a patterning of small, black ants. They rove in panicky lines along the bottom edges of the exposed walls.

'These ants are the locals,' Fortunato explains. 'They have been in the house the longest. They used to stay only in the kitchen. Some months ago, they expanded into the lounge.'

Fortunato abruptly swerves the torch upward, finding a hole in the ceiling. Brick follows his light. Larger, red ants cluster around the ragged hole. They ferry crumbs and some dead black ants.

'These have also been here long,' Fortunato tells him. 'They used to stick to the garden, but found their way into the roofing. Through that hole—they have discovered the house. For months, they managed to co-exist peacefully with their neighbours, until...'

The torch beam moves again. It settles on the floor. Large greyish ants cluster beneath the couch, moving in strong lines toward the center of the room.

'...the building next door was fumigated. These fellows used to own that block. Now they need to establish new territory. They came in through the cellar and are set on taking the whole house. The center of this room is the main battleground. You are standing in a war zone.'

The flashlight roves as he speaks. Hundreds of battle-ravaged corpses litter the killing floor. They concentrate toward the center. Brick lowers the glasses, glancing at the men on the couches. They slouch, eating cheesy crisps out of packets, morbidly entranced by the miniature conflict.

'Colonialism at work,' Fortunato announces, bored.

He moves off. Brick sets down the viewing apparatus and follows him deeper into the house.

They go down, toward the cellar, arriving eventually at a metal door. The door has been bolted in several places. It takes Fortunato a few minutes to get it open. They pass into a somewhat surreal chamber, lit by UV lamps. The room is filled with aquariums and a tiny hydroponic garden. Brick looks around in surprise. Fortunato locks them in. Brick follows him through another door. They pass through a short corridor, into a surprisingly well-equipped edit suite. Brick eyes the hardware, impressed.

'This is high-end gear,' Brick comments. 'Industry standard.'

'Delilah arranged it,' Fortunato explains.

'Alright, enough mystery,' Brick says. 'Tell me what's going on.'

'I'll do better,' Fortunato grins. 'I'll show you.'

He indicates the control chair. Brick obliges him by sitting in it. Banks of sophisticated sound monitors face him. The viewing screen is comfortable and large. Fortunato starts up the machines and begins to load a large file.

'So, what are we watching?'

'Do you know Anita?' Fortunato asks, getting some programs online.

'I don't think so, no.'

'You knew about the other film though?'

'Christ! Was I the only one who didn't know?'

'Anita wanted Trill to steal fish for them. We let them have them. The fish are here to teach us things. Delilah understands that.'

'Tell me about the film.'

'Anita made a secret deal with Delilah. She stole all the secret footage…'

'*All* the footage?'

'Everything.'

'Aren't there safety protocols in place, to prevent this sort of thing happening?'

'Usually. Croeser changed that. He wanted to have the only copies. Anita used this against him. She fed the raw files to Delilah and substituted blank drives. Of course, as you know—you cannot use anything less than the raw files to create a finished product. She left the low fidelity rushes to avoid rousing suspicion. This charade ended a few days ago. Croeser found out what was happening. All hell broke loose.'

'This is why he vanished?'

'I'm sure of it. Maybe he needed to get away from his investors. Who knows.'

'So, Delilah gave you the footage?'

'Not just the secret footage. She's been feeding me *all* of it. Anita had no idea what we were doing.'

Fortunato points at some black, armoured suitcases stacked neatly in the corner.

'That's Club Ded,' he declares.

'This is so illegal,' Brick mutters.

'It doesn't compare to what Anita and Croeser were doing. For the producers, this would be just one more dirty secret. They can't afford to expose us.'

Brick starts to realize what's going on.

'So, Delilah gave you the footage and asked you to cut it?'

'She felt exploited. All the same, she felt that she had done some of her best work in Club Ded. Their illegal activity gave her leverage. She approached Anita. Anita loved the idea.'

'Is this why Delilah sent her agent away?'

'She needed to keep her activity secret.'

'What did she ask you to do with the footage?'

'She wanted me to integrate the two films into a whole, excluding the X-rated elements and reinforcing the fantasy elements.'

Brick perks up. He cannot believe what he is hearing.

'And you've actually done this?' he exclaims.

'Yes. Obviously, it's rough. The sound needs to be synched properly. It's ungraded.'

'But the structure is there?'

'Absolutely.'

'Show me,' Brick says.

He settles back. Fortunato dims the light, presses play and leans against the wall to watch as well.

Brick doesn't speak for an hour and forty-three minutes. He is completely engrossed. It is as though Fortunato has managed to tap a hidden key. Unlocking Croeser's signature personality. By carving off all the fat and candied sentiment, Fortunato has amplified the essence of Croeser's visionary appeal. Even the action sequences are tighter. More intricately balanced. The whole thing has pace and elegance—a far cry from the heavily laden behemoths that have plagued the franchise since 'GAME OVER'. The inclusion of the secret footage is the *pièce de résistance*. It adds a whole new scale. Delilah's character has flipped. From two-dimensional eye-candy, into a post-modern, emotional time-bomb. Again—it's as though Fortunato is reading Brick's mind:

'If I can include the new work with Sasha Styles, this thing could really fly,' he says.

'You heard how well it went?' Brick asks, surprised. 'Who told you?'

'No-one. I just knew that you would pull it off.'

'I appreciate the vote of confidence.'

'So, what do you think?'

'Let me get this straight—Delilah was playing Delaney this whole time?'

'She's a smart girl. She'll make a good producer one day.'

'And the sex? Was that also just for show?'

'I think they had a real connection.'

'You think?'

'Croeser is a monster. There is no doubt about that. But, I knew him first as a film-maker. Working on this mad vision of his...well, it was an honour. There are aspects to his personality I still admire—despite everything.'

'What you and Delilah have achieved is incredible.'

'How do you plan to use it?'

Brick regards him, automatically probing for hidden motives.

'You're really both going to trust me with this?'

'If anyone is going to save the day, it's going to be Brick Bryson— That's what Delilah said.'

Brick laughs.

'And you agree with her?'

Fortunato nods.

Before they drive back, Brick gets Fortunato to burn him two low-res dumps of the edit. He plots the angles all the way back to Lido. Fortunato is going to follow him back to the hotel and check on Delilah. He has herbs that he claims will assist her condition. Brick can't help being impressed with the guy. If ever they needed a miracle, this was it. Delilah Lex!—he shouts internally. Croeser finally meets his match. They reach Long Street and pick up the Mustang. Fortunato follows him to Camps Bay, where he rousts Greenie from the beach house he is using. Brick had asked him about the address. Greenie explained how he had an old friend who owned a bungalow on Clifton's fourth beach. The area is a maze of luxury houses, set in cobbled alleyways. They skirt a cascade of small beaches, leading up to Camps Bay. Greenie answers the door in a tartan robe and headset.

'Watch this and get back to me asap,' Brick tells him, handing him a DVD.

'What is it?' Greenie shouts after him.

'Salvation!' Brick calls over his shoulder.

In the car, Brick calls Sal and fills him in.

'It's a winning hand,' Sal agrees. 'But a dangerous one.'

'What are you thinking?'

'...That whoever paid for that shit storm is going to want their money's worth.'

Brick hasn't considered this.

'It's on Croeser though, I suppose. If Delilah doesn't want the

X-rated version circulating and has taken control, there's not much anyone can do.'

'There could be ramifications about the secret footage being used in the official release. If you have a co-directing credit, it could reflect badly on you—if things go pear-shaped. The low-res rushes could also get leaked.'

'True. But the bottom line is, it's our cut or a half-assed fiddle on the tanker that was pushed onto me. They can use the legal footage, but we have all the high-budget secret stuff.'

'Send the cut to me as soon as you get back to the hotel. I'll meet Luminstein tomorrow and see what we can get out of this hostage situation.'

'I didn't think of it as a hostage situation…'

'Well, you better start, buddy. Because that's exactly what you and Delilah are doing. You are holding a major production…and Christ knows whoever else's raw footage hostage—and the *only* thing in your favour, is the fact that their hands are dirtier than yours. This could play out any way.'

'I'll chance it, I guess. It's either that or back to the fucking pasture.'

'That's the fighting spirit.'

'One other thing….'

'Shoot.'

'I want to try get Fortunato a credit. He's really the one who got us here. Wait till you see what he's done with this….'

'I don't represent him, Brick.'

'He's Delilah's golden boy, Sal. This guy is going places, I'm telling you.'

'Ok, let me watch his edit. Send links to his other films as well. I'll see what I can do. Fair's fair.'

When they get to the hotel, Brick starts to get a feeling that's somethings wrong. The sense intensifies when he and Fortunato cross the corridor leading to his suite. The door is ajar. Brick pushes in. Delilah is sitting naked on the edge of the bed. She looks up when she sees them. Brick notices an upturned mirror, covered with untouched lines of cocaine. Delilah is also, inexplicably, wearing make-up.

'Coke?' Brick frowns. 'What happened here, Delilah?'

'It's not mine,' she mutters blankly.

Fortunato drapes a blanket around her shoulders. He produces a bottle of some herbal infusion. She allows his ministrations. Brick notes their conspiratorial interaction with interest.

'Who was in here?' Brick asks her again.

'Don't worry about it,' she replies tartly.

Her face is expressionless and sickly. Despite his irritation, Brick realizes that she is going to stay mute no matter how much he pushes. When Fortunato has checked out her condition, he turns to Brick.

'I'm taking her back to Langa.'

'You ok with that, sweetheart?' Brick asks Delilah.

She nods.

'Safer there, that's for sure,' she mutters cryptically.

The next day goes like clockwork. Again, the energy is good. They wrap early. Brick corners Luther afterward.

'I know about the second film,' Brick informs him.

Luther blinks a few times.

'Never took you for a detective, Brick,' he smiles.

'Do you know that Delilah has all the footage you guys shot?'

'I know it went missing. I also knew it would turn up again. I don't ask questions, my friend. I just get paid to shoot movies.'

'Where is this Club Ded, anyway.'

'Ah, it's really dead now. You can't go there.'

'What happened?'

Luther shrugs.

'Who knows? One day we got the call not to go back.'

'And Mo?'

'I heard he's back in LA.'

Thursday and Friday are even better workwise. Still no word from Luminstein. Sal tells Brick that their meeting was a poker face party. The outcome is pending. They manage to finish the reshoots. Greenie is supportive of Brick's play to get Fortunato in after seeing the cut. He wangles it so that Fortunato has access to the reshoots. Fortunato gets to work. He works so quickly that they have a completed rough cut by Saturday night. On Sunday, the bomb drops.

The story breaks at an international level—courtesy of the Two Des's. Brick is in his suite when the crisis unfolds. His phone starts ringing off the hook. Intimate photographs of Delilah and Brick show up. The story offers sordid details about a hotel love nest and a psychedelic 'African drug cult'. Various nudes are leaked. Photographs of cocaine sliced mirrors and sex toys. Delilah's exposed pictures are so pornographic that they crash servers. The story is that they were accidentally uploaded to a cloud and before being leaked to the Two Des's. Some of the stills were captured in the flat on Brownlow. Trill is in a couple. It's hard to tell who Delilah is sucking on in others. Clearly, the inference is that it is Brick. When Brick sees the photos of them together, he realizes that the hotel suite must have been bugged from the very beginning. It could have only been Croeser. It wouldn't be difficult to composite shots from fixed camera mounts to create a false narrative. It all starts to unravel.

Croeser must have fed a false story to the hounds, to distract attention. The FX images would have clinched it. For some reason Delilah has been compliant. This is what irks Brick the most. He calls her in Langa to confront her about it.

'You knew?'

'You have to see the big picture. These leaks will bump ticket sales through the roof...'

'I mean, I just don't get it Delilah. You don't want the porno version circulating, but you'll stoop to *this*?'

'We need to push the picture. This could be massive. Grow up, man! This shit will pass and your bankability will soar, I promise...'

'After I left you alone that night. Did Luminstein or Croeser contact you? Did they talk you into this?'

'This guy came in the room. He had a key...'

'Who?'

'This PI called Struik. Wilbur Struik. He was just going to plant the coke and some other props. Maybe make sure I was naked—I don't know. When he saw I was awake, he called Luminstein. We spoke then...'

'And you just went along with it!' Brick yells, incredulous.

'It was just supposed to be me and Delany, at first. But I told Shane that it would work better with you. I made a deal with him.'

'Why?'

'Fuck, dude! I was *helping* you and dissing Delaney. Wake up! We need to sell this thing. I need to sell this thing! My whole career is on the line. If Club Doofus tanks, I'm finished. If we win, I'm a motherfucking player...and I never forget my friends.'

'Delilah, this isn't some teenage drama. You can't just play fast and loose...'

'This is showbiz, spaceman...'

'It won't make any difference if you confirm or deny,' Sal explains. 'The images are out there. Of course, the studio is making a big hoopla about invasions of privacy and legals, etcetera. But it's just smoke. They are only vulnerable if you out them. And you *can't* out them.'

'Why the hell not?'

'Because backing Fortunato's cut, makes you complicit. You're now part of the conspiracy, whether you like it or not.'

'Karma is quick these days...'

'It's also good strategy—diverts attention from the real shit-nest at the heart of this.'

'This is so bad.'

'There's no such thing as bad press!'

'You're actually in favour of this?' Brick asks, flabbergasted.

'Hey, we've been getting offers, pal. Heavyweight offers—straight off the back of the leak. People thought you were a washed up drunk. Now you're a Hollywood bad boy, back from the grave and *writing* again. Delilah wasn't lying when she said she did you a favour. Production has also gone all out to push your writing cred. You'll take some minor hits, but at the end of the day this is good business.'

'This is fucking exploitation!'

'This is...'

'Oh, spare me.'

'You'll lose the credit. They haven't said anything, but that's my feeling. It doesn't matter though, because after this film comes out, you're going to be hot property again.'

'I'm fucked,' Brick mutters, exasperated.

'You just got your career back, Brick. Go celebrate.'

Brick stays in. He tries to distract himself. He takes the phone off the hook. The nice thing about a hotel is how you could screen out reality. This is all the inner voice can offer. *Make a microcosm—maybe a little whiskey will help...* Of course, even microcosm's have their shelf life. When night finally falls, Brick finally gathers up enough courage to open the video from his wife.

Lisa-Marie is in the kitchen. She's been crying. She's smoking.

'God, it's just like a film, isn't it?' she laughs. 'The speech the wife makes—starring me as the wife. I used to play the hot homewrecker. I guess I'm too old now. Maybe this is karma? What am I saying... Everything is karma! I'm just a cameo now. Only two appearances. One at the beginning to set a tone of morality and another at the end to deliver judgement. I guess that's what hurts—losing screen-time. You can understand that? It's not like I look down on you for what you did, but just...seeing it splattered *everywhere*... I can't even show my face at yoga! Phone is ringing sideways... Fuck, Brick, I don't know. Maybe you should just come home? Or maybe you shouldn't...Is that what I'm supposed to say? I used to get all the witty one-liners. Now I get this jilted wife shit. I haven't trained for *this*! I should get drunk, but it's still so early...'

She reaches abruptly for her laptop. The image goes blank.

Fallout

Nights blur in the city. Ziq wanders aimlessly. Basic needs provide him with purpose. He is thankful when these motorized necessities call him out of the fog. He operates in flight patterns when they do. He catches himself muttering in a bar. He doesn't usually talk to himself in front of others. People are wary of him. He wonders what it would feel like to be drunk. Alcohol has never comforted him. He glimpses himself in neon grimed windows. There is a chaotic tint about him now. He could break something. He bumps into people by mistake. He shrinks like a cat. One night, he sees a brawl through dirty panes. He watches the bodies grind against one another like cigarettes in an ashtray. The uselessness of these nameless hours—they enshroud him in nothingness.

He calls the Oracle helpline from payphones, leaves messages. Dawn sees him sleepless in cheap cafes. His clothes are soiled and rumpled. He watches sunlight trickle over the mountain. It fills his empty cup with glare. The light swells in a teardrop. It catches in the rime and remnants. Ruthlessly illuminating the passage of what has come before.

Ziq is standing in a restroom cubicle. He is arranging fifteen to twenty wallets on the closed toilet lid. Sleeplessness has dulled him. His reflexes clash with his mind. Frustrated comments escape his mouth. He can hear people outside the stall. Pausing to listen. Some wallets fall. One falls into the toilet bowl while he trying to urinate. The water removes shadows from its weave. He stares at it for several seconds before abandoning it, clattering out of the stall.

He is loitering in a cinema crowd. Maybe a day or two later. Sober and paled. The smell of popcorn teases him. He realizes he hasn't eaten for a very long time. He drifts over to the brightly lit snack arcade. Then stands for long minutes, picking at white nubbins with distaste. He crosses the facades. Stares at patrons. Wondering if fate might somehow direct him back to Jennifer. He keeps expecting to bump into her. He throws the popcorn off a bridge. Swarms of pigeons and seagulls come from all over the city. They descend furiously upon his leavings.

He is illuminated in a phone-booth. There aren't very many of them left now. They keep vanishing. Leaving naked sockets. Night traffic. Hunched over a phone. As though weeping. Sometimes his logic is precise. He presents perfect arguments to the answering machines of the Oracle's helpline. Sometimes he just screams at the empty spaces beyond. Then he stops. Thinking that she might hear his voice and judge him. He leaves the phone booth abruptly. Then walks for miles, looking for another one.

Jaybird stands naked in an open, sunlit meadow. Wind ruffles dry grass. It snakes up the soaring faces of the mountain before him. Sunlight sharp and fresh. It catches in long sprays—orange and yellow flowers. He wears his bird mask. He hefts a can of petrol. A zebra grazes in the near distance. The city keeps a herd on the foothills. For tourists to gape at. Jaybird stands serene. Watching. All knock-kneed and dreamy. Eventually, he continues up the meadow. He trails bright blue petrol in his wake. Completely absorbed by the landscape.

Ziq awakens to the sound of helicopters. Sprawled beneath a willow tree at the very edge of the Pharm. Opening his eyes, he notices the mountain is on fire. Crawling to the stream, he washes his face amongst the goats. Within minutes, he is on the streets again. Everyone is talking about the fire. Choppers rotor to and fro. They ferry water to the disparate blazes. Fires aren't particularly unusual for the season. Ziq watches smoke formations. They unspool against a cobalt sky. He begins to move in the direction of the fire. He walks slowly at first. Then with a growing anxiety. And as he draws closer, an unnerving sense of knowing charges him. Jaybird is responsible for the disaster. Ziq can feel it, clear as day. He stumbles up toward the cable-car station. The view becomes clearer as he rises. The buildings give way to pines. Ziq can see the billowing pillars of smoke in great detail now. The main node of activity is centered below the cable-station. Fire trucks jam like packaged candy. People scurry to and fro. They remind Ziq of ants beneath a magnifying glass. He takes the first road he sees, leading to the suburb beneath the mountain. He then heads directly towards the fire trucks. There is excitement in the faces of the people that he passes. It irritates Ziq. It is the kind of bloodthirstiness born out of boredom. Fat pipes begin to clog up the road. They leak and spurt, creating puddles everywhere. Smoke rifts in ghostly masses between the houses. The acrid perfume of resin burns the eyes. Every now and then, a chopper cuts overhead. Blades churn the smoke. Charred remnants thrash. A telephone pole lies on its side, sparking in the underbrush. Ziq passes soot-caked fire-fighters. They shout. They barrel. Dragging filthy machines. Some burned people emerge from the smoke. Medics hoist them onto khaki gurneys. They elbow pedestrians aside. Ziq emerges through a knot of bystanders, immediately spying Jaybird. He hovers in a grassy space between houses. A helicopter passes low. It whips up the trees, raining debris. Jaybird is burned along one side, streaked with soot. He clutches the remains of his bird mask, laughing gaily. Ziq drags him deeper into the channel between the buildings. Jaybird cackles limply. He is thrust against a wall.

'There were people!' Ziq shouts uselessly.

'They're only people...' Jaybird chuckles.

Ziq breaks Jaybird's nose with a piece of charred wood. He digs the wood into the smiling face several times before he realizes what he is doing. The thin figure giggles in the grass. Ziq begins to kick into the rubbery ribcage. Until he feels something break. Phantoms rush. None seem to see. Their screams are erased by the rushing helicopters.

A scorched black hill. Cresting toward blue sky. Pockets of flaming matter cough. The air is cindered. A distant line of masked fire-fighters, struggling up a steep slope. They resemble beetles, hauling detritus. Ziq drifts aimlessly across the blackened earth. He is weeping like a child, blood across his fingers. One of the fire-fighters spots him in the danger zone. He calls out frantically. But his voice fails to penetrate the scorched air. Eventually, he gives up, losing sight of Ziq in the ragged flags of smoke.

Ziq notices that the hem of his coat has caught alight. In his struggle to put it out, he loses his balance. Tumbling down a slope of sticky ash, he eventually comes to rest in a shallow ravine. Dragging himself to his knees, Ziq stumbles around. A twisted, blackened shape resolves ahead. The smoking corpse of a zebra. The air is rich with the stench of roasted meat. Ziq sinks to his haunches. Currents of air burn his eyes. Blinding him with tears. Despite this, he forces them open. He stares into the incinerated carcass. Overhead, choppers deploy chemical foam. The toxic substance settles. Long, soothing, poison clouds of iridescent whiteness.

Ziq is side-lit. By the blue and pink neon of a karaoke hole. Japanese salesmen argue onstage. His sleepless eyes focus on three pink pills. Balanced along the palm of his hand. He has been watching the suicide pills for an hour now. The song changes again. A large screen flickers. A pretty hologram-girl appears. Yellow lyrics flutter. Drunken hands struggle for a microphone. Ziq watches. He slowly leans down. Like an exhausted dog, he licks the pills up.

A wave of gravitational force shudders inside him. It starts at the base of his spine, multiplying upward. Dispersing into his fingers. He stumbles in the street. He leans against a lamp-post. His hands and jaw are trembling uncontrollably. Paranoia erupts. But no-one is staring at him. People pass. Slow boats in a diffuse glare. They pass with heavy droning noises. Like large bees or aeroplanes. Faint, photographic trails.

Ziq blinks. Paws at his face with rubbery palms. Fear drives into him, then leaves. It reminds him of a flighty moth. In and out of a window at night. He continues down the street, becoming aware of the intense *unnaturalness* of the scape. The structures and scalding lights stand in direct contrast with the natural order of things. They cascade forever—permanent as teeth. Even bombs could not cleanse their deeply rooted calcification of the world. He wonders how he could walk, day by day, through this defiant wreckage and not see the sacrilege of it all. Then he recognizes that he is part of the problem. He feels the city mirrored deep inside him. Feeling filthy at a cellular level, he starts to crave clean water. The immense, ruthless purity of the mountain oppresses him. The sticky city gathers around its base. Garbage around a crystal spring. An electric web, in which he is hopelessly tangled. He can feel the garbage moving around, inside his cells. Ziq is struck by a mythological shame. He must get clean. He passes into the gleaming obelisk of a shopping mall. He steals through static, fridge-white corridors. Signals scream at him. People pass like animals. He barricades himself in the toilets and opens the taps full. He practically bathes in the sink, but feels dirtier. The water is not clean, here. How could he think that water out of a pipe could be clean? The only water that can help him is natural water. He must get to the sea. But the sea is too cold... He begins to seethe and panic in the glowing bathroom. Mirrors ripple like jelly. Ziq pulls himself together in their quicksand. He does not look even vaguely human. Or, perhaps, he looks too human... The primordial mud clings inescapably to him. He recognizes another filthy denizen of civilization. Sub-human and bewildered. Gathering reality around him like a raincoat, he glides back out. Into a Babylonian parade of clothing stores, advertising billboards, candy, cinemas, electrical appliances. Teenagers hunt in packs. Everything is embalmed in plastic. Even the air is tainted.

Ziq escapes down a flight of stairs. He enters a huge, echoing parking lot. There, he spies Jennifer's blonde hair. Emerging from an escalator. He shivers in apprehension. He hides behind a door. Jennifer is with another girl. He peers closer. Actually, he can't quite tell whether it is her at all. She looks so different. Like a different person. But, in a way, it *is* Jennifer, he reasons. The narcotic has conjured a doppelganger—woven from the medium of night. Ziq accepts the duplicate—as a symbol. Or perhaps even the real thing. The suicide-pills riddle everything with meaning. Even the rusty banisters and corroded bricks are coded with ancient knowledge. Before Ziq is even aware of what it is he is doing, he is moving toward the doppelganger and her companion. Mannequin faces glance up as he approaches. He must look disturbing, he realizes. He brushes past the Jennifer-girl, snagging her purse with numb, automatic fingers. He walks on. He looks over his shoulder. The girl is talking to her friend in an agitated manner. She signals to him. He draws further and further afield. Their voices are like distant birds. The girl suddenly breaks from her friend. She approaches him with a determined stride. Her impending arrival shocks him back onto the reality of the parking garage. The proximity of another life-form overwhelms his senses. She approaches like an alien world, viewed through the cockpit of a plummeting spaceship. Her face, mannerisms, clothing and scent draw into sudden, sharp focus. Her friend lingers in the background—still a bit-part.

'Excuse me,' she says.

Ziq doesn't fully accept that she addressing him. Her volatile presence swamps his universe. It's been so long since someone spoke directly to him. He stands, paralyzed by her eyes. They gleam. Violent blue jewels in a mask. He falters, his throat too dry to vocalize. A spell has been broken somewhere.

'Laura!' her friend calls from another universe.

Ziq mumbles something, tries to shrink back to the safety of shadows.

'My cards are in there,' The doppelganger pleads.

She follows him as he retreats.

'Look it's alright,' she blurts suddenly. 'Just give it back...I won't say anything.'

Her friend calls her name again. The sound of her voice echoes. It chases itself around the concrete. The doppelganger's eyes shine— unstable metal.

'Just give it back. I know you took it, I just want it back.'

He continues to shamble backward and she follows—some huge, mesmerized puppet. She reeks. Alcohol and hormones. Blue eyes laced with red. Suddenly, she grabs his sleeve with all the fury of a hunting bird. He recoils. She hangs on murderously. He calculates every chance of escape. The faraway friend begins to approach. Moving from the backstage, asserting herself into their vivid circle.

'Laura!' she calls desperately.

Ziq stares at the furious eyes—eyes set like nails. Eyes which even bombs could not dislodge. The friend takes the doppelganger's elbow. Together, they all form a strange, clinging chain. Ziq begins to stammer something. It comes out as complete gibberish.

'You probably left it at the bar...' Her friend lies, her eyes locked fearfully to Ziq's.

She is lying because she is afraid of him. The fact that someone could be afraid of him, amuses him. He smiles stupidly.

'He took it!' the doppelganger shouts. 'I can see it *bulging* in his coat!'

She turns on him.

'How can you fucking laugh at me? I know you took it! Just give it back!'

Her repetition numbs him. He feels himself wilting. But his eyes are locked to her face. Jennifer's expressions travel like fish across it. He is tempted to take that face and cry into it. Paralysis grips him. She pulls at his arm, pushing them deeper and deeper into subterranean regions.

'Maybe you left it at the bar...' the friend repeats uselessly.

'Jesus, Sandy! Of course I didn't leave it at the fucking bar! Why would I lie? He has my purse! Why would I lie?'

She turns back on him. A paradoxically helpless expression. The helplessness breaks his heart. She takes his arms, yanking him closer.

'Just give it back!' She begs. 'I won't say anything!'

'Let's just go...' Her friend interjects.

'No!' The doppelganger shrieks. 'This fuck took my purse! I want it back!'

She grabs his collar. She claws at his face.

'Thief!'

The weight of the situation suddenly occurs to him. He panics. Adrenalin floods his system. He breaks free of her grasp. Stumbling back as she lurches forward. They stop some paces apart, facing one another like gladiators. She is coiled—a hungry bird, desperate, unflinching. The friend flusters uselessly. Again, Ziq sees Jennifer. Ziq remembers his horrible anger. He remembers breaking things in the kitchen. Suddenly he finds himself wanting to break something in her too. His face must have changed because the doppelganger is now wary, hesitant—and fearful.

'I'm going to get the car,' the friend declares, disappearing.

The universe shrinks again. It encapsulates the pair. Delivering them back to a tiny, apocalyptic stage. She points at him, her finger shaking.

'You've got my purse.'

Magnetic anger flares uncontrollably between them.

'Give it back!'

Before he realizes it, he has pushed her to the ground. She flails—a spider on its back.

'Don't you touch me!' she wails.

The sound of her voice gets him in his soft center. It pushes home the brutality of his actions.

'Don't you dare fucking touch me!' she screams, rising like an unstoppable phantom.

She grabs his coat again. The smell of her fear sweat freezes him.

'You don't push a woman, you fuck!'

He wrestles automatically. His elbow strikes her accidentally, across her head. She ricochets off and the lack of her is suddenly terrifying to him. He looks up to her shocked eyes. She fumbles in her handbag with shaking hands. Withdraws a small, black pistol. A hooter erupts through the lot. The friend is reacting to the sight of the gun. The doppelganger stares down her pistol.

'Get in the fucking car,' she splutters.

The car swoops out of the shadows. Draws alongside. The friend is shouting, gesticulating. But her noise cannot penetrate the stillness between them.

'Get in the fucking car,' the doppelganger repeats.

'Laura! What are you doing!' her friend screeches.

'Get in the fucking car!'

Her command shatters Ziq's reverie.

She grabs his collar, bullies him into the passenger seat. Inside, the friend is deafening.

'What the fuck are you doing!' She shouts, over and over again.

The doppelganger scrabbles into the back.

'Drive,' she instructs.

Ziq is staring at the parking lot as the doors slam. Through the glass and noise, the lot seems like another dimension—a universe in which he has suddenly ceased to exist. Something cold and hard clangs against the back of his head. The world flashes blinding white. He tastes a rusty suction. Blood follows the blow. It oozes out of him, into the world.

A head-lit highway. The dark sea—visible over a security barrier. Their shouting match has intensified. Nameless hysteria. At one point the doppelganger goes through his outer pockets. She finds his phones. Throws them to the floor in rage. He weeps wretchedly. She pistol whips him again. His bleeding head cups like an egg in his hand. Bare rock, dangerously close. The girls argue viciously. He proclaims his innocence. Ragged outbursts. The stench of poisonous sweat. They drive faster. Words slur, becoming useless, crumbling in the jet stream.

The car turns recklessly. Onto a look-out crescent. Gravel scatters. The passenger door flies open. Ziq jumps. He staggers with velocity, passing out of the headlights like an animal. The doppelganger throws open the back door too. She leans out after him, screaming. The swerving causes her to lose her grip. She also rolls out, onto the sand. The pistol bounces through the headlights. Spinning into shadow. The car wrenches to a halt. Half-on, half-off the road. The doppelganger begins to scurry, through the blaze of light. She searches frantically for her lost gun. Ziq stops running.

'Help me!' the doppelganger calls pitifully to the car.

Her friend sees Ziq reappear and panics. Gunning the engine, she reverses. The back-bumper smashes down a safety barrier. The doppelganger scrambles to her feet, chasing into the light. She runs onto the road. But the car has already skidded down the highway. She runs after it. One of her heels snaps. It sends her to the tarmac. Darkness falls as the car recedes. The doppelganger-girl's head and shoulders shake in the dying light. She shouts after the vehicle. The headlights swerve around a distant bend. It is gone. Ziq watches from the crescent. He sinks slowly down to the gravel and clutches it in his fists. He heaves a ragged sigh of release, falling back. When his injured scalp strikes the sand, he stares drunkenly. A spinning maelstrom of stars. Gratitude floods him. He floats in outer space—lighter than he has ever felt. He embraces this nearness of the divine with shaking hands. Distant, jagged screams filter back. They pull him back to earth. The ordeal has weakened him. He could lie there the whole night, waiting for the dawn. Sweat cools sharply as he rises. He is bathed in goaty perspiration. Another scream out of the star-drenched dark. The doppelganger is on the tarmac. Once again, it is as though a faery pall has descended, transforming the girl into Jennifer. When Ziq calls out, it is Jennifer he is addressing.

'Calm down,' he reassures her.

The doppelganger freezes. He feels her fear.

'Stay away from me, you fucker!' she shrills.

'I won't hurt you…'

They watch each other across the divide. She breaks into tears. In the dimness, a hairline crack. Forming deep within his chest. He is the one who has done this to her. He wants to put his arms around Jennifer and almost acts on this lunatic impulse.

'I'm not going to hurt you…' he calls again.

'Stay away!'

She backs away as he attempts to approach. She is limping on her one good heel—a wounded bird. He stops. She stops too, swaying in the wind.

'It's not safe here!' he shouts over the gusts.

She hesitates.

'There's a small hotel—a few kilometers away. We can walk there, call you a taxi.'

He attempts to approach again. But she staggers away—an uncatchable mirage.

The night porter is half-awake. He watches a rom-com on a small pad. A pair of figures enter through the doors at the end of the lobby. He leans up, blinking. A girl remains half-way down the hall. She hovers, arms wrapped around herself. A male figure in a dirty coat. He approaches. He looks homeless. An unshaven lunatic.

'Evening,' the porter greets warily.

The coated figure nods. He leans on the counter, hands trembling.

'We had some car the trouble,' He coughs.

'Will you be staying the night?' the porter enquires. 'Bridal suite is available.'

The girl barks out a bitter laugh. The porter decides that he doesn't like the pair very much. The male figure seems dazed, disorientated. He stares intently at some detail on his sleeve. There is beach gravel in his hair. His cheek is grazed. The girl leans icily. She massages her wrists in manic fashion, clearly drunk.

'Our car broke down. We lost our phones,' she snaps irritably. 'Please, can I just use your phone?'

The porter looks her up and down. He takes in her costly cocktail dress and ruined designer shoes.

'Certainly,' he replies, offering her a receiver.

'Where are the bathrooms?' she asks.

The porter directs her. She vanishes through a pair of sallow doors.

'Could you call us a taxi?' he stutters.

'Sure. Are you ok, sir?'

He looks up sharply. The porter sees that his pupils are dilated to wide black holes. His head is crusted with blood.

'Shock probably...' he answers slowly. 'We had a bad spill.'

'Right,' the porter says, dialling.

'Is there a bar?'

'Sure, through those doors.'

In the bar, Ziq begins to settle back into himself. Like milk, curdling in reverse, he gradually unifies his polarities into an objective whole. He is beginning to understand the fervour of religion. That peculiar shock of being birthed into a strange, new world. He might as well be sitting in a diner on Mars. He nurses the cup of coffee as though it were his first. He is about to take a sip, when he spots the piano across the room. He goes over to it. It is a boudoir model, one below a baby grand. A little scuffed, in relatively good condition. He sits down wearily, opens the key-lid. The barman is about to protest when he begins playing Bach. The music flows out of him unimpeded. If only he could have played like this in New York. He might not have quit then. The doppelganger enters abruptly. She appears surprisingly refreshed. Hair is slicked back into a sharp, blonde bullet. Her dress hangs tidily. She shoots Ziq an unfathomable look, sits at the bar. He stops playing immediately. She orders a double whiskey, bristling with tension. The tired barman abandons his text message. He starts slowly for the bottles. Ziq sits next to her.

'Taxi is on its way,' he says, anxious to prove his solidarity.

She nods sullenly, transformed. Catching a glimpse of her in the mirror across the bar, he begins to wonder how he could have mistaken this stranger for Jennifer. Aside from the colour and cut of her blonde hair, there really isn't much of a similarity. The whiskey arrives. She swallows it in a single gulp, blinks heavily, orders another. The bartender observes with some interest, pouring out another. This time she swallows only half. She nurses the tumbler.

'Sorry about the gun thing,' she says unexpectedly.

'Forget it,' he replies, stunned.

She swallows the whiskey, orders another double.

'I must have left it at the other bar,' she says.

After a while, the porter comes. He informs them that their taxi has arrived. The barman produces a saucer. The doppelganger swipes a slip of paper from it, reaching for her purse. She realizes that she doesn't have it.

'Oh fuck,' she slurs.

Ziq wordlessly tosses her purse onto the bar before her. She stares speechlessly at it for several seconds. Then punches him in the side of the head. He falls off his stool. When he gets up again, she is laughing.

She passes out in the back of the taxi. He watches the dawn light rise behind the mountain. They stop at the Three Towers and he opens his door in relief. The doppelganger is asleep, hair draped carelessly across the seat. Ziq looks at the blonde fall, feeling once again that strange link with Jennifer. He experiences a curious sense of release as the car pulls off. He watches it disappear, stands very still in the morning light. After a while, he pulls the gun from an inner pocket. He stands for a long time, looking at it, savouring it's heaviness. A breeze starts up. It brings with it the strange scents of a new day.

Game Over II

Brick had been at this pool party. He'd been so busy trying get his nose to the grindstone with the film, that he'd forgotten to check if he had people in town. Of course, he did. Next thing he was at a party. He met some swimwear models. They took him to another party. He stayed at someone's house near the sea. He ended up in a threesome in a Jacuzzi. He was drinking heavily. His phone kept ringing. So, he threw it off a balcony. A few days went by in a haze. He won ten grand in a poker game, pretending to be Fast Eddie Felson. The pool party was the high point—or a low point. Depending on one's politics. Brick certainly felt that he nearly went to the 'next level' at that party. It had been wild. Rich kids. He remembers a deckchair on fire. A white, stone statue of Apollo had fallen to the bottom of a waterfall pool. Brick was holding onto its arm, to stay at the bottom. He was starting to get an idea of what Delilah went through in that godforsaken, made-up country of Croeser's. As usual he was a little too in character. He passed out underwater. Luckily someone was on hand to resuscitate him. The event sobered him up. So, he started drinking more.

Brick wakes up a few days later, in a Rastafarian Saloon. The bartender tells him he is near Scarborough (wherever that is). Apparently, he already has a room upstairs. He gets a couple of beers and goes out to look at the sunset. The only problem is that it's dawn. He can't bring himself to open up beers for breakfast. So, he gets a Bloody Mary instead. Rummaging around in his pocket, he discovers a cocktail napkin. Someone has scrawled 'GAME OVER', in pale blue lipstick.

He goes up to his small, beach-facing room. He doesn't recognize it—even though he's apparently been there two days. The phone wakes him up around noon. The manager tells him he has a visitor. He shambles down to the bar, where he finds a short man in a raincoat. The man's hat and mustache are both neat and grey. He smiles amiably. When Brick first arrived in the Cape, he had been shocked to find that people were still being described as 'Cape coloureds'. He contemplates asking the man, whether he would describe himself that way. In the end, he decides that it is perhaps a little forward.

'You're a hard man to find,' the man says, extending his hand.

'Wilbur Struik.'

Brick looks at the hand, but does not take it.

'I suppose you think it's alright, then—coercing a young girl into leaking compromising photographs of herself?'

'I'm just the messenger. I would never force anyone to do anything against their will.'

Brick studies his face. He looks honest enough.

'Ex-cop?' Brick asks.

'Navy. I trained and worked at the base in Simonstown.'

'Why'd you leave?'

'I was discharged.'

'What did you do?'

Struik shrugs. But his voice betrays a steeliness.

'I found out about something. It happened by mistake.'

Brick sighs and puts out his hand. Struik shakes it peaceably.

'Get you a beer?' Brick asks, sitting next to him at the bar.

'I'm fine.'

'So, what brings you to my doorstep?' Brick asks, signaling the bartender.

'Luminstein wants to talk.'

Brick gets his beer and takes a swig. He considers the message.

'What does he want to talk about?'

'Why don't I call him now?' Struik offers.

Brick asks the bartender for a plate of fries. He offers Struik the menu, but the detective declines.

'Ok,' Brick says, after a moment. 'Call.'

Struik nods. He pulls a pad from his coat. Balancing the device against the wooden bar-post, he rings the producer. Luminstein picks up quickly. He's at home, in a large, but messy kitchen. There's a maid in an outfit, doing dishes.

'Brick,' Luminstein smiles. 'Nice to see you. Been getting some R&R?'

'I guess you could say that,' Brick grunts.

'You've discussed the offer with Sal?'

'What offer? Sorry, I've been unreachable.'

'Well—just to catch up, we are going with Fortunato's cut. Croeser okayed it. In fact, he loves it.'

'What choice did he have?'

Luminstein grins uncomfortably.

'Well, he really did love it, Brick. I mean, we all did. We couldn't swing the credit, though.'

'You said something about an offer?'

'I suggest you speak to your agent—or maybe just contact Delilah.'

'Delilah?' Brick frowns.

'Yes. Delilah.'

Struik tells Brick that he can drop him back at his suite. He mulls it over while he finishes his beer. In the end, Brick agrees. He hasn't carried anything with him except his wallet. So, he settles everything and leaves with the detective.

In the car, he uses Struik's phone to call Delilah. She's happy to meet with him in a couple of hours. She'll bring Fortunato. It feels like a whole month has passed since he was in the hotel. A lot more people seem to recognize him. The girl at the desk informs him that the hotel was very happy to hold his suite for him. Everything should be 'just as he left it'. Somehow, it does little to reassure him. He is on the way to the lift when, out of the blue, he runs into V. She wears a tailored suit and reeks of money.

'Brick!' she exclaims, putting her arms around his neck and kissing both cheeks.

Brick is dumbfounded.

'I never thought I'd see you again,' he confesses.

'I had to come back for a funeral.'

'I'm sorry to hear that.'

'Let's have dinner and catch up,' she suggests. 'I have to meet some Oracle friends now.'

He gets her new number and goes upstairs, shaking his head. In his room, the giant lipstick V is still there. He gets a wad of tissue paper and smudges it irreparably. Somehow this makes him feel better. Then he notices that the Oscar statuette is missing.

The hotel tells Brick that they didn't touch the award. He believes them. He showers and puts on his white suit. His nose is healing quickly now. He almost feels like himself again. He meets Delilah and Fortunato by the pool. By some humorous twist of circumstance, Fortunato is also wearing a white suit. Delilah loves that they are matching.

'It's a sign, bitches!' she yells, causing everyone to look up.

They take a table near the water and order green juices. Brick notes how much calmer Fortunato seems around Delilah. He gets the sense of how vital the concept of conspiracy must be to their partnership. They seem to have about them at all times, a revolutionary look (*from a film about revolutionaries*—the old inner voice addendums snidely).

'Fortunato, Sasha and me have been plotting,' Delilah explains. 'We want to pitch Shane on the next movie. Sash and me want to go in as producers. Also, I have big money guys eating out of my hand now. So, we don't need to beg.'

'Let me guess,' Brick says. 'You recruited your own billionaires in Club Ded?'

'Oh, as money mixers go—that space-base was aces.'

'Delaney won't go for it,' Brick replied.

'Shane and the production team have had enough of him,' Delilah confides. 'He played it too close to the bone. They want fresh meat for the next one.'

'So, what's the offer?' Brick smiles.

Fortunato leans forward.

'I want to direct a sequel to GAME OVER,' he says. 'With Sasha and Delilah. Written by and hopefully…starring you.'

Brick looks at them both. There is something quite touching about the way they both seem to be holding their breath while they wait for a response. Fortunato's unexpected display of worldly ambition, strikes a chord in Brick.

'I never thought you would try pitch me, Fortunato,' Brick teases.

Fortunato chuckles, embarrassed.

'Is that a yes?' Delilah asks.

'Don't be offended, but they'll consider you a first-time director. They might insist on going with someone they trust.'

'They'll go for it if we all back him,' Delilah says.

'Also…' Fortunato mumbles. '…if you consider co-directing it with me.'

Brick bursts out laughing.

'Say yes, fuck it!' Delilah shouts.

'Of course, yes!' Brick nods.

Fortunato extends his hand awkwardly. Brick takes it.

'If you will excuse me,' Fortunato coughs, getting up abruptly.

They watch him walk slowly to the bathrooms.

'He's probably going to throw up now,' Delilah snickers. 'You have no idea how nervous he was that you might refuse.'

Brick leans back comfortably in his chair. The ocean view really *is* spectacular from up here.

'How could I refuse,' he sighs, with something approaching satisfaction.

Brick meets V in Greenmarket Square towards sunset. The market stalls are packing up. Pigeons flock pleasantly around the Church's bell tower. Brick breathes it in. All in all, it's a nice, sugary slice of retail tourism come splendidly to life. Indeed, V's new hyper-styled appearance only accentuates the tawdry, glossy magazine aspect of the location. She fits in all too well with the tourism cliché, he notes—especially with a movie star on her arm.

'Been out of town then, I take it?' Brick asks, as they stroll.

'Out of my mind!' she sings.

'Pray tell…'

V inspects some hand-carved idols with distaste. Already, Brick feels himself being managed comfortably into the role of an assigned suitor (or future husband), so powerful is the affectation of V's new orbit.

'I was in Milan—mostly,' she confesses, a little theatrically.

She grabs Brick's arm and looks into his eyes.

'I got married, Brick!'

'Congratulations,' he replies drily.

'It's not what you think. Etienne and I have been seeing one another for some time. He's in cryptofinance. He travels a lot.'

'Almost exactly what I envisaged for you…'

'No need to be that way.'

'Sorry. That was uncalled for.'

'Tell me, how is Fortunato?'

'Very well!'

'I would love to catch up with him.'

'Really? I was under the impression that you had been avoiding him.'

V makes a face.

'He is too sensitive. A real artist. I mean, you know what they can be like?'

'Sure,' Brick nods. 'Anyway, so tell me more about your husband.'

'Etienne? Oh, Etienne is in crypto.'

'Yes, you mentioned that.'

'Such a fabulous human being, Brick. Really, quite spiritual. He likes to sail. Has houses all over Europe…'

'Sounds like a real catch.'

'Oh, it's not like that.'

'I'm just glad that you're alright. We were all a bit concerned, you know.'

'We? You mean Fortunato? I would really love to see him, you know. I saw some pictures of him—with Delilah—in an Italian tabloid! I was so proud.'

'He's in the society pages already!' Brick laughs. 'That fucking guy…'

'To tell you the truth, he's been avoiding my calls. Why would he do that, you think?'

'I really wouldn't know. So, will you both be settling in Italy?'

'I suppose. I'm trying to push Etienne to get a place in the States. I mean Italy, god! It's like a third world country…'

'If you say so.'

Their conversation is interrupted by a woman in upmarket jogging gear.

'Child molester!' she shouts, in a stultified Afrikaans accent.

It takes Brick a moment to realize that the remark is being directed at him. People are starting to look in their direction.

'Delilah is a child, you pig!' the woman declares furiously.

They are caught off-guard, beside the tables of an outdoor café. V casually reaches over and picks up a glass of water. She flings the liquid at the heckler, drenching her.

'Get out of here, you, ignorant woman,' she mutters regally.

Shocked, the woman retreats.

'Shame on you both,' she calls over her shoulder.

V looks back to the watching tourists.

'And, what are you savages staring at?' she snaps

Taking Brick by the hand, she yanks him down a side-street.

They stroll up the tree-lined avenue of the Company Gardens. V has her arm linked with his in a show of support.

'I sold myself, didn't I?' she laughs.

'What's he like then, really?'

'Boring. Stuffy…unattractive. But he is safe. And quite sweet. He's not involved in any illegal activities—that I know of. He's loyal. I know that he would never hurt me. I also…Well, don't fear for my life anymore.'

'You're not hurting anyone,' Brick reassures her.

She bites her lip lightly. In the dark, beneath the gloaming trees her guard seems to slip.

'I should have stuck with Fortunato…'

'You're not thinking of him!' he laughs. 'You're thinking of all those Hollywood pool parties and awards ceremonies you'll be missing…'

'I could get him back.'

'Don't even think about it, baby. You've tortured that poor guy enough. Let him have his day in the sun.'

'What will you do?'

'Back to Paris. Fix things with my wife.'

'You love her still?'

'Not in the way I used to.'

'How was that?'

'Like we were in a movie, I guess…'

'What about Delaney? Will you still see him?'

'After what he did! I'm not sure… I mean, He bugged my hotel suite, for Christ's sake!'

'Yes, I was aware of that.'

'Why would he do such a thing? And more importantly—why didn't you tell me?'

'Ah, he became obsessed with that old film.'

'Two weeks in another town?'

'He thought if he could engineer circumstances to mirror the narrative, with secret cameras, he could do some sort of closed circuit, post-Dogme homage on the backburner…'

'A third film!'

'Hey, he's your friend!'

'I suppose that speech he gave should have tipped me off.'

'He wrote that stuff while we were having sex. Told me the winged helmet would swing it. And what a good actor you were—that you would come up with spontaneous gems if you didn't know you were being filmed.'

'At least I managed to lose his Oscar.'

V sniggers.

'You didn't.'

Brick stops in his tracks.

'What?' he says. 'What do you mean?'

'Struik retrieved it for Croeser, when he briefed Delilah.'

Brick blinks a few times, speechless.

'Sorry, I thought you knew…' she smiles, pulling him along.

Sleepwalking

Chloe pilots her pink and powder blue Kawasaki down the coast. She passes the cube that used to provide access to Club Ded. The walls are smashed. The structure now appears derelict. Chloe was there the day the elevator mechanisms were sabotaged. People had been trapped in the compound below. They had to wait two days to be rescued by boat. Two whole days and nights with all those dead bodies. Luckily, Chloe knew another way out. She'd been able to escape with two of the girls.

Half a kilometer from the cube, she turns down a dirt trail. The passage leads to a grotto of alien pines. A graffiti stricken concrete station, situated at the far end of a small clifftop. Overlooking the sea. The structure has a heavy metal door, a sturdy padlock. Chloe parks outside, dismounts. She inserts a key into the padlock. The front slips off, revealing a complex keypad. She enters a combination. The metal door unseals with a gasp of pressurized air. She wheels her bike into the shed. Locks herself in by the light of her phone. The interior is bare concrete. The only feature is a metal trapdoor. In the center of the floor. This is fitted with another keypad. Chloe kneels and unlocks it. A lighting system activates, revealing a metal spiral stair. It sits in the center of a narrow shaft, leading down into the rock.

Chloe has been back a few times since Club Ded shut down. The memories of that day continue to plague her. The staircase seems to go down forever. It never fails to remind Chloe of the steps in the Leicester Square tube. The shaft terminates in the back of Anita's old walk-in closet. A combination lock provides access. To a long, narrow space full of designer gowns in plastic sheaths. Chloe emerges from the rustling garments and pauses to listen. She stalks cautiously around the dark spaces. Her stun-pistol is on full charge. She carries an electroshock-tonfa as back-up. Most of the glass shattered when they torched the place. The walls are mostly black, broken. Some areas remain eerily preserved. At one point, Chloe senses movement. She spins, paranoically fires. The discharge lights the broken hall for a second. A section of blistered plaster sizzles, scorches. Penguins shamble towards a ruined water feature. They splash in the polluted water, anxious to escape. It's unusual seeing them on this side of the peninsula. Someone must have been keeping them as pets. Relieved to have missed them, Chloe descends a few levels. She is heading for the remains of her bar. Seabirds have already begun to nest in the cracks. A real, ruined queendom, she thinks. She passes what's left of the bank. Mostly rubble. They took everything—even the paperwork. She locates the bar. One of the walls has collapsed. The cavity looks pleasantly out over the sea. There's a lot of dry food and alcohol. Human scavengers haven't managed to find a way down the cliffs yet. If you wanted to be down here, you had to have the means. Chloe mixes herself a lukewarm cocktail. She kicks a wicker chair to the edge of the missing wall. Putting her boots up on the ruined concrete, she settles in for the sunset. She's been back six times now. Each time, with the intention of calling Jennifer—to tell her what happened. She hasn't made it that far yet. Each time, she ends up getting drunk, postponing. But now, halfway through her third cocktail, she finally works up the nerve.

Jennifer likes the capsule hotel. Each pod is sound-proofed and has a window. The circular porthole is at the head end. It looks out onto the neon signage of Kabukicho. The foot-end terminates in a solid airlock. The walls are pearly white. The mattress, tatami. A ventilation shaft, shelving and a smart-screen are the only features. Men are not allowed in the building. When Jennifer is inside, she feels like a wasp in a cell—something that is melting down, changing shape. It takes her back to the pods in Club Ded. She used to love the excitement of being in those. They would acclimatize her body before releasing her into the tank system. She bleached her hair back to blonde within a day of landing in Japan. Now it is short at the sides, gelled back on the top. When her phone beeps, she moves stiffly. Her joints feel as though they were encased in plastic.

'Moshi moshi.'
'It's Chloe.'
'Oh fuck…'
The call catches Jennifer completely by surprise. She hasn't spoken English in weeks.
'How are you?' she asks.
'I'm ok. How's Japan?'
Jennifer looks out into the neon night.
'It's busy here,' she replies hazily. 'Real busy.'
'You in Kyoto?'
'I stay in Tokyo some week-ends'
'Shinjuku?'
'Yeah.'
'Nice.'
There is an uncomfortable pause. For a moment, neither of them

seems able to commit to what must, by necessity, come next.

'How's Anita?' Jennifer asks. 'I can't reach her.'

Chloe closes her eyes. She drains the cocktail and hurls the glass to the rocks below.

'I've been meaning to call, actually,' she replies stickily.

Jennifer hears the distant smash of glass. It numbs her somewhere inside.

'What's happened?' she whispers.

Chloe has been over that day so many times. She has analyzed it, turned over all the different ways it could have played out. She even dreams about it.

'Things started falling apart. I was there that day, but I didn't see it go down.'

Jennifer is silent, so Chloe continues.

'Nobody knew who they were. Customs didn't see them coming. They landed in a speedboat. By that stage, there were no books, no records, most of the original people had pulled out. The military had bailed—with all their gear. We lost most of the consulates over a weekend. Security was down to a handful....'

She pauses, slowing down.

'Whoever it was, they were very professional. Even in riot gear, our people went down in seconds...'

Chloe stares into the sea, remembering the sounds and closed-circuit feeds. She remembers running.

'Anita was really falling apart,' she mumbles uselessly.

'What happened?' Jennifer breathes.

'I wasn't there,' Chloe repeats. 'But Audrey was hiding. She saw them take Anita. They put her in a bag and they just...took her. They took all the girls, Jen.'

Jennifer lies motionless in her pod, imagining.

'I think Croeser offered us all up as collateral to traffickers or someone worse. Maybe to save his own hide after the footage disappeared. I mean, he *hated* Annie...'

Chloe pauses for a moment, then continues.

'They didn't touch the punters. Took out some staff. A clean-up crew was dispatched in the next few days. They got the survivors, dealt with the bodies.'

Jennifer visualizes Anita, somewhere in the world. Trapped in some indescribable hell.

'I'm really sorry...' Chloe flusters.

Jennifer breathes in slowly, composing herself.

Thanks for the call, Chloe,' she says, preparing to hang-up.

'Listen, Jen. There's something else.'

Jennifer pauses.

'Some guy's been phoning the helpline, leaving messages for you.'

'Messages?' she repeats vacantly.

'Long messages. Some of them aren't so pretty.'

Jennifer remains silent, digesting this.

'I archived them for you,' Chloe says. 'Some of the girls...Well, some of the girls read a few—by mistake.'

'I see,' Jennifer eventually replies.

Chloe toys with her stun-gun, waiting to see if Jennifer has more to say on the subject.

'He seems very upset,' she blurts.

'Delete them,' Jennifer says.

Chloe frowns. She had been hoping that the messages would somehow dull the blow. Instead they have only added to it. Too late, Chloe realizes how tactless she has been.

'I can send them to you. It's no problem...' she adds hurriedly, a little drunk.

'Listen, Chloe, I have to go. Thanks for calling. Please just discard those mails.'

The phone cuts out. Chloe stares at the device for a moment, before replacing it in its holster. Rising, she crosses the room to fix herself another round. As she is doing so, she realizes, quite suddenly and clearly, that she will ever speak to Jennifer again.

The Oracle's Kyoto house is sixteenth century. It sits on the slopes of Mount Ogura, overlooking the city. The Edo-period garden has some historical significance. Its centerpiece is a moss garden. This has taken centuries to develop. Ornamental stone bridges stitch the area prettily. The entire garden is at an incline, incorporating a view of Mount Hiei in the overall pattern. Now, when the rain is only slightly more substantial than mist, and the dawn is softened to a grey, diffuse glow, the garden takes on a tranquil, slightly supernatural air. The atmosphere is enhanced by its silence. This is broken only by water and the creaking of wood. In such a harmonious environment, an incongruent presence is easy to detect.

A discordant sound travels though the mist. Agonized, slurred weeping. Jennifer staggers across a bridge. Her hair is a mess. Kimono hanging open, revealing bruised flesh. A bottle of cheap liquor in her fingers. It clinks against the balustrades, frightening a pair of egrets. She takes another long swallow, vomits across the lotus pads of a carp pond. She's been crying through the night. Her face is red and white. Entering a series of filigreed arches, she eventually emerges into a hedged-in area. A dry rock Zen garden sheltered by the greenery. The tablet of impeccably raked sand stops her in her tracks. For some reason, she is offended by its monumental stillness. She feels the bottle slip. It shatters. Bright blue fluid leaks into the patterning. She wades down into the Zen garden. At one point, she loses her balance, falls. Rising crookedly, she hurls a fistful of sand at the tallest of the standing stones. Her cries rise above the trees, disturbing more birds. She stumbles over to the closest standing stone and topples it. It falls ungraciously, gusting sand everywhere. She collapses to her knees. Granules enter her clenched fists. She can feel them embed into line-work of her palms. Are they changing them—she panics? Are they changing her future?

Nobody in the house mentions the incident. Jennifer awakens on a woven mat in a quiet chamber. Somebody has cleaned her, wrapped her in blankets, left food beside the bed. She sleeps throughout the night. Then returns to her room the next morning. She meets several girls along the way. Everyone smiles courteously, as though nothing has happened. Jennifer senses that they want her out. She doesn't care. The estate is enormous and silent. Easy to hide in. It's haunted by cats and speechless women in traditional dress-code. She is generally ignored, or treated in a polite, but deferential way. It has been all too easy to slot into the slow clockworks. Someone had once told Jennifer that she had the character of a creeper vine—always questing for something to grow around. The truth is that she will settle for almost any system, simply to quieten her mind. The routines of the house have slowed her. The estate houses the central hub of Japanese Control. Jennifer arrives there for work each morning, in white. She's only tentatively explored the city— one or two local festivals, some tourist sites. Her Japanese is limited and the sensation of being a stranger leaves her feeling stranded. One day, by chance, she discovers a smack pipe in one of the toilets. Investigating further, she befriends a dour girl called Mitsuko, who begins to supply her with heroin. Her memory starts to disintegrate. Just as she had so fervently prayed it would. She hasn't seen the Oracle since arriving. After hearing about Anita, she ceases to care whether she will ever see her again. Jennifer becomes a perfect cog. She performs her duties with detail and care. She sleeps deeply, watches fish for hours in the garden. She becomes almost content. She begins to forget the blue world by the sea. It becomes like a dream, or a film she had seen once. She has more money than ever before. But can find nothing to spend it on—except heroin and elaborate sweetmeats. All her needs are taken care of by the machinations of the house.

At some point, soon after her arrival, Jennifer had been asked to courier black boxes to the offices in the Tokyo. She would wear black on these trips. She quickly realized how much she missed being in a city. She began to return in her free time, sleeping in the same capsule.

Eating alone in expensive restaurants. She missed Anita the most on these jaunts. The temptation to call had been great. She didn't dare. It would have taken only one word from Anita to make her return. But she knew that she could not survive a return to the blue light. It haunts her dreams still. When she dreams of Anita, blue light shines from her eyes, navel and fingertips. Like St Elmo's fire. It gusts around an entire universe, trying to find its way back into her waking world.

Jennifer sees herself as a kind of mannequin now. In a way, she has become more of a machine than Anita could have ever hoped to be. Jennifer is a robot. She is tuned to efficient programming. In a house, full of strangers. The form hardens with each passing day. It renders her sexless and emotionally impenetrable. Jennifer knows that she will never again engage in intimate relations. She will never make love or kiss, feel or experience affectionate with anyone else ever again. These things are relics now—the husks of a former existence. She has become as dead and beautiful as a seashell. Fully content to exist in a nun-like state of retreat for the rest of her life. She sees it as a fair trade. The price she must pay for her transgressions. Hers is now a strange and cold paradise—a paradise in which she will remain, forever, a stranger.

In the quiet of the garden, Jennifer deadens herself with ecstasies of peace. She inhales milky erasures. Koi suspend in a dappled universe—a universe that she was once familiar with. Leaves fall like pale fire. She finds it brutally ironic that Chloe should call, precisely at the moment when she is missing Anita the most. She had dined alone the night before, pleasantly adrift in the code-work of the city. She's eating meat again. It doesn't seem to matter anymore. She has to keep it a secret at the house. Carnivorous consumption is against the Oracle's rules. She laughs at how Anita would scold her. She came so very close to calling her the night Chloe rang.

Afterwards, when Anita's demise starts to sink in, it isn't as though Jennifer feels something die. It is more that she finally realizes that something *has already* died. It has left its festering corpse, deep within her breast. She finds it strange that she hasn't thought of Ziq. Not even once. It took Chloe to remind her that he even existed. She feels vaguely sorry for him. Perhaps even amused at the way Anita keeps beating him to the punch—even now. The truth is that Anita takes up so much room. There is no place for anything else. She has simply eclipsed Ziq. Just like everything else she came into contact with. Jennifer almost laughs at thoughts like this. Then she will catch herself on the word 'death'. It's like getting snagged on broken glass. It makes her suffer. Not because Anita might be gone forever, but that *she might still be alive*. The thought torments her—almost to madness. She becomes overwhelmed by scenarios, possibilities. She sees Anita as a broken slave in a hell of starving shadows. The thought drives her to drink and self-mutilation. It drives her to a quiet, secret insanity, nurtured at the heart of the world itself. There is simply no room. There is no room for anything anymore, ever.

Control is classically furnished. Paper walls divide the spaces. They diffuse light into sequences. Large windows overlook the garden. Computers are set at regular intervals throughout. Girls in white kimonos kneel before the screens. They fill the spaces with a pleasant buzz of activity. A hummingbird darts around the room, unable to find its way out. Jennifer kneels in one of the rows. She types slowly, but fastidiously. Her hair is neat again. Her face powdered to porcelain. At first, she thought the house over-styled. Something a foreigner would do. Later she discovered that it was a historical recreation. A sort of snow-globe world. A bubble. A girl in black robes enters. She scans the chamber, picking out Jennifer's blonde head. Padding silently down the row in spotless tabi socks, she kneels briefly. Jennifer pauses, looking up. A tired expression. The girl in black whispers something to her and leaves. Jennifer rises slowly, following her out.

The bath-house is separated from the central structure. To reach it, you have to take a path. Down into a small, wooded area. The bath-house comprises several circular structures. The interior is purposefully dim. In the steam and darkness, the dimensions become ambiguous. Dragonflies get lost in the bath-house. Bamboo screens slat out the garden. Large leaves filter the light. The girl in black helps Jennifer to undress. She folds her kimono. She scrubs Jennifer with salt and icy water. Then leads her through a dark gallery of steaming wooden vats. They take a short stair to a sunken level. The steam makes it difficult to see. The lower level is also darker. Jennifer enters the still, scalding water. She inches in by degrees. Until the heavy, resonant water has claimed her entirely. She submerges, then reclines against the wood. The girl in black is gone. The steam obscures the far end of the bath. Jennifer realizes that she is not alone. There is another presence in the water.

'I'm sending you back, little bird,' The Oracle tells her quietly.

Jennifer exhales heavily across the surface of the water. Vapour eddies. Somehow, it soothes her to know that judgement has finally come.

'This spirit, that talks to you in your sleep,' The Oracle says. 'It has told you its name—but you will not speak it.'

Jennifer listens to the passage of distant birds.

'It is written,' she replies, uselessly.

She books too late, has to fly via Dubai. She ends up caught in transit for hours. It all comes as a shock. Especially after the sleepy alienation of Japan. She finds herself crying in the departure lounge, dying for a soft screen of smack. Jennifer's return to the Three Towers is marked by an intense sensation of artifice. The structures have taken on the unnerving, two-dimensional qualities of a backdrop. Even the mountain looks fake. In the lobby, she feels like a ghost. She rides the elevator, turns her key in the lock. Light slices into the tomb-like space. A sour, dusty smell. The plants have all died. She sets down her luggage. Wretched with fatigue and sporadic withdrawal symptoms. The apartment is a wreck. Furniture lies overturned, broken. The television squats—an enormous, broken eye. Wallets and purses scatter—fallen birds. She wanders bleakly through the ruins. The bathroom is a cornucopia of shattered mirrors. A black briefcase sits ominously in the empty bath. She picks her way over to it, kneeling cautiously between broken glass. Inside she finds the billfolds of foreign currency she had left for him—all painted pink. A small pistol lies accusingly on top the ruined money. It has also been painted pink. The paint has glued it to some of the cash. A note reads: 'THE END'. She sighs, sitting like that for a while. Breathing slowly. Observing the wreckage.

Awakening

Ziq left the tower after his encounter with the doppelganger. The suicide pills had begun to re-wire his neural network. New branches of thought were flourishing—away from the cataclysmic horizon of Jennifer. He moved back to the Pharm. He had nowhere else to run. Jaybird had vanished entirely. Nobody had seen him since the fire. Ziq noted the disappearance with fear. He wonders whether he murdered Jaybird in that grassy cleft between worlds. He even tried to find out if a murder had been reported. But there was nothing. His life had become a quiet graveyard of painful events. Some weeks passed. His money dwindled. He could not bring himself to pickpocket again. The mechanisms were dead. The processing plant had been shut down. For good. Chickens now invade its buckets. The pink paint left a garish rime. Desperate days brought him down to the boulevards and arcades, where he eyed human transactions with an unbearable nervousness. A thin layer of fear had caked around him. Psychic ice. Whenever he thought to slip back into that sinewy exchange of hands and wallets, the fear would surface again. Some heavy, unendurable fish. It paralyzed him entirely. Somewhere, a spell had been broken. He had traded his cat-like invisibility for hesitation. And a fresh palette of raw emotion. With these pigments, he began the arduous task of painting his life anew. He was forced, for the first time to follow the dictates of society. He applied for and somehow succeeded in acquiring a job in a small bookshop. The monumental personal significance of this task passed unnoticed to the rest of society. To Ziq, however, it was an almost unbelievable milestone. He realized that he was beginning to empathize and indeed exist again, amongst humanity. This stripping of armour and fearful re-entry was Jennifer's legacy to him. He had gone out into the icy blackness of space with nothing and returned. Injured but alive. Each social act, however menial, was filled with a strange potency. His heart had begun to live again. To move with its own power. He made one or two casual acquaintances at work. They spoke to him about books, the weather and other mundane things. Yet, despite the banality of the conversation, each interaction was somehow imbued with a kernel of intense value. It was something he had simply been unable to sense before. People had been nothing more than cardboard cutouts. They existed beyond a fog. It shamed him to see how he had stood in icy judgement above the world, like some fatally flawed angel, breaking apart in the atmosphere. He had flown too close to the sun on wax wings and fallen, burning, back to earth. Now he grew, green as a plant out of the ashes of his crater. He was able, within a month or two to find himself a room in a house. He remained on friendly terms with the other tenants. He passed his time in paperbacks. Drinking tea beside a window overlooking the mountain. The mountain had begun to appear in his dreams. Sometimes it would seem to be burned. A volcano vista, etched with the progress of simple, amoebic lifeforms. He would struggle and split in the protoplasm with them. Merging slowly and deliciously into the soil, where the seeds lay. The mountain would continue its glacial progress throughout the corridor of time—a passenger in some other, indescribable cosmic story. Ziq would always awaken from these dreams, feeling strangely fulfilled. As though an awful rage had abated, somewhere within his breast.

After a month or two however, the routines of society set their roots. He found himself being quietly re-programmed. By the protocols of those around him. It was almost impossible for him to maintain his own thoughts anymore. Each conversation, each work-day became a tiny stumbling block. He had to work to recover his mental stride. Hanging onto his inner rhythms became a new kind of religion. He sliced up time like a cake, desperately trying to save the choicest pieces for himself. But, despite his efforts, the rats of his mind left only crumbs and savaged segments. His rebellion provoked a weary return to dark thoughts. He found himself walking past the Pharm at odd times. He would hover there. Usually around twilight. Communing with the animals. Loitering beside his favourite trees. The visits were always laced with masochism. It was a kind of doubt. In which he feared the loss of former purity. He sensed the beginning of a perilous self-hate. He began to think about Jennifer again. At first, in an almost whimsical way. Then later, with intoxicating nostalgia. The road to Deer Park reappeared in his eye-line. He refused to take it. Dangerous trapdoors lurked beneath those Towers—the ghost of violence. A depressive air entered his nights. It was like the perfume of distant flowers. He took to smoking marijuana. He began to pull reality around him like a blanket, quilted with dazzling, secret images. Time slowed down again. It began to suggest pockets of hidden intensity. He watched the quiet, secret work of ants. He listened to Chopin on rainy nights. He catalogued book after book after book after book...He found himself drifting again. Where before, his exile had been external, Ziq was now adrift. On the slow, sluggish tide of internal rivers. These were rivers which grew steadily stagnant the deeper he travelled. Their banks were festooned with crocodiles of doubt. Crossed regularly, by the ghost-barge of regret.

One day Ziq passes the Deli, on one of his aimless excursions to the Pharm. He hasn't been to the cafe in months. He is mortified to discover that it has been sold. The comfortable, paint-peeled exterior is gone. Replaced by designer signage and expensive fronting. Tables crowd with upwardly mobile consumers. Somehow Adrian is still there. Ziq sights him, but is too disgusted to approach the place. He gets another shock when he finds Jaybird's sister in one of the lower fields of the Pharm. She is feeding horses with coloured cubes of sugar. Tabitha is unlike her brother. She exudes bright, apple-cheeked health and has one of those automatic smiles. Ziq was under the impression she had been doing care-work in the States. He hesitates when he recognizes her, beginning to reflexively withdraw. Tabitha smiles enormously when she notices him. She extends both arms, as though signaling on an airplane runway. Ziq approaches cautiously. Catching him in an energetic hug, she beams.

'Pat! You look so different!'

'I don't live here anymore,' he murmurs. 'I've also cut my hair. It's probably that.'

She still has him, in her warm, puffy sleeves.

'It's so good to see you!' she laughs.

They walk awhile. She tells him that she is around for some work. She plans to return to the States in a couple of days. He hedges uncomfortably around the subject of Jaybird, waiting for her to bring him up. Eventually, she does.

'He's doing good you know,' she nods. 'He told me to say hi, if I ever saw you.'

'He did? Where is he?'

An almost mystic expression glazes her face.

'It's really peculiar. He was diagnosed with an illness.'

'An illness?' Ziq mutters, feeling suddenly uncomfortable.

'A rare sort of disease. A parasite, in his brain. Some kind of worm. I mean, you must have noticed?'

He isn't quite sure how to respond.

'It was what made him act the way he did,' She explains.

Ziq nods, confused.

'But Jason's alright now!' she smiles broadly. 'He just needed a very specific treatment. The doctors diagnosed him stateside and he's... Well, he's just himself again now!'

'Where is he?' Ziq asks again, feeling the onset of a headache.

'Oh, he's back on the Upper East Side. He enrolled in Art School again. Isn't that great? Wait! Let me show you a picture...'

She pulls out a leather wallet and digs around. Ziq watches with mounting tension.

'There!' she announces, holding up an image.

Ziq doesn't recognize the person in it at all. The photograph depicts a plumpish figure in a jacket and horn-rimmed spectacles. He is eating a sandwich in a trendy, student cafe. His hair is long. A manicured fringe dangles over his eyes. This character is smiling, halfway through a joke. He wears a white polo-neck sweater. It is the first time Ziq has ever seen this person. He feels as though he has switched over to an alternate universe. A vacant space that has lain, folded and ready to spring. Ever since his first meeting with the bird-headed figure. That creature did not exist anymore. It was an illusion, a social sickness. For a moment, Ziq suspects some kind of crazy prank. Any moment now, Jaybird will pounce out of the undergrowth and begin to screech like a maniac. He will start setting fire to the horses. Tabitha squints in concern. She is surprised by his reaction. Placing a hand on his shoulder, she looks into his face. He sees, for the first time, a family resemblance between the siblings.

'I didn't realize,' Ziq says very quietly.

A tear forms in his eye. Clearly, she imagines that he is overcome by some kind of emotional reaction to the news. In fact, his distress stems from a more disturbing reason. Ziq had, after all, existed quite comfortably in Jaybird's appalling reality. Indeed, it was a reality they had shared, equally. He understood and accepted the perversities of his companion—as a reaction to the skewed logic of the world. Now he is being told that it was *they* who had been skew—all this time. The machine has finally come for them. With loving, healing hands. Ziq cannot accept the revelation, no matter his temptation. The madman has abandoned him in the asylum. The only thing left to guard is that vague notion of resistance which originally moved him. Yet, it is a notion which has grown muddy of late—like a relic in a wilderness. He looks down at the photo again. The inmate is cured. Now Ziq is the lunatic.

He roves seaside pavements. It is his custom around dusk. He'd left his job weeks ago. Wandering occupies the majority of his days. His thoughts revolve like dirty moons around some fascinating, yet somehow dying planet. He would have to move again. The rent is due. Even so, he can't bear the notion of a return to the waking world. He does not know where he will go. In a way, he doesn't care. He watches people walk into the fading sunlight. They carry ice-creams, towels. Children spill onto silvery sands. The boardwalk neon flickers up. Lines of blue, yellow and pink trace vividly against a sunset sky. They light the parched mouths of cocktail bars and dubious seafood restaurants. He pulls his collar tight as a chill wind blows in off the sea. The pavements rise, circumnavigating the public pools. Salt bleached railings, looking down. Over the last remnants of sun-slick bathers. The seedy, kidney-shaped pools elongate from his raised perspective. They catch the scarlet off the sky. He slows to watch the sunset. All of a sudden notices Jennifer.

She poises on a diving board. She stands still and straight, arms up in a perfect cruciform. Ziq does not completely register her at first. As in a dream, awareness blossoms slowly. The pool beneath is vacant gold. She flicks into space with perfect, economic motion. Bronze highlights glint. They flicker across her turning form. She breaks the water, shaking him from his trance. Ziq has imagined this moment many times. He had always thought that he would turn and walk on. Now he sees the immense futility of his daydream. The luxury of choice had never existed. All he has left, is the curse of inevitability. He leaves the railing like a sleepwalker, making his way toward the entrance. He glances down regularly, to check that she is still there. He loses sight when the railing becomes a wall.

Jennifer breaks the surface, treads water. Her nose has ruptured in the fall. Blood runs out of her, into the salt water. She swims quickly to the edge and clambers out. Grabbing her things, she locates the nearest bathroom—halfway across the complex. Ziq breaks through the queue at the top. He doesn't have any money, so he vaults the gate and runs. A security guard is sent to apprehend him. He navigates a series of staircases, fords his way through a small crowd. Eventually, he finds his way to the dive pool. By the time he arrives—Jennifer is no longer there. Thinking perhaps that he imagined the entire episode, he begins shrieking her name. Security drags him out. They might have left it at that. But Ziq tries once again to break in. A nearby patrol van picks him up. He is making such a fuss that they cuff him and lock him in a holding cell for the night.

Jennifer left the Three Towers the day after arriving. She didn't even bother to touch anything in the apartment. She booked herself into a hotel in Bantry Bay and barely left the room. She did take her car however. Chloe had thoughtfully made sure it was fixed. She'd even found a reputable chop shop to ensure that her tune-ups were in good shape. They immediately saw the problem created by Cookie and fixed it. The car was no longer a danger. Jennifer got in the habit of taking long drives down the coast, to see how fast she could go. She liked Chapman's Peak Drive—a famous, high mountain road, whose edges, at certain points, plunge hundreds of meters to the Atlantic Ocean.

One bright day, she accelerated purposefully off the side. Her car nicked a couple of rocky outcrops, but otherwise managed to hit the water unscathed. Her body was never recovered. Not particularly surprising. The area is known to have one of the highest densities of great white sharks in the world.

They wear white to the funeral. Chloe makes the arrangements. The ceremony is held on a private yacht, some distance out to sea. It is a chill and sunny day, chipped with cloud. A muscular wind comes in over the chop. Whipping their clothing this way and that. They all wear sunglasses. Clinging to railings and walls like an outlandish species of gull. The Oracle is not present. Someone speaks through a microphone. Chloe had seen V earlier. She was vomiting in the galley. When she looked up, a grim communication had flashed between them. Anita again, Chloe realizes. The presence of Anita is so thick and subliminal. Like the stench of burned things. No-one had mourned Anita. Because none of them could say for certain whether she would be back or not. Others speculated cheerfully. That she had disappeared with millions and was now living in luxury. Some tax haven in the tropics. They couldn't know. But Chloe did. She had been there. And so, Anita passed into her very own underhand mythology. Half-existing, not quite dead. A private medusa, whose memory bred secrets and turned things to stone. Jennifer's death momentarily ruptured this womb of not-knowing. That half-feeling of loss when someone vanishes. Are they alive—are they not? The funeral spills a double-yolk of shock. Down upon them all.

Chloe watches V. She scatters Jennifer's symbolic ashes off the prow. The ashes are silver birch-wood. They'd been supplied so that a token burial could take place. Many are in tears. Chloe can see that some of the tears are being wept for Anita. Even in death, Jennifer is somehow supplicant to Anita's dense, gravitational presence. It angers Chloe. She separates from the knot of mourners, making her way to the opposite end of the boat. Following the railing to the far end of the vessel, she stops to watch the wake of froth. After a moment, she removes a bundle of envelopes and printed pages from her purse. She has not been able to bring herself to burn the Ziq's messages. Despite Jennifer's instructions, she has held onto them. Now, she unclips the bands. The pages disperse, butterflying down to the spume, where they are churned under. The messages scatter wildly underwater. A few of them trace lightly against the smooth bottom of the craft. Others whip deeper. Some of the pages flit past Jennifer, who bobs lightly in the crystalline water. She hangs suspended against the open sea. The pages trickle past, but she takes no notice. The craft above ploughs away. She remains floating. In blue shafts of sunlight. After a while, she begins to move, into vaster depths.

Of course, Ziq returned to the towers the moment he was set free.

He was barred from entrance by the guards. His card no longer worked. He elected to return every night, to watch for her. A few weeks later, he is still in the darkened underbrush, waiting. He realizes she has probably moved out. But cannot bear to break this last tenuous link. Tonight, the forest is peaceful and temperate. He gazes dreamily at the Towers, adrift in thought. Beside him, a beetle glitters wildly in the moonlight—a droplet of cold fire. Then, a strangely familiar sound from the wood. He becomes gradually aware of it. A slow, uniform shuffle of feet. Ziq rises quietly. Threading toward the sound. The radiance of many candles. Glistering through the trees. He trails the procession from a distance. After some time, he draws closer. Is able to discern some of the figures. There is no immediate similarity. Men, women, both young and elderly. Some carry candles. Others do not. Ordinary clothing. It is only their total silence that unifies them. They blend into the stillness of the forest. Ziq finds himself breaking from the tree line. He drifts into view of some of the people, but is awarded no special attention. One or two glance up. But that is all. He joins the edge of their column. Moving slightly apart from the cluster. He follows for a while. Just to see where they are going. But soon, the silence and repetitive motion mesmerises him. He finds himself forgetting the distance they have covered. He drifts closer and closer. Finally, he is amongst them, watching the passage of closely illumined branches. Someone hands him a candle. He accepts it comfortably. A bird calls from deep in the woods. He is not sure what type of bird it is.

At the Beach

Volker has entered an unforeseen chapter of his life. At first, it had been easy, to quarantine Sulette in his mother's shadow. But she indulged his various whims and fancies so well. He found himself warming to her—almost against his will. It wasn't long until she had the run of the house. Of course, she suffered a minor breakdown when she realized that her pregnancy was planned and paid for. He believed that he had broken her and took great pleasure in her defeat. But she was quick to adapt.

'A real black baby!' she began to gush to her circle. 'Angelina had to adopt, but you know, Volker and I—we're going to do it *properly*...'

Everyone was impressed with her lavish new address. One day she stormed in and demanded that Volker marry her. He was responsible for her child and should therefore provide security. She caught him off-guard. He found himself accepting. The truth, of course, was that he wanted her around. That was the worst of it.

Now they sit, husband and wife, breakfasting on the terrace. Some teenage skaters pass on the street below. Some security guards follow. Then a waiter from the new Deli (which she adores). She waves prettily at them all. Volker knows that she is fucking most of them. He doesn't complain. She brings him photos. Sulette stretches pleasurably, surveying her domain through designer sunglasses.

'What will we do today?' she yawns.

He fiddles with his spoon, loathe to bring it up.

'We could go to the beach?' he suggests.

She slams her china cup down.

'We *always* go to the beach.'

He looks away. He doesn't feel like getting into another argument. Suddenly, her expression changes. She's had an idea.

'We could go to the *beach* beach,' she smiles slowly.

He struggles with his cutlery for a moment, clearing his throat, unsure how to resist. His discomfort invigorates her.

'We *never* go there,' she insists.

Somehow, she gets her way. Even his manservant is confused. He keeps shooting Volker questioning looks in the rearview. He chauffeurs them over Kloof Nek, towards Camps Bay. They pass the ridge. The

Atlantic opens up like an eye. It's a massive shock for Volker. He has avoided the ocean for decades. Seeing it only from airplane windows, or in tiny cutlets between buildings in town. Sulette squeezes his hand. He looks over. She smiles reassuringly. He is reminded again, strikingly, of his mother. They drive down the main road of Camp's Bay. Really, it isn't that bad, he begins to think. He likes the royal palms and the hotels. He is surprised at how much the area has developed. He starts to think about investment. They have a nice lunch in one of the better restaurants. At one point, he has to visit the bathroom. Inside the cubicle, the panic returns. The crucible of his secret life has, for decades, rested on the preservation of a secret dream—a vision. Yet, in the very pursuit of it, the vision tarnished. Reality has rusted over, obscuring its view. He regards himself long and hard in the mirror. Is he a man or a boy, he asks? Perhaps his wife is right. Perhaps it is finally time to put aside childish things. He exits the bathroom. Cold, impeccable and confident. She sees him coming and lights up. Somehow, in his approach, she recognizes the defeat of ancient demons.

After they eat, they stroll through one of the newer malls. She selects some dresses, jewelry and swimwear. He indulges her. The manservant takes her shopping to the car. Sulette announces that she'd like to walk on the beach. He nods in agreement, riding the wave of his new liberation. He even stops to buy them gelato. She goes ahead. After Volker has paid, he crosses the road, balancing the cones in both hands. The beach is not particularly full. He steps gingerly onto the sand. Then he sees her.

It is like an electric jolt. She stands, some distance away, between him and the sea. She stands with her back to him, on a deserted dune. Completely unconscious of his observation. Everything seems to retract. Except her, and the vision of the beach framing her. He is back in the basement. How naïve of him to think that the dream had withered. It has lost none of its potency. He realizes he has dropped the ice creams. He steps away from them, staggering, unused to the sand. He draws closer. Still, she does move. She stands with one hand on her hip. The other shades her eyes. She stares, captivated by some indefinable point on the horizon. He hesitates right behind her. He is breathing raggedly now. Her hair flutters in a steady breeze. He can scent it on the wind. He reaches out slowly toward it. But at the last moment, closes his hand to a fist. Touching her would destroy the image.

Hitchhiking to Heaven

A sheer of moving dust chromes the horizon line. The wind-whittled rocks of the Northern Namib waste rise like bones. A cargo of loose particles trawls between. Creating long, serpentine movements across the baked earth. A procession shifts in the distance. The figures flicker in a metallic rift, gradually taking form. Ziq has a shirt wrapped around his head to keep the sun out. He moves with dogged deliberation, keeping pace with the caravan. His mouth is dry. He chews the remnants of Sceletium, as do they all. It helps focus on long distances. There is grit in his eyes. In the beginning, it had annoyed him. Now he uses aloe beneath the lid. Raw silence fills the world outside their trudge. The void lends each sound a luminosity. A fine cake-layer colours them uniformly. It accumulates in Ziq's unchecked facial hair, pasting with sweat. Noon is intense, yet bearable. In their ragged robes, and after so many days of travel, they have acclimatized. The sun coasts. An eye of white fire in a white sky. Distant, biscuit slopes turn bare flanks against it. Tufts of pale herbage. Tiny lichen-blasted rocks speckle the wilderness.

A week passes. Perhaps two. Perhaps three. They have been living off cured kudu meat, roots and herbs. One of the party comes from the region. He knows the desert flora intimately. No one is suffering. One night, they camp in the lee of an enormous rock formation. The fluid rock contorts against the twilight. Others, like it, recede into an immense evening. The monoliths make a mockery of scale. Campfires gutter at their base. Embers starburst, traveling for many meters on the wind. Ziq lies in his sleeping bag, thinking. The tent billows. Endless walking has unlimbered him. A glowing looseness fills him with satisfaction. The physical relief sinks him down, toward a cavern of sleep. One of his Sudanese traveling companions sits outside the entrance. The short, muscular man puffs a fragrant cheroot, gazing into the gathering dusk. Ziq listens to the wind. He closes his eyes against its lilting songs.

It takes a few more weeks to reach the greener, mountainous regions south of Angola. The land is wilder here. Even less populated than the lower regions of Namibia. Some members of the caravan peel off early during the trek. Some strike east for Botswana. Or one of the northernmost Namibian settlements. Others make for the coast. The rest are joined by Himba tribesmen, who agree to show them a way through the mountains, to the Kunene river.

Large raptors circle, loose as scraps of paper. They have been in the mountains for days. Tonight's campsite is in the lee of a monolith. Hemmed by sheer faces of stone. A thin waterfall of inexpressibly sweet water trickles down one of the quarries. The leaves of the plants are vivid, pastel, dotted with an intensity of colour. One of the Himba shows Ziq what looks like a stone. His Sudanese friend explains, in Swahili. It is a kind of mushroom. It can cure cancer. Later, Ziq lies in his sleeping bag, beside a fire. Someone plays a flute in the shadows. The sound of it reaches into the upper distance, becoming immense.

Ziq's eyes glitter brightly as he walks. Something light has entered his step. He has a beard now. He stopped trying to hack at it. His coat is tattered. The other pilgrims share his loose, wild-eyed gait. They cross the edge of an enormous cliff. Below is vegetation in abundance. It cuts through a winding of ancient peaks. The next day, they are on a high verge. Ziq looks down and sees something which makes him stop. The others shuffle onward, oblivious. It is close to twilight. A single shaft of sunlight has pierced through the clouds. It illuminates a pale tree in a small, verdant pasture. Ziq sits down on his haunches. He stares for some time. While the rest of the caravan trickles past. The beam widens. It encompasses a larger measure of grassland around the tree. The area lies beyond some gradual elevations, nestling in a shallow cleft. The last member of the caravan passes. He tramps up the rocky path after the others. Ziq is thinking of his hitchhiking to heaven game. Smiling, dwells on the fact that the tree is, without a doubt, the most heavenly thing in his current sphere. A crossroads manifests. Looking up the path, he sees the train rounding a sharp corner. The walkers erase momentarily into the wilderness. Ziq stands up gradually and shoulders his pack. He begins moving in the opposite direction from the others. At one point, he has to leave the path. In order to descend to the grasses. It takes him about an hour. He keeps an eye on his bearings as he crosses into meadowland. Tiny red, white and yellow flowers imbed. Like paint in the turf. Once he has crested the second hillock, he glances back at the mountain. After a few minutes, he locates the caravan. They trail like ants along the side of a tortuous rock face. Soon they will be out of sight entirely. Ziq jogs down the slope, clambers up the next. Some small, startled animal brushes through the grass. The nearby tinkle of water.

It's twilight when he finally sights the tree. It reaches majestically above a vale of flowers. He slows his pace, approaching reverently. Its sides are smooth, almost pearly from sun and wind. Despite this, the tree is somehow not dead. It has vegetation. This tapers dizzily outward. Like the tendrils of a sea fan. The lavender sky has intensified—to an enormous, cold orange. It spheres the heavens in glimmering silence. Ziq rests for a moment beneath the tree. He watches the colours darken. Sleep creeps up on him. He awakens in a luminescent night. A fresh breeze unrolls drapery across star-washed grassland. The sky is a pelt of diamonds. Ziq unfolds his sleeping bag. He crawls in, falling instantly to a deep slumber.

At dawn, as soon as he wakens, Ziq gathers his things. His plan is to follow the trail. Catch up with the caravan in a day or two. He doesn't believe they will deviate from the mountain path. He is collecting water when he glimpses something beyond a crack in some boulders. Looking up, he sees in the distance, a vivid, golden mountain. It cradles beyond a range of cascading mauve cliffs. Ziq is stunned. He wonders if it is simply the dawn's light which lends it this sheen. It couldn't possibly be snow. Yet, the colour is so strong. So pure, that it almost infers the reflectivity of ice. Its majesty is undeniably grand—heavenly, in fact. Ziq watches for a while. Some clouds begin to form. He steps back down off the rocks and digs around for roots. He eats some dark berries from a nearby bush. Then returns to the tree. The mountain is faraway—more than a few days walk. He slowly collects his things and sits for a moment, watching the play of water against rock. In a while, he crosses over the boulders. Moving in the direction of the golden mountain.

Acknowledgments

I have worked on this book, on and off, since 2001, in many cities. Carmen Incarnadine was beside me from start (where I saw her first in a photograph, dressed as a mermaid) to finish. I would not have been able to complete it without her support and razor insight.

Whilst writing, I employed a method of filming certain sections in Cape Town (before writing as prose), with crew and actors. To use as raw material, in order to manifest a more resonant literary canvas.

For the initial filmed sections, I extend thanks to Johan Horjus, Hannah Barnard, Claire Angelique (who needs to be doubly thanked for talking me into moving to Cape Town in the first place), Nico Krijno, Jason Aeschliman, Bona and that crazy Canadian aerobics girl Mel.

For TRILLZONE, thanks to Justin Allart, Niklas Wittenberg, Bingo, Robert (The Robfather) Scholz, Claire Holtak, Jenna Bass and Nadine List. Also, thanks to Trevor Steele Taylor and Cedric Sundstrom for screening and hosting the picture at the National Arts Festival.

Special thanks to Lise Slabber, for her amazing performance and inspired improvisations – a wonderful actress.

Shot to Ryan (the original gangster) Sanders for all the stock car jargon and tuning tips.

Thanks to Moonchild (Charlotte Free) for inspiring Delilah Lex

And to Aryan Kaganof, for serialising early sections on his blog, as well as Steve Shultz – for all the Saudi intel.

Thanks to my fantastic agent Sarah Such for fording the way, and to Francesca T Barbini (and Robert S Malan) and everyone else at Luna for championing the book. Much gratitude. Thanks also to everyone at the African Speculative Fiction Society and the Nommos, for their dedication and assistance to a great myriad of African voices. Also, to Ruby Gloom, for the ice-cool cover art.

And lastly, to 'The Chap', the Zen Cowboy, Agent 00666, the droll imp of the perverse, he who I named Balthazar, by way of the Alexandria Quartet and Balthus the painter:
Mthandeni.
You are missed, old chap. Give the devils hell.

Lightning Source UK Ltd.
Milton Keynes UK
UKHW012007141222
413947UK00019B/302/J